Heaven's Warrior

Ken Baker

Printed in the United States of America
First Printing 2025

Publisher: Loft Light Books
Orem, Utah
www.loftlightbooks.com

Library of Congress Control Number: 2025920851

ISBN: 979-8-9930587-0-2

Book jacket design by Ken Baker

Dedication:

To Denise, for her patience, strength, support, laughter, and love.

Chapter 1
Qiu Meilin – True Nightmares

"Death's vision strikes sure and quick.

Torture's blood flows fast and thick.

One chance. One path. One escape.

To flee the fatal dreamscape."

- Private Journal of Qiu Meilin

I ball my fists in an attempt to hold back the flood of fear and anxiety welling up in my chest. How do you tell your older sister she's going to be murdered if she doesn't run away from home? I breathe out long and slow, trying to reassure myself that the murder part isn't certain. It's little consolation, since the near-death torture and bloody suffering are definite. A lump forms in my throat. What if she doesn't listen to me?

I try to come up with the right words as we catch our breath. My legs ache and my heart beats fast after our predawn hike through the damp ancient woods of Gudai. Lian and I sit on the low stone wall that borders the forest and the shrine gardens of the weather goddess while we wait for the other villagers to gather for morning exercises. We watch with anticipation as rays from the rising sun touch droplets of water from last night's rain cling to leaves and blossoms all around us.

Excitement rises in my heart, almost dispelling the fear that holds me. At once, the droplets pulse. They glow like liquid gold. The glow intensifies, the water droplets pulse faster and faster until they burst into one hundred different tints and shades of colored mist that swirl upward like fireworks. Shen Breath.

When we were little, Father would pay us a copper Zhu for each paper lantern that we had scooped full of Shen Breath. Then, he would hang the rainbow swirling lanterns at the edge of the growing fields in hopes that the Shen Breath's Chi would enhance our crops' growth, or at least invite the Two's blessings.

Hope rises inside me as I push my face into a small cloud of swirling mist and inhale deep. Right now, I could use as many of the Two's blessings as possible. I've never had much faith in the parent gods or their children, the Shen gods, but I'm desperate. Somehow, I have to convince Lian to accept my plan to protect her. Maybe the Two will show me the way.

My body jerks at a monkey screeching in the woods behind us. It sounds too much like the shrieking golden dragon in my nightmares.

"Is everything alright?" Lian asks with a look of concern.

I take a deep breath. "No. Everything is not alright. I've had a true dream."

I half expect Lian to grin with interest. True dreams are rare, and when we were little we'd giggle together at our aspirations to be the recipients of true dreams. But Lian's face tightens into her latest habitual frown.

The words rush out. "You're no longer safe here. We need to hide in Gudai and run as far away from Ning valley as we can."

"What?" Lian snaps. "What are you talking about? We can't abandon Mother and Father. They need us."

I want to correct her. Mother needs us. Father cares nothing for me, his delinquent daughter. But I hold my tongue, knowing how Father coddles Lian, his favorite and perfect daughter. I can't argue. Lian is practically perfect. But this has nothing to do with Father and Mother. Lian's life is at stake.

I tell her about the ravaging golden dragon in my nightmare, Lian's screams for help, and the bubbling pools of blood that engulf Lian. True dreams rarely play out in literal fashion, but the danger to Lian is clear. The longer she stays in Ning the harder it will be to evade it.

Her eyes turn hard. Is it because of Cai? She still mourns his death, her fiancée, lost in the Lord Emperor's war with the Yemaren on Dashi's northern border. For some reason, she blames herself for his death.

"I won't run away!" she blurts. "I deserve whatever evil fate the Two have for me."

"But Lian…"

I want to pound my head and shout, "You witless fool!" This isn't like Lian. I rebuke her.

I give her a soft smile, trying to show empathy. "The Two offer only gifts of love. This evil does not come from them. They want you to flee it. Why else would they send me this dream?"

Serenity returns to Lian's expression. "Yes, the Two love us. That's why they sent you this dream. So, you would not despair the day it comes true. So, you would know that all will be as it should be."

I shake my fists. "No!" But Lian has already broken free of my grip, jumped down from the wall, and sprinted toward the exercise lawn.

I watch her sprint through a meadow of bright blue poppies sloping down toward the shrine gardens and through its elegantly ordered precise sections of dwarf pine forests, bamboo groves, ficus, ancient willows, flowering plums, and vivid flower gardens. They all combine to create a striking medley of deep and bright colors. The cobblestone paths, footbridges, and winding streams form an intricate stroke design of the two-character symbols the represent the weather goddess' name – a bird rising up to heaven for Tiān and streams of rising mist for Qì— Tiānqì.

I let out a loud sigh. By the time Lian reaches the garden's exercise lawn, most of the other Ning villagers have already assembled. I have no choice. I hop off the stone wall and chase after Lian, wincing at the risk and likely suffering that my backup plan will require.

Once on the practice lawn, I take a place near Lian in one of the evenly spaced ordered rows in front of Master Wang Jin. Compared to our drab gray tunics and trousers, he stands out with his lavish, bright green priest robes.

He smiles and winks at me, a teasing gesture that says, "Meilin, you're late again, but I'm glad you're here."

I smile and wink back. I like and respect Master Jin. He respects and honors women as the Two would desire, never demeaning them as the Lord Emperor's code of Innate Honor too often requires.

In near-perfect unison, the villagers and I follow Master Jin through a series of Fei Chi forms from Wind Bends the Willow to Fold the Dragon's Wings. When we complete the last form, we steeple our hands in front of our faces and give Master Jin a deep reverent bow. He returns a slight nod to formally signal the end of the exercise.

All bow in return. The men hold their bows for only a second before leaving the exercise field, laughing and talking among themselves as their wives and children remain in their low bows still as statues. According to Magistrate Pang Yan's interpretation of Innate Honor, the women and children must not release their bowed postures until the last man dons his hat and sandals, and starts on the path back to Ning.

But I don't care what Pang thinks. Since Lian wouldn't listen to me, it's time for plan B. I release my bow and stand up straight as soon as the men do. The women gasp. Lian stares at me with daggers that shout, "What are you doing Meilin?"

The men shout "Xie spawn!" "Worm!" "Kaioda!" "Betrayer!"

I keep my gaze from them, fearful that Father will be among those cursing me. Master Jin frowns—not because he feels disrespected, but because he knows what will soon happen to me.

Dressed in his blue silk robe, green sash, and winged black hat, Magistrate Pang marches onto the exercise lawn, silencing the curses and chatter. The women and girls hold their statuesque bowing poses. The men return to donning theirs hats and sandals. No one dares look at me but Master Jin and Magistrate Pang—the first with a sorrowful frown and the last with the scowl of a Beifang Cat.

"Kneel!" Pang hisses with his sneering lips. I stand up straighter, locking my defiant eyes with his. He grins wickedly, savoring this moment. He removes the bamboo thrashing rod hanging from his robes, steps behind me, and raises the rod to strike.

"No!" Lian shouts, still bowing in perfect form. "It's my fault she released her bow. Strike me, not her."

I can't see Pang's face, but I sense him considering what to do. Though she secretly despises Innate Honor, Lian devoutly obeys its tenets. I lift my chin up and straighten my shoulders in defiance, hoping Pang will decide to spare his model citizen and thrash me—the village rebel—as planned.

Whack! Stinging pain lashes below my shoulder blades. I wince but refuse to stumble. I straighten my shoulders and brace for the next blow. For Lian, I tell myself. For Lian.

Whack! Whack! Whack!

I grin through the tears that I can't hold back. The sting of each lash deepens.

"No!" Lian screams again, putting herself in danger of the thrashing rod. Pang ignores her, exulting in thrashing me.

On the tenth stinging lash, I fall to my knees, my willpower no match for the slashing agony that rips open lines of blood across my back. The pain is so much more than I had imagined. By the fifteenth lash, I writhe on the ground, trying hard not to squeal or moan, My body shakes and trembles at the incessant stabs and throbs of pain. For Lian, I tell myself. For Lian.

When Pang raises his rod for the sixteenth lash, Master Jin shouts, "Enough! That is enough of your cruel justice for the day."

Pang still holds his thrashing rod high, but pauses with an intense glare at Master Jin. "Innate Honor demands twenty lashes and a day in the pain yoke for her crimes. You dare defy the emperor's law."

Master Jin steps between me and Pang. "I defy only you and your vile interpretation of the law."

The tension increases, but I'm happy for the pause in the beating. Pang continues with venom in his tone, "I am Ning's Magistrate. I am the law here."

Master Jin laughs. "Yes, you are Ning's magistrate, but this is not Ning. These are the sacred grounds of Tiānqì Shen. I am her priest and the master in this place. I do not agree with what you have done this day, but I have allowed it in respect to the emperor. The lashings stop now, or by the Two I will appeal to the emperor to have you stripped of all authority and imprisoned in the deepest prison cesspools."

Silence hangs between them for several heartbeats until Pang relents. "Fine. The lashing stops. But she will still receive a day and night in the pain yoke. And I will not forget your defiance this day."

"Nor will I forget your cruel ignorance," Master Jin responds.

Both retreat from each other, but almost instantly the provincial guard in his jade-colored uniform clamps the large square, pain yoke around my neck and shackles my ankles. In my weakened state, I can't move under the yoke's weight. But the worst of the yoke's punishment are the collar's needles that poke and prick my neck with the slightest of movements.

A few minutes later I feel a tinge of relief as a cold wet rag gingerly washes across the wounds on my back.

"Why, my willful little duck?" Lian whispers close to my ear. "You should not have done this. I love you, but I cannot protect you when you behave so."

I smile on the inside. "Oh, Lian. You will see. I do this to protect you, since you will do nothing to protect yourself."

Lian stays with me while the men, women, and children head back to Ning valley for their day's chores. I can feel the guard's eyes on us, making sure Lian doesn't secretly give me food. Starvation is an added punishment of the yoke. Its big square shape makes it near impossible for your hands to reach your mouth to feed yourself. And it's the provincial guard's duty to keep anyone from feeding me.

"Time for you to leave, missy," the guard orders Lian.

"Please, let me stay with her longer," Lian pleads.

The guard grins in amusement. "Now why would I do that? She defied Innate Honor. Get or I'll thrash her even more myself."

Lian lowers her head in respect. "My apologies, sir. I will go, but please, harm her no further."

Then, before leaving, she turns to me, "Sorry, Meilin. I wish I could do more. May the Two watch over you."

I grin through the pain. "All will be well," I mumble. "This is my fault, not yours."

The last part is a blatant lie. I wouldn't have had to resort to this, if Lian had agreed to run away. But she doesn't need to know that. Neither does she need to know the next step in my plan. If she did, she might thrash me herself.

Chapter 2
Qiu Meilin – Defying Deity

"Like heaven's breath, mists swirl and rise.
Spring chill silences deep woods cries.
Rays of dawn dance down leaf and limb.
Scorned prayers whispered pierce the skies."

- Private Journal of Qiu Meilin

The day passes painfully slow. The enforced fasting adds to the torture. I wait and wait for the provincial guard to leave his post on the shrine's step for his daily nap in the pear orchard, but he never goes. Why did he have to choose today to be vigilant? Perhaps, he's afraid the pain yoke and shackle around my ankles aren't enough to keep me from wandering off. If so, he has more wits than I gave him credit for.

When the night guard arrives to take his place, the vigilance continues. What happened to the guards' reputation of being laxed and lazy? Now, even if the new guard decides to take a break, I might not have the strength to carry out my plan. Did I purposely let myself get thrashed fifteen times with the rod for nothing?

Near midnight, a torrential rain pelts my face and numbs my fingers and toes unmercifully with its chilling drops. Two's mercy, though, it sends the guard running for cover in one of the garden pavilions.

In spite of the sixteen years of tales that Mama told me of the Two and their divine children, the Shen, I have never had much faith in those gods and goddesses, nor any other supposed deity. Although I lack Mama's faith in the Shen, I'm desperate enough to believe that a blessing from the goddess, Tiānqì Shen, is my only hope—rather, Lian's only hope.

So, gathering all my strength, I fight to my feet under the yoke's weight. My peasant gray tunic and trousers are soaked even though the pain yoke shields my body from most of the downpour. I press forward, determined to reach the shrine of Tiānqì Shen, goddess of weather. Every step brings a prick or stab from the yoke's sharp needles. I try to smile even though the chained shackles around my ankles cause me to stumble every few steps, jolting me with more piercing pain.

I refuse to be miserable. Gales and hails, but smiling would be easier if the back spasms and throbbing from the beating Magistrate Pang gave me would let up. I force my smile wider at another pinprick of pain at my neck. Okay, maybe I am miserable. But it's a happy miserable. If it weren't for the near-constant wincing, I'd be all smiles. I try to convince myself that things couldn't have worked out better if I had planned it. Pang's punishment has given me the needed excuse to be outside after women's curfew and in the shrine gardens after dark.

The pouring rain drowns out the rattling of my chains across the stone path as I hobble through the garden toward the shrine. Master Jin should be sleeping in his cozy cottage near the garden ponds. And hopefully, the guard is asleep and snoring louder than thunder. If he wakes and finds me in the shrine, I'll face immediate execution. The emperor's mandate of Innate Honor forbids all women from entering any holy shrine within Huyan's borders. I don't know if it's because Lord Emperor Xiang Hu, Chosen of Heaven doesn't believe women are worthy of Shen blessings or if he thinks girls and women should only pray to him. It doesn't matter. I care little for what the three-hundred-year-old Lord Emperor thinks. But tonight, my feelings for the Shen are a bit different.

As I hobble up the shrine's steps, lightning flashes and thunder booms. I freeze. Did I see movement below? Has the guard returned? No, I'm worrying about nothing. Except that maybe the lightning is the weather goddess' way to warn me to stay out of her shrine.

I force a smile. "Everything will be fine," I tell myself. "Nothing to worry about."

I try to hurry my pace up the steps, but stumble. Needle pricks stab my neck. I wince at the pain as I rise and continue upward. I grin through the stings and aches when I finally reach the top. Lit by gold and red-papered lanterns hanging from the shrine's crossbeams, plump granite statues of the Two greet me with their wide smiles—the first Mother on the right and first Father on the left. I bow to each one, trying hard not to topple over from the weight of the pain yoke.

After I hobble past the Two, I ignore the scowls of the golden dragons painted on the pavilion's rosewood posts and crossbeams. My skin tingles as I step inside the shrine. Hanging from the walls and lining the floors, nearly clear, white-papered lanterns glow with swirling streams of rainbow-colored mist inside each one— Shen Breath.

My feet chill and my chains rattle as I step on the porcelain tiles leading to the shrine altar, each tile decorated in geometric patterns representing different stages of weather. More paper lanterns glowing with Shen Breath line each side of the aisle floor. Behind the lanterns, paintings hang on the walls depicting scenes of the Two and some of their children, including several paintings of Tiānqì Shen wielding her gifts of lightning, rain, wind, hail, or sunshine to bless or curse the people of Dashi.

At the end of the shrine aisle stands a magnificent gold statue of the beautifully plump Tiānqì Shen. A headdress inlaid with tendrils of the sun sits upon her head. A fierce wind billows through her royal robes and blasts her long locks in whipping waves behind her. Like glistening pearls, a string of raindrops hangs from her neck. Bracelets formed of clouds swirl around her wrists. Sharp icicles dangle from the fingertips of her downturned left hand while she holds a lightning bolt in her right.

When I come within three paces of her statue, I struggle to my knees and try to kowtow in respect. The pain yoke keeps me from being able to touch my forehead to the floor, but I hope Tiānqì Shen accepts my efforts as I bow as deep as I can three times. Slowly, I rise, hobble another step, kneel, and kowtow three more times. Once more I rise, hobble toward the statue, kneel, and kowtow three last times.

Still bowed, I pull eight hazelnuts and five peapods from my trouser pocket. They were supposed to be my morning breakfast. Thank the Two for the forced fast. Otherwise, what sacrifice would I have to offer Tiānqì Shen?

I rub my thumb over the nuts and peapods, hesitating to place them on the elaborate rosewood altar tray in front of the weather goddess' statue. The tightening in my stomach reminds me that there are still several hours till morning when I will finally be free of the pain yoke. Maybe I could toss one or two of the nuts into my mouth. Tiānqì Shen wouldn't mind.

The words Mama rehearsed to me many times after my complaints about household chores whisper past my lips. "No sacrifice requires no pain. The best gifts blossom from the soil and toil of hardship."

I sigh as I somehow manage to place the nuts and peas on the tray. My stomach hurts even more at the sight of them. I try to smile. This is a good thing. Lian needs the best gift that Tiānqì Shen can offer.

I make a fist with my left hand, cover it with my right hand to make a fist in hand salute. I press my fists against my chest as I close my eyes. What do I say to Tiānqì Shen? I've never offered a formal prayer to any of the Shen before. I want to believe she will help. I hesitate. Part of me feels like a fool. The other part is desperate. Lian is in danger. In a rush, these simple words roll from my tongue.

"Oh, great Tiānqì Shen, Lian needs your help, but she cannot come to you. Law forbids it. It forbids me too, but I had to come. I have to help her somehow if I can. I don't know if you are real, but by the Two, if you are, I will do all I can to save her if you will help me. This is the gift that I ask. All thanks to you and the Two."

I open my eyes and raise my head. I'm not sure what I expected, but nothing happens. No blinding lights. No shaking of the earth. No godly voice thundering, "Lian is now safe!" Nothing happens. The dreams of the past nights continue to prickle the back of my thoughts, telling me Lian is still in danger.

I wait. Maybe this is a test of faith. I sit in silence, hoping and praying for the weather goddess' help. My heart pounds in my chest. Time passes slowly. My hope dims. Discouragement grips my chest, squeezing and suffocating any faith in the Shen that I might have. I wait a few more heartbeats, but then shake my head. With slow effort I rise to my feet and turn my back to Tiānqì Shen. I'm on my own.

Eyes lowered, I hobble back across the porcelain tiles, but stop halfway from the pavilion opening when my eyes fall upon the Shen Breath lanterns at my sides. Their colored mists glow much brighter than before, and their tendrils seem to stretch and pull as if reaching out for me.

I crouch beside one to examine it more closely. The mists glow brighter. The tendrils stretch, and then push flat against the side of the lantern, bulging outward toward me. A soft "wooo" trills from within the lantern. I push my face closer and the trilling sings stronger, rising and falling in a beautiful melody.

A loud crash from behind startles me. Ignoring the fact that the sound came from the back of the pavilion, my first thought is that the shrine guard woke from wherever in the gardens he was slumbering and has now discovered me. Moving much too fast for my shackles and stepping on a wet spot on the tile as I try to turn in that direction, I crash toward the floor. I try to regain my balance. My legs kick. My arms flail. I manage to smash several of the Shen Breath lanterns that line the aisle.

"Gales and hails!" I curse. The Shen Breath starts to break free of the lanterns. If the soldier doesn't figure out I was here, surely Master Jin or the Magistrate will.

A laughing squeal turns my attention toward the statue of Tiānqì Shen. Snubby. Master Jin's favorite golden snub-nosed monkey dances in front of the upturned altar tray. I can't help but grin at the monkey and his mischievous smile, that is until I see that he's clutching my hazelnuts in one hand and stuffing his mouth with my peapods in the other.

"By the Two I'll…" I slam my mouth closed before I can finish cursing Snubby. My eyes shift to the broken lanterns and Shen Breath at my feet. Instead of rising high in the air like escaped Shen Breath often does, its brilliant glowing swirls circle around me like glowing hurricanes of colors. What is happening?

My skin tingles as the glowing mists course beneath my clothes and wrap my whole body in warmth. The tendrils dance upon my skin, searching and pushing their way into the pores of my flesh. The trill of the Shen Breath song thunders in my ears. My hands and feet glow brighter and brighter. I imagine my whole body is glowing.

I should be terrified, but the warmth and energy flowing within me is exhilarating. Beneath my skin, my insides burn with fire, but it's a soothing fire.

When every trace of mist has vanished, I stop glowing. The fire beneath my skin stops burning. The song of the Shen Breath stops singing. My exhaustion is gone. The throbbing in my back and pin pricks of pain around my neck have vanished. Except for the broken lanterns at my feet and Snubby laughing at me in front of the upturned altar tray, everything is back to normal.

That's when I realize the pounding rain no longer drums on the roof above me. How long has it been silent? Coming from outside the shrine, I hear the guttural sound of what can only be the shrine guard clearing his throat of mucus and spit. Snubby bounces up and down, screeching and laughing at me. It doesn't matter that the monkey can't talk. I know exactly what he's trying to say. "Ha, ha, I ate your food and now you're going to die."

Chapter 3
Qiu Meilin – Life for a Life

"Midnight rain and morning sun are not sufficient. The requirement to have all five elements in close proximity is why the Shen Breath transformation only occurs in certain fields and forest areas."

- Hidden Scrolls of Quingping: Study in the aspects of Shen Breath

Chattering and squealing with delight, Snubby picks up the altar tray and starts banging it on the floor's porcelain tiles.

Relax. No need to worry. He'll stop. Snubby's a good monkey. A nice monkey. Right?

Snubby doesn't stop.

"Please hush," I whisper, trying to sound as pleasant as I can. "The guard will hear and that will be trouble for both of us."

Snubby doesn't hush. He screeches louder. He bangs the tray harder on the floor. Maybe the guard won't hear. Maybe he went back to sleep.

"Flaming pits of Kaioda!" The guard's cursing sounds clearly from outside the shrine. "By the Two, if that monkey's messed things again, I'll skin him."

Heavy footfalls move upward on the steps outside the shrine. The guard is coming, and I have nowhere to go. My ankle chains rattle and the pain yoke needles prick my neck as I rise to my feet. With hopeful eyes, I look to Snubby as if he might somehow be able to help me escape. He wags his head and chatters at me.

"Stupid girl. Stupid girl," he seems to say.

I smile back, trying hard to remind myself that the orange ball of fur is really a nice monkey no matter how much I want to strangle him right now.

"Be a sweet boy," I say softly. "Help me escape and I promise I'll get you more hazelnuts. Okay?"

Snubby throws the tray on the ground, but grins wide, dancing up and down.

"Maybe if you run outside, the guard will chase you," I say. "You're so fast he won't be able to catch you. But while he's trying, I can sneak out without him seeing me? What do you think?"

I can't believe I'm talking to a monkey, but the snub nose looks at me as if he understood every word I said. Then, he begins to squeal with laughter as if I'd just said the most witless thing he has ever heard. The soldier's lumbering footsteps draw closer to the top of the shrine steps. I have to do something.

"Please, Snubby. I need your help."

Snubby grins, turns around, scurries between a small gap in the wall and the statue of Tiānqì Shen, and disappears behind the statue.

"Wait! Come back!" I want to yell, but the guard will hear me, and I know Snubby won't come back. So, I pick my chains up off the floor so they won't rattle and hobble as fast as I can to the gap between the wall and statue. The gap is narrow, but I'm slim and if I tilt my head forward the edges of the pain yoke dip down enough for me to squeeze through. As I do, my lips tighten, forcing back a squeal of pain. The forward weight of the pain yoke pulls the collar needles deep into the back of my neck. I hold my breath, fighting cries of pain as I barely make it through the narrow gap.

Relief comes and breath returns when I'm finally able to raise my head in the cramped space behind the statue. There's no sign of Snubby. Eyelevel, on the back wall is an open window that looks out into the darkness of the garden. Snubby's escape route.

"Snub-rat! Where'd you go?" sounds from the other side of the statue. "You better hope Master Jin doesn't make me clean this mess."

I hold as still as I can with a smile of gratitude on my lips. The plumpness of Tiānqì Shen's statue conceals me and my pain yoke from the guard's view. The guard stomps about and curses a few moments more before I hear the clomping of his boots leave the shrine and head down its steps.

When I can hear his steps no more, I painfully squeeze out from behind the statue and hobble to the shrine entrance. The rain clouds have cleared, and the stars shine bright in the moonless sky. I hear the guard curse Snubby before I see the man's shadowed silhouette rushing through the dark toward the pine groves and apricot orchards on the back side of the shrine.

Thank you Snubby. I owe you a pile of hazelnuts.

As fast as my shackles and pain yoke allow and grinning through pricks of pain, I hobble down the steps and make my way to the exercise lawn. Thankfully, I don't see or hear the guard. At the lawn's edge, I sit beside a flowering plum tree and try to sleep.

Shivering from the cold and grimacing at the pinpricks at my neck, the hours pass slowly with fitful sleep. The fragrance of soaked wood from last night's rain still weighs heavy in the garden shrine air when I wake. Hints of red and purple begin to brighten the eastern sky. The shrine garden and nearby Gudai forest have already started to come alive with the morning chirps and whistles of wagtails, jays, thrushes, and other birds.

"Meilin, are you well?" Master Jin's soft voice startles me. Barefoot on the edge of the exercise lawn, the Fei Chi master crouches near me in his lavish, bright green priest robes. "I am so sorry you have suffered this past day and night because of me."

I can't help but smile at the kindness in Master Jin's voice. "The fault is mine, not yours. I need to be more respectful."

Even as the words leave my mouth, they feel wrong, especially in Master Jin's presence. He has never sought for respect or honor. And while he would never openly defy the principles of Innate Honor, he has always treated me and other women with uncommon respect. I have often wondered if it's because he has dedicated his life to serving Tiānqì Shen, one of the many female Shen.

I have never heard him utter the words, but I would not be surprised to hear him privately say, "Lord Emperor's mandate of Innate Honor teaches that woman must reverence man. Yet we reverence all children of the Two equally, both male and female Shen. Why is that so?" Whether intentional or not, the way Master Jin acts and speaks has somehow made me silently consider that question many times—a question that no one else in Ning seems to have ever considered. A question that too often pushes me toward trouble.

Master Jin smiles. "You are a girl of rare character, Meilin." He rises from his crouch and continues with a pinched expression, "No matter how good that rarity may be, others may not see it as so."

Master Jin walks away to the middle of the exercise lawn to await the arrival of the villagers for morning exercises. When they come, few look my way. It's as if I'm invisible to them. I smile. That's fine. I'm disappointed, but not surprised that Father and Mama are not with the villagers. Seeing me yoked would only remind Father how I have shamed him.

But Lian came, probably against Father's demands. When she sees me, she rushes toward me and wraps her arms around me, causing the yoke's needles to prick my neck. I try not to let her see the pain she causes. I want to sink into her embrace.

"Oh, Meilin, I am so sorry," she whispers. "Are you well? Have you eaten yet? I brought you a little something."

She slips a few hazelnuts into my mouth out of sight of the guard and Magistrate Pang before joining the others on the exercise lawn. After they finish moving through the Fei Chi forms, Master Jin dismisses the men and boys as the women and girls hold their bows.

Leaving their families behind, the men stroll down the angling path that leads through the shrine gardens toward the main road to Ning village. Master Jin walks at the rear of the group, conversing with the village elders. He'll walk all the way to the village square with them, anxious to debate the virtues and powers of the different Shen while enjoying morning tea with fruit buns, sweet dumplings, and sesame cakes.

As the men walk away, the women and children leave their ordered rows to retrieve their own hats and sandals. The women huddle close in pairs and trios, chatting and laughing with each other. The young ones giggle and shout, running in circles, spontaneously beginning a game of tag. I no longer see Lian. She must have hurried off to quell Father's anger at her disobedience. A few minutes pass before the other women finally begin to corral their children and make their own way to the garden path and the road back to Ning.

As soon as the women and children disappear from view beneath the canopy of weeping willows near the garden's entrance, Magistrate Pang strides toward me. I keep my head bowed, my eyes on his toes, and my lips in a thin line careful not to show any emotion. For Pang, a frown is sign of disrespect and a smile means I haven't suffered enough. Either one will give him an excuse to beat me again or keep me in the pain yoke longer.

"Have you learned your lesson, child?" The scorn in his voice has a sharp edge. "Do you need more time in the pain yoke?"

"That would be delightful!" I'm tempted to say, but I'm not that witless. I'm tired. I want the pinpricks to be gone. I want to go home. I don't want another thrashing. So, I offer one of the few practiced replies that I know Pang likes.

"Magistrate, your merciful punishment has inspired me to show greater honor and respect, yet I will yield to your judgement."

He grunts, which is a good thing. No screeching. No yelling. No beating me with his thrashing rod. All signs that he's in one of his better moods. I hold as still as I can as he unlatches the pain yoke and removes the shackles from my ankles. The freedom and relief feel divine, but I hold in the sigh pushing against the inside of my lips.

"Mind yourself, Qiu Meilin." The words sound more like a threat, than an order. "Don't make me regret being so easy on you."

I don't move until Pang marches away and vanishes from sight among the cluster of weeping willows near the garden exit. I rise slowly after I put on my sandals and wide brim bamboo hat. My neck and ankles throb, but it feels wonderful to be free.

"What in the Two's name is that?"

Around where I sat, the character symbol for wind has been scrawled in the dirt over and over again. I don't remember drawing the characters, but they look like they were done in my own hand.

I look closer. A meaningless curved slash has been drawn beside each wind character. No. The character isn't meaningless. It's the Mother stroke, the right slanting stroke that makes up the female half of the symbol representing the Two. I've never seen the Mother stroke written by itself, let alone paired with the wind symbol.

I shake my head. "Meilin, what were you doing? Are you going crazy?"

I must be. I have no memory of making those characters, but I did. Why would I do that? Even stranger, I've also drawn the wind and Mother stroke on my hand with one of my charcoal sticks. Could it be a sign from Tiānqì Shen? I think of my prayer to Tiānqì Shen and my strange experience with the Shen Breath in her shrine. What did it mean? Is the goddess of weather somehow going to help Lian after all?

Pondering the characters' meaning, I start my walk home. My spirits rise as I pass beneath the canopy of willows and my sandaled feet touch down on the dusty road that runs along the edges of Gudai Forest and leads to Ning. I grin. Even though a long day of work lies ahead, I'm happy to be going home. But the grin lessens when I remember that Lian is still in danger. Today is the day my nightmares come true.

My ponderings are so stirred up with thoughts of the Shen and Lian that I barely notice the escalating rants of a squealing monkey coming from the gardens behind me. The squealing grows louder and louder, turning into wild screeches. I grin as it reminds me of the pile of hazelnuts that I owe Snubby for saving my life. As obnoxious as the golden ball of fur is, he really isn't that bad for a monkey.

I turn back toward the garden entrance, wondering if it's Snubby making all that noise. Suddenly, the screeches stop. Instead of feeling relief, I tense. I watch and wait for the stream of squeals and shrieks to start back up. They don't.

After a long wait, raucous laughter booms from the garden entrance. I dart from the road toward the cover of Gudai forest and hide behind a massive oak. The shrine guard walks up the road, swaying side to side as if he's the happiest man alive. With one hand on the pommel of his sword, his other hand tightly holds a bag. He swings the bag in a wide circle and laughs loudly.

He repeats this several times, but it's not until he's quite a bit closer that I hear a soft whimper every time he swings the bag. My gut clenches. Something moves inside the bag. No. The guard has caught Snubby.

Chapter 4
Qiu Meilin – Deadly Confessions

"Oh, hated foe you laugh you taunt.

My wretched woe, you live to flaunt.

Your helpless pleas should cheer my heart.

But throes I sow I will not vaunt. ."

- Private Journal of Qiu Meilin

Having fun, Snub-rat?" the guard laughs as he swings the bag again. "Ho, I doubt Master Jin will even miss you. I won't. No more squeals. No more messes. Oh, but you'll make a fine meal. I'll slow roast you, that's what I'll do. Oh, and we can't let your fur go to waste. Maybe I'll make myself a nice winter hat. Or a handbag for my lady. That'll put the charm in her. What do you think of that?"

The guard strides from the road toward Gudai. He belly-laughs and I tense when he throws the bag high in the air. He reaches his hands up to catch it as it falls, then chuckles when he almost doesn't catch it. "Oh, that was a close one, wasn't it? Don't worry, it'll be over soon enough."

The guard begins to whistle a familiar tune as he steps into the cover of the forest. I've never heard the words to the song before, but it's one that makes Master Jin frown whenever the guards whistle it. The tune grows fainter the further the guard goes into the woods.

Being as quiet as a speck mouse, I follow the guard across a blanket of purple flowers, beneath a wall of dangling vines, through a cluster of giant ferns, over orchid covered deadwood, and around a mossy mud pit.

I'm ten steps away when he begins again to swing the bag with Snubby in it. "Stop it!" I yell. Tears well in the corners of my eyes. "Stop it!"

The guard stops and turns to face me. I can't believe I yelled at a man, a guard no less. If he chose to, he would have every right to beat me with a thrashing rod. I should run and hope he doesn't catch me. But I don't. My knees shake, but other than that I don't move. Forcing my tears back, I keep my gaze on his cruel dark eyes.

His grip on the bag tightens. The laughter on his lips turns to a sneer. His free hand goes to the pommel of his sword. "Ho, girly, you don't want to be here. Scat before I forget my manners."

I stand firm. That is, if you call shaking like a bowl of jelly firm. My gaze moves from his face to the bag and then back to his face. His lips compress, tightening his sneer further. Thick, scruffy stubble dots his hard face. Not only has it been days since he's shaved, but his nauseous stench affirms it's been much longer since he's bathed.

He waves his hand at me. "You deaf? Get!"

He's right, I should get. Before that, I should drop to my knees, bow my head, beg forgiveness, and then run like Xie spawn and pray he doesn't come after me. But I don't do any of those things.

With my hands hanging to my sides and trying to stand straight, I say with a firm calm. "Let. Snubby. Go."

The guard cocks his head to the side. His sneer relaxes into a mean grin, and he tightens his grip on his sheathed sword. "Girly, who do you think you are? I could skin you alive for talking to me like that."

My insides scream at me to turn around and run away, but I don't listen. I stay in place. My shaking slows. I breathe in. I breathe out. Slow. Still. Relaxed. Calm. No anger. No edge. I repeat, "Let. Snubby. Go."

The guard snorts, letting out a guttural chuckle. He shakes the bag, and a quiet whimper comes from inside. "This is my lunch. It's not going anywhere, but on the spit. Slow roasting. Mmmm."

A vile glint shows in his eyes. Leaves crunch beneath his boots as he steps toward me. Why did I follow this monster of a person into Gudai's shadows? Why am I still standing here? I ignore those thoughts. Breathe in. Breathe out. Calm. "I'll tell Master Jin if you don't let Snubby go."

The guard chuckles again. "Ho, girly. We can't be having you do that. Can we?"

He steps over a rotted stump and continues toward me. Now what do I do? He pulls at the knot on the top of the bag, making sure it's secure. A nearby thrush whistles. The guard whistles, mimicking its song. Less than five steps away a harmless brown rat snake slithers past his boots into the cover of a patch of purple crocus. I frown. Where's a pit viper or banded krait when you need one?

The guard continues, the smile on his face widening, "Maybe my lunch can wait. You and I should talk. Get to know each other better. You'd like that, wouldn't you? I know I would."

My knees shake again, no matter how hard I try to keep still. Breathe in. Breathe out. Relax. I shift my left foot slightly forward, planting both feet hard in the soft ground forcing my knees still. I've faced Magistrate Pang's thrashing rod dozens of times before, but I always knew my heart would still beat when he finished. I have no hope of that now. Fear and terror howl and quake inside me.

Calm. I can't let the guard harm Snubby. I can't let him do whatever atrocity he plans for me either. The guard steps closer. Step. Step. Step. When he's within a pace away I do the only thing I can think of to save Snubby and me. I smile.

The guard stops. His expression relaxes in confusion. In that moment, years of Fei Chi practice and sparring take over. I rock back slightly on the balls of my feet and jump kick, whipping my foot into his face. His head snaps back and he drops the bag.

I grin. It worked. I reach for the bag, but his thick fingers wrap around my wrist before I reach it. The guard's crushing grip squeezes a whimper out my lips. I try to kick him in the groin, but he grabs my ankle with his other hand.

He chuckles, and he tightens his grip on both my ankle and wrist. I squeeze my eyes shut, pushing back tears.

"You are a feisty one, no?"

I want to scream at the top of my lungs. I jerk and pull my hand and foot, trying to break free of his grip. It's no good. I feel helpless.

The guard smiles and winks at me. "Maybe we'll have our fun later. After you've settled down."

Swinging me by my wrist and ankle, he throws me. My arms and legs flail as I fly through the air. I crash back-first into a clump of pine branches. Pine needles scratch and cut my face and arms as I fall toward the ground.

I land with a plop into the mossy mud pit. My feet sink as I try to stand. Some forest mud pits can be as deep as twenty-five arm lengths. Still, I've never heard of anyone drowning in one. Father told me once that Tian Long, a burly old farmer who hunts wild boar in the remote areas of Gudai, once stepped in a mud pit. He was stuck in it for two days before someone found him.

Now I believe it. I sink fast and I can barely move. The mud reaches above my waist before I stop sinking. I try to slide my foot forward. My muscles strain and ache to move a mere half step. Huffing and puffing, I try to move my other foot, but it's like walking with the arms of a two-ton Pang Bear wrapped around my legs.

I make little progress. I'm still five paces from the edge of the pit. I'm so tired it might as well be a league. I drive my legs forward. The mud grips my legs and sucks the strength from me. I want to lie down and give up. I can't. My legs burn, but I keep driving and pushing forward little more than a few toe-lengths at a time.

The soldier laughs. "Ha. You keep trying, girly. By the time you get out you'll be too tired to fight. Then we'll have some fun, no?"

I grit my teeth and keep plodding through the mud, ignoring the guard's leers.

"'til then, I'm going skin me a snub-rat," he continues, licking his lips. "Now that my shifts done, I can slow roast him in my little fire pit while I have a nap. Ah, and when wake, he'll be ready to eat. If you like, I might even let you have a little taste of your friend."

I scoop up a glob of mud in my hand and throw it at him. He snickers as the mud falls short of hitting him. He pulls a butterfly knife from one of his boots and waves it in the air.

"You best play nice," he says with a sneer. "Or I won't be so nice when I let you out."

He clears leaves and pine needles off a fat stump and sits down. He pulls the bag snug around Snubby so it shows the outline of his body. The guard moves the point of his knife near where Snubby's eyes are. I push harder through the mud. I have to get out to save him, but I'm still at least three paces from the edge.

"Stop!" Tears stream down my mud-caked face. "You have to let him go."

The guard swivels on the stump to face me with his sneer. "Why? This beast is nothing but trouble. His laughs and screeches are bad enough, but ho, the messes are the worst. And who gets to clean them up? Me. Oh, and Master Jin will have my hide for the disaster the monkey made last night. So, I'll take the snub-rat's. A hide for a hide, that's what I say."

The guard's eyes turn back to the bag. I picture Snubby trembling and terrified inside. Does he even know what's about to happen to him?

The soldier grips the bag tight with one hand and with the other hovers the knife tip near Snubby's eyes. A soft whimper comes from inside. "Say, goodnight snub-rat. I won't be missing you."

I frantically push my way through the pit and make more progress. Driving my legs forward, I move a little closer. The pit edge is almost in reach, but not close enough to save Snubby.

"No!" I shout. "He didn't do it. I did!"

The guard lowers his knife. He turns to me with a confused look on his face. "What are you talking about, girly?"

I push harder. My leg muscles burn. My lungs ache, gasping for breath. My heart pounds so hard it hurts. Mud cakes my body. I reach the edge of the pit, but I don't have the energy to pull myself out. My chest thumps onto a bed of moss as I collapse, falling forward.

The thud of the soldier's boots moves toward me. I lift my eyes to see his boots stop inches away from my nose. He looms over me. He squats down his bulking frame and grabs my chin with his thick fingers. He jerks my head up so we're eye to eye.

"What did you do? Tell me, girly. What are you talking about?"

He squeezes my chin harder when I don't answer. "Tell me!"

I want to reach up and punch him in the nose, but I'm too tired. The guard lets my chin go and stands. I can barely hold my head up to watch him. He steps back, retrieves his butterfly knife and pushes the flat of the blade against Snubby's bag.

"You going to talk, or do I get back to making dinner?"

I squeeze my eyes shut. If I had the strength, I'd leap to my feet, kick the guard in the face again and run to Master Jin with Snubby in my arms. But as Father would often say, "Light doesn't always brighten the path we want most."

"Fine!" snaps the guard. "I'll make dinner."

I blink my eyes open. "No!" My fingers dig into the moss as I clench my fists. "You can't punish Snubby. I made the mess in the shrine, not Snubby."

The guard's body goes taut. His eyes fix on me like dark coals about to erupt into fiery flames. The bag slips from his hand. Snubby screeches as the bag bounces on the ground. The guard slips his knife back into his boot. The fine steel of his sword hums as he pulls the long, straight blade from his sheath.

I squeal when he grabs my ponytail with his other hand and pulls me completely free of the mud pit. When he lets go, I flop onto the moss and roll onto my back, muscles burning and still panting and gasping for air, but relieved to be free of the mud.

He leans over me. His eyes narrow as he raises his sword high. His lips move slowly as he speaks. "You went into the shrine? You tainted the temple with your female filth?"

I want to scream, "What filth? There's no filth about me." But then I realize I'm caked in mud. Not a great time to argue about cleanliness.

His sneer hardens. The grip on his sword tightens. "The Two curse you. The Shen curse you. And I will carry out that curse."

His sword looms over me. My end is near. But all I can think of at the moment is what Lian will suffer when my nightmares come true. My thoughts accelerate while the sword falls toward me as if in slow motion. If the guard kills me, who will save Lian? No one. The warning dreams came to me. It's my duty. No one else's. That's why I risked death to enter the shrine. I can't let it end here. I have to keep my promise. I have to save Lian.

As those thoughts speed through my mind, a soothing warmth shoots through my body, healing and reviving my muscles. It gives me enough strength to roll to the side. The soldier's eyes widen in anger as his sword brushes past me and buries deep into the muddy moss.

The energizing warmth continues to pulse and flow through my veins and muscles, revitalizing me at a rapid rate. Agile as a Beifang Cat I leap to my feet. The guard stares at me in surprise. Before he moves, I jump kick and whip my foot into his face. This time not only does his head snap back, but he stumbles backward several steps, crashing into the thick trunk of an oak.

He glares at me when he catches his breath and then roars, waving his sword and charging toward me through the brush like a crazed water buffalo.

An overload of warmth and strength continues to build within my muscles. My mind tells me I should run while I have the chance, but the pulsing energy inside me makes me feel invincible. I hold my ground while the guard charges. When he's almost on top of me I dart sideways, evading the slash of his sword. I move so fast it surprises me and I almost stumble. Still, I catch myself with an agility I've never known before.

The guard turns and takes advantage of my pause. He swipes his blade at my chest. I twist out of the way, but not soon enough. I scream. The tip of his sword slices above my bicep. Blood streams from the gash, soaking my sleeve. Like steam from a boiling teapot, a blast of glowing Shen Breath erupts from the wound as well.

The guard's eyes transfix on my bleeding gash as it almost instantly heals. "What in Kaioda?" he curses.

As the mist leaves my body, the sting of the wound recedes. Eventually, so does the flow of both blood and mist. The surge of energy lessens within me too, but I still feel strong and invincible.

The guard slashes again. I move back, duck low, and with a dragon-tail back sweep I knock his feet out from under him. He flops on his backside into the thick of a giant fern. He quickly rolls to his feet with a speed that I thought impossible for a man his size.

"Ho, girly," he says, backhanding sweat from his forehead. "Demon blood must flow inside you." Then he grins wide. "But don't worry. I've slain more than my share of demons before."

No. Not demon blood. A boon from Tiānqì Shen. This must be her gift to me to help Lian. The boon of power pulses hotter and stronger as my thoughts acknowledge the Shen. With a renewed confidence, I crouch into the Fei Chi dragon stance.

The guard scowls not impressed. But his demeanor has changed, as if he now considers me a possible threat. Instead of charging wildly, he circles around me in a slow disciplined manner. With the tip pointing forward, he grips his sword in a controlled horizontal backhand position above his head. He moves with the grace of a Fei Chi master.

I turn with him as he circles me, locking my eyes on his. I've always been proficient at Fei Chi for my age, but even with the extra boon of power and speed roiling inside me, can I beat a master---especially one twice my size?

To make matters worse, even though my arm wound no longer hurts or bleeds, the boon weakens inside me every moment that passes. Even though Shen Breath no longer leaks from the wound, I still must be using up whatever remnants of the boon that remain inside me. Once it's used up, I'm guessing any chance I have of overcoming him will be gone too. I have to act fast.

Out of the corner of my eyes I scan the area for anything to improve my odds against his sword. The moment my gaze shifts he lunges. I step forward and inside the attack, grab his wrist and force it down. If not for the energy surging inside me, he could have easily skewered me or at least flung me aside. But in the same movement of forcing his sword down, I drive my knee into his stomach and thrust the palm of my free hand into his chin.

He drops to his knees. His sword falls. I smile as I elbow thrust to finish him off. I scream as I make contact. Sharp pain pierces my gut. With his eye's half-closed, the guard lies in a bed of purple of crocuses, but his butterfly knife sticks out from my stomach.

My body trembles and convulses. I collapse to my knees, struggling to stay conscious and calm. The thick layer of mud covering my clothes from the chest down keeps me from seeing how bad it's bleeding. But a stream of Shen Breath pours nonstop from the wound, stealing my strength faster and faster. I grab the knife hilt and scream at the burning pain as I pull it out.

Panting and wheezing, I fall forward, planting my face in a pile of pine needles. The boon pulses around the wound in my stomach, its warmth healing my wound, lessening the pain, and strengthening me. But its influence weakens.

I rise to my knees, but jerk back. Wild-eyed and enraged, the guard presses his face up to mine. His thick fingers close around my throat and squeeze. The lingering warmth of the boon keeps him from completely crushing my air pathway, but I still struggle to breathe. Little black dots flash before my eyes as light-headedness sets in.

"You should've run while you could've, girly. You've about breathed your last."

I sense the truth in those words. Focusing on the last bit of power from the boon flowing within me, a simple prayer forms in my mind. "Tiānqì Shen, please help. For me and for Lian."

The warmth of the boon surges again beneath my flesh and flows to my left hand. The charcoal-drawn characters of the wind and Mother stroke on my palm glow. The boon rages and burns along each stroke line, screaming to be released. I have no idea what it'll do, but I'm desperate for any help the boon from Tiānqì Shen might offer. I place my palm on the guard's chest and will the boon to act.

Wide-eyed, the guard releases his grip on me. A howling wind storms from my hand. It blasts and lifts him off his feet, slamming him hard against a broad oak.

Chapter 5
Qiu Meilin – Dreams Revealed

"Great wall rises tall, our home shield.

Firm bricks yield not once, foes repealed.

No heart no ears no eyes to see.

Cruel wall spites own, lost love sealed. "

- Private Journal of Qiu Meilin

A blue butterfly flutters above the guard's cheek as he lies on his side beneath a giant fern. I'm relieved at the slight rise and fall of his chest. Even though he planned to kill me, I don't want to do the same. Still, I might wish I had once he wakes up. But that doesn't mean I can't make it harder for him to chase me down.

Using his silk waist sash, I bind his wrists tight against each other and then his ankles. After that, I debate trying to roll him into the mud pit. That would definitely keep him from coming after me for a while. But with the power boon completely gone from my body I doubt I have the strength to do more than roll him onto his back. Besides, what if he drowns in the pit? I can't live with that.

A soft whimper from behind reminds me about Snubby. I find his bag a few steps from the mud pit. It lies on its side on a bed of moss amid a cluster of large toadstools.

"Everything's going to be okay," I say. I gently pick up the bag and lay it on a stump. "I'll tell Master Jin about the guard, and he'll never bother you again."

Hopefully, that will keep the guard from bothering me too. But will it be enough? I violated Innate Honor. If the guard tells Magistrate Pang, what happens then? It doesn't matter. I won't kill the guard. Besides, I have other things to worry about right now.

When I loosen the drawstrings and pull the bag open, Snubby pokes his head out. He bares his teeth and hisses. I jump back and stumble. Snubby hops out of the bag, grins and squeals in delight. He sticks his tongue out at me, making me laugh. Before I can stick my tongue out back at him, he scurries to the nearest tree. He hops up onto a branch and leaps from tree to tree until he's out of sight.

"You're welcome!" I grin, shouting after him. "Don't worry! It wasn't any bother!"

His squeals sound in the distance somewhere near the gardens. I shake my head and laugh. He's definitely not the most grateful beast, but I think I paid my debt to him for saving my life. Although, giving him a pile of hazelnuts would have been a lot easier. But my bigger worry is my boon from Tiānqì Shen. Did I waste her gift to me just to save a monkey? Will she still help me save Lian?

Those thoughts weigh on my mind as I trudge from the forest and onto the road to Ning. I can't worry about that now. I have to hurry home. I have no idea when the danger to Lian will come. I quicken my pace down the road, but don't get very far before I glance down at my clothes.

"Smart, Meilin," I say, rolling my eyes. "Go home caked in mud and blood. Pshhh! That's a great idea. What will Father think?"

As the road starts to bend toward the Pangbo River I race forward until the dirt path runs beside the tall grass and reeds that grow along the river's shoreline. I dash across the grass, slip off my sandals and shudder as I step into the chill shallows of the river. Once the initial shock passes, the cool Pangbo waters swirling around my feet and legs feels refreshing. Still, I shudder again when I push through the reeds into the water over my waist and then over my chest.

Shoulder deep in the water, the tall reeds engulf me. Shielded from the eyes of passing fishermen poling their small flatboats up the shallower reaches of the river's wide expanse, I quickly slip off my clothes. I rub the clothes together fast and hard to work off as much mud and blood as I can. Most of the mud comes off, but my clothes definitely look more drab than usual.

The sound of distant chanting pulls me from my reverie. With its fierce looking dragonhead prow and multi-story towers, one of Emperor Hu's warships glides upriver. Little more than a breeze fills its massive fan-shaped sails, causing most of its power to come from the chanting oarsman propelling the ship forward by working the ship's long paddles in unison.

I sink deeper into the Pangbo's shallows. It's a reflex. No one on the approaching warship can see me bathing among the river's reeds, but I feel safer not taking chances.

With its massive fan-shaped sails unfurled, oarsmen chant as they propel the multi-towered ship up the great Pangbo. The swift, majestic warships often cruise the river. They're powerful reminders to the citizens of the Huyan kingdom of the immortal Lord Emperor's might, and what he can do if a village refuses to pay taxes or disobey the mandates of Innate Honor.

My chest tightens and my stomach sickens as I stare at the ship's fierce dragonhead prow. Relax Meilin. It's not a real dragon. Still, it reminds me of the razor-clawed, fiery-eyed dragon from my nightmares.

A hint of fear nicks my heart when the warship slows and turns toward the docks of our little village. Why would it dock in Ning? It's weeks before our next tax.

A slight breeze whistles through the reeds around me, sounding like my older sister's cries for help in my nightmares. I scream. The water swirling around me darkens and thickens with more blood.

No. No. No. I push through the reeds, my toes sinking and squishing through the mud as I hurry to shore. The darker blood and my sister's cries aren't real, but they feel genuine. That's how true dreams and nightmares work. A warning. Lian's in danger.

I gaze again at the warship, avoiding looking at the dragonhead prow. My chest tightens more when I notice the golden dragon on the ship's tallest mast—the emperor's flag. Snails for brains! How could I have missed that? The true dream couldn't be any clearer. The warship is here for Lian.

I hurry from the river and throw on my still-wet peasant grays and bamboo hat. I have to get to Lian. To protect her. When I reach the rise in the road that overlooks Ning valley. The shops lie quiet. Empty. It's not market day. So, the women will be home, while the men and boys work their assigned farm plots that stretch across the valley in precise gridwork squares. Half of what we harvest goes to taxes. The rest we can eat or trade for other food and needs.

The village gong sounds before I'm halfway across the valley. At the end of the river pier, the Imperial Warship looms tall. Dressed in bright red uniforms, Imperial Army soldiers file from the ship into the village square, forming exact ordered rows. The mid-morning sun reflects on their gold-painted steel helmets, making them look like walking candles.

"What are they going to do?"

I meant the question only for myself, but Lo Jing, an aged tea farmer standing nearby, shakes his head and scowls at me. He doesn't speak. He doesn't have to. His face shows what he's thinking.

"Meilin, have you no honor?" Lo Jing would say, if he already didn't think of me as lower than a worm. "You dare speak without the bidding of your betters? Your insolence dishonors me and all the men of Ning. Bow and beg my forgiveness before I have the magistrate give you fifteen strikes with a thrashing rod for your impudence."

I want to scrunch up my nose and stick out my tongue at the old man. Instead, I force my lips into a tight thin line to hold back the words I wish to say. I bend my knees, bow my head, and lower my gaze to the dirt in respect.

Lo Jing grunts and spits at my feet. Silent. I don't move. When he storms off toward the village square, I grin smugly, as if Lo Jing just gave me the best gift I could ever hope for and then whisper, "Thank you, Lo Jing. You have a wonderful day too."

Against the flow of villagers headed toward the square, I race across the village and up the switchback roads toward our home on the hillside. I hope I'm not too late. The village gong sounds again as I pass clusters of bamboo and thatch-roofed homes packed close together on the hillside.

On the third switchback, small, but firm arms embrace my shoulders, stopping my progress. "Meilin, young friend, where are you going? The village is the other way."

I look down into the kind eyes of Sun Yi. Strong wrinkles crease the small, elderly lady's face, accentuating her brilliant smile. Blue poppies adorn the buns of her bright white hair, making her beautiful and majestic all at once. Even though she's married to the village's most influential elder, she doesn't act like the other high ladies. She's the most thoughtful and loving lady I know.

Best of all, Sun Yi has always treated me as a friend. If I had time, I would sink into her embrace and tell her all my worries.

"Sun Yi, good morning," I say with a quick bow and smile. "Please forgive me, I must find my sister and mother before they leave for the village gathering."

Tiny wrinkles at the corners of her eyes tighten in worry. "Meilin is all well? How can I help?"

My smile wilts for a moment, but I force it back. "With the Two's blessing, all will be fine. But please excuse my leave—I must hurry."

A concerned frown crosses her lips as she lets me slip from her embrace. I wave to her over my shoulder and then push my way up the crowded road.

When I reach the little porch of our bamboo house I skid to a stop. My eyes widen. An icy chill squeezes my heart. Cold shivers take hold of my entire body. Mama steps from the house dressed in her working gray shirt and trousers. Sadness shows in her eyes and the downturn of her lips. Lian steps behind her dressed like a frowning princess in an elegant white dress with a swirl of embroidered cherry blossoms running down from her shoulder to her waist. How did Father ever afford such a gown? Even Lian's hair is pinned up like a princess with lotus flowers and fancy cherry wood combs.

For over a month rumors have passed through all the villages along the Pangbo River that one of Emperor Hu's many Wives Divine had died, and he plans to take another Wife Divine to replace her. I never would have imagined they would seek her among the lowly people of Ning, but with the Imperial Warship unexpectedly docking near our shores I'm certain that's the danger to Lian my dreams have warned me about.

But how did Mama, Lian and Father already know they would come to Ning? And come today? Lian couldn't have dressed up so fancy this quickly unless… Had Father had a dream too?

If so, he would never see this as the threat that it is. For him, it would be a fantasy made real. Lian has always been Father's pretty petite flower. In spite of Lian's feelings for Cai, Father had always hoped to marry her to a noble in one of the nearby big cities, or even a promising village elder. She would become a high lady, and Father would receive a hefty bride price. If Lian were to become one of the emperor's Wives Divine, the bride price would make Father the richest man in Ning.

"No!" I shout, leaping onto the porch. "You can't go the square. You must hide."

I grab Lian by the wrist to pull her back inside the house. As I turn and step inside, my face smashes into Father's broad chest. His tight frown and stern eyes stare down at me in a way that shows he's more displeased with me than usual. His dark ponytail is tied up in a top knot with the leather wrap from his youthful days in the military, an adornment he only wears on special occasions.

"Meilin! What are you doing?"

I release my grip on Lian's wrist, push my fist and palm together against my stomach, bow low, and then stand to attention under Father's hard gaze. What do I say? How can I convince Father of the danger Lian is in?

To not offend Father, I don't meet his eyes, but stare at one of the ringed ridges on our bamboo floor. I hesitate to speak. I don't want to disrespect Father. But he did ask me a question. Out of a respect, I must answer. He can't be angry at me for that, can he?

Breathe in. Breathe out. Calm. "Father, I had a true dream." The words come out slow and controlled. No emotion. No disrespect. "I fear it is not safe for Lian to go to the village square. If we let the Imperial Guard take her, she'll be in danger."

Father laughs. I glance upward to see his tight frown relax and widen into a grin. "Meilin, you know nothing of true dreams. I have had a true dream too, and Lian is to become a Wife Divine. Honor will be hers and ours. It is a time to celebrate. Not to fear."

I lift my gaze, but still do not look into Father's eyes. Instead, I look past him where Mama's scroll painting of the mist shrouded Mount Qiangu hangs on the wall. "Father, I believe Lian becoming a Wife

Divine is the danger."

Father scoffs. "What danger? To live in the palace dressed in fine silks, feasting at lavish banquets, lounging on couches and goose-feathered pillows, and having servants kneel at her feet, caring to her every need? I thought you of all people would be happy for her. As a Wife Divine she will live above many of the obligations of Innate Honor."

I move my eyes from the wall scroll to the crooked little table where we eat, prepare our food, and learn art and characters from Mama. I put my hands behind my back and squeeze my fingers tight against each other. I have to be careful. This is not going well at all. "Forgive me, Father, but I heard that the life of a Wife Divine is much different than that."

Father waves a hand at me. "Bah! What did you hear? That the Lord Emperor, Chosen of Heaven locks his wives in squalid dungeons beneath the palace until he has need of one? Or that he butchers those who fail to please him?"

I squeeze my fingers tighter. That's exactly what I heard. But I don't dare admit it to Father. That would be blasphemy worthy of at least twenty-fives strikes from a bamboo thrashing rod. I lower my eyes to a worn tattered rug covering a small space of our bamboo floor.

When I don't answer, Father almost shouts, "Crone prattling and heresy! That's what that is." I tense, almost expecting him to strike me. Instead, he continues in a softer voice, "My great aunt was chosen as a Wife Divine. Her family enjoyed great honor, and she lived a life of luxury."

I take a deep breath, deciding whether I dare say my thoughts. How far can I push Father? Will he listen to anything I say? How will he punish me? "Father, you told me yourself that once your great aunt left to become a Wife Divine, her family never saw or heard from her again.

You said, they even went to visit her, but were turned away."

I risk raising my eyes slightly. Father's frown tightens. Anger burns in his eyes. His face blossoms red. But several heartbeats pass before he answers. When he does, he speaks low, controlled, and with an edge to it.

"What do you expect?" he says. "She was a Wife Divine. Not just anyone can see a divinity?"

I let go of my fingers and drop my hands to my sides in balled fists before opening my hands forcing my fingers to relax. Relax. Rein in my temper. Do I dare say more? I have to. I can't put Lian in danger. "Father, that's the puzzle," I say slowly, trying hard to keep emotion out of my voice. "No one sees the wives. No one has even seen Divine Lady Empress Ling Yuan in over a hundred years. Why not? If she's immortal and rules as a goddess beside Emperor Hu, why does no one ever see her? Where is she? Where are all his other Wives Divine?"

Father takes a deep breath and lets it out slowly. "Your words dishonor the Lord Emperor, Chosen of Heaven. They disgrace me and our family. I will not allow further dishonor from your lips."

He steps past me as if I'm no longer there and stops beside Lian, offering his arm to her as an escort – an honor often reserved for royalty. Lian neither frowns nor smiles as she turns to walk with him. It's the same emotionless face she has often worn since she learned of Cai's death.

"Father, wait," I say, not willing to give up. "Please forgive my dishonorable words, but what about Lian? Have you asked her what she wants?"

Father turns to look at me. A smug smile stretches across his face. "I am not like other men. I am not so uncaring about my family's feelings, especially those who do not disgrace me. So, yes, I have asked Lian her wishes. If the Chosen of Heaven desires her as a Wife Divine, she wishes to honor his desire. Isn't that right Lian?"

She doesn't turn to face me. She barely moves. But she nods slightly. I'm not surprised. Lian would never openly disobey Father, but not long ago she would have used her grip on his heart strings to sway him to her way of thinking. Months before Cai had joined the army, she had made progress with Father that a match between her and Cai might be an honorable one. I could sense that Father was almost ready to agree to negotiate their marriage with Cai's father. But all that ended when Cai abruptly decided to start his eighteen months of military service early.

I kneel at Father's feet and bow low, my nose touching the dusty rug. I crinkle my nose to hold back a sneeze until the urge passes. "Father, please believe me. It's not safe. Trust me this once and I will never speak out of turn again. I will become the most honorable daughter you could dream of."

"I am your father!" I can't see his face, but I hear the anger in his voice. "Must I barter like a peddler to receive your honor? I cannot even walk the village square without the eyes of scorn following me. To my ears come their whispers, 'Qiu Feng cannot even teach his daughter respect and silence. He is not a man in his house. He has no honor.'"

Part of me wants to rise from my knees, glare at the disdain in Father's face, and shout with clenched fists, "So, you sell your daughter to the emperor like a water buffalo to a slaughterhouse? Will her death bring the honor you crave?"

But I do not let the anger take me. I stay on my knees. I keep my nose to the floor. Tears drop from my eyes to the rug as I speak in a soft whisper. "I have never meant anything to you, Father. But I know you care for Lian. Please, do not do this. It will be her death."

"Enough!"

I glance up. Father's eyes widen. His face flushes redder than a radish. The vein on his forehead bulges. His entire body tenses. He raises an open hand to strike me. I brace for the blow, but it doesn't come. "Your disrespect ends now, as does your meddling."

He lowers his hand, steps toward Lian and offers her his arm. "Come, Lian. We are done here." Lian's eyes lower. She won't look at me but takes Father's arm. When she does, Father turns back toward me. "Meilin, I will hear no more from you in this matter. Nor will anyone else. To be sure, you will not step from this house before the gathering ends. Do not disobey me in this. If you do, do not bother coming back."

He turns his back on me, interlocks his arm with Lian and they leave without another word.

Ken Baker

Chapter 6
Qiu Meilin – Rising Storm

"Of combs and wings and childhood dreams.
Useless treasures my heart did cling.
Kind words unheard, smiles left unseen.
For these my barren heart did sing."

- Private Journal of Qiu Meilin

Despite what Father might think, I have always tried to obey his commands. But this one I can't.

Packing takes only a minute. All my belongings lie in a box on the floor of the cramped room that I share with Lian. A change of clothes. One wooden comb. A few scrolls of paper. Some charcoal sticks, a sharpening knife, ink sticks, my broken fish hawk figurine, a grinding stone, and bamboo pen that Mama gave me for practicing characters and making art. Plus, a jade butterfly that Father carved for me for my eighth birthday—the only real gift I remember Father giving me.

I pinch one of the butterfly wings between my fingers and debate throwing it out the window. Instead, I wrap my fingers around it and clutch it tight. A small smile shines through the tears streaming down my cheeks. After several heartbeats, I drop the wings in the bottom of a cloth shoulder bag. I quickly stuff my other belongings in the shoulder bag and hurry out the front door.

As I step onto my porch, the bright lavender moon, Shi, rises in the morning sky above the rocky cliffs across the Pangbo. Without her lover San, the single moon looks as lonely as I feel. But since it's a Shi-day, the two moons will reunite this evening at twilight after being separated for two full days. Shi and San are lucky. I fear my separation from my family will be more than a few days. It will be a lifetime.

Imperial soldiers fill half the village square. They stand on the square's cobbles in four precise rows. They wear steel helmets and body armor painted gold and trimmed with red fabric. With their heads bowed, the other half of the square is empty except for an ordered line of twenty-three village girls between the ages of seventeen and twenty-one —all the marriageable maidens of Ning. Dressed in her dazzling colorful dress, Lian shines like a flower among weeds compared to the other girls dressed in their drab work grays.

All the villagers of Ning wait and watch in tense silence. They crowd in front of the market's small bamboo buildings or colored tent stalls, or huddle on the patches of grass beneath the various shade trees that surround the square. I don't know what the wait is for, but I watch hidden behind and above the crowds in the crook of my favorite elm tree.

As the minutes pass, the soldiers stand in their ranks like frowning stone statues. The marriageable girls stand in their line still and silent. The men among the villagers begin to fidget with a buzz of whispers rising and falling among them. To ease the wait, I pull from my bag my knife and a charcoal stick to sharpen.

Between strokes of the knife, I study the rows of soldiers and gaps between the crowds of villagers surrounding the square. I try to imagine some way of spiriting Lian away. With all eyes on the girls, no attempt would go unnoticed especially with Lian standing out in her gorgeous dress.

"Gales and hails!" I mutter aloud. "Tiānqì Shen, how do I save her?"

I don't really expect an answer, but I squeeze my eyes shut and listen hopefully. A slight breeze swirls through the leaves of the elm, but no answer from the weather goddess comes.

What now? I think about the wind character paired with the Mother stroke that I had drawn in the dirt on the shrine grounds. Why had I done that? I tuck my sharpening knife into its sheath and put it in my bag. I have paper in my shoulder bag, but I don't bother to get it out. Instead, I draw the symbols side by side on the palm of my hand with my charcoal stick and study them. What could they mean?

I study the symbols for several moments, but no hidden insight comes. They're just characters, but I know they have power. I experienced that in my fight with the guard. Still, I sigh in frustration. I barely overcame that guard. How can I hope to take on entire squad of the Imperial Guard. I close my eyes, trying desperately to figure out how to save Lian. Several heartbeats pass before a vision of the shrine of Tiānqì Shen invades my thoughts.

The shrine's insides lay as I left them this morning. Broken paper lanterns lay scattered across the porcelain tile floor. A few whole lanterns hang from the ceiling and line the aisle nearest the altar, their swirling-colored mist sending dancing prisms across the wall paintings of the Shen and ancient Dashi history. Before the magnificent statue of Tiānqì Shen, the altar tray still sits upturned with one corner on the floor and another propped on a corner of the low altar shelf.

Soft footsteps echo through the shrine as a man in ragged and heavily stained working grays steps across the tile toward the shrine statue. His broad shoulders and confident gait seem familiar, but his back is to me, so I can't see his face. No hat covers his dark black hair tied back in a single ponytail that reaches below the middle of his back.

The man kneels reverently before the statue and returns the upturned altar tray back on its shelf. He pulls from his pocket a handful of orange berries and places them on the altar tray. Bowing low, face to the floor, he kowtows three times while a stream of too quiet to hear murmured whispers flow past his lips.

Even though the whispers end before too long, the man keeps his face to the floor several moments more. When he finally lifts his head, tendrils of Shen Breath in the few remaining whole lanterns push against the insides, stretching and reaching for him much like they did for me. He rises slowly and as he turns from the altar, my heart pounds and my entire body tenses. Though streaked with dirt and a long cut above his eye, I know the face in an instant. It's Cai.

The village gong sounds. My eyes fly open, jerking me from the vision. The village square goes silent as the gong quiets. My thoughts race in a muddled mess as I try to make sense of what my mind saw while my eyes shift to the events in the village square.

Wearing long sky-blue robes and round black caps, two skinny servants—one short and one tall—stand near the entrance to the square. The tall one calls to the crowd, "Behold, citizens of Huyan, give honor to General Meng De and High Lord Zheng Gong."

The crowds bow as General Meng marches into the square wearing a shimmering steel helmet and black leather armor with overlapping shiny plates of steel protecting his shoulders, torso, and thighs. He's followed close behind by High Lord Zheng, an imperial official riding a large black horse. The horse's hooves clop loudly on the stone cobbles. A stiff black square hat with narrow wings poking out the sides adorns Lord Zheng's head. A long purple robe with a golden belt, golden cuffs, and a golden collar cover him from shoulders to ankles.

As Zheng slowly rides into the square, I grin as a plan sprouts in my mind. "Oh, Meilin you are too clever." I just have to wait for the right moment.

When Zheng reins his horse to a stop near the line of girls, the two skinny servants rush to his side. The tall servant helps Zheng down from the horse and then leads the horse to the far side of the village square. The short servant pulls out a piece of gray paper and a long skinny knife from a pocket in his robe. He unsheathes the knife and gives it to the official, but keeps the paper clutched tight in his own hand.

Without even a brief glance at her face, Zheng grabs the wrist of the first girl in the line. A gasp rises among the villagers when he pokes the tip of the girls' finger with the point of the knife. The High Lord ignores the gasps and smears blood from the girl's fingertip onto the paper held by the short servant. Zheng and the servant stare at the paper for a few heartbeats before the Zheng shakes his head and they move onto the next girl.

Not once looking into the face of any of the girls, Zheng and the servant repeat the knife prick and blood smear routine on each girl. There are only four girls left when they reach Lian. After they smear blood from her fingertip on the paper, barely a second passes before the High Lord raises his eyes from the paper with a grin.

He hands the knife to the short servant and clasps his hands above his head. The servant shoos away all the girls but Lian. Most look relieved. Some act confused. But none appear sad that they weren't chosen to be one of Emperor Hu's Wives Divine.

High Lord Zheng turns his back on Lian to address the crowd of villagers surrounding him. His high-pitched voice squeals as he talks. "Blessed citizens of Huyan, humble villagers of the notable valley of Ning, the Two have bestowed great honor upon you today." He pauses and gestures toward Lian. "The Two have made known their will. Seven nights from now a spring royal wedding will be held beneath the emerald glow of the lone moon, San. And this young flower shall take the holy oaths to become a Wife Divine to Lord Emperor Xiang Hu, Chosen of Heaven..."

I've heard enough. I drop from the elm to the ground and leave my shoulder bag at its base. I barely take two steps before I trip on of one the tree's many raised roots. So much for not drawing attention to myself. I've climbed this elm thousands of times and no matter how careful I am, almost every time I manage to trip on one of its roots.

Ignoring the villagers' glares, I run from the tree toward the shop tents and stalls that line the western edge of the village square. I slip behind the tents and crouch low to stay out of view of the villagers and soldiers as I hurry to the other side of the square. If anyone spots me, my impromptu plan will fail before it even starts.

My nose crinkles when I duck behind the bright green tent where Cai's father sells fish. I half expect to find Cai gutting and filleting the morning catch. As with all the village girls, gazing at his athletic frame and handsome face was always a pleasure. But when Lian was not around, we would sometimes joke about how the fish stink that clung to his skin and clothes was so strong it would kill all the mosquitoes in Ning and attract every Pang Bear in Gudai. I feel bad for how we joked, but that same odor oozes from the tent making his memory even fresher in my mind.

What if he's not really dead? Though much different than a true dream, the vision of him in the shrine felt real—like he was really there. I shake my head. No. He's gone. An imperial messenger wouldn't lie about such a thing.

I tiptoe through the narrow gap between the fish tent and candle stall. Tethered to a lantern post ten steps away, the High Lord's horse grazes on the scant blades of grass growing between the cobbles. The rows of imperial soldiers are a short twenty paces to the horse's side, but all their eyes fix on the official as he presents my father a small wooden chest filled with gold—the bride price for giving his daughter to the emperor. A curse of Kaioda forms in my mind, but I push it away. I want to believe Father truly thinks he is doing what is best for Lian, even if it does make him wealthy, too.

Up this close, the horse looks like a monster. I've never ridden a horse before, but it can't be too different from riding a water buffalo from the rice fields to the village. The horse eyes me as I step close, but she continues to scavenge for stray blades of grass. None of the soldiers look my way as I grab the horse's reins and un-tether her from the post. A low snort flares from her nostrils for a moment when I step beside her.

"Peace, noble one," I say as I stroke her mane. "You're going to help me save a life."

I grip the reins tight and close my eyes to offer a silent prayer. "Tiānqì Shen, please help."

My skin warms. I can feel an inkling of the boon stir within me, pushing at me to let it spring into action instead of holding it back until I really need it. From how it pushes, I can tell the reservoir of power is much smaller than when I fought the shrine guard. Could it be because I only absorbed a little Shen Breath since then? Hopefully, if I need the power boon, it'll be enough.

I raise my foot high into the horse's stirrup and swing into the saddle. The black mare snorts loudly, stomps her forelegs and rears back. I fight the urge to pull back on the reins to keep from sliding off. Instead, I lean forward, pressing my cheek against her warm neck and whisper softly, "Peace, girl!"

She drops back down on all fours, but a cry of alarm rises from the ranks of the soldiers. All eyes turn to me. Swords unsheathe in a resounding hum. Weapons rise. I offer another quick prayer, press my heels into the mare's flanks and shout, "Yee!"

Before the soldiers can block the way, I prod the black beast into a gallop. Shouts and curses trail behind. Surprisingly, it only takes gentle turns on the reins and slight heel pushes to steer the mare where I want to go.

Father and Lian's eyes widen as I charge toward them. Lord Zheng raises a fist at me. Anger reddens his face. But as I draw closer the anger melts to fear. Lord Zheng shrieks before sprinting away. Lian holds her ground. Her face stone.

With another silent plea to Tiānqì Shen, the boon surges within me. My muscles swell with power. I swerve the charging mare alongside Lian and scoop her up with one arm. With strength from the boon, she feels as light as a rag doll. I set her in front of me with one arm around her waist, so she won't fall off. Guards shout and race toward me from all directions. I steer the galloping mare across the square toward the gap in the stalls that lead to the main road.

With a mixture of anger and shock, Lian shouts in my face, "Meilin! Why? How?"

I still haven't quite figured out the how, but Lian should know why. Like me, she's heard the stories of how Emperor Hu mistreats his Wives Divine. She just doesn't care anymore. I want to tell her of my vision of Cai. Maybe that would give her hope. But not now. First, I have to get us free. I charge the mare forward. We swerve in and out of the mass of imperial soldiers. They rush and dart in front of us from all directions.

Lian pushes and tugs at my arm to break free of my embrace. I tighten my grip and beg her. "Stop it! This is our only chance."

Once we are beyond the village square our escape will be sure. We'll head to a remote village. The imperial soldiers won't be able to catch us while on horseback. Maybe we'll hide in Gudai. They'd never find us in the vast ancient woods.

Hope of escape fades fast. A thick wall of soldiers now blocks the gap. Their swords drawn and ready to strike. Magistrate Pang stands with them, his sword drawn too and anxious to use it. What do I do? Make the mare jump over them? Too risky. Retreat? No. Too many soldiers in the rear. I'm such a fool. I'm trapped.

Still, I charge forward. My only hope in saving Lian lies ahead. The warmth of the boon surges beneath my flesh. It flows in an instant to my left hand. The charcoal-drawn characters of the wind and Mother stroke on my palm glow. The boon rages and burns along each stroke line, screaming to be released. I have no idea what it'll do, but I'm desperate for any help the boon from Tiānqì Shen might offer. I raise my arm, turn my palm toward the soldiers blocking the gap, and will the boon to act.

Wind blasts from my hand and lifts the soldiers and magistrate off their feet, throwing them to the side. In a blink the gap is clear. In that same blink, the force of the blast backlashes, pushing back at my hand and twisting me backward. With my other arm around Lian, I can't keep my balance. I jerk back and tumble off the horse, crashing hard on my backside atop the cobbles. Lian falls too, landing on top of me.

The fall could have easily broken my back or knocked me unconscious, but the remnants of the boon surge within me quickly repairing any harm. Lian rolls off me, hurries to her feet, and scowls down at me before sprinting away. I slowly pull myself upright. I shake my head as the black mare gallops rider-less through the gap and toward the main road. Before a curse can even form on my lips, a dozen Imperial soldiers surround me. The tips of their swords hover inches from my neck

.

Chapter 7
Qiu Meilin – Slayers of the Defiled

"Rubies perish.
Power wanes.
Lost love cherished.
Endless pains."
- Private Journal of Qiu Meilin

Except for the distant shrieks of cormorants flying along the riverbanks, silence grips the village square. I slow my breathing and hold still. I have no desire to be skewered by a fidgety armed soldier whether on purpose or accident. If I had some of the boon left, I might have a chance to escape, but now I'm at the soldiers' mercy.

Scurrying foot falls across the cobbles and shrill hollering announces the rapid approach of Lord Zheng. "Execute her! Execute her at once!"

The soldiers tighten their grips on their swords. Some grin, anxious to get back at me for making them look foolish.

"No! Wait! Do not hurt her." I can't see him, but I recognize Master Jin's voice.

The sword tips still hover near my throat, but none of the soldiers strike. I can imagine the indignant look on Zheng's face to have a lowly village priest obstruct his orders.

"Honorable one, young children are in the square," Master Jin pleads. "Would the Lord Emperor, Chosen of Heaven want their young minds scarred at the sight of blood flowing on the cobbles of their village? No harm has been done here. Let her go free."

The shrill voice of Lord Zheng rises. "No harm? She committed treason! Kidnapping the emperor's new Wife Divine. Stealing my horse. All crimes punishable by death."

Master Jin chuckles. I imagine a wide grin stretching across his face as Zheng's sneer deepens. "From the cradle the girl has always been crazed. Her brain is not right. She has fits and tantrums. Sometimes she acts protective of the village girls, especially for the new Wife Divine. She probably didn't understand why you were taking her away. The girl likely feared for the new Wife Divine's life. It put her in a mental frenzy. It happens all the time. How could there be any treason? The girl has no notion to what she was doing."

I don't like Master Jin's lies about me, but the tension drops at his words. The soldiers' expressions subdue. The tips of their swords withdraw a bit. Silence follows as Lord Zheng doesn't respond immediately.

When Zheng talks again the shrill in his voice is replaced by a quiet firmness. "How do you explain her witchery? She made the soldiers scatter."

I'm not sure how I would explain it. Having wind blast from the palm of my hand doesn't happen every day. But I guess I shouldn't be too surprised. The boon is from the goddess of weather after all. I glance at the palm of my hand. No trace of the charcoal-drawn characters remain on my hand. Not even a smudge.

"Witchery?" Master Jin laughs. His laugh usually makes me smile, but I draw my lips into a thin smile. I don't need to give Zheng any other reasons to punish me. "Honorable one, even the bravest of men would scatter in the face of a crazed girl stampeding toward them on a frightful steed such as yours. Certainly, some of them even feared the new Wife Divine might be harmed if they held their ground. Put no blame on this girl or the soldiers."

Grips on some of the swords surrounding me tighten again. The scorn on their faces makes it clear they think Master Jin's words paint them as cowards. Given the command, they wouldn't hesitate to prove otherwise and end my life.

In the silence that follows, the loud clopping of hoof beats on the cobble sounds across the square. Master Jin laughs again. "See, honorable one, your steed has been recovered. As I said, no harm has been done. Let me see to the girl. Fifty blows with a thrashing rod will teach her of her wrongs. I'll see to it myself."

"Humph! Make sure nothing of this kind happens again." Lord Zheng clicks his tongue. With disappointing scowls, the soldiers withdraw their swords and leave me alone sitting on the ground.

Master Jin waits several heartbeats before he steps to my side. All smiles, I open my mouth to thank him, but he silences me with a wave of his hand. He doesn't even spare me a glance. With a displeased grimace on his face, he stares after Lord Zheng, who stalks toward his horse—the hem of his purple robes snapping behind him as he goes.

In precise lines, the ranks of soldiers start to file out. Their heavy boots stomp across the village square as they head toward their ship. Amid a buzz of quiet, yet excited chatter, the villagers too begin to leave the square, returning to their chores in the fields or homes.

Father grins in the center of the square, clutching his chest filled with gold as he talks with one of the official's servants. A few paces from him, Mama embraces a trembling Lian, although no sobs escape her lips.

In his shimmering steel helmet and black leather armor, General Meng marches up to Mama and Lian. Four blue-robed servants follow close behind the general carrying a luxurious purple sedan chair. Gold tassels hang all along the edges of the sedan's peaked roof. Made of thick silk, its closed curtains are decorated with dragons, peach blossoms, and the phoenix.

With hand in fist, General Meng bows to Lian and Mama. I can't hear his words, but he gestures for Lian to enter the sedan. The general waits at attention as Lian slowly leaves Mama's embrace. She has stopped trembling, solemn confidence on her face as she moves toward the sedan. When one of the servants pulls open the curtain for her, she looks back over her shoulder. At that moment our eyes meet, she smiles briefly. I don't know how to react. She's about to go to her death or some untold torture that the Lord Emperor has planned for her. What is there to grin about? Still, I want to run to her and give her one last hug.

Sensing my intentions, Master Jin firmly places a hand on my shoulder to keep me from rising. I suppress a sigh and lift my hand to wave goodbye. Lian waves back, but her solemn in control face has returned. The purple silk curtains close. The servants lift the sedan and follow the general across the cobbles of the village square behind the ranks of retreating soldiers.

Mama stands alone watching the imperial sedan bearing her oldest daughter away, leaving her behind forever to become a Wife Divine. A line of tears falls from her eyes.

I've seen that look many times before when Father has punished or yelled at me. It's a sadness mixed with fear and helplessness. A desire to step in and intervene in my behalf, but knowing that doing so will shame Father, shame our family, and give Father every right to administer thirty blows to her with a thrashing rod before severing all ties with her. Even though the threat has always been there, Father would never do so. He has a kind side to him, especially towards Mama. Deep down he loves her. When I was younger, I thought I saw glimpses of a similar love toward me, but now I wonder if he really felt anything more than disdain for me.

Mama's eyes stay on me when Father finally takes her by the arm to lead her back home. I want so badly to feel the warmth of her embrace squeeze my shoulders. But even if Master Jin's hand wasn't holding me down, there would be no hugs between Mama and me. Not that she wouldn't welcome it, but Father spoke, and I disobeyed. The tears streaming from her eyes are not just for Lian. Some are for me. Mama has lost both her daughters this day.

Master Jin doesn't remove his hand from my shoulder until all signs of the imperial forces have left the village square. Magistrate Pang is not in the square either. If he were, I'm sure I'd already be in the pain yoke again with fresh thrashing wounds on my back. Then I remember he was with solders I wind blasted. Is he okay? A smile forms on my lips, but I push it down.

Master Jin helps me to my feet and stares at me for several heartbeats. Worry lines crease his bald forehead. A mix of concern and seriousness haunt his eyes, making me wonder if he plans to comfort me at the loss of my sister or make good on his threat to give me fifty blows with a thrashing rod.

I shift uncomfortably on my feet, waiting for whatever he's going to say or do. I don't want to be here. I want to race after Lian to try to save her again, no matter how foolish it might be. I could run to the fields to get more Shen Breath from the paper lanterns hanging at the rows. If I get enough, I could sneak onto the ship and try again to rescue Lian.

But I can't do any of that until Master Jin finishes with me. If he's going to punish me, I want him to hurry, and do it so I can go after Lian. I have to get her free before the Imperial Warship leaves dock with her. Every second wasted waiting for my punishment lessens my chance of saving her. Oh, but what if he puts me back in the pain yoke. I'll lose every chance I have to save Lian.

Master Jin folds his arms across his chest and wrinkles his eyebrows, giving me a stern look. "Meilin, trouble has always been your shadow."

I bow my head. He's right. And all of the sudden I wonder if it's my fault that the emperor has stolen my sister. Maybe if I tried harder to be respectful, to bring more honor to my family, Father wouldn't have felt the need to give Lian up. No. That wouldn't have stopped him. He believes this is the most wonderful thing that could have happened to his prized daughter.

Stop it. Feeling sorry for myself won't help Lian. I need to take my punishment and move on. The sooner I let Master Jin say what he's going to say and punish me, the sooner I can go after Lian.

"Rebellious. Impudent. Bad mannered. Shameful. Disrespectful. These are just a few of the Magistrate's and Elders' regular complaints against you. But, after today, they are the least of your problems."

Behind my back at my waist, I clench the folds of my gray work clothes, trying hard to hide my impatience. Please, get on with your punishment and let me go. I need to go after Lian.

"Meilin, you are in grave danger. Stories will spread about what you did today."

"What? Because I borrowed a horse and tried to save my sister?" I know I shouldn't speak so freely. Even though Master Jin has never had a problem with women speaking their mind to him—as long as no other men are around—right now it would probably be better to show more restraint than usual.

Master Jin frowns. "Do not make me the fool. You know we talk of something more. Do you think Lord Zheng truly believed my pleas in your behalf? Lord Zheng knows what he saw. As do I."

I tense. The tone in Master Jin's voice and the expression on his face stir a tinge of fear inside me. The way Jin had defended me against Lord Zheng had made me think that perhaps he hadn't really noticed the wind blasting from my hand. How could I be such a fool? Everyone noticed. So, why did Master Jin act like nothing had really happened? Zheng had called it witchery. What did he mean by that? All I did was use Tiānqì Shen's gift. Why should that be a problem?

"What…"

Master Jin cuts me off. "These things are not lawful to talk of."

"Why not?" I want to shout. It's a gift from Tiānqì Shen. Why can't it be talked of? And why would Zheng call it witchery? I want to understand this gift. How can I better use it to save Lian?

Master Jin drops his voice to a whisper. "How you became Shen-Blessed, I do not want to know. To be so blessed is forbidden, save for the Lord Emperor, Chosen of Heaven."

Shen-Blessed? Is that what I am? If so, how can it be wrong? All I did was pray. I don't care what the emperor says. How can asking help of the Shen be evil?

"I just want to help Lian."

Master Jin shuts his eyes. "Stop! Tell me nothing more." He exhales a long breath and opens his eyes again. "Listen to me. You were right to try to help Lian. She is in danger, but now you are too. You must leave Ning. But do not go after your sister. You cannot save her now."

"I can't give up on her."

"She is beyond your reach, but you still have a chance." The wrinkles on his forehead crease. "It might take a few days, or maybe a week, but they will come for you. You need to get away. Far away. Maybe upriver to the Yemaren border or beyond."

"Why? Who will come for me?"

Before Master Jin can answer, the boom of a drum strike sounds from the river, followed by the chant of oarsmen. The Imperial Warship moves away from the dock. Its dragonhead prow slowly turns downriver toward Quanli, the City of Heaven, capital of Huyan. I'm too late. Lian is gone.

Master Jin grabs my wrist and places a small, weighted bag in my hand. Its contents jingle with the sound of coins. "Take this. The silver and copper zhu's will be enough to live on for a few weeks. Walk or catch a ride with a river gypsy. But get away. You are not safe here."

"Because of Magistrate Pang?"

Master Jin shakes his head. "Pang is the least of your worries. Yes, he will be angry when he wakes from being knocked out, but without proper evidence he has no authority to execute you. When news of today's deeds travel, those who will come for you, will end your life swiftly."

Before I can ask him why, he lets go of my wrist and walks away. I stare after him, wanting answers. But if Master Jin had been willing to say more, he would have. I'm on my own.

Still, I'm surprised at the help he's given me. I'm a girl after all. The fact that he did help scares me. Am I really in that much danger? It doesn't matter. I can't run away. Somehow, I have to rescue Lian.

I retrieve my shoulder bag from near the elm tree and slip the bag of coins inside. I wander from the square toward the fields. I don't really have a plan other than to get more Shen Breath. I'm not sure what good it will do me now, but it's all I can think of. I feel so helpless.

Bees buzz and grasshoppers leap in front of me as I walk through the wildflowers and tall grass toward the growing fields. I stop when I reach the grid work of family plots. The eyes of every villager working their fields fall on me. Anger shows on the faces of most the men and boys, and even a few women. It's the expression of anger that shouts, "Meilin, where is your honor? How could you shame us again?"

Confusion or fear show on a few others. But none show any empathy for me having lost my sister today. It's clear. I'm no longer welcome—if I ever was. I've disgraced them. They want me gone.

I look past their stares to the lanterns of Shen Breath hanging near each row of crops. That's why I came here, to harvest the Shen Breath. Do I dare collect it with so many eyes on me? Would they notice? What would they think? Freak! Thief! Witch! Are a few of the epithets I imagine them hurling my way.

Maybe the villagers are the danger that Master Jin warned me about. Or does he share their feelings of disgust for me? Is that the real reason why Master Jin told me to flee? Does he simply want me gone? I'm unsure what to think anymore.

I turn away and walk. I'll get the Shen Breath later. I head toward the rise that leads toward Gudai Forest, leaving behind my neighbors' stares. I kick at a patch of weeds, angry at my failure at saving Lian.

"Why, Tiānqì Shen?" I cry aloud. "Why didn't you help me? What good were your gifts if they failed to help me save Lian?"

"Silly, child."

I jerk to a stop. I almost trip over a young girl sitting hidden amid the tall grass. She clutches a tattered rag doll to her chest like it's her greatest possession. The girl's name is Jia, the candle maker's four-year-old daughter. Her intense dark eyes send chills up my back. But it's the voice that spooks me most. Not Jia's normal playful voice, but the voice of an aged woman floats past the little girl's lips.

"I did help you," the unnatural voice continues. "Did my gift displease you?"

My eyes go wide. I have to fight the urge to run away. "Tiānqì Shen?"

"Well, did it?" the girl asks again.

I blink several times. I have to be imagining this. But when the little girl stands with hands on her hips, she gives me a stern look that would have a Fei Chi Master begging forgiveness. I drop to my knees and bow my head slightly, but with my gaze still meeting Jia's.

"Forgive me, Blessed One," I manage to say. "Your gift did please me. It was wonderful."

The intensity in young Jia's eyes softens. A sly grin turns the corners of her lips upward. The elderly voice of Tiānqì Shen comes out almost as a chuckle. "Yet, it was not perhaps what you wanted. Is that it?"

I hesitate at first, but then I lift my head. My thoughts rush out in a flurry. "With all your power, you could have stopped them. But you didn't. Lian's gone now. Gone! I thought your gift would save her, but it didn't. Why? Why didn't you help me more? Why didn't you stop them? That's why I came to you! That's why I risked my life to pray to you! To save Lian. Why didn't you save her?"

Little Jia purses her lips and shakes her head. The voice of Tiānqì Shen breathes out slow and firm. "Did you think it enough to simply ask, and all would be given? Some gifts are freely given. But to learn their true value, some require patience. Most require work. All must be shared. You must not only receive, but you must also do."

"Do what? What must I do?"

Jia smiles. "Use the gift mark of the Wind well and always keep your oath."

The Wind gift mark must be the wind symbol paired with the Mother stroke, but what oath is she talking about? I crinkle my nose and tilt my head sideways as I stare at the little girl. "How will some oath save Lian?"

Jia flashes a grin and winks. "Now that you have the gift, it is for you to decide."

What does that even mean? Why the riddles. I just want to save Lian. I want to know how to save her.

In a panic I grab little Jia's shoulder and shake her. "I don't know what to do! You have to tell me! Please, tell me how to save Lian."

Jia's lips tighten. The intensity in her eyes vanishes, replaced with fear. "Mama! Mama!" Jia screams in her own high-pitched voice. "Meilin is hurting me."

I jerk my hands off her shoulders and step back. Jia squeals, tucks her rag doll under her arm and sprints toward the growing fields. I turn and sigh, watching the young girl run to her mother. That's just what I need—one more reason for the villagers to hate me.

"Everything will be fine," I tell myself, but I struggle to believe it. I try to smile, but I can't see how it will do me any good right now. Then Mama's words whisper at the back of my mind, "Better to smile through hopelessness than frown in surrender to misery." The corners of my lips rise a little, but not much.

I turn away and continue through the wildflowers and tall grass up the rise toward Gudai. Halfway up the rise, I hear a buzz of chatter from behind me. I ignore it. It's probably the villagers squawking and muttering about how they think I mistreated little Jia. But the squawks rise to panicked shrieks and screams.

I spin on my heels. Sprays of dirt and greens fly in the air as frenzied villagers scatter from the growing fields. Fathers and mothers scoop up their young ones. Older children rush behind close on their heels. Some head toward their hillside homes. Others dash and dart anywhere they can to distance themselves from the fields.

As the fields clear, five armed warriors appear. They sprint through the middle of the fields from the direction of the village square. Dressed in black flowing robes and leather breast and shoulder armor, they race over the green fields with the grace and speed of Jade Leopards. The closer they come, the trill melody of the Shen Breath song whispers inside my head. That's when I notice the Shen Breath.

My chest tightens. As the warriors pass each crop row, every paper lantern bursts in an explosion of color. The glowing Shen Breath fills the air around them with a swirling storm of color. It's a dazzling spectacle. The air above the growing fields curls and streaks with a rainbow of snaking tendrils.

At first, I think the warriors must be Shen-Blessed, like me. But I'm wrong. The escaped Shen Breath doesn't flow into their flesh as it did mine. Instead, the colored mists stream into the black-hilt swords sheathed on their backs. By the time the warriors reach the edge of the fields closest to me, their weapons glow with power, having drained every paper lantern of its precious Shen Breath.

In that moment I notice two things. First, the guard from the shrine of Tiānqì Shen runs about fifty paces behind the warriors, struggling to keep up. His eyes fix on me. Second, each warrior wears the red and gold demon-wolf masks of the Shashyao, slayers of the defiled. Like every child in Huyan, from the cradle I heard the stories of the Shashyao—half demon, half wolves—who hunt day and night for any who revile the Shen or the lesser gods.

As a child, the threat "Mind the Shashyao!" echoed in my ears dozens of times a week or day. Mama would say it in a tease to get me to obey. Father would use it as a stern rebuke when I failed to show enough honor. As a child my friends and I would cover our faces with homemade red and gold demon-wolf paper masks of the Shashyao. We would howl and scream as we'd chase each other in circles, trying to tag others before being tagged.

The Shashyao aren't only child's play. Actors in travelling shows wear the masks of the fierce Shashyao as they act out being the Shen's angels of destruction who punish villains or devastate whole villages. Musicians sing heart rending love ballads of the Shashyao slaying one's lover for some forgotten wrongdoing.

I even remember sitting hidden in the branches of my favorite elm as the village Elders sat on the grass below in a circle around Master Jin. They laughed as Master Jin told them in a hushed warning that the Shashyao existed. Not as mythical creatures, but as a secret band of elite Fei Chi assassins. I giggled quietly along with the Elders' chuckles. Master Jin did not laugh. I thought then that he only pretended to be serious as he told how these Shashyao assassins were endowed with power from Emperor Hu to silence any who question him or his claim to godhood.

As these masked warriors now rush from the growing fields toward me, I doubt Master Jin had meant that warning of years ago for me. But now I know who his warning of not many minutes ago was about. It would not be days or weeks. The Shashyao are here now. And they are here for me.

Chapter 8
Qiu Meilin – Death Hunt

"Forlorn forgotten, shadows shun.
Friendless fearful, hope fades, hope runs.
A pauper's hand, a stranger's smile.
Steps through darkness, a friendship won."
- Private Journal of Qiu Meilin

I turn and run. The dense foliage of Gudai Forest lies less than thirty paces away. If I can reach its borders, I might be able to escape. I know this part of Gudai better than most, especially outsiders. If I can't outrun the Shashyao, I might be able to hide from them.

The Shashyao run less than fifty paces behind me when I step into the cool moist air beneath the canopy. Thick strands of moss cover the trunks and hang from the massive oaks and other ancient trees that twist heavenward and tower over me. I sprint across the forest floor. The balls of my feet spring off the soft cushion of decayed leaves and lichen. The whole forest comes alive as I dart through the trees and swerve between thick shrubbery and brambles.

Blue thrush take flight above as I duck beneath hanging vine loops. A covey of green grouse scatters as I push through head-high fern fronds. A bush tail squirrel chitters at me, then scurries away as I leap over a thick clump of rotted deadwood.

At every step, birds whistle and chatter. Insects buzz. Animals squeak and chatter. Even if the Fei Chi assassins can't track my path, the rising sounds of Gudai will lead them right to me. I had planned to hide in a small dugout beneath a cluster of boulders deeper in the forest, but now I doubt I can reach it before the Shashyao catch up to me. I'm sure they're gaining on me, and I'm already panting, and my legs are tiring. I don't know what to do.

Suddenly, a golden ball of fur drops from the branches above, lands in a clump of leaves in front of me, bares its fanged teeth, and squeals. Snubby.

I wave him away and shout whisper, "Get!"

His grin widens and he dances side to side. Then he lets out an even louder shrill.

"Quiet!" I shout whisper again. "You'll lead them right to me."

His dark eyes brighten. He sticks out his tongue, curling it up, and then laughs in a taunting chatter that's meaning is clear. "They're going to find you. They're going to find you."

Before I can tell him to go away again, he turns his back and scampers ahead through the green brush. He stops about eight paces ahead and looks back at me over his shoulder. He opens his mouth in a thin wide line, showing his teeth in a manner that could be either a menacing threat or an encouraging smile. I'm not sure which. But his eyes focus on me with a determined look. He's waiting for something. He's waiting for me.

When I don't move, he lets out a murmurous chatter, jumps up and down, and shakes his hands at me. It's like he's saying, "Hurry, you dough head! Are you going to follow me or not?"

"Please, Snubby" I whisper. "Go away."

He sticks his tongue out at me through the narrow gap in teeth. His dark round eyes beg me. "Come on. Come on."

I hear the swoosh of leaves and of crunch of underbrush not far behind me. The Shashyao are getting close. Snubby jumps up and down again, and chatters urgently at me.

I shake my head. It's crazy, but I run toward Snubby. He smiles, chatters happily, and scoots quickly ahead. I follow him deeper into the cool shadows of Gudai. We zig zag through tree and bush, up and over uneven ground, boulders, and decaying logs. The course he takes feels random at first, but he never hesitates. The golden snub nose acts as if he knows exactly where he's going.

The songs and chatter of forest life still rise wherever we go, but the zig zag pattern that Snubby leads me on makes the sounds surge and drop in so many different directions that it will make it much harder for the Shashyao to tell which way we've gone. It almost makes me wonder if this monkey is actually a genius.

Snubby slows down near a wall of vibrant violet orchids. From the twisting branches of gnarled trees, the colorful flowers dangle in large clumps amid long tresses of hanging moss. The orchids and their sword-shaped leaves sprout in dense jumbles from the trees' protruding roots and up their trunks. In spotty patches they even mix in with large golden mushrooms that grow in terraced layers atop rotted logs, bark chunks, and the scattering of other deadwood.

Snubby bounds over to the rotted remains of a fallen tree enclosed in a thick layer of stringy moss and carpeted with clusters of orchids and mushrooms. He scurries onto one end of it and starts hopping up and down from one leg to the other. He bares his teeth at me and chatters. A nearby stream babbles, but not loud enough to drown out Snubby's chatter.

"Shush!" I whisper and hurry over to him, hoping to quiet him.

He stops chattering as soon as I reach him and flashes a huge grin, pleased with himself that he can so easily get me to do what he wants.

"Snubby, what do you want? We need to go."

He grins again, leans over the end of the fallen log, sticks his head into the hollow of it, pulls his head back out, and opens his mouth wide like he's silently laughing. I stare at him. There's nothing to laugh about.

The Shashyao have to be getting close. I can't wait here any longer trying to figure out what Snubby's trying to say.

Before I take a step to run away and ditch him, Snubby sticks his head back into the hollow of the log and pulls it out again. This time his big round eyes give me a look that says, "Come on dough head. You are the daftest girl I have ever met."

I want to scream, "What? What do you want?"

But then I smile. I get it. I hurry over to the end of the log and peer inside. A huge banana slug slithers across the inner edge. A pair of xudupedes scurry up the walls. It's dark further in, blinding me to other creatures hiding in its depths, but the opening is plenty large enough for me to crawl inside.

Delightful. I shake my head, but smile. I'd rather spend another night in the pain yoke then crawl in there. Snubby wags his head and squeals. Before I can hush him, I hear the voice of the shrine guard call, "Over there."

Snubby stops howling and gives a smile that says, "You better hurry or I'll howl again."

I can't tell how far away the Shashyao are, but they're too close. Trying not to cringe, I pick the banana slug up by its end and throw it as far away as I can. Then I reach inside the log and flick the xudupedes out of the log with my fingers. I hope there aren't any others further inside.

I put on my bravest grin, drop to my belly, take a deep breath, and crawl inside. My fingers sink into the moist, goo-like wood. My nose twinges at the stench of rot and decay that fills the log. I try not to think about all things my elbows, belly, knees, and toes squish and push through as I squirm further in. I finally stop where a faint beam of light shines through a knuckle-size knothole in the log. It's not a great view of the world outside the log, but it helps lessen the feeling of being trapped.

As I settle into place, I'm thankful for Snubby's help. The monkey howls and screams as loud he can. My entire body clenches. The insides of my stomach squeeze and twist with anxiety. What is that monkey doing? I thought I could trust him.

He squeals louder and louder for several moments, and then suddenly goes quiet. I hear him hop off the log and scurry away until the I only hear the babbling stream and the buzz and click of bugs inside and near my log. Moments later, movement in the nearby brush break the silence.

I push an eye closer to the knothole. Five pairs of black boots step softly across the forest floor. The Shashyao. Another pair of long, wide boots with more shine, but poorer quality lumber behind them.

"Ho, that girly be close by, I tell you," sounds the voice of the shrine guard. "If that foul monkey is near, she probably is too."

The Shashyao say nothing. They each take a step in different directions, pause and take another step. Three pairs of boots step out of my view. The shrine guard and the other two stay in place. The shrine guard rocks back and forth from heel to toe on his big boots. The remaining Fei Chi assassins pivot in place on their boots, turning slowly in complete circles.

I wish I could see their eyes as they search for me. Will they find my tracks leading to the log? Any moment I expect hands to grip me by the ankles and yank me out. What will they do when they find me? Take me prisoner? Execute me? Is Master Jin right? Do they know I'm Shen-Blessed? Is that why they're here? How did they get here so fast?

"Your time is wasting," the shrine guard continues. "They're an evil pair, I tell you. Demons. Each defiled the shrine. Each helped the other escape. The further that snub-rat gets, the further that girly gets too."

"Thank you, soldier," says a low, hard voice that sounds more annoyed than grateful.

"Just doing my duty," the guard continues. "The moment I saw you skulking about the gardens, I knew you would want to know about the girly. And if there be a little something in it for me, well, I wouldn't say no."

"You'll be rewarded," the assassin says, still sounding annoyed. "But are you sure you haven't seen the deserter we described?"

The guard chuckles. "No, but I can ask about him in the village. All the villagers love me. If they've seen him, they'll tell me. Don't you worry."

"No!" The Shashyao answers firm. "This is military business. Just keep a lookout for him."

"Ho, I will…"

A howl sounds deeper in the forest. It's Snubby. It silences the guard, while stirring up more sounds of the forest. The Shashyao spin on their boots to face the direction of the sounds.

The guard continues, "I tell you, if you…"

"Enough!" The Shashyao says. "Your help is no longer needed. Return to your post."

"But..."

A pair of boots steps toward the guard. "Leave us, now! Do I need to repeat that order?"

Silence follows. Finally, the guard turns on his boots. He kicks up leaves and dirt as he shuffles across the forest floor until he's out of view. The Fei Chi assassins stand in silence several moments longer. Snubby howls again. When he quiets, the Shashyao whisper among themselves, but too quiet for me to tell what they're saying. Before long, their boots step from view. I listen to their footfalls and movement through the brush until once again I only hear the rumble of the nearby stream and the buzz and clicks of insects.

Still, I don't dare move or make a noise. Only four pair of boots passed my view. One of the assassins could still be here looking for me, or at least close by watching. Several minutes pass as I lay as still as I can inside the damp and dark confines. Before long, Snubby howls again. If there's still a Shashyao here, I don't hear him. I continue to keep still.

Every ten minutes or so, Snubby howls further and further in the distance. An hour passes before Snubby's howls grow too faint to hear. I stay put. I only move when a xudupede crawls across my calf up my pant leg. I shiver as its thousands of tiny legs tickle my flesh.

Trying not to make a sound, I rub my legs together to squish the bug. Its guts slime my skin in an oozing glob. I desperately want to brush off the slime, but it's too far down my leg to reach.

I spend the next hour trying not to think about the slime on my leg. Or how many other bugs might be crawling around me. Or how the inside of the log seems to grow smaller and smaller around my arms and legs, making me feel trapped. Or how hot and stuffy it is inside the log. Breathe in. Breathe out. Smile. All will be well.

I focus my thoughts on a way to escape the Shashyao and rescue Lian. Before long, another xudupede interrupts my thoughts. It crawls up my other leg and I squish it too, leaving more bug guts on my leg. Four more times that happens. I shudder each time I squish the bugs, fighting the urge to crawl out of the log screaming.

More bugs crawl across my face. Some on my cheek. One on my nose. Another behind my ear. These I reach by working my hand up the tight confines of the log. Some I flick away. Others I squish between my fingers and wipe the slime on the moss of the log.

I try to stay calm, but the hours pass slowly. The tight and humid confines of the log grow more uncomfortable. Gudai's dense canopy of leaves and branches usually keep the forest cool spring and summer, but inside this log I'm roasting inside a steaming pot. A layer of sweat coats my skin and soaks into my clothes clinging against my flesh. Little heat or moisture escapes the log's insides, making it warmer and more humid the more time passes. But that's okay. I'm safe… at least for now.

Every time I tell myself it's okay to crawl out of the log, I hear a noise in a nearby bush or tree. Each time I'm certain it must be one of the Shashyao still lurking nearby. Even if there are no more Shashyao nearby, there's no need to leave my log. I've come up with the crude beginnings of a plan, but I need to wait until after dark to act on it.

Eventually my stomach tightens with hunger pains. I haven't eaten since the night before last. Several times I put my hand to my stomach to muffle its grumblings. But it does little good. The rumblings sound like the cry of a sick water buffalo. Every time my stomach grumbles, I expect a Shashyao blade to slice through the log into my flesh. I keep hoping my stomach can't be heard much further than the log.

To take my mind off my hunger, I think of Lian. When we were little, she used to pinch my nose and call me her "silly little duck." She's only a year older than me, but she's always treated me like a baby sister, spoiling me like a princess. And she always watched out for me. Now it's my turn to watch out for her, if she'll let me.

I think about Shen Breath, the Wind gift mark, and the boon Tiānqì Shen gave me. In spite of the power they bring, I know there's more I need to learn about them. I worry it won't be enough to help me save Lian.

When, the shadows of Gudai darken with nightfall I consider leaving the log. It has to be safe now, but I don't move. I have no desire to face a Shashyao assassin in the dark of night. Besides, it's still too early to carry out my plan. Even so, the combination of Gudai's darkness with the cramped confines of the log's insides rattle my nerves. I have to try harder to calm myself. I take slow, deep breaths, hoping they're not too loud. Somehow, I relax enough that my eyelids droop closed.

Chapter 9
Qiu Meilin – Caught

"Storm rains death.
Night conceals.
Outlaw seized.
Truth revealed."
- Private Journal of Qiu Meilin

The staccato of heavy raindrops wakes me. I have no idea how long I've slept or how long it's been raining. A slow trickle of drops falls from the peephole in my log, running down my shirt from shoulder to waist, adding to the dampness of my still sweat-soaked clothes.

I take a deep breath. It's time. The dark night and the heavy rain will hopefully make my escape easier. I shimmy backward out of the log—my legs, torso, and head immediately getting drenched once I'm free of the log. The cool spring rain feels refreshing after being in the hot quarters of the log for so long. Still, I hurry toward the trunk of a nearby oak to get a little shelter beneath its branches from the pouring rain.

"Kaioda!" A mass of orange fur with round dark eyes pops in front of my face. I jump back startled. Snubby hangs from a branch right in front of me, baring his teeth in what I hope is a smile.

He swings on the branch and flies toward me. He lands on my chest before I can move out of the way and wraps his long arms around my neck. He's heavier than I expect. I cradle him in my arms to keep from tipping forward and to take some of his weight off my neck.

I grin wide. "Snubby, what are you doing?"

He snuffs his white bulbous nose a couple times before burying his soft fur into my neck. He rubs it gently against my skin. I'm guessing this is his way of telling me thank you for saving him from the shrine guard.

"Thank you, too," I whisper, in case any of the Shashyao are nearby. "You've saved me twice now. Maybe I still owe you that pile of hazelnuts I promised."

Snubby widens his mouth into a narrow grin and waggles his tongue at me as he shakes his head. He releases his arms from around my neck and drops to the rain-soaked ground. Now that he has thanked me, I expect him to run off and disappear into the woods. Instead, he grabs my wrist with his long fingers and places something in my palm with his other hand.

Six shelled hazelnuts. I can't help but grin. I'm starving. Even though it's not much, it looks like a feast. I crouch down and wrap my arms around the monkey in a tight hug. "Thank you, Snubby. Thank you."

I pop the nuts into my mouth, not even caring that Snubby probably shelled them with his saliva-dripping teeth. They taste better than a fruit bun with honey. I chew them slowly, enjoying every bite. Snubby watches me as I eat, a big grin on his face.

When I finish, I crouch down and pat Snubby's shoulder. "Thank you, Snubby. You are a good monkey. Take care of yourself. I hope to see you again if I ever make it back to Ning. May the Two watch you."

I take a deep breath, rise and sprint away into the dark and pouring rain. Water soaks the ground and my sandals slosh with every step. But as long I stay where the leaves and undergrowth are thick, I shouldn't have to worry about getting stuck in a mud pit. I push through the dense foliage of Gudai, heading mostly northeast and toward the Pangbo River and the village pier. My rain-soaked clothes hang heavy on my arms and legs, making the effort to run much harder.

I don't have to worry about making noise as I move through the brush of the forest. The pounding rain drowns out any sound I make. I could scream and no one would hear me over the torrent. But that also means the Shashyao assassins could be lurking anywhere, and I would never hear or see them until it is too late. They're also less likely to see or hear me unless I step right into their camp.

When I reach the edge of Gudai I stop. The darkness and downpour make the growing fields to my left a muddled blur. The switchback hillside where my home and all the Ning villagers' houses stand can't be seen at all. Not a single flickering dot of light shines. Either all the villagers have gone to bed for the night, or the rain and wind doused all the lanterns.

No lanterns shine in the village square. The lavender moon, Shi, should still be high in the sky, while her emerald lover, San, prepares to set in the next few hours, if he hasn't already. But the thick rain clouds block any light the moons' rays might offer. Still, I can make out silhouettes of a few buildings near the village square. Beyond the village where the Pangbo River flows is a wall of black. That's where I need to reach. I brush a stream of rainwater from my forehead and eyes and launch into the open.

The fields between here and the river provide no shelter. If the Shashyao are watching for me, I can only hope the sheets of rain and black of night hide me as I run. I slosh and splash with every step. The field's bog-like mud sucks at my feet. Haphazard streams and puddles often cross underfoot before I see them.

At any moment, I expect a Shashyao warrior to charge in front of me and slice off my head. Near the village square, I hear the tingle of chimes blowing in the wind. I hurry past. My eyes scan the shadows of the old buildings and market stalls for the assassins. My hopes rise. No sign of them.

On the village pier, the rain pounds on the bamboo deck like a million drums. A dozen or so fishing boats tied into their narrow slips rock and rise on the churned-up waves of the river. The water flows harmlessly over the flat decks of the fishing boats. Most of the boats are simply long, narrow rafts made of thick bamboo trunks capped at each end and bound together side by side with rope. Some are longer and wider than the others and have a small open-ended shelter on the middle or near the back of the deck. Two of these even have a small mast and sail that can be raised when the wind is right. I hurry toward the closest of these.

I leave a couple copper zhu's on the deck near a wooden cleat that the boat's rope is tied to. I don't know how much it costs to rent a boat, but that's all I dare spare. I have no idea how long the coins need to last that Master Jin gave me.

The boat rocks and wobbles under my feet as I step on, and I almost fall in the water. I quickly squat low to catch my balance. I've been on a fishing boat plenty of times before, but never in a rainstorm or on rough water. I'll have to be more careful. I won't do Lian any good if I drown before I have a chance to save her.

I lean toward the dock to untie the boat. Strong fingers grab my wrist, clamping hard on my flesh. My heart stops. I'm caught. The Shashyao found me. I expect a knife to the throat or to the heart. None comes.

I raise my eyes, expecting to meet the hard gaze of eyes peering from behind a demon-wolf mask. But there's no mask. Even through the flood of rainwater streaming through my eyes and blurring my vision, I know that face—dark, serious eyes, full lips, dimpled chin, and rigid jaw line. Just as I saw in my vision of him in the shrine, he even has the long cut above his eye. My heart flutters. Gales and hails, Cai lives.

Chapter 10
Qiu Meilin – Night Flight

"Shen are not picky gods, caring little about petitioners' character. An oath by one of the blood need only be made with true and honorable intent. Albeit, under scrutiny the Shen's perception of honorable may appear fluid."

- Hidden Scrolls of Quingping: Study in Oath Criticalities

Even drenched in rain and with his lips tightened in a grim frown, Cai still looks as handsome as ever. When he wasn't working, Cai always had one of the most attractive smiles I've ever seen. Sometimes I imagined that smile was reserved only for me. But when gutting and filleting his catch of the day, he would wear a nasty expression that shouted, "Don't bother me or I might gut you too!" His expression now is ten times nastier and more lethal. But I'm not sure what makes me more nervous, the danger or beauty in his look.

"You're supposed to be dead!" I blurt.

His frown tightens, as does his grip on my wrist. "You're a thief. This is mine and my father's boat."

Shivering, I tilt my head toward the coins I placed on the dock to pay for borrowing the boat. "I left some copper zhu's."

His eyes shift to the coins and back to me. His frown doesn't relax. "That makes you a thief and a cheat."

"I need the boat. The Imperial Guard took Lian."

His grip on my wrist doesn't lessen. Neither does his frown. "I know, but what does that have to do with you?"

"She's in danger!" The desperation in my voice rises. "In three nights, she'll be forced to become one of the emperor's Wives Divine. I have to save her."

Cai's frown twists to a mocking smile. No. Not again. Am I the only one who realizes that being chosen as a Wife Divine is not a good thing? How do I convince Cai of the threat to Lian? Then I realize that's not the reason for his mocking smile.

"Go home Meilin," he says, with a laugh in his voice. "You're a girl. How do you expect to be able to save her? Leave me to go after Lian."

I want to strangle Cai. I've never heard him talk like that before. If I had Shen Breath flowing in my veins, I'd teach him that I can do a lot more than he realizes. Then I remember the vision I had of Cai in the shrine. I look at him more intently. Does Shen Breath flow in his veins? Is he Shen-Blessed too? If he is, how am I any better able to save Lian than him?

Nothing that I say to Cai will convince him to help. Even worse, behind his mocking smile I see resentment in his eyes. Is he upset to have a girl talk so freely to him? Before he left for war, he didn't mind when I would talk to him openly and tease him about Lian. Did the military change that?

Or does he feel I shamed him? Does he know that I tried to protect Lian in the village square? She's the love of his life. Honor dictates that he should have protected her. Or does he feel dishonor that I'm determined to save her when he should be the one to come to her rescue?

Men can be such goat heads. Why should it matter that I'm a girl? I'm trying to save Lian. That should be all that matters to Cai. I can't let him stop me. I have to try a different tact.

I bite my lip, let it quiver a bit, and give him my best pouty face. I hope shivering in the pouring rain with drenched hair and clothes makes me look more pathetic than normal. "The Shashyao are after me. I need the boat to escape."

I half expect him to laugh at any tale of the Shashyao, but his eyes widen. His entire body tenses. "They're here? You saw them?"

Now what do I tell him? I can't tell him about my visit to the shrine and being Shen-Blessed. He might turn me over to the Shashyao himself. A half-truth maybe? I give in to the cold of my wet clothes clinging to my flesh and allow myself to shiver even more, trying to look more vulnerable.

"When the Imperial Guard took Lian, I tried to stop them. The next thing I know, five of the assassins in demon-wolf masks show up and chase after me. I ran to Gudai before they could catch me. I hid there all day and night until now. I need your father's boat to escape. If I don't escape, they'll kill me. I know they will."

He looks over his shoulder, moving his head side to side scanning shadows in the rain for any sign of the assassins. Concern shows in his eyes when he turns back to me. I must be imagining it, but for a moment I see a trace of guilt in his expression before it hardens.

He lets go of my wrist. "Get inside the shelter. You can come, but don't make me regret this."

The boat rocks as I crouch-walk to the shelter. When I stick my head in, I jerk back, rocking the boat even more. A huge dark bird sits in the shadows of the shelter's corner squawking at me. It's Cai's trained fishing cormorant. It's usually a well-behaved bird, but it's not happy that I'm intruding its territory.

"Watch it!" Cai calls to me over the sound of the rain. "You're going to drown us."

I grit my teeth. "Sorry." I slowly duck all the way inside the shelter, keeping my distance from the bird. It stands tall, spreads its wide, black-feathered wings, lifts its head high with its beak pointed to the roof, and squawks one more time at me before settling back in its corner.

Cai unties the boat and poles us out a little further to the current and shallows of the Pangbo. When he finishes, he doesn't bother to light the lantern that hangs on the hook-post on the boat's bow. He simply crouches down and makes his way back into the shelter, sitting in the back near his cormorant. He grabs the handle of the long stern paddle that pokes through an opening in the back of the shelter and steers the boat as it floats downstream toward Quanli.

The cormorant arches its neck as Cai runs the fingers of his free hand along the back of the bird's neck. A low croak sounds from the bird's throat, pleased with Cai's attention. "You missed me, didn't you Peck? Baba never strokes your neck like I do, does he?"

Peck wiggles its head and lets out another soft croak and settles in close to Cai. Cai smiles and continues to stroke the bird's feathers. "That's my good girl."

I've never heard Cai talk like that before. In fact, Lian and I would often tease him about being so proper. We would even compete to see which of us could make him laugh first or break from his serious way of talking. Lian usually won, but that was because he liked her.

"Wow! I didn't know you were such a sweet talker," I say with a grin. "You're going to make Lian jealous."

Even though it's dark in the shelter, I clearly see Cai's smile flatten into a thin line. It's his serious face. One he wears like a mask to hide his feelings. What did I say that upset him? Is he angry? Sad? I want to apologize, but I'm not sure what I did wrong.

His eyes meet mine and for a moment they plea for help. Just as fast the look disappears. It's dark. Did I imagine that? Cai has never been one to ask for help.

He turns away from me toward a storage box in the corner of the shelter and begins to rummage through it. After several heartbeats he pulls out a blanket and a small package wrapped in paper.

He tosses the blanket and package at my feet. "There's a rice cake in there if you're hungry," he says. "And wrap up in the blanket before you freeze."

"Thank you," I say, taking the blanket and package. I meet his gaze again and give him a comforting look.

He lowers his eyes and quickly turns to leave. He stops at the shelter opening, crouching. Without looking back at me, he says in a voice almost too soft for me to hear, "Get some sleep. We have a long trip ahead. In the morning, you'll need to take a turn steering so we can keep moving."

When he leaves, I pull the blanket tight around me. Its warmth feels wonderful. I hurriedly open the paper package and grin as I devour the rice cake. It's dry and stale, but it's food and I'm starving.

While I eat, the rippling of the river's current serenades me with the splash of Cai's steering pole occasionally interrupting the river's song. I can't help wondering what's bothering Cai. He's so angry, and maybe a little scared. What's going on with him? Does he know the Imperial Army told us he died? Why did they do that? He's obviously alive. What really happened and why is he here now? So many questions. Somehow, I'll have to get him to tell me the answers. But not tonight.

Part 2

Chapter 11
Fan Suyin – Assassins Duel

"As with any Shen granted powers, each gift in Luxíng Shen's traveling pentad has its own strengths and limitations, as well as potential different methods of preparation and operation between females and males."
- Hidden Scrolls of Quingping: Study in the gifts of the Shen

Sitting in the fading dark before sunrise, I rock back and forth with my arms wrapped around my knees to stay warm and to keep my impatience in check. Alone on this hilltop with the edge of the woods at my back, I have a good view of the little thatched-roof houses nestled along the hillside beneath me. Flickering dots of lights snake their way down the hill from the lanterns that shine behind the houses' paper windows.

Roosters have already begun to crow. A few goats bleat. Water buffalos huff and snuff waiting impatiently to be milked and fed. The impatience. The waiting. I know that feeling well. I could live without it. Waiting is most of what I've done during my young life. From the time as a scrawny five-year-old girl when I first spoke the Deliverer's Oath beside my twin brother, I slaved and trained for the next twelve years, waiting for the day I could free my people. But in not too many days the waiting will end.

Below me, sleepy farmers will be shuffling about inside their houses getting ready to work their meager fields or care for their haggard animals. It's a poor ordinary farming village, not much different than the dozens of others I've passed since escaping the emperor's quarries. I snicker. They all think their lives are so hard under the emperor's rule. But they know nothing of his cruelty. They wouldn't last a day in his quarries.

Still, what makes this village different? Why did the Shashyao stop here? Since I first found the trail of the demon warriors, they had never stopped anywhere long enough for me to catch up to them, let alone give me time to make a plan of attack.

When the horizon begins to brighten, I place a piece of paper little bigger than my hand on a hard patch of ground at my feet. I pull my grinding stone and brushes from my belt pouch. What ink sticks will I need this time? Black, green, gray, and brown should do. Well, maybe a little red. Once the sun rises, I'll know for sure. I shiver, anxious for the sun to chase away my chills. The peasant grays I'm wearing are still damp from last night's rain.

Time to get to work. I spit in the grinding stone and begin grinding black. Out of habit I make sure to only grind what I need and no more. Ink sticks were rare in the quarry camps. More than a few fellow slaves risked their lives over the years to get me the ink sticks and painting supplies I needed. It doesn't matter that even colored ink sticks are plentiful outside the quarry camps. Habit has trained me to always use each one prudently.

Shafts of orange light from the rising sun streak across the sky. As the sun's rays touch the woods' mists behind me, I sense their transformation. The chorus of Shen Breath sings in my mind. The glowing swirls of color flow toward me and seep into my flesh, warming my insides and fueling my gifts. I welcome the boon and its strength. I'll need as much of it as I can get.

With a prayer in my thoughts to Yanlì Shen, I use my gift of Farsight to look downriver and scan the up-close details of the rocky cliffs rising high above the other side of the Pangbo. To make my escape, I need a Leap destination far from the Shashyao. Being high on the cliff tops will also give me a nice vantage point to pick out my next destination. The only problem will be if my boon runs dry. Then I'll have to go on foot until I find more Shen Breath. If that happens, hopefully I will be able to find an easy path down from the cliffs, as well as a dense wooded area where Shen Breath can spawn after a night's rain.

I focus my Farsight on a large flat boulder outcropping atop the cliffs far downriver. A distinctive lone pine grows beside the boulder. Few branches adorn the lower portion of its tall scythe-shaped trunk. But its top has a lush wedge-shape crown that juts over the cliff edge as if to get a better look at the Pangbo far below. It's perfect. The distinctive pine and flat boulder make it easy to paint.

I'm no artist, but my skill with the inks is better than most people. Training as a Deliverer never allowed me much time for painting practice. I'm glad of that. I'd much rather spend my time developing my other gifts, especially mastering Fei Chi.

It's good that Leap paintings don't require the same precision that artistry requires. A fair depiction of the destination does fine. No need to be beautiful or exact, just uniquely recognizable. There's rarely time to get a painting perfect anyway. But there is always the worry about what will happen if a depiction isn't accurate or unique enough. That's something I hope to never find out. So, I do the best I can with what little time I have.

I move my brush in quick, fluid strokes across the small piece of paper. The lines and shades of color shape the boulder's contours, the mineral veins spidering across it, random blades of grass surrounding the rock, the leaning of the curved pine with its lush bough, and a hint of the rock formations and plant life covering the cliff face below. I glance back at the spot often with my Farsight to make sure I get it right.

As I paint, the villagers below care for their animals and head to their fields. A few exchange greetings, but most keep quiet as if in reverence to the peaceful morning. The animals show no reverence. The bleating, clucking, snuffing, and huffing grow loud as if begging for attention as their masters emerge from their homes. But there's no sign of the Shashyao. They spent the night in one of the finer houses at the hill's base, probably that of the village elder. But they have yet to appear.

After my last stroke with the brush, I softly blow on the paper. The ink doesn't need to be dry to activate it, but even a small smudge in the wrong place can ruin a Leap. I reach behind my neck for my necklace's leather cord and pull it off over my head. At a glance, it's easy to mistake the discs on the necklace for large coins. But these are ceramic rather than metal. To make it easy to find the right disc, I've glazed the different sets into different colors so each pentad of gifts as its own color, such as emerald, sapphire, amber, ivory, lime, and ruby. Each disc also has a hole at the top instead of at the center to allow them to hang on my necklace. But most important, instead of having raised characters bearing the emperor's name and coin value, each disc bears the symbols for its particular gift.

My fingers find the raised ridges of the Leap gift mark before my eyes do. Careful not to get ink anywhere else on the emerald glazed disc, I brush a thin layer of ink on the raised ridges of both the Mother stroke and the Leap character. Pressing the disc on the painting barely above the boulder's middle, I stamp a perfect image of the Leap gift mark.

Lifting the front collar of my shirt, I use the leftover ink on the disc to also stamp the gift mark above my left breast, the place where both heart and soul reside. With a quick thought, I will my boon to dry the mark on my flesh. I can't risk having my clothes smear and ruin the mark's power.

With a quick glance, I double check the condition of the several other gift marks printed above my breast. Most are Step marks, as well as Leap and Return marks I've yet to use. Nearly all were stamped over a week ago. Even with bathing, none have faded. But last night I did have to restamp other gift marks on my arms and soles of my feet. It's always good to have them in place in case I ever need them. It would be nice if I could ready myself like that with all my gifts, but like the Leap mark, many marks must be stamped in a certain order.

Watching the village below for any sign of the Shashyao, I put my inks and brushes into my belt pouch and pull out a small, hollow clay tube. I blow the ink dry on my small painting one last time before rolling it up and sliding it into the tube. With a quick strike of a fire stick, I create a small flame and light my painting on fire.

Thin wisps of smoke spiral heavenward from the burning painting while I clean any leftover ink from my grinding stone. My brother, Wei, has always teased me that I'm too meticulous, but I don't like messes. Life can be as chaotic as a raging thunderstorm but being able to keep at least some things in order brings me a sense of calm. That's one of the many ways that Wei and I differ. No matter what, Wei can flash a sly grin and kick up his feet for a relaxing nap while all the forces of nature go on a rampage.

When the smoke from my burning painting settles and nothing but gray ashes remain in the bottom of the tube, I pour them into a tiny cloth bag, tie it shut with a blue string, and put the bag in my belt pouch with all my other bags—each one tied with strings of different colors to help me remember what they're for.

Hefting a bundle of sticks onto my shoulder, I make my way down the winding path that leads past the villagers' homes toward the village square. My peasant grays and broad rimmed bamboo hat make it easy to blend in with the other villagers on the path. Still, I'm careful to keep the front of my hat tipped down. I don't need anyone seeing my face. One glance at my birth mark and they'll know I'm not one of their own.

Shen-cursed. That's how the quarry guards refer to any slaves born with the unusual birthmark. Marring the right side of my face, the mark's bright red symbols read "Make right the wrongs." Always on the right side for females and on the left for males. Almost half the slaves bear the marks. The guards believe it's a curse for something our ancestors did long ago. It makes them feel justified for treating us worse than the other slaves.

Some of my cousins think if the guards knew the real truth about the curse, they would ease up their brutal treatment of us. Perhaps they would even consider freeing us. Not a chance. I scowl at the thought. They still brutalize the other slaves, just not as bad as us. Besides, why else would we need Deliverers?

On my way down the hill a few of the villagers greet me "Good rising." I keep my head down, mumbling a reply and often parroting back their own greeting. I can't let my face or voice betray me. Would the villagers alert the Shashyao if they discover I'm not one of their own? Probably not. Anyone with snails for brains keeps their distance from the emperor's assassins. Still, I need to be careful.

At the bottom of the hill, I'm greeted by the colored shop tents and bamboo buildings surrounding the cobblestone square. They look little different than those of other villages I've seen. I laugh. Does the emperor dictate the design of every village square? Or do these simple people just have no imagination?

Beneath a broad shade elm near the village square, I set down my bundle of sticks and watch for the Shashyao. To keep from looking suspicious, I sort the sticks into piles as if I'm doing a normal villager task.

Nearby, a bronze door knocker with the face of Xié Shen, the demon god, clangs loudly as its big red door opens and swings to a stop. The house is an elegant one built with rich gold-colored bricks and roofed with a red glazed tile instead of thatch, bamboo, and mud like most of the village houses.

Shashyao warriors march out the door dressed in black robes, black leather armor, and demon-wolf masks. They scan the village and its surroundings from the square to the growing fields, the hillside homes, back across the fields, all along the edge of Gudai, and to the southern portion of the main road that runs alongside the great Pangbo River.

The Shashyao exchange a few quick words before separating into two groups to scout the area. They move like Dark Hounds fast on the blood scent of their master's enemy. Three spread out, angling between the growing fields and the south river road toward the towering tree line of Gudai. The other two spread apart as they move toward the village square. Villagers scurry out of their way, distancing themselves from the emperor's assassins.

I keep my head down and stay calm as one passes a few paces away. Would he recognize the Shen-cursed mark on my face? I don't want to find out, at least not right now. Though I have no fear of the Shashyao, they are still dangerous. I need to pick the time and place to engage them.

So, I keep sorting sticks, moving them from one pile to another. After the assassin passes, I lift my gaze and watch the Shashyao move through the market stalls, looking in the tents, under tables, and behind boxes searching for someone or something. The other Shashyao zig zags through a manicured lawn to the side of the village square, following a pattern toward the river and the village docks.

After a few heartbeats, I gather my sticks back in a bundle, lift them to my shoulder, and head toward the main road leading south. I keep my head down, but from the corner of my eye I watch the other Shashyao scouting the growing fields and tall grass as they move closer toward the edges of Gudai.

After I reach the road and create some distance between me and the assassins near the village square, I quicken my pace and focus on the warriors headed toward the forest. Even though they zig zag in their search for their prey, I don't like how close they already are to the massive oaks, cypress, and pines of the ancient forest. It will be hard to catch up to them. Luckily, the closer they get, the more they spread out from each other. The more distance they create between each other, the easier they make my job.

Fighting my impatience, I force myself not to walk faster. I can't afford to draw attention to myself. Still, I worry that the warriors already have too great of a lead on me. The closest warrior is about one hundred paces ahead and more than three hundred paces away to my right. I should still be able to catch him if he keeps angling toward the river, which with every step he takes narrows his distance away and brings him a little closer to me.

When all three of the Shashyao step past the forest line and disappear into its shadows and dense foliage, I give in to my impatience. I throw down my bundle of sticks and sprint from the road toward the spot where the closest assassin entered Gudai. As much as I want to, I refrain from using my boon to speed up my pace. Even though I've been storing up Shen Breath for days, I can't afford to needlessly waste any. Besides, while I'm still in the open, the extra speed might draw even more attention to me, especially to the eyes of the two Shashyao in the village square.

Once inside Gudai, the morning light quickly fades behind me. I push past hanging vines and layers of giant triangular fronds. A chorus of Shen Breath songs greets me as wisps of the colored mist spiral toward me, infusing me with even more boon. I scan deeper into the forest, looking for gaps in the Shen Breath. Wherever the Shashyao passed, his sword—Zhangchi or Chi Wielder—will have drawn in any nearby Shen Breath, making a narrow corridor void of mist and giving me an easy path to follow. That is until it warms up enough that all the Shen Breath evaporates for the day.

It only takes a few heartbeats to find the Shashyao's mist-less trail. Before I move after him, I take out my necklace and quickly search through my emerald discs for the one with the Return gift mark—my most used disc. I don't bother to ink it. Instead, I search for a moist patch of ground. In the damp rainforest, I find one easily between a rotted old stump and carpet of moss. I press the disc firmly into the damp soil, making a clear impression of the gift mark.

With the Deliverer Oath rising in my mind, I seize upon a thread of the boon swirling inside me. The Rise gift mark stamped on the soles of my feet warms slightly. My steps grow lighter, helping me move quieter and twice as swift through the forest.

With practiced grace, I weave between thick dangling vines, dense brush, and haphazard columns of ancient trees wherever no swirls of Shen Breath rise. The Shashyao's back is to me when I spot him in a small clearing before a wall of hanging vines.

I pull a dart from my belt and throw. My aim is true, but the Shashyao turns to face me and easily evades the dart.

A snort of laughter comes from behind the demon-wolf mask. "Fool, child. It is death to attack the emperor's chosen."

I grin, letting slip a quiet, but clear snicker.

The Shashyao grunts. "You laugh the fool. You shall die the fool."

Zhangchi hums as the Shashyao draws the long, straight sword from its scabbard. A glowing halo of Shen Breath surrounds the sword as more colored streams of the mist swirl and stream toward it. My grin widens. This is what I came for. This prize will let me accomplish all that I have worked for since I first started practicing the forms and making oaths to the Shen.

The Shashyao raises the sword above his head and howls a war cry that thunders through the silence of Gudai. Then he charges. He's not much bigger than me, but he moves with twice the grace and speed of any Fei Chi master. Although not Shen-Blessed, with Zhangchi in his grip it's as if he were.

I hold my ground, leaning forward on the balls of my feet. The Deliverer Oath still ever-present in the recesses of my mind. My eyes flick between the glow of Zhangchi and the dark eyes glowering from behind the demon-wolf mask.

Fear has always been an alien emotion to me. Like many of my fellow slaves, I welcome death as a release from suffering. As a Deliverer, that release simply comes sooner. Why fear the inevitable? A type of freedom comes from embracing its inevitability.

Even now I feel no fear of the Shashyao and his abilities. Zhangchi is the real threat. Not just the power that the glowing sword gives its wielder, but one touch of its sharp steel against my flesh will rip away any trace of Shen Breath boon inside me. That's what makes it the perfect weapon for the Shashyao to hunt down and destroy the Shen-Blessed.

When he's almost on top of me, I tap into my boon. I move a hair faster than the Shashyao. That's all I need. In a quick burst, my left hand slams against his right elbow. I shove it upward and lock it straight. At the same time, my right hand blocks his wrist. I reach over it, grab the hilt, and force it upward. I lock the Shashyao's other wrist, bending it up and backwards until he releases his hold on the sword.

Even with control of Zhangchi, I still flinch as the sword's steel almost touches my torso. In that moment, the Shashyao sweep kicks my feet out from under me. The sword flies from my hand. Even without the power of Zhangchi, the Shashyao is faster and stronger than most warriors. He somehow retrieves the sword before I have a chance to react.

The assassin hisses as he slowly circles me. "You have stolen gifts from the Shen. You will pay for your sacrilege."

I laugh, leaping to my feet. I crouch low in the leopard stance, keeping my eyes on him and turning in place as he circles me. "How can one steal what the Shen so willingly give?"

Few know the truth of the Shashyao. The emperor not only encourages tales of how the legendary demon-wolves hunt down those that blaspheme the Shen, but he also started those stories. It's not enough to revere Lord Emperor, Chosen of Heaven as a god. His people must fear to disobey his laws, especially those laws that allow him and his Wives Divine to be the only ones to receive the gifts of the Shen. Few really understand what it means to be Shen-Blessed. But most that do, know the Shashyao's main directive—hunt down and eliminate any besides the emperor and his Wives Divine that have been blessed.

The Shashyao slices Zhangchi inches from my chest. "You dare defy the Lord Emperor, Chosen of Heaven? How many temples have you defiled with your presence? How many Shen have you blasphemed? With your blood, the Shen will take back the gifts you stole."

I scowl, shaking my head. "You believe the emperor's lies? By the Two, I have stolen nothing. If you seek a thief, go to the palace in the City of Heaven. You'll find one sitting on the throne."

The Shashyao slices again. I back away out of reach. I have to be careful. I'm barely faster than him. And all he has to do is touch me with the blade and the fight will end.

When he lunges, I slide forward under the attack, grab his wrist, twist it, and pull him down. Somehow, he keeps his grip on Zhangchi. He rolls to his feet. Zhangchi slices down toward me. I roll out of the way, rise to my feet, and leap over his head.

Before I touch ground, he spins and renews his attack. I dodge lunge after lunge. I duck and twist away from slices. I grab a thick branch to parry his attacks. Zhangchi slices through it like it's a barley stock. Any thought of simply overcoming him with my boon has vanished. I have to try a different tactic.

On his next stroke, I rush in. Like before, with a slam and grab, I lock his elbow with one hand and his wrist with the other. While he tries to break free, I focus the boon on my Return gift. With a quick, silent prayer to Luxíng Shen, the air around us bends and shimmers. In an instant we both transport to the patch of mud near the edge of Gudai where I stamped my Return mark.

The sudden change in location combined with the sudden flood of nausea that accompanies the use of travelling takes the Shashyao by surprise. In that moment, I shove a dart from my belt into his gut. Its tip has enough sedative to knock out a water buffalo. The Shashyao struggles for a moment, wavers, and falls limp to the ground.

Hours will pass before the slumbering Shashyao wakes. I kneel beside him and remove his mask. I expect to see the hardened face of a veteran warrior. Instead, a handsome young man in his early twenties lies on the ground beneath me. He's probably not more than five or six years older than me.

I shake my head. What a pity to hide such a pretty face behind such a hideous disguise. A slight grin turns up the corner of my lips. What would others think more repulsive, my own red marred face or the mask of the Shashyao? The thought sparks an idea that will make it even easier to reach my goal.

Before long, the sleeping Shashyao lies in a patch of mud wearing my peasant grays. With my hair redone in a male topknot, I hover over the assassin wearing his black robe, leather armor, demon-wolf mask, and his weapons, including the now sheathed Zhangchi.

My fingers glide over the line of paired ruby and emerald teardrops that run from the bottom of the hilt to the top of the hilt. Round-side-up with the emerald on the left and ruby on the right, the gems angle toward each other, symbolic of paired Father and Mother strokes. Six paired gems on each side of the hilt could make holding Zhangchi a bit uncomfortable, but it's worth the price. Without the gems and whatever gifts Hu somehow bound to the sword, Zhangchi would be nothing more than a common blade.

"Thank you, young warrior," I whisper to the sleeping assassin. "Sleep dreams of peace. Soon my people's curse will be lifted, and all will know freedom."

After I move my assortment of ash-filled cloth bags from my old pouch to the new black leather pouch on my belt, I retrieve the bag tied with a blue ribbon. I pour the ashes into the palm of my hand and squeeze tight. I will my boon to charge the Leap gift mark stamped on my breast. The mark swells with warmth and spreads through my body to the ends of my toes and fingertips.

I let the ashes in my hand grow warmer until they feel like they'll burst into flames. I throw them in the air. With another prayer to Luxíng Shen, the air bends and shimmers around me for a moment. When the shimmering stops, I stand on the other side of the Pangbo, high atop the cliffs beside a scythe-shaped pine on a flat boulder overlooking the river far below.

Chapter 12
Bing Shi – Quingping Massacre

"Unlike some of the witless followers of the Two's more favored children, even in Xié Shen's imprisonment he has never concealed his gifts from those who seek a more empowering path."

- Forbidden Writings of Zha Zhi

The barren plains of Quingping are a despicable place for a lady with my refined tastes and exquisite nature. No proper beds or silk pillows. No one to bring me mangoes and shrimp, let alone drinkable water. You can't really even call what flows down the creek, water. It smells like rotten eggs and tastes like rust. The food is the worst. I don't care if General Cheng Lu and his soldiers think cicadas are a delicacy. That doesn't make it acceptable to have them for the main course of every meal.

Patience. Just like always, it takes time to make the best of one's situation, in spite of how horrendous it might be. And Quingping is truly horrendous. It's still morning, but I'm already sweating like a ditch digger. At least the yellow-blossomed silk trees along the creek provide some refuge from the dry heat.

But what I need now is refuge from boredom. There's nothing to do since General Cheng stopped the cricket duels. "The crickets are getting too scarce and we need them for food," he said. He's a terrible liar. Crickets overrun the camp. I think too many of his men complained of losing their wages to me and my crickets.

No one will play stones with me either. Not even the mastermind general. It's so silly that their pride wounds so easily just because a delicate flower like myself outsmarts them on every move. I've often wondered if I wasn't so stunningly attractive if their pride would still suffer so much by losing to me. Of course, Ye San would play with me if I didn't insist on his constant diligence in executing our plan. My plan really, but its success all depends on his execution.

"Sweet love, are you close to finishing this week's report?"

San sits in the red dirt and sand, his scroll spread atop a flat boulder. He's so gorgeous and distinguished in his red silk scholar robes. Of course, purple grade robes would make him even more distinguished, but the red dirt stains would stand out more. Besides, the purple robes will be his once Emperor Hu becomes convinced of how instrumental San has been in General Cheng's successes.

As the battalion's historian, it would seem easy for San to color the truth about the vital strategic insight and intelligence that he has provided the general, but General Cheng checks every character and symbol for accuracy and fact. And it's only been in the recent weeks that General Cheng has started to trust the information we feed him enough to actually use it. Even so, San still has to be careful that he only makes small mentions of his contributions in the reports to the emperor. In time, those contributions and mentions will enlarge, and San will wear the purple robes and I will be surrounded by silks and real delicacies within the palace's luscious comforts.

"Sweet love, did you hear me?" I say, when he doesn't look up. San gets so caught up in his writing. "How is this week's report coming?"

San looks up from his paper and ink, and smiles at me. My shoulders shudder and my spine tingles at the perfect, caring smile. Oh, how I love this man.

"A few more heartbeats are all I need, my lovely," he says, twisting his smile to a wry grin. "Then I shall be more than pleased to stroll with you beneath the emerald fronds and golden blossoms of the most sickly silk tree grove in all of Dashi. Or perhaps we could scale the magnificent red rock crags of this barren paradise and dance with scorpions to the rattle of vipers. Whatever you please, that shall I do."

With a wink and a stretch of his grin, he bows toward me and returns to his writing. I stifle a giggle. San has always been much more than a clever scholar. One of the things I love most about him is his ability to make the most detestable things sound so beautifully romantic and humorous at the same time.

After rescuing me from years of forced servitude in Lord Zheng's harem, we knew we would need to change my name. So, in his romantic way, he said, "As the moons in the sky, you can be my Shi to your San. And like the emerald moon, I will seek your love till the Heavens and Dashi be no more." We laughed and kissed, and my old name was forgotten and I became Bing Shi from that day onward.

As promised, only a few more heartbeats pass before San puts down his pen and sprinkles red sand on the paper to blot it dry. After he shakes off the excess sand, a dark blue lady beetle with big red spots on its back lands on San's hand. San stiffens and his eyes close. The power brand on the bottom of my left foot begins to burn with a light itch. It always does when San uses his gift. I assume his foot itches when I use my gift too, but I've never asked him.

San's face grows paler and paler the longer his eyes are closed. I want to shout at him to hurry and finish. The last time he stayed in his vision too long, he was so sick he vomited on my favorite green slippers. We don't need him vomiting on this week's report and having to spend all those hours rewriting it.

When San opens his eyes, he doesn't vomit, but there's panic on his face. "What's the matter?" I ask, anxiety rising in my voice.

"It's not good," he says. "It's better that I show you. Then you can decide what we tell General Cheng to do."

San cups the lady beetle in his palm so it won't try to fly away. Leaving this week's report on the boulder, San hurries to his feet and rushes past different groups of soldiers. Some are just finishing breakfast. Others move through the forms of Fei Chi, some duel with swords, and a few practice the bow. One small group crowds behind a tent playing dice.

San stops and sits at one of the cook fires still blazing. I stay standing. I'm too anxious to sit. What has San so concerned? He throws the lady beetle from his hand into the fire and his vision appears in the flames. Out of habit, I look over my shoulder to see if anyone around notices the vision, even though San has reassured me several times that only those he wishes to can see what his gift shows.

When I turn back to the flames, my eyes go wide and my fear rises. It's not possible. It shows thousands of Yemaren archers in the cracks, crevices, and ridgelines of the craggy red rock range just east of our camp. Cheng had two battalions guarding both the northern and eastern access to that range. How could they possibly have gotten by?

The vision shifts to the deep red rock ravines to the north that have served as the natural barrier between the main armies of the Huyan and Yemaren. The ravines have been a constant sallying point. Every week or so, the Yemaren have managed to construct a bridge or two somewhere along the miles of rocky ravine and get as many infantry troops across as they could before we could detect them, wipe them out, and destroy the bridges. Right now, ten different bridges are in place. Three battalions of infantry have already crossed as well as more than three thousand cavalry.

Where are our spies? How did they get so many bridges up without us knowing? And how did they get their cavalry across. No sane horse would cross those bridges. My eyes narrow and my lips thin in concentration as I rub the tip of my forefinger across the cleft of my chin. I don't understand. How did they do it?

"Well?" San reaches up for my hand and gently takes my fingers into his. "What do we tell the general?"

My shoulders slump and I sigh as I stare into the flames' vision several more heartbeats before answering. "It doesn't matter what we tell General Cheng. We are lost."

Chapter 13
Lord Emperor Xiang Hu – Tales of a Sheepherder

"Blossoms pink and airy dance from bough to breeze. Butterflies blue and deep float, and circle. Sweet jasmine weaves its spell, casts its charm. Jasper eyes sparkling smile, sparkling glow. Our fingers touch. Our hands enfold. Your rose lips brush soft and gentle our love's first kiss."

- The Empress Letters

I cringe at the quiet that grips the Divine Empress' royal chambers. If I could, I would command an orchestra to serenade Yuan nonstop. But few can know where my Most Holy Wife, the Divine Lady Empress sleeps both night and day. It's for her safety. And that of the empire. No windows. Plain gray walls. Simple bed of pillows. No decorations or art. Nothing to hint of the royalty of the room's occupant. Not even the monastery's nuns know Yuan's true identity. They only know to keep her comfortable, make sure the tube stays in her mouth, and the solution of liquid food and sedative in the tube's jar never runs dry.

The cold stone floor sends chills up my legs as I kneel beside Yuan, Divine Empress and the only one I love of all my wives. Certain that Yuan and I are alone, I pull off my black leather gloves to take her hand in mine. I frown. Her hand feels almost as cold as the stone floor. I'll have to tell the nuns to cover her in more blankets.

I kneel beside her, lean in close, and lay my cheek against hers. The sweet smell of jasmine fills my senses. "Sweet Yuan, your face so smooth. As beautiful as the day we met."

She doesn't answer. She never does. Eyes shut. Face pale. Lips closed in a thin line. Her robed body still except for the slow rise and fall of her chest.

I lift my head and hold her hand. "Oh, but I miss your smile. Remember how I would sneak your mother's warm walnut dumplings off your porch? You always knew it was me, but your mother would blame the golden jays. Your father would get so mad. He would stomp his feet, grab his sling, and hunt down as many jays as he could find. You would always smile because you knew that would give us a few more precious moments without your father's watchful eyes. Your father never did approve of me. He wanted better for you than a zhu-less sheepherder. I never blamed him for that."

I squeeze Yuan's hand and rise from my knees to sit on the pillows beside her.

"Did I tell you that Du Bao passed a few weeks ago? She came to the palace only thirty years ago. It's so sad. The Wives Divine pass so much younger now. I promise, the nuns keep them safe and comfortable, and make sure they receive all the nourishment they need. I visit them every week and no matter how painful it is, I use my touch to heal any ills they might have and revive their muscles' vigor. But the healing touch cannot erase their years or stop the wilting of their flesh. Only you and I are so blessed. Or sometimes I wonder if it's a curse."

I release Yuan's hand and stare at the blank wall. "I pray you can forgive that your room has never had windows. You would love the monastery's orchards of flowering peach and plum trees, as well as the snow peaked mountains that tower close by in beautiful majesty. And I had the nuns plant all your favorite flowers in the garden. You would love to see it all."

I frown, the lack of windows don't matter. In the continual sleep I have imposed upon her, Yuan will never know the difference.

"You would have liked Du Bao. She came from a small village in the northwest where they know snow more than sunshine. She was so proud to serve her country. But a new Wife Divine will serve in her place. She should arrive any day. But do not worry. I will still be faithful to you. The young girl will sleep the living sleep with the others."

"Oh, I do miss you." I take Yuan's hands again and kiss each knuckle.

"We used to share so much joy together, so many adventures. Do you remember when I first told you I loved you? You took me to the ruins of Danwang. Butterflies flit about as we chased through the ancient groves. Moss and ivy covered the crumbling palace walls. You led me to the gardens that had become more of a jungle with its wild and dense overgrowth.

"We swung on vines. Waded in the creek. We even climbed to the top of a giant cherry tree, its pink blossoms in full bloom. We could see the entire Danwang valley. The lake shimmered like a plate of silver. I pointed to a knoll by the lake covered in daffodils and told you I would build you a palace there someday.

"'Silly sheepherder!' you said, and then laughed your whimsical laugh. I kept my promise though, didn't I? I always keep my promises. Especially that first promise we made together. It was that same day.

"After we came down from the tree, I found a patch of peonies and picked a handful for you. I opened my mouth to tell you of my love, but before I could, you put a finger to my lips.

"'Not here,' you whispered.'

"You took me by the hand and led me to the far edge of the garden. Like a green veil, ivy draped and covered every inch of stone and tile of the old shrine. It was the only building of all of Danwang still intact.

"It should have been dark inside, but from cracks in the walls small purple and golden flowers glowed, lighting a carpet of moss that led to the back of the shrine where a green-tinted copper statue of a tall, slender woman stood. A veil covered her face. Dozens of sun, star, and crescent moon jewels decorated her pinned-high hair. The palms of her outstretched hands held beams of light. Silk strips wrapped around her from shoulder to toe like the dresses old barbarian Yemaren queens used to wear.

"'She's Guāng Shen,' you whispered before I could ask. 'Goddess of radiance.' I knew nothing of the Shen, or even the Two. Few did then. But I could tell from your tone she was someone to be reverenced.

"You told me the first of the many legends of the Two that your grandmother had taught you. You said Two formed Dashi's first mortals in Danwang using clay and breathing Chi into their souls to give them life. The Two sent more than one hundred of their children, the Shen, to watch over our mortal ancestors and teach them to seek the Light and live in it daily. Dìyī Shen and Guāng Shen were the oldest and wisest of the Shen. With their help, Danwang became a great kingdom. But during the Great Shen War, Dìyī Shen died and it broke Guāng Shen's heart. She left Danwang and since then has wandered the universe until the Two call her back home. But from time to time, she still grants blessings to those who pray to her.

"'Such a storyteller,' I called you.

"You pinched my cheek so hard, it hurt for days after. 'It's not a story! It's true.'

"I laughed.

"Your lips tightened, and your nose crinkled up the cute way that it does before you scold me. But instead of wagging your finger and promising you'd never let me kiss you again, your eyes sparkled, and a beautiful grin crossed your face.

"'I know! I'll prove it to you. We'll make an oath to Guāng Shen.'

"You knelt before Guāng Shen's statue and placed a spring roll in one of her hands, bowed your head, and said, 'With your help, I promise to stand in the Light as long as I live.' Then you turned to me and said, 'Your turn. Make a promise to her.'

"I knelt beside you and bowed my head. Before I could open my mouth, you elbowed me in the ribs. 'Make an offering first. Give her your spring roll.'

"'It's all I have for lunch. Besides, you made my favorite this time.'

"Your glare told me there would be no more spring rolls and definitely no more kisses if I didn't give up my lunch. I scowled, but put my spring roll in Guāng Shen's other hand and made my oath.

"'I love Yuan with all my soul, and will always cherish her and protect her. And if you really do give blessings like Yuan says, I'll believe all her silly stories about you and the Shen, and maybe even share them with others.'

"Of course, nothing happened, except I could barely keep from laughing and you elbowed me in the ribs even harder. You wouldn't talk to me for days, no matter how many times I apologized. It wasn't until the gift showed itself, that you would even see me. And that was just to gloat. It took…"

The gold of my Tongshi locket warms my chest, interrupting me. My fists tighten as I rise from the bed. I stride away from Yuan, not wanting to disrupt her slumber. I push down the anger at the interruption. My right hand squeezes the hilt of my sword. This better be an emergency.

My fingers brush across the locket's paired ruby and emerald stones as I pull it out from under my robe and flip open the lid. Inside the lid appears the image of Imperial Commandant Wu Kang. His gaze is lowered, even though his locket does not let him see me. I wish he could see the fury in my eyes. If he were here, it would take all my self-control not to slice off the man's head, no matter how competent he normally is.

"Did you forget, this is my private hour? What is so urgent, that you dare intrude?"

His face tightens, lowering his gaze even more. "Please forgive me, Lord Emperor, Chosen of Heaven. The flash towers bring urgent news."

I release my grip on my sword, but continue to scowl. Sometimes I wish I had not devised such effective communication. Messages make their way to me even when I wish to not be found. "Well, what is it then?"

Wu Kang clears his throat. "The Yemaren have breached the forward strongholds at Quingping. General Cheng Lu has fallen. The secondary strongholds hold, but not for long. If they break through, they'll gain control of the quarries and access to the Pangbo."

I clamp my hand back on my hilt and clench my teeth. Do I have to do everything? What good are my armies if I have to keep winning their battles for them? I blow out a long stream of air to calm myself enough to not take my frustration out on Wu Kang. It's not this man's fault. Besides, it's the Yemaren that I need to save my anger for.

"Thank you, commandant. I'll join them shortly."

Without waiting for a response, I click the locket closed and stuff it back under my robe. I step back to Yuan's bedside, lean over her, and kiss her cheek. "Time to keep my promises again, but I'll be back."

From one of the large pockets in my robe, I pull out a small bag with the characters for Quingping inked across it. I pour the bag's ashes into my bare hand, tighten my fingers around them until they burn, and throw the ashes in the air. A moment later, the shrieks and cries of war thunder in my ears. I stand alone on a high watchtower overlooking the rugged wasteland of Quingping where the advancing legions of Yemaren barbarians cut a bloody path through the ranks of my imperial forces.

I summon dark storm clouds to gather. Streaks of lightning flash through the sky and scorch the battlefield. Flash after flash burns through the rear ranks of the Yemaren. As fast as I use it, a constant stream of Shen Breath replenishes my boon from the hundreds of paper lanterns hanging on the watchtower.

Smoke and the smell of burning flesh fill the air. The forward Yemaren ranks halt their attack. They watch in horror as their barbarian brothers incinerate by the hundreds. My imperial forces rush back to their defenses, a safe distance from my attack. But a few don't retreat fast enough. Fools. They burn with the remaining Yemaren as my attack quickly rolls over them. In minutes, the skies and battlefield fall silent.

Chapter 14
Qiu Meilin – Vile Treachery

"The Shashyao are one of Ye Ye's most cruel creations and a major obstacle to our deliverance."

- History of the Descendants: Volume 4, Page 116

Void of hope or emotion, Lian gazes down at me. My fingers reach up to touch her face, but jerk back as it tightens and contorts in pain. An agonizing scream shrills from her lips. Before I can reach back to comfort her, her soft olive skin hardens, transforming into the rough, black demon mask of the Shashyao. I scream a soundless cry for help and jerk awake from the dream.

The rocking of the boat and the shelter's low roof disorient me at first. But the murmur of river birds, chatter of wildlife, and sound of water lapping over the boat deck stir my memories of last night's events. It's still dark, but traces of early dawn have begun to chase away night's shadows.

A few feet beyond the shelter's front opening, Cai stands in silhouette with his back to me, steering the boat with his river pole. I try not to grin, gazing at the lean muscles that define his frame. Beyond Cai, his hunting cormorant, Peck, perches like a dark shadow on the prow's edge. She holds her black wings outstretched as if she's a majestic figurehead like warships use to intimidate enemies.

Such a blessed bird. If not for her, I'm sure I would have slept too peacefully. Her squeals, cackles, and croaks throughout the night woke me so often that I was able to be extra vigilant. I'm sure that's way more important than being comfortable and rested, especially when you're on the run. Right? Of course, her chatter would wake Cai, too. He cooed and spoke softly to the bird, like she was his true heart. Peck would quiet down, and Cai would fall right back to sleep, while I fought off worries about Lian and the Shashyao until I could finally find sleep again.

I rub sleep from my eyes and stretch. Then my chest tightens in panic. Outside the shelter's side windows, dense woods close in tight on both sides of the riverbanks—too close. Instead of seeing lofty mountains and sheer cliff faces on one side of the Pangbo's wide expanse and fields and villages on the other, there's only a shadowed forest. There is no wide expanse. We float down a river that's little wider than a boat length. Gnarled branches of ancient oaks and willows create an arched canopy above the small river blocking any glimpse of sky. Vines dotted with orchids of bright yellow and blue dangle from above, most out of reach, but some almost low enough to kiss the river's ripples. It's a beautiful sight, but not the right sight.

The boat rocks sideways as I quickly rise to my knees. "Where are we? This isn't the Pangbo!"

"Watch it!" Cai shouts back, trying to keep his balance. Peck echoes Cai's shout with a squawk and flap of her wide wings. "Juxing water snakes own this part of the river. I don't want to be their breakfast."

I crawl to the edge of the opening. "We only have six days to get to Quanli. Why aren't we on the Pangbo?"

Cai keeps his back to me, concentrating on keeping the boat in the center of the narrow river. "We will get to Quanli before the wedding. Only a few fishermen know about this branch of the river. It will take us four days to get to the City of Heaven, a day longer than the Pangbo proper, but the Shashyao won't know we went this way. That takes care of at least one danger we won't have to worry about."

"What do you mean one danger we won't have to worry about?"

"This branch cuts through the heart of Gudai that few travel. We should be fine, as long as we stay on the river and keep moving."

Like near my village, the fringes of Gudai are relatively safe. But it’s never wise to wander too deep into Gudai. Pang Bears, Jade Leopards, Dark Hounds, Beifang cats, and dozens of different deadly snakes and insects are a few of the ancient forest's dangers. But stories say it's the unknown dangers that lie in its deepest bowels that you have to be most concerned about. I hope Cai is right, that as long we stay on the river we’ll be safe.

Danger or not, it doesn’t matter. We have to get to Quanli. And once Lian hears that Cai still lives, she might actually let us rescue her. Maybe hope will return to her eyes, and smiles will brighten her face once again.

The boat rocks a little as I crawl further out of the shelter. The thick forest canopy filters most of dawn’s growing light, but it’s light enough to see where I’m going. “Excuse me,” I say as my shoulder brushes against the side of Cai’s knee as I crawl by him.

“Hey!” He jumps a little. For a moment I think he might whack me with the steering pole. “What are you doing?”

“I’m tired of talking to your backside. I’m moving to the front for a better view.”

His body tenses. “It’s not proper to talk that way, especially to me.”

Is that embarrassment or disapproval in his voice? Regardless, I lower my eyes and press my lips in a thin line as I carefully crawl to the front of the boat. I sit with my back to Peck and face Cai. Even though this is Cai, I still need to be careful what I say. He’s a man and by all rights could choose to punish me if I don’t show him proper respect.

I guess if he tried to punish me, I could overpower him with my boon from Tiānqì Shen. That is, unless he has a boon too. While I debate whether I should beg his forgiveness or push him off the boat, he crouches down eyelevel with me.

"Sorry, that came out wrong," he says. "We've always been friends. You can talk to me however you like. But you should be careful. You never know who might be listening."

I relax, meet his gaze, and laugh. "We're on boat in the middle of Gudai. Who's going to be listening?"

His cheeks color with embarrassment, but he laughs too. "You know what I mean."

I nod. "Yeah. I do. Thanks."

That's when I notice the long gash above his eye and a half dozen other smaller cuts and scrapes marking up his face. How did he get so many wounds? But that's not the question that's been nagging me. As hard as I try, I can't think of a polite way to ask what I want to ask. Mama used to joke that I have the manners of a badger. She never meant it as compliment, but right now I'm glad I have no problem being blunt.

"Why aren't you dead? A month ago, they told us you had died in battle."

Cai grimaces, rises from his crouched position, and tightens his grip on the steering pole as he renews guiding the boat down the river. From the look on his face, if we were to meet any water snakes right now, I doubt they would stand a chance. With the anger that burns in his eyes, I'm glad he turns his gaze far beyond me.

"I should be dead." His words have a controlled edge. "But it doesn't matter. No one will believe what happened to me."

Silence passes for several heartbeats. I don't want to upset him further, but I want to know what happened. "Okay, maybe I won't believe you. Tell me anyway."

His cold gaze shifts down to mine. I return it with a hopeful smile. His grimace relaxes with a hint of a smile for a moment, but then he lifts his gaze past me again. Several more heartbeats pass before he continues.

"The first two weeks we travelled on a warship up the Pangbo, heading northwest toward the Yemaren border. Our regiment had nearly one hundred men. Except for the officers, we were all new recruits. Every day we'd rise at dawn and train for combat until the sun set with only short breaks for meals. We went ashore the third week, but our routine changed little until about the fourth day.

Cai ducks to avoid a pair of low hanging vines thick with bright blue orchids. The boat rocks a little as his feet shift. When he resets his footing, he continues, "Imperial riders rode into camp during lunch. Riders had come into camp before, but these were different. Only one of them was military—a colonel. The others included a court official, a couple servants, and nine Shashyao warriors. None of us had ever seen a Shashyao before. Few of us had believed they even existed.

"The colonel ordered us into ranks, and one by one the court official and his servants pricked our forefingers with a needle, squeezed drops of our blood onto a piece of paper, and sent us back to lunch. We all wondered what it was about, but knew better than to ask questions. When lunch ended, everyone was ordered back to training exercises except for thirteen of us."

Cai's expression turned thoughtful. I wonder if he had been hiding near the village square yesterday when High Lord Zheng Gong took blood drops from Lian and Ning's other marriageable maidens. I'm pretty sure I know what the finger pricking is about, but does Cai know?

A large purple dragonfly glides above the rippling river's surface and suddenly zips upwards, buzzing near Cai's face and taking him out of his reverie. He swats at it before continuing his story.

"After the colonel took the thirteen of us aside, he told us with a grin that we had been selected for a special mission. He ordered us to gather our belongings and prepare to leave immediately, but to leave our weapons behind. He explained we would be provided special weapons at our new post."

"That was odd. Imperial officers never explain orders. Do as you're told. No questions. Why would one justify an order now? It made no sense. When we left camp, they had us to walk ahead of the riders, not in the back inhaling their dust like usual. Something felt wrong, but I had no idea what.

"Less than an hour from camp the Shashyao attacked. No warning. No mercy. They came at us from behind in complete silence. I didn't know what was happening until blood sprayed me from both sides. My friends fell around me in a slaughter. I would have died too. I should have, but…"

Cai's lips tighten. His eyes lower to meet mine. Their steady, always serious look gone. A haunting uneasiness takes its place. He studies me, trying to decide whether to continue. The chatter, howls, and cries of Gudai intensify in Cai's silence. Scarlet thrushes whistle in the branches above. Dawn's rays filtering through the thick canopy light the edges of Cai's hair, giving him an ethereal glow.

"The ground burst apart," he continues." Rock erupted from the soil. Fragments of stone and rubble struck the Shashyao from all directions. Fissures ripped open beneath the colonel and court officials, swallowing them and their mounts. It lasted only heartbeats, but when the tremors stopped and rock settled, only three of us recruits stood. I've been running ever since."

I say nothing. I see a hint of vulnerability in Cai's gaze that I've not seen before. He's trying hard not to show it, but he's scared. He should be. Two days ago, I would have laughed at such a tale. But I know there's nothing funny in his story. His world has crumpled. Shashyao exist. At the command of the Lord Emperor's officers, they tried to kill him. He's now a fugitive and I doubt he even understands why. And the girl he loves has been taken to become wife to the emperor who ordered Cai's own slaughter.

Should I tell him he's Shen-Blessed and that's why he was almost killed? For some reason I keep that to myself. It's almost as if I don't want him to know he's Shen-Blessed.

Still, I need to somehow comfort him. Even though it's against social protocol, I reach up to touch his arm. He tenses a moment at the touch, either from surprise or because I messed up his steering. But then he relaxes. His eyes soften, as do the worry lines on his face.

"Things will be okay," I say. "They won't find us. And we'll save Lian. That's all that matters now."

Chapter 15
Qiu Meilin – Eyes of Gudai

"While the exact essence of Shen Breath mists has been debated for over a century, it is understood to be a visible, more tangible form of Chi in a highly concentrated presence."

- Hidden Scrolls of Quingping: Study in the aspects of Shen Breath

The sounds of a waking forest surround us as we travel in silence down the narrow river. The rising sun's rays have penetrated more of Gudai's shadows. Wisps of mist stream above the river in shades of pale gray, but above Gudai soil, where last night's rainwater still clings to trees and plant life, the twisting tendrils of mist begin their colorful transformation to Shen Breath.

Their song whispers to me, calling me to come and accept their boon. I glance at Cai. Does he hear it too? His head swivels from side to side, searching. Uncertainty shows on his face. If he hears the song, I don't think he knows what it means. It's odd, but that makes me feel relieved. For whatever reason, I don't yet want him to know he might have powers from Tiānqì Shen.

Only yesterday, I first felt the warmth and strength of the Shen Breath and its Chi swell inside me. But now I feel weak without it. I want its strength again. If I don't answer the call of the Shen Breath now, it might be days or weeks before I have another chance. While Gudai has frequent midnight downpours, they don't happen every night.

"Stop the boat!"

My outburst startles Cai. Worry wrinkles crease the corners of his eyes. "What's wrong?"

I bow my head, not sure how to answer, but softly say, "It's personal."

Cai rolls his eyes. A smirk plays on his lips. "Personal? There's a chamber pot in the shelter. Don't worry. I'll keep my back to you."

I bite my bottom lip. That's not what I meant, but the deceit will work. I keep my eyes on the bamboo deck of the boat, trying to look both meek and embarrassed at the same time. In a soft voice I plead, "Please don't make me use a chamber pot!"

Cai laughs. "I thought we were in a hurry?"

I feel bad for fooling him, but not enough to not. I lower my eyes further and add a mix of fear and anxiety to my voice. "Please stop the boat."

Cai steers the raft to the riverbank atop some gnarled roots, peeking above the water's surface. I tense. Something scaly and thicker than an elephant's trunk slithers along the side of the boat, before slipping under the water with barely a splash. It's just a fish, I tell myself, trying to convince myself it wasn't a Juxing water snake.

Thick patches of broadleaf grass and bright red flowers cover the bank. The boat wobbles only slightly as I rise to my feet. I hesitate, wondering what beasts wait for me beyond the strings of moss and vine that dangle in scattered waves from branch to ground.

My body jerks at Cai's voice. "It's not safe to go ashore alone. Gudai can be dangerous in these parts."

With the need for pretense gone, all traces of meekness and timidity vanish from my expression and voice. "I'll be fine myself." But then with grin and playful warning I say, "Don't you dare follow me."

I really do need to relieve myself, but privacy is not the whole reason I want Cai to stay put. I can't keep Tiānqì Shen's gift a secret if he sees the Shen Breath draw toward me. And if he really is Shen-Blessed, it will draw toward him too. Why do I care so much about keeping this knowledge to myself?

I give him one more look of warning before I hurry off. My foot sinks slightly as I step on the damp grass. Once on solid ground, I push through the hanging vines and hurry away from the riverbank, as well as any lingering Juxing snakes.

I'm no more than a few steps in when tendrils of Shen Breath envelope me. It seeps into my flesh, tingling my skin and filling me with its warmth and music. Strength surges within me as I run deeper into Gudai, jumping over bushes and dodging in between trees to distance myself from Cai's view. No matter how fast I run, the tendrils reach me and infuse me with more of the boon.

I eventually slow to a walk, enjoying the rush of power that swells inside me. The feeling of invincibility exhilarates me.

When the warmth of the sun finally chases away the last traces of Shen Breath, the inflow of Chi stops. The song of the Shen Breath fades. Still, its power swirls inside me, waiting for me to release it. The familiar and not so familiar sounds of Gudai grow stronger. The forest here feels more alive. More exotic. More foreboding.

At once, I sense unseen eyes watching me. The sense of danger surrounds me. I should be scared, but I'm not. The constant pulse of Shen Breath inside me makes me fearless.

"Come on!" I smile, calling to any eager threats. "You want me? Try to take me."

The songs of the forest don't miss a beat. Their tone and volume go unchanged. My invitation goes unheeded.

I laugh. "That's right. I'm the master. Best keep your place."

In spite of my overconfidence, it's not wise to stay any longer than needed. Even though I'm pretty sure the closest human waits for me back at the boat, I stop within a tight circle of towering trees surrounded by dense brush for a degree of privacy.

After I take care of my business, I find a fallen log to sit on. I pull a charcoal stick from my shoulder bag and draw the paired Wind and Mother strokes on the palm of my left hand. Tiānqì Shen called it a Wind gift mark. My confidence rises even more, knowing I have another weapon at my disposal. I try to draw the strokes on my right palm too, but my left hand can't get the lines right. I need to find a way to draw the gift mark easily on both hands.

I leave the circle of trees and retrace my steps back to the river. Then panic strikes. Everything in this part of Gudai looks so similar. It's not like back home where Gudai has been my playground since I knew how to walk. Which way do I go? I think about shouting for Cai, but he's too far to hear me. Besides, I don't want him to thing I need his help.

I head back the way I think I came, but I'm not certain about it. The hanging moss and vines from tree to tree all look the same. The dense hedges, red and purple patches of flowers, and thick fronds of ferns all blend together in a confusing maze. I keep walking.

I listen for the babble of the river, but I only hear the buzz and chittering of the forest. I continue walking. The feeling that I'm lost grows stronger. I think about climbing a tree to get a better view. But shake my head. I'd have to climb several hundred feet before I could get a clear view of the river.

I still walk, but slower. Should I go back to the circle of trees and start over? No. I could get even more lost. In spite of the warmth of the Chi pulsing inside me, my confidence fades. Tiānqì Shen's boon can do little to help me find my way back to the boat. I'm on my own.

The noises of the forest seem louder now, more deadly. It's as if they can sense my fear. I have to fight the urge to run. Running away is like shouting, "Hey, beasties, look at me. First one to catch me gets dinner." Even if no beasts gave chase, I'd probably end up even more lost.

I almost give into the desire to call for Cai when I notice a gap in the vines to my right. A grin slips onto my face. I head to it and walk straight past. I walk and watch. Another broken vine, a bent branch, trampled fern, and other signs of my earlier tromping through Gudai restore my confidence. I'm headed in the right direction.

My confidence is complete when I hear the river's babbling. That's also when I hear movement in the trees behind me. I pick up my pace, trying not to worry. The sound follows me. I've never seen a Jade Leopard before. Few have. Their forest green fur sprinkled with a slight mix of brown and black highlights makes them almost invisible to spot in Gudai's branches. Add to that their grace and speed, and it's no wonder they're one of Gudai's most lethal beasts.

I scold myself. "It's not a leopard. It can't be. It's just a squirrel. A very big and loud squirrel."

I walk faster. I shouldn't be afraid. I have my boon after all. A Jade Leopard shouldn't be a problem. But my confidence weakens again. I no longer want to test my abilities. I want to get back to the boat and head down river. Even a Juxing water snake sounds more inviting than a Jade Leopard.

I get a glimpse of the river ahead and break into a run. The rustling of tree branches behind grows louder and increases in speed, easily keeping up with me. It's going to catch me I know it. I think about tapping into my boon to run faster. No. I'd rather have as much boon as possible if the leopard actually catches me.

I zig zag between trees. Leap over bushes. Duck under vines. The noise draws closer. My heart pounds. My lungs pump harder and harder. I fight to keep from drawing on the boon.

"Save it for the fight," I tell myself. "Oh, I really don't want a fight."

I push myself to run faster. I can see the boat now. I shove aside more vines and moss as I run. The sound following me has grown fainter, falling further behind. Jade Leopards don't like water. Maybe the river's scent has made it grow wary.

I keep running. When I push through the last veil of vines, I leap onto the boat. It rocks, but the roots beneath it keep it fairly stable.

"What's wrong with you!" Cai shouts. "Are you trying to put a hole in my boat?"

"Go!" I shout back. "Get us out of here!"

One glance at my face tells Cai everything he needs to know. He grips his steering pole and shoves us away from the bank as fast he can. The boat moves slowly as it scrapes atop the roots breaching the river's surface. It finally breaks free of the roots and moves faster downstream. My body relaxes. I breathe out a long, slow sigh of relief.

I sit in my place, facing upstream and looking up at Cai steering us downriver. I smile up at him, all trace of panic clear from my face. "See, I told you I would be fine."

Branches above rustle and shudder violently. A blur of color bursts through. Bright white fangs and claws leap through the air toward me. A high pitch squeal rings in my ears as I scream. I forget about Chi. I forget about Tiānqì Shen's boon. All I can think is, I'm dead.

Chapter 16
Qiu Meilin – Defying Expectations

"The stink of Innate Honor suffocates any speck of actual honor that might have ever been imagined to exist within its foul mandates"

- Secret Musings of Wang Jin

I squeeze my eyes shut and scream again. I cower, shielding my head beneath crossed arms. I anticipate claw and fang tearing into me. I tense, waiting for the crash of the massive beast to smother me. But it doesn't.

Eyes still shut tight, my mind replays the blur of attacking fangs and fur. The blur of color was bright orange not the forest green of a Jade Leopard.

"Get off my boat!" Cai shouts, cutting through my thoughts.

I open my eyes. An adorable orange ball of fur dances and hops before me. Snubby. The little snub-nosed monkey's back is to me, but squeals at Cai. He shakes his arms upward as if he's trying to protect me from Cai.

"Get!" Cai repeats, raising the steering pole above his head like a weapon. Behind him Peck spreads and bats her huge black wings. She croaks and grunts, sounding more like an angry pig than a majestic fishing bird.

Snubby squeals louder and swings his arms wildly.

I reach up, wrap my arms around Snubby and pull him into a tight hug. "I'm so happy to see you," I say, nuzzling my nose in his fur. "But how did you find me?"

Snubby smiles, his cute round eyes looking up. I stroke the fur behind his hears and he relaxes on my lap, cooing pleasantly.

Cai folds his arms across his chest. "You know that stinky beast?"

"You don't stink, do you Snubby?" I say, grinning at the little orange fur ball. My nose crinkles and my smile wilts a little as I look up at Cai. "Well, not too much anyway. He's my friend, aren't you Snubby?"

Snubby smiles, then lifts his head and makes a face at Cai, chattering triumphantly. Just as quickly, Snubby sinks back into my arms, cooing as I continue to stroke his fur.

Cai frowns. "It can't stay. It'll make a mess of my boat."

I ignore Cai and smile at the little monkey. "My beautiful little Snubby won't make a mess, will you?"

Cai grunts under his breath and turns his back on me. He dips his pole in the water and continues to steer us downriver as if nothing happened. Snubby flutters his eyes and coos as I softly tickle the fur behind his ears. The little monkey's presence comforts me. I'm glad he's here.

All the colors of Gudai's trees and plant life continue to brighten as we float further down the river. If Cai is right, we'll reach Quanli in four days—two days before Lian's marriage to Emperor Hu. Will that be enough time to rescue her? What will I do once we get there? How will I even rescue her? Always keep your oath. That's what Tiānqì Shen said I needed to do. What oath?

My thoughts go back to my prayer in Tiānqì Shen's shrine. What did I say? It seems so long ago. Was that really just two nights ago? Not even that long. More like yesterday afternoon? Everything happened in a rush. What oath did I make? Why would that be so important?

My mind relives kneeling in Tiānqì Shen's shrine before her fierce golden statue. My offering of hazelnuts, peapods, and bread lay on the rosewood altar tray. I pause my reverie for a moment to cast a quick glance at Snubby cuddled in my arms. I don't know whether to scowl or smile at the little beast as I recall how he tipped over the altar tray and ate my offering. The little monkey made me furious, but Tiānqì Shen didn't mind. She still gave me a gift. Maybe the willingness to sacrifice matters most.

No. The oath must matter too. Why else would Tiānqì Shen tell me to always keep my oath? What did I promise? My thoughts return to the shrine. I steepled my hands before my face, closed my eyes, and bowed low to the ground. What were the words? I asked for a gift—a gift that would help me save Lian. What did I promise in return? Warmth tickles the back of my shoulders as I finally remember. I promised I would do all I could to save Lian if Tiānqì Shen would help me. That was my oath —do all that I can.

"How did you get the hairy demon to like you?"

I blink. Cai's question jolts me from my thoughts. "What? You mean Snubby?"

"Yeah, the snubnose." Cai has turned to face me, his back to the direction we're floating. He continues to dip his long pole in the water, but it must be out of habit. There's no way he can steer without seeing where we're going.

"Mischief imp," he continues. "Worse than Xi born. Those furry monkeys get into everything. Always causing trouble. But in your arms, he looks tame. Almost angelic."

I laugh, but quickly cover my mouth out of habit and respect. "Snubby is no angel, but he likes me."

"I've never seen that before. You must be Shen-Blessed."

I tense. He knows. How? Then I relax. The fishermen sometimes call each other Shen-Blessed after a good day of fishing. A phrase of good luck. Cai doesn't know the phrase's true meaning.

"No," I say. "I saved Snubby's life, and he saved mine. So, I guess we kind of have a life bond."

Cai arches an eyebrow. "A life bond with a monkey? That's a new one."

I shrug my shoulders, then look past Cai. The boat floats downstream in the center of the river beneath arching branches of Gudai's dense canopy. How does Cai keep us from crashing into a bank without looking where he's going? It makes me wonder if he has eyes in the back of his head.

"Anyway," he continues. "I guess the monkey can stay. I didn't know he meant so much to you."

"Thanks." I smile. But wonder why I would need his permission to keep Snubby?

Cai's expression turns pensive and an awkward silence hovers between us. His shoulders slump and his eyebrows furrow. "I'm sorry about last night," he says, his voice somber.

My eyebrows arch. "What?"

Men never apologize to women, at least none that I've ever known. I cock my head to the side, wondering what could have guilted him into breaking a three-hundred-year-old cultural tradition. I'm also trying to remember what he did that he needs to apologize about. "What exactly are you sorry about?"

He straightens up, tense. His mouth opens wide as his jaw drops. His eyes widen in an amusing panic "Um… I …Well…"

I laugh. "Did you forget?"

His mouth works up and down without making any noise. His grip tightens on his steering pole and quickly glances back over his shoulder. I'm not sure if he's suddenly worried that someone might have heard him apologize or if his rear-facing vision has stopped working and he's suddenly worried about steering us into a bank.

When he looks back at me, my grin widens. "Well? Are you apologizing or not?"

"Yes… I mean…It's only that…I shouldn't have called you a thief. That was wrong of me."

Oh yeah, he did call me thief, as well as a few other things. I decide to have some fun with him. I scrunch my nose, furrow my eyebrows, and try to scowl, but the corners of my mouth still turn up in a smile "You called me a cheat too. You sorry about that?"

He tilts his head and squints, giving me a sideways stare. "What?"

I clear my throat to mask a chuckle. "You said I was a cheat for only leaving a few copper zhu's to borrow your boat. Are you sorry about that too?"

His eyes widen, but when I can't hold in my laughter he says with a grin, "Yes. I'm sorry for that too."

His smile flattens into a frown. After a long pause, he adds, "I'm also sorry I said you couldn't help save Lian because you're a girl. That was wrong of me. That's something the village elders would say. I don't want to be like that."

My mouth drops open. Did I hear him right? In spite of the tough image he portrays, I've always known on the inside that Cai is kind and caring, but I never expected this. He could be beaten with a thrashing rod for speaking out against the elders. Worse, some could say he's criticizing the mandate of Innate Honor. That can bring severe punishment, even execution.

Maybe since the emperor's Shashyao are already trying to kill him, he doesn't see any harm against speaking out against it. Still, I can't imagine he would ever say such a thing unless he really felt that way. That in itself is remarkable.

My gaze lowers out of true respect and honor for Cai's words. As I do, he faces forward again, steering the boat in silence. Several moments pass as I ponder the idea that at least two men that I know don't necessarily agree with Innate Honor. I'm not sure what to think of that. More questions than answers rise in my mind. As I try to make sense of them, my eyes eventually fall on the scuffed and worn leather of Cai's soldier boots. It's only slight, but every few moments Cai's feet and legs spasm. What's wrong with him? His movements are sluggish and uncertain. His body droops.

By the Two! How selfish of me. Cai's been steering the boat since last night without any sleep. Before that, who knows how long it's been since he's slept. How thoughtless I've been. I should apologize, but the words feel hollow. Instead, I clear my throat to get Cai's attention.

With a sympathetic smile, I whisper, "You've had a long night. You should get some sleep. I can steer for now."

Cai turns around and with a tired smile says, "Thanks." He crouches to lay the steering pole by my side before shuffling to the back of the boat. Peck flutters her wings then marches behind Cai, following him like a faithful acolyte. The bird bobs her head at me as she passes and gives a scolding grunt. One after the other they disappear into the shadows of the shelter to sleep.

Chapter 17
Qiu Meilin – Death Kiss

"Think of the oath as a spur. A mule won't budge without a good kick."
- Hidden Scrolls of Quingping: Study in Oath Criticalities

The hours pass slowly as I guide our boat downriver through Gudai's deep. It winds and twists, only occasionally following a straight course. The sun's rays filter in broken streams and brilliant flashes through the dense canopy, but the sun itself remains blocked from view.

The forest plays its steady chorus of chirps, squeaks, trills, clicks, whistles, growls, croaks, leaf rustling, and river babbling. A rainbow of bright colored birds preen, flit, and feed among the ancient forest's thick and gnarled branches. Deep red and dark blue butterflies dance in the air above rich bouquets of violets and orchids.

Around almost every bend in the river new wildlife appears. Spotted deer graze on grass and plants growing near the river's edge. Black squirrels scurry up trees and vines. Pink-faced monkeys troop single file through dense evergreens not far from the bank. A red panda spies me from within a small bamboo grove. A striped fox prowls the riverbank, hunting fish and frogs.

I peer into the river depths. If I look hard enough, I see the shadowed shapes of fish swimming about. The dark shapes call my attention to the hunger pangs that have grown stronger as morning passed into afternoon. The last things I ate were Snubby's hazelnuts and the rice cake Cai gave me late last night. Just one of those fish swimming below would easily squash my hunger. Reaching down and grabbing one seems so easy, but I know better.

Even the best fishermen of Ning can seldom catch a fish barehanded. Of course, that might be because they rely more on their trained cormorants to catch fish rather than their own skill. Even so, I have no idea which parts of the river the Juxing water snakes hunt. I might lose a hand or arm with little chance of even catching a fish.

I keep hoping we'll pass a patch of berries growing along the banks. A few handfuls would satisfy my stomach for hours. But I haven't seen a single sign of any berries. Several varieties flourish in Gudai, but the trick is knowing where.

If I can't fish or gather berries, I have to do something to take my mind off my hunger. I try to think of how I'll rescue Lian once we reach Quanli, but it's hard to plan when I have no idea what the City of Heaven is like. I've never been there before. I've never been outside of Ning valley. I can only count on my gift from Tiānqì Shen.

I smile. It might seem hopeless, but if it was simple, what would be the fun in that? So, what if Tiānqì Shen didn't rescue Lian for me? She gave me the Wind gift. I just need a little practice using it.

I look down at the charcoal drawing of the paired Wind and Mother strokes on my left palm—the gift mark of the wind. The lines have smeared from using the steering pole. That won't work.

I glance over my shoulder back at the shelter to check on Cai. He's flopped on his back still sound asleep. Peck sleeps, standing beside him with her head twisted behind her nestled between her folded wings on her back. Snubby sits atop the shelter like an emperor overlooking his domain.

I look ahead at the river's course. This section flows fairly straight. I might be able to take a short break from steering without running ashore. I set down the steering pole, take a charcoal stick from my shoulder bag, and redraw the gift mark on my palm.

In the short time it takes, the boat begins to veer toward the right bank. I grab the steering pole, careful not to smudge the characters on my hand, and get us back on course. When we reach another straight section, I set the pole down again.

This time I take the charcoal stick in my left hand and attempt to draw the gift mark on my right palm. I concentrate hard and focus on keeping my left hand steady as I make the lines. I try not to worry about crashing the boat as I take my time to get the characters right.

I breathe out a long sigh as I study the sloppy strokes. "Not too dreadful, but it will work." Now it's time to practice.

Facing forward, I sit cross-legged on the bamboo deck. The warmth of the Shen Breath I gathered this morning still pulses inside me, waiting to be called upon. I raise my arms and aim my palms at a tangle of branches above. I try to tap into the boon and will a gust of wind to blast from my hand. Nothing happens. I try again. Still nothing.

"Pshhh!" I mutter. "What's the matter?"

I focus my thoughts on the Wind and Mother strokes of the gift mark on my palms and try to mentally make a connection between the characters and Shen Breath. I aim at a new set of branches and try to will my boon into action.

"Gales and hails! What am I doing wrong?"

"Remember your oath!"

My oath. Okay. This time as I focus on the strokes and the Shen Breath, I think of my oath to Tiānqì Shen. I repeat in my mind, "Do all I can to save Lian. Do all I can to save Lian. Do all I can to save Lian."

Still, nothing happens. No swelling warmth of Shen Breath. No wind blasting from my palms. Nothing.

"By the Two, Tiānqì Shen! How can I save Lian if you don't let me learn how to use my gift!"

Suddenly, as if my words forge a missing link between my oath, boon, and desired action, the Shen Breath surges within me. The gift mark on my palms glow with warmth and power. The boon burns along the stroke lines, aching to break free. I aim at another tangle of branches above and will the boon into action.

Wind blasts from my hands, knocking me flat on my back, breaking my concentration and the flow of air. For a moment, the front of the boat dips down under water, flooding the foredeck and drenching the cuffs of my pants, before bobbing back above the surface. A flurry of bright ficus leaves swirl from the branches above and orange figs plop like hailstones into the running river.

Snubby howls atop the shelter, clapping his hands. His smile shouts, "Do it again! Do it again!"

In the shelter beneath him, by the Two's luck Cai continues to snore. I grin. That wasn't too terrible for a first practice. But maybe a little less power and a different direction to aim so I don't get knocked flat next time.

I lay flat on the deck with my head hanging over the front of the boat. My face hovers only a few hand spans above the water. I spread my arms out wide, hands extending barely over the sides of the boat and palms facing the water a little behind me. I think of my oath to save Lian and how this practice will help me save her, and then I tap into the power of the Shen Breath to energize the lines of charcoal on my palms.

As the power pulses in my palms, I focus on releasing only a little. A light breeze flows from my skin making bubbles across the surface of the water.

"Yes!" I laugh. "I did it!"

Little by little I increase the flow of wind, hoping that its force will propel the boat forward faster. At first, it only makes more bubbles in the water. But as it gets stronger, instead of propelling the boat, it propels me. Its force pushes me forward, almost sending me headfirst into the river. I cut off the wind flow with half my upper body hanging over the front of the boat.

That was too close. If not for the rope that binds together the ends of the bamboo logs slowing my progress, I would have definitely fallen in. I shimmy backwards all the way back onto the boat wondering how in the Two's name I can keep from blowing myself into the water. As I stare at the binding ropes, an idea comes.

The rope wraps tight around each individual log, but the section of the rope that runs in a line over the top of the logs from one side of the boat to the other has some slack in it. I slide my arms under the rope and wrap them back over it, so the rope holds tight against my chest and shoulders. That should keep me from sliding off.

Now as I increase the flow of wind from my hands, the force pushes my chest and shoulders tight against the binding ropes, keeping me on the boat and moving the boat a little faster. Success. The more wind I blast, the faster the boat goes. It also pushes me against the ropes, which is increasingly more uncomfortable, but I don't mind. My Wind gift is making the boat go faster. Little by little I increase the wind flow in both hands. I grin as the boat speeds faster and faster, leaving large churning of bubbles and a deep wake of water in our path.

A sudden bend in the river causes the boat to head for the left bank. I decrease the flow of air from my right hand to turn the boat more to the right Too much! Now we're heading fast toward the right bank. I increase the air flow from my right hand to compensate. Too much again. the boat heads back too far to the left.

It takes several attempts, adding more wind power with one hand and easing off on the other, and vice versa, until I finally get a feel for how to make the boat go the direction I want.

I giggle with delight as the boat zips over the water, turning and swerving at my will. Amazing. The boat speeds faster than it could with the sail up on a blustery day. Flying fast across the water exhilarates me. I feel so alive. Free. Powerful. Invincible. I've never felt this way before.

"Thank you, Tiānqì Shen!" I shout whisper, not wanting to wake Cai. I'm almost surprised the boat's high speed doesn't wake him. As tired as he is, he could probably sleep through almost anything.

We glide and zip across the water for more than a few minutes. Although my Shen Breath reserves have lowered, their power still pulses strong within me when all at once the wind stops blasting from my hands. The bubbles stop and the boat slows to match the current of the river.

I try to will the wind to blow again, but I can't create the mental link between the Shen Breath and the gift mark on my palms. I pull my arms free of the binding ropes and a quick glance at one hand tells me why my gift has stopped working. The strokes of charcoal are gone. At first, I think the water must have washed them off, but my palms only have a few moist spots on them. Somehow all traces of the charcoal writing is gone. I stare at my palm, debating whether I should redraw the gift mark to practice more.

A rippling in the water draws my attention. A gold tentacle shoots out of the water, wraps around my wrist, and pulls me off the boat. Snubby's squeals as I'm dragged beneath the water's surface.

Holding my breath, I thrash and kick beneath the water. I try to pull the tentacle off with my free hand, but it's too strong. More tentacles grab my ankles and my other wrist. I pull and kick, but the tentacles hold me fast beneath the water.

The face of a handsome young man pushes through the water close to mine. His kind eyes, shining like sapphires, hold my gaze. His thick inviting lips smile. His bare broad chest ripples with the muscles of a warrior. Peace and calm flow through me. I'm safe now. Why was I afraid anyway? I don't remember. I don't care. I want to stare into those eyes forever. My lips long to press firm against his.

Something pulls on my feet and ankles, dragging me through the water. Where is it taking me? I don't care, as long as I can keep staring into that divine face. My lungs tighten in pain. I don't know why. I don't care. I want those lips.

I push my face closer. One kiss. I only need one kiss and I'll be the happiest girl on all of Dashi. Bubbles stream from my mouth as I pucker. Should the bubbles worry me? No, I'm being silly. What's to worry about when you're about to kiss a god.

The god's divine lips part to meet mine. His teeth shine like silver. Except, they're not teeth. They're needle-like fangs. That's okay. They're lovely fangs, behind irresistible lips. I need those lips. But first, I need one more look at his enchanting eyes.

The gaze of those sapphire eyes sends a rush of euphoria through my veins. I want to look at them forever. What a decision—to stare into heaven forever or kiss the lips of a god. How did I get so blessed with two such wonderful choices?

Cold chills tremor through my body. My lungs feel like they're going to explode. My throat burns. My head pounds. None of it matters. Everything is wonderful. Everything is perfect.

While he holds my gaze, he blinks. It's a mere moment, but in that moment transparent eyelids close over those sapphire eyes and the eyes flick to a dull orange before changing back to sapphire. The eyes become beautiful again, but just for a moment. The spell is broken. Hunger rather than kindness shows in those eyes as the illusion fades.

My lungs burn for air. I need the surface. My breath is nearly gone. I try to kick my hands and feet free. The tentacles are too strong. The lips that I desperately wanted to kiss moments ago grow larger and open wide revealing several rows of needle-like fangs. The bewitching face and upper body transform into that of a gold demonic looking gargoyle. Huge orange eyes. A big flat snout. Saucer-shaped ears. Two long, thick tentacles sprout from each side, still holding me fast. The fishlike scales of his lower body reflect rainbows of light as its shark-like tailfin propels it through the water.

Jianzha Jiang. The demon river rogue. Beguiler of humans. Devourer of souls.

Dizziness clouds my thoughts. My vision blurs. I'm dying. But I can't die. Lian needs me to save her. Focusing on my oath and the need to survive to save Lian, I reach for the small supply of Shen Breath still lingering inside me. Warmth and strength flare through my body. Somehow, I can breathe again.

I don't have time to waste. With a surge of strength my fingers grip the tentacles that hold my wrists. With all the force I can muster, I yank hard right and then left. The tentacles snap off like a lizard's tail. A high pitch scream reverberates through the water. Jianzha Jiang's lower tentacles release my ankles. A haze of blood swirls and floats in the water for a moment, but the monster's wound quickly heals.

In a burst of speed, gargoyle fangs lunge for me. Even with the Shen Breath, I can't move in the water as fast as the Jianzha Jiang. With no way to evade those teeth in time, I grab the sides of his head to hold the fangs back.

It shakes and thrashes as it drives me backward beneath the water, trying to break free of my grip. It wraps its two remaining tentacles around my waist to pull free. I think about snapping them off like the others, but I'm not sure I can before its fangs take a bite out of me.

My Shen Breath wanes. If I don't do something fast, I'll quickly become dinner. Concentrating all the power of my boon to my hands, I release my hold on the Jianzha Jiang's head. As it lunges, I throw a double palm strike—a punch to each of its eyes.

The punches hurt it enough that I break free of its tentacles. I swim for the surface, hoping I've blinded it or wounded it enough that it won't come after me. But my forehead barely touches the water surface when a tentacle wraps around my ankle and pulls me back down.

Chapter 18
Qiu Meilin – Hopeless Frenzy

"Can one stand in the Light when silencing a truth to spare a hurt? Which tenet is more important, honesty or hospitality of heart?"
- Pan Ru: Essays on the Tenets of Light

My lungs burn as the tentacle pulls me back under the chill river. I try to kick free, but it's no use. I used up my Shen Breath. I have no power. My thoughts grow muddled from lack of air and fatigue. I have to stay focused. I have to survive.

The gargoyle face and fangs of the Jianzha Jiang rise quickly. Its large orange eyes burn with anger. The corners bleed from my earlier palm strikes. I jerk and twist to break free of the tentacle, but without success. In my mind, I plead for Tiānqì Shen to help me. No help comes. I'm on my own. I have to escape.

As it pulls me close to its fangs, I make a frenzied attempt to survive. I drive the heel of my free foot onto the center of its ugly snout. My heel batters and drives, over and over again. I don't dare stop. Once I stop, it'll be over. It will have me. So, I kick and don't stop kicking.

My lungs scream for air. Chilling cold burns my flesh. I kick harder and faster.

Dizziness swirls in my mind. I keep kicking.

My vision blurs. I can't see my target, but I kick and kick.

Its tentacles release my other foot. I kick with it too.

My thoughts grow foggy. I can't think straight. I only know that I have to keep kicking. I can't remember why, other than my life depends on it.

Where am I? Am I still kicking? I think so.

I no longer feel my legs or arms. Why am I so cold?

Everything goes black…

Water spews from mouth. I cough and gag. I take in air between more spews of water. I'm on my hands and knees, shivering and shaking. The sun warms the back of my neck, but my wet clothes hang cold and heavy on my skin, dripping pools of water. My fingernails dig into a bamboo floor. No, not a floor. A boat deck.

The warmth of a blanket encircles me. Strong arms lift me to my feet. Like a distant echo, someone says, "You're going to be okay,"

With blurred vision, I turn to the source. I try to focus. The stunning face becomes clearer. Then I remember. Jianzha Jiang! Fear and panic strike.

"No!" I scream. I try to hit and kick, but the blanket holds me fast. "Let me go! You won't have me!"

The arms and blankets enfold me closer. I can't move. I have to get out.

"Meilin! You're safe now!"

I have to get away!

"Meilin, stop! It's me, Cai."

I look closer. The face grows clear.

"Cai?"

He nods. I stop fighting. It is Cai. All my emotions rush to the surface. With everything else that has happened—Lian, Father's shame, the Shashyao—and now almost dying at the hand of the Jianzha Jiang, it's too much for me. I want to scream. I want to hide somewhere safe. But nowhere is safe.

I fight to hold back the tears. I have to be strong. I try to smile away the panic and overwhelming fear. But when I see the concern in Cai's soft eyes, I can't stop crying. I lower my head, so he won't see the flow of tears. Still, my cold shivers grow to violent trembles.

Cai holds me closer. I want to melt into his embrace. Its warmth feeds me strength. Hope.

He guides me to the back of the boat, beneath the shelter. I tense as he helps me lay on the floor in a corner of the shelter. I don't want to leave the safety of his embrace. Snubby waggles his way past Cai, sits beside me, and lays his head on my shoulder. I smile. Snubby's presence brings a little comfort, but I want Cai to hold me again.

This isn't like me. I'm strong. I can do things on my own. I don't need anyone's help. But right now, I don't care. I want Cai to sit close to me. But he doesn't. He sits across from me in the other corner. He faces forward and grabs the stern paddle to steer. Splashes sound behind us as he pulls and pushes hard on the paddle. The boat jerks and bumps, and eventually begins to move slowly as it floats away from the bank.

The concentration on Cai's face tells me it's much harder to steer with the stern paddle in this narrow channel. But I'm glad he's here in the shelter rather than steering out on the boat's bow.

"The Two must love you," Cai says. "I doubt we would have found you if your little beast's screams hadn't woken me. What happened?"

The crinkle in his forehead, the intensity in his eyes shows true concern. I want to tell him what happened, but I can't. How can I say that I escaped a Jianzha Jiang without revealing my gift from Tiānqì Shen? Maybe I should tell him. Would it really be bad if he knew that he might be gifted too? If he is, he'll eventually find out. No. I can't. At least not now.

"I fell off the boat," I say, revealing only part of the truth. "After that, it's a blur."

Some of it is a blur. I really don't know what happened after I blacked out. Did Cai see the Jianzha Jiang? How did I get away from it? Did my kicking hurt it?

Cai nods at Snubby with a half-smile. "You were gone when I woke. Your snub-nosed kept pointing in the water, squealing like a shrill rat. I looked up and down the river for you. There was no sign."

He pauses as he forcefully blinks his eyes a few times and clears his throat. When he speaks again, his voice sounds softer, and each word comes out slow and controlled as if difficult to speak. "I thought you had drowned or worse. I was certain we lost you."

He stops again, this time taking a deep breath before continuing, "You floated to the surface ahead of us. There was no way you should have still been alive, but you were."

The last sentence comes out more like an accusation. His gaze grows intense as if demanding to know how I survived. I shrug, staying silent. I pull the blanket tight around me, to fight off the shivers. Cai says nothing more. In the silence, my eyelids grow heavy, and I succumb to sleep.

I'm unsure how much time passed, but when I wake Cai is no longer in the shelter. He stands at the front of the boat again with his back to me, steering us down the river with his pole. My clothes are still damp, but I shed the blanket as I stretch and yawn.

"If you're hungry, there's some fish up here," Cai calls to me over his shoulder. "Peck's been working hard, haven't you girl?"

A guttural croak sounds above me on top of the shelter. I imagine the large cormorant bobbing its head and spreading its huge wings, pleased at Cai's attention.

The boat rocks side to side as I crawl from the shelter into the sun's warmth. Gudai's thick canopy blocks my view of the sun, but the slightly cooler temperature and smell of approaching rain tells me dusk is not too far off. I kneel down, sitting on my heels a few paces behind Cai. I'm barely settled before Snubby hops off the shelter, scrambles toward me, and crawls onto my lap. I smile at the little monkey, and he smiles back as I stroke the fur behind his ears.

"The fish are in the basket," Cai says without looking back. "I hope you don't mind them raw. We can't risk the attention a cooking fire might create."

Inside the shelter opening, nine fish tails poke up from a big basket of curing salt. The salt preserves the fish, so it doesn't rot. Whatever we don't eat tonight, Cai can hang up to dry tomorrow to finish the curing process. Fully salt dried fish is okay. Plain raw is not too bad. But neither come close to Mama's ginger and garlic boiled fish slices covered in sweet soybean paste. Oh, I already miss Mama's cooking.

But right now, raw is better than none at all. I grab one of the fish tails and pull out a yellow-spotted bream, a little shorter than my forearm. Using a knife hanging by a string on the basket, I quickly scrape off the scales and excess salt before sinking in my teeth. The skin's a little chewy raw, but full of flavor. I devour the bream quickly, spitting out bones and too tough fins. When I'm done, only the tail and lips remain. I brush those off into the water for whatever hungry scavengers glide beneath us.

I eye one of the other bream in the basket, but decide I've had plenty for now. The pangs in my stomach are gone and I feel a resurgence of energy now that I've had plenty of food.

With his back to me, Cai guides the boat downriver deeper into Gudai. I thought this far into Gudai would be darker or scarier, but it's not that different from the woods near home. The howls, chitters, and whistles of some animals differ, but most are still familiar. The shape and twist of trees, density of vines, vibrancy and colors of flowers, and shades and thickness of greenery constantly change as we travel, but that's the way Gudai is at home too.

They say the deep of Gudai hides multitudes of dangers and mysteries, but I feel peace here. Is it a false peace? Or are the tales of Gudai's exaggerated? What really lies beyond the wall of trees and vines that lines each section of river we pass?

"Did you enjoy the bream?" Cai asks, his face still facing forward. "Peck always appreciates a thank you."

The lighthearted, playful tone in Cai's voice makes me smile. I look over my shoulder at Peck, perched on top of the shelter with his wings still spread wide. With a capricious smile, I bow my head at the black bird and with a slight lilt say, "Why thank you, Peck. That was the most divine bream I've had in days."

Peck stretches his neck up and arches his head back before letting out a guttural croak in thanks. I giggle. Cai joins in, laughing and smiling over his shoulder at both of us. My smile broadens. I love Cai's smile.

"What?" Cai asks, his smile still wide. "Why are you looking at me like that?"

My lips flatten and I lower my eyes. After a moment, I raise them back up, trying not to act embarrassed that I've been caught staring. "Sorry," I say. "I was thinking about Lian. If she knew you were here, she'd be smiling too. That's something she hasn't done for a while."

The grin on his face disappears. A wall of silence slams between us. The joy in his eyes dims. A somber mask covers his face, before he turns to look forward and steer the boat again. I'm not sure what I said wrong?

"Cai, Lian will be okay. We will rescue her. I promise."

His body stiffens a moment. With little emotion, he utters, "No doubt."

How do I respond to that? What is going on in his mind? I have no idea why my words upset him. But I get the hint that talking time has ended. I shrug my shoulders and try not to let it bother me. But I wish I could fix whatever I did.

More out of boredom than hunger, I grab another bream from the salt basket. This time I nibble on it, savoring the skin and meat. A content smile plays on my lips as I gaze up at the canopy with its mix of willows, gnarled oaks and cypress trees arching overhead. Bright orchids color the branches with bright pinks and purple. Their fragrance fills the air, almost overpowering the fish scent beneath my nose.

The next hour passes in silence as I watch the deep greens of Gudai turn darker and darker. Early evening changes to dusk and then to night. The river surface shimmers with enough specks of filtered light from the lone moon San to discern the black of the water from the shadowy banks. The noises of the forest grow quieter, but in a way more intense. The buzz and chirps have lessened, but the howls, clicks and whistles have become more pronounced with fewer sounds to compete against. Only the most stealthy or deadly dare move about in Gudai's dark.

I shiver. I want to crawl back into the cover of the boat's shelter, hidden from the glowing eyes of red and yellow that peer hungrily at me from the forest's shadows and the river's shallows. I push up the corners of my mouth. Hiding would be too easy.

"Get some rest," I call to Cai. "You've been steering for hours. Let me take a turn."

Cai tenses, my voice startling him for a moment. Without a word, he lays down the steering pole and turns toward me with a slight nod. The boat barely rocks as he moves toward the shelter. As he passes, our eyes meet in the darkness for a moment. I expect to see anger for whatever it was that I said earlier to upset him. But there's not a hint of even annoyance. I'm not sure, but he looks almost sad. It might even be wistful sorrow. What is going on in Cai's mind?

Once he's passed, I stand and use the long pole to keep the boat centered in the river's flow. I have no desire to come within reach of any night creatures hiding in the riverbank's shadows. I stiffen at the slightest rustle of leaves or creak of branches. I jump at the tiniest splash of water. I cringe at the squeaks and currents of air swirling about from the erratic glides and dives of bats hunting bugs and other prey in the night. Noises and moving shadows taunt me from around and above.

With no reserves of Shen Breath, I have little defense against any creature that might decide to attack me from the shadows above or the river below. Still, I straighten my posture, push back my shoulders, hold my head high, grip the steering pole like a weapon, and grin. Fear cannot defeat he who stands tall. At least that's what Master Jin would often tell the village boys as they were sent off to war. I'm not sure I believe it. But if it will help keep me from scurrying back to the shelter like a frightened dot mouse, I'll give it a try.

The fear never leaves, but somehow pretending like I'm brave makes it easier to keep it at bay. I try to keep my eyes on the river ahead, ignoring the movements and sounds to my sides. The hours pass slowly. My body stiffens from standing and steering so long. My eyelids droop. I want to sleep, but I can't stop worrying about unseen predators. At least that helps me stay wide awake. Still, I desperately want to wake Cai and shout at him, "I'm done with this! It's your turn!" But no. I have to be strong. I refuse to give in to fear and fatigue.

All of a sudden, the night air cools and grows heavy. The noises of the forest go still. The awesome smell of midnight rain fills my nostrils. I love that smell. At least I love it when I'm warm and dry in my room with a sturdy roof above my head. It's not so great this many leagues from home in the middle of Gudai with the likelihood I'll be standing in its wet torrents for who knows how many hours.

Like pounding drums, the sound of the approaching showers grows to a deafening roar until it's upon me. The rain pelts my head and shoulders, drenching me instantly. I laugh. At least I should be safe now.

Even the most dangerous beasts of Gudai take shelter during midnight downpours.

A tap on my shoulder startles me. I almost drop the steering pole in the river, but regain my grip in time. Ready to use the pole as a weapon, I turn. Of course, it's Cai. Who else would it be? Rain soaks his dark hair and flows in rivers down his face.

"Forgive me. I didn't mean to scare you," he says. "Go inside. It's my turn."

I'm tempted to shine a big smile at him and tell him, "No thanks. I'm fine." But that would be dumb. I braved the terrors of the night. I have nothing to prove. If Cai wants to brave the showers of the night, who am I to stand in his way?

With water streaming down my nose and across my lips, I flash a big grin at him and say, "Thanks."

I hand him the pole, bow slightly, and hurry to the warmth and dry of the shelter. Snubby cuddles up beside me as I wrap myself in a blanket. Even with the loud staccato of pelting rain on the roof above, sleep takes me in a short few minutes.

Chapter 19
Lord Emperor Xiang Hu – To Taste Immortality

"Nursing wolf her prey devours. Caring thief pilfers succor. Truth of nature? Truth of man? One to justify the other? Goodness shaped to please our image? Smiling lies still deceive. When light first breathed across the heavens, what truth shined? What goodness reigned?"

- Personal Meditations of Xiang Hu

Adding to the flicker of a dozen porcelain oil burning lamps, a few golden rays of early morning sun stream into the royal chamber through windows covered in sheer silk. Bare, except for my underclothes I recline on a cushioned couch. I try to hold still but it's near impossible as Wang Hai tickles my belly with the hairs of his cursed pen.

My chief scholar hovers over me, redrawing or adding new layers of ink to my gift marks. Five hundred fifty-five. That's the number of different gift marks that cover my body from shoulder to toe. But Hai only works on those that have faded from use or my morning bath.

I despise this morning ritual, but I would be a fool to neglect it. At least the character strokes last longer since Hai has begun using the new ink mixture of soot, acacia sap, and sesame oil. Anything that lets me use my gifts longer and lessens how many marks need to be redrawn or re-inked is a blessing from the Two.

Trying not to upset Hai's work, I take in a deep breath. To sweeten the room's air, musk and frankincense mix with the aroma of hemp oil that burns in the lamps. The scents usually relax me, but not today. Once again nightmares of the demon dragon's rampage tormented my sleep again. I wish I could push out the visions of slaughter and wreckage that fill my mind, but they're ever present. The best I can do is try to think of new ways to stop the dreams' prophecies from coming true.

I keep frowning. It's not just because of the tragedies that I must somehow stop. It's also the constant memory of how the dreams' interpretation drove a wedge between Yuan and me.

Oh, sweet Yuan, why could you not understand what I see so clearly? Why could you not see that everything I do is to protect you and to protect Dashi?

After Hai finishes redrawing the last gift mark, he meticulously cleans up his inks and brushes, and stows them in a red silk satchel. He takes from the satchel a large red fan bearing two golden dragons and waves it above the newly inked symbols. Like usual, they only take a few minutes to dry, but it seems like forever. Hai finally finishes and hurries out the door after honoring me with three floor-level kowtows.

Anxious for my morning visit with Yuan, I struggle to quickly dress in my yellow royal robes. "Xie spawn!" I curse as I try to get my gold and silver belt on right. Some days I wish I hadn't long ago banned my servants from dressing me. Dressing myself is such an inconvenience. But it's necessary to keep my gift marks secret, as well as my healing touch.

Once dressed, I gather up in my arms the new screen painting I had commissioned. It will eventually have a prominent place in the Imperial Gallery, but first I want to share it with Yuan. She would so much enjoy it. I tap into my return gift mark linked to the orchard monastery and travel to the Divine Empress' room in an instant.

"Sweet, Yuan! I brought a surprise to brighten your room for the day!"

I place the screen in front of the plain wall opposite her bed. If not for her forced sleep, she'd have a perfect view of the painting. To anyone else, the painting portrays a mythical tale of a young warrior braving the dangers of the golden dragon and red phoenix that stand guard on Mount Qiangu, so he can steal a peach from the Tree of Life for a beautiful princess.

I slip off my leather gloves and sit on the bed beside Yuan and stroke her long dark hair. "Do you remember that time, my sweet love? I was not yet a warrior, but still a humble sheepherder. Though only a sheepherder's new bride, you were indeed a princess to me, and you will always be that and so much more.

"What adventures we had those early months of marriage. Your grandmother's tales of the Shen inspired us to search out their lost shrines. We knew so little of the oaths and gifts back then. Thanks to the Two, we uncovered secrets that lay hidden for centuries. Oh, and when we found the shrine of Luxíng Shen more of the world opened to us. Gifts from the god of journeys made no place or destiny too far."

I rise from the bed and walk to the painting. My fingers trace around the image of the princess sitting peacefully beneath a cherry tree in full blossom at the foot of the mountain, waiting for her hero to return. It actually was not a peaceful time. Yuan did not wait at the mountain foot. She lay in bed hundreds of leagues away at home, near death with rose fever. The doctors had given up on her, but I refused to.

"I was so thankful you bullied me into studying the writings of Pan Ru," I say with a laugh. "If not for that, I never would have found his description of the hidden gorge high on Mount Qiangu where the legendary peach tree grew. The details were exact—another blessing of the Two. For if not for that, the Leap gift never could have taken me there.

"The gorge lay hidden between two looming crags—one shaped like the howling wolf and the other a curled-up slumbering lamb. At each end of the gorge, nine tear-shaped cypress trees stood branch-to-branch like sentinels blocking entrance to the gorge. Bubbling up from the high end of the gorge, a crystal spring flooded it, turning the gorge into a muddy, but beautiful bog carpeted with a glorious field of lily pads and yellow lotus.

"A grassy mound rose in the gorge center, where the majestic peach tree stood. As the stories say, a deadly snake-like dragon curled itself around the tree and a vicious phoenix perched among its ever blossoming and ever fruit-laden branches. The ever-vigilant beast and fowl guarded against any who dared steal the fruit's gift of immortality.

"Ha! But they could not stop what they could not see. A quick pick of the biggest peach and I was back home before that red-winged bird or golden-scaled dragon could blink."

My gaze turns from the painting to the slumbering figure of Yuan. "By the time I returned, you had fallen into a fitful stupor. Your fever rose dangerously high. Your body convulsed. Screams pierced your lips. I could only imagine the nightmares the fever inflicted on your mind.

"I did not wait. I cut into the peach, forcing small slices past your lips, moving your mouth up and down, helping you eat one after the other. With only half the peach eaten, your body began to glow. Your screams and fits stopped. Color returned to your cheeks. Your fever left. Your eyes focused. Your lips smiled. Your health and life restored.

"I encouraged you to eat the rest of the peach to make sure the healing was complete, but you would not. 'Would you curse me to immortality without you?' you asked. 'No. You eat the rest that we may share eternity together.' I did as you bade, but now look at us. I have cursed us both."

My lips tighten as I stare at Yuan in silence, wishing that the Shen or even the Two might speak to my thoughts as they once did. Why had they stopped speaking to me so long ago? I keep the oaths. Everything I do honors those oaths. Otherwise, how could I wield the Shen's gifts? Oh, why would they not tell me how to convince Yuan to join me in their cause? It makes no sense. The last thing I wanted was to force Yuan into a never-ending sleep and me to never-ending loneliness. But I had no choice. How I wish there was another way.

My frown deepens. "I must leave you to your sleep, my sweet Yuan. The empire we built cannot run on its own. There is much work to be done. Officials to keep happy. People to feed. Yemaren to defeat. A demon dragon to stop from rising. How I wish you would help me. But that is not to be."

Chapter 20
Qiu Meilin – Fool in the Forest

"Hospitality of heart means more than kindness. It is putting all others before our own convenience, desires, and safety."
- Pan Ru: Essays on the Tenets of Light

Curled up in the warmth of my blanket in the back of the shelter, I wake a moment before Cai shakes my shoulder. He smiles down at me, but the droop in his half-closed eyes shows fatigue from a long night of steering.

I'm already pulling off my blanket and getting to my feet when he whispers, "Your turn."

It's still dark out, but the rain has stopped. I pull a bream from the salt basket as I crawl from the shelter to the boat's front to take my turn poling. Before long, flickers of morning light begin to make their way through the canopy branches above. As the sun's rays grow brighter, wisps of Shen Breath begin to rise and swirl along the green of the woods.

The mists call to me, reminding me of the power they offer. With Cai sleeping soundly between Peck and Snubby in the shelter, it's a perfect opportunity to go ashore and replenish my boon, but I hesitate. Yesterday's adventure ashore unnerved me. What if I really encounter a Jade Leopard? Still, I need more Shen Breath, and I won't have to go far to replenish it.

Careful not to jostle Cai and his sleeping companions, I steer the boat toward a flat patch of clover growing along the bank. The boat glides with barely a bump and creak onto the shore. Nice job. Better than I thought I could do.

Using a simple sewing knot, I tie the boat to the closest willow and step ashore. I walk slowly through patches and swirls of Shen Breath, letting them infuse me with their strength. I love the feeling. Invincibility. Power. Grace. Confidence. All of them combine and grow stronger and stronger inside me.

Only a few minutes pass before the inward flow of Shen Breath stops. My body has taken in all that it can handle of the boon. But it's more than enough.

Pushing branches and vines out of the way, I hurry back to the boat and hopefully away from any nearby Jade Leopards. I breathe easier when the boat and river come into sight. I smile. Cai will never know I left.

Before I take another step, a child's cry for help brings me to quick a stop beneath a branch of purple orchids. The cry sounded close. Not too far back into Gudai. I hold still, listening again for the child. I hear only the whistles and clicks of the forest.

I glance back at the boat. I need to get back before Cai wakes. But I can't abandon a child in need. Memories of the Jianzha Jiang's trickery return. Could this be a deceit of some other deadly creature hoping to make a snack of me?

It could even be a savage of the deep hoping to ambush me. Little is known about the people of Gudai's deep. Most simply want to live in seclusion. But there are stories of slave takers and worse.

"Help!" sounds again. Sobs and a sense of panicked urgency attend the voice.

Gales and hails! It doesn't matter. I have to help. Besides, I have my boon. Trampling flower and grass, weaving through oak and pine, skirting dense bamboo groves, ducking clusters of hanging vines, and pushing through thick brush, I hurry toward the cry. My eyes shift back and forth between the way ahead and the branches above, on constant watch for near-invisible Jade Leopards or any other threat.

I curse myself for having left the boat without a weapon. I think of the fish knife hanging from the salt basket. Even my small sharpening knife would give me a little comfort, but it's in the boat shelter inside my shoulder bag.

More sobs sound the moment before I duck under a clump of drooping moss and step into a clearing circled by a mix of towering ancient oaks and pine trees. At the far end of the clearing, near a thicket of red-yellow tiger roses, a girl no more than three years old sits on her heels in kneeling position.

Too short for a proper ponytail, her dark hair doesn't reach her shoulders. Her tunic and trousers match my traditional grays, except they're dyed dark green. With her head bowed and chin tucked against her chest, tears roll down her pale, rosy cheeks.

"Little one, what's wrong?"

The girl's head jerks up. A gasp blows past her lips. Her dark eyes widen when she meets my gaze. Her body tenses. She looks left and right, deciding whether to scream or run.

I kneel in a clump of damp leaves to show I'm not a threat. "I won't hurt you," I whisper. "Where is your mama and baba?"

Her chest heaves as she sniffles and wipes her nose on her sleeve. Her cheeks puff and her eyes bulge with fear. She sniffles twice more before speaking between stuttered gasps. "I…don't…know."

"Do you need help finding them?" It sounds like such a dumb question, but I want her to feel safe."

She blinks several times to bat away tears. Her bottom lip pushes up over her upper lip into a scared pout. She wants to say something, but the words don't come. Instead, she slowly nods her head.

I smile to reassure her, and I rise to my feet. I take slow, measured steps to not scare her off. I kneel in front of her, picking a tiger rose and offering it to her. She hesitates, but takes the rose—a hint of a smile turns up one corner of her mouth.

"My name's Meilin," I say. "What's yours?"

The girl fixes her eyes on the rose as she twirls it between her fingers. Her voice trembles as she whispers, "Ling."

What a pretty name," I say. "Ling, where did you last see your parents?"

She doesn't take her eyes off the twirling rose, but her trembling has lessened. "At home."

I squeeze her knee and smile. "Where is home? Can you show me?"

Her lips tighten and her gaze on the rose intensifies. She shakes her head.

Now what do I do? Maybe her village is close by. I think about taking Ling by the hand and wandering Gudai with the hope that we'd soon stumble on her home. But that'd be as smart as walking into den of Xie Wolves, Pang Bears, or Jade Leopards. Those are a few of threats that make Gudai their home. How many of their different hunting grounds might we pass wandering to find her home?

Maybe Ling can give clues to her home's location to help us avoid Gudai's monsters. "Do you remember how you got here?"

A huge smile brightens Ling's face. Excitement shines in her eyes as she lifts her gaze up at me and nods. "Butterflies!"

My nose crinkles. "Butterflies?"

She nods enthusiastically. "Pretty blue butterflies. Lots of them."

My nose crinkles even more. I cross my arms across my chest. "What? Did they fly you here?"

Ling covers her mouth and giggles. "Meilin silly."

My lips tighten, frustrated that I have no idea how to get simple answers from a three-year-old. "How did the pretty butterflies bring you here?"

Ling giggles louder. Her eyes sparkle like polished coal. "Butterflies pretty. I chase chase chase." She pauses. Her eyes darken. Her grin vanishes. "Branch break. Fall down boom."

My lips purse as I try to make sense of Ling's words. What little I understand doesn't do much to help me figure out how to get her home. And I can't leave her here alone.

Tiānqì Shen, how do I help this girl?

No answer comes from the weather goddess. Not that I really expect one. And I'm not sure I really want one. I shudder. It was more than creepy when she spoke to me back home through the mouth of young Jia. Still, I wouldn't mind a little guidance, especially if it came by way of few well-placed ideas inserted into my thoughts.

While my mind struggles for any sign of a decent plan, Ling gasps and buries her face in her hands. Her body stiffens. Her hands and arms tremble even more.

She jerks when I touch her shoulder. "Ling, it'll be okay. We'll find your mama and baba."

She leans forward, burying her face and hand into her lap. I wrap my arms around her, but freeze when a muted thump sounds behind me. I slowly glance over my shoulder to the side. I tense with a quick intake of breath.

An enormous Pang Bear lumbers into the clearing. Dark brown fur with flecks of gray covers its body. Streaks of dark green flare at angles from the top of its head and across its face from the edges of its eyes. Even though it's on all fours, it walks taller than the tallest man in all of Ning. Its massive paws leave imprints in the moss and damp underbrush larger than a wok.

I turn to face the massive bear, shielding Ling and trying to hold her still behind me. Years back when I used to eavesdrop on the village elders as they sipped tea and chatted beneath the shade of my favorite elm, they would sometimes discuss the best ways to survive a Pang Bear in Gudai's deep.

Sun Guo would pound the grass and shout, "Run and don't stop running!" He argued that the large bear's size made it too difficult to maneuver well through the dense trees and brush of the forest.

Master Jin would chuckle and take a long sip of tea until all eyes and ears leaned toward him. He would gingerly set his tea on the grass, clasp his hands in front of his chest, and in a hushed voice say, "The Pang Bear mind no branch nor bush. Run if you would be lunch. Be still and silent as a pebble if you would live another day."

I doubt any of the elders or Master Jin ever really faced a live Pang Bear, but I trust Master Jin's counsel over Sun Guo's, or any other village elder. Besides, I'm not sure how fast I could run carrying Ling in my arms.

Trying to make myself as small and still as a pebble, I hold my breath and watch the Pang Bear plod through the clearing. It stops to sniff the air a few times, and even looks my way. But it acknowledges me no more important than it would a tree. Master Jin was right. The Pang Bear passes no closer than eight paces away from me without a threatening glance.

Ling's little fingers grab a fistful of my trousers right behind my knees. Her cheek presses against the side of my leg as she peers around me to watch the massive bear. As the Pang Bear reaches the other side of the clearing, it slowly swings its head in our direction. Its eyes pass over us with little interest, but a slight twitch of its mouth reveals its huge teeth and long side fangs. In that moment, Ling tugs hard on my trousers and lets out a shrill shriek.

The bear shifts its focus to us. I try to hold still, but Ling pulls on my trousers. Her breathing quickens. Panicked sobs grow in intensity and volume. The bear's lips pull back in a menacing growl. Its turns toward us and rises on its hind legs, towering twice as tall as a man. If we weren't in a clearing, the upper third of its body would rise above all the lowest branches. It walks toward us with nothing but a few ferns, rose bushes, and clumps of moss barring its way.

Now I see the wisdom in Sun Guo's advice, and I'm tempted to pick up Ling and flee from the clearing. The Pang Bear would have a difficult time making its way through the thick of the forest, but only if it stayed on its hind legs. If it came to a chase, I'm sure it would drop on all fours and charge us with more force and strength than a raging water buffalo. It would easily plow through brush and thicket, and small trees. Only where large trees grow close together would it have any real difficulty in catching us.

The warmth of the Shen Breath pulses through my body. If I have to, I'll fight the bear. Even with the strength of the boon, I'm unsure if I can survive. But just in case, I offer a silent prayer.

Tiānqì Shen, if this bear kills me, I can't keep my oath to save Lian. So, if it comes to a fight, don't hold out on me. I need that boon, please!

I'm sure it's not a proper prayer. Still, the power of the boon flares up inside my chest, arms, and legs, waiting to be engaged. I'm tempted to charge the bear and strike it before it can reach us, but that would be witless. I hold still.

Snarling and growling, the bear crosses the clearing and stops right in front of me. Ling sobs and trembles behind me. I can't remember if it's better to avoid eye contact with the bear or look it in the eyes. I decide I don't care. If the bear attacks, I want to see it coming. It takes all my willpower to not scream and run away.

More to help calm myself rather than out of any hope that that my words will make difference, I whisper with a meek grin, "Master Bear, you are so tall and handsome. What an honor to have you greet us. But you really don't need to bother. We will be fine here by ourselves. You can go back to your business."

The Pang Bear sniffs the air above me as if considering if my words are tasty or not. It pulls its lips back, revealing its huge sharp teeth and snaps them in the air.

I smile, even though I feel sick. "Master Bear, I promise we taste as bad as snails. Unless of course, you like snails. Then we taste as bad as eels? You don't like eels, do you?"

The bear tilts back its head and roars. The thunderous noise drowns out every click, whistle, and growl of Gudai. Trees and branches shudder. Eerie silence follows, quickly ended by Ling's screams from behind me. She wraps her arms around my legs in a hard embrace. I'd run and scream, but my muscles freeze. I can't move. I can't speak.

Before I can blink, a paw bigger than my face slaps my shoulder. I fly several paces and crash into a tree trunk. The blow could have killed me if not for the warmth of the boon healing and surging inside me.

Ling screams, huddled on the ground beneath the massive bear. Saliva drips from its bared teeth as it leans down closer. The Pang Bear eyes her like a hungry beggar would a sweet bun hot and fresh from the fire. A single strike from its claws would rip the life from Ling. Her screams grow louder as she backs against the thicket of tiger roses. The Pang Bear has her trapped with nowhere to go.

I charge. Four paces away, I leap in the air leading with my feet. Powered by the Shen Breath, I fly high. Focusing the boon on the snap of my right leg, I jam the heel of my foot against the side of the bear's head. It's like kicking an iron pot, but the bear's head jerks to the side. It tumbles sideways like a falling tree.

It roars, telling me I didn't hurt it as bad as I wished. It's madder now. Luckily, wisps of the morning's Shen Breath still float among the forest flora and quickly flow into me, replenishing any of my boon that I've used. Before the bear can recover, I quickly pick up Ling and run to other side of the clearing and set her out of the bear's view behind a large rotted fallen tree.

"Stay here and don't make sound!" I tell her. "Everything will be okay."

Tears stream from her fear-filled eyes, but she nods in quiet obedience. I wish I could believe that everything really would be okay. I hope that even if I don't survive the Pang Bear, it will forget about Ling and leave after it finishes me off.

As I turn from Ling, the ground shakes from the pounding of the bear's paws. It rushes toward me. On all fours, it charges like a mad water buffalo. Moss and brush fly in the air from its wake. Its teeth snap, eager to crush me in its bite. I circle away in a sprint to lead it away from Ling.

I spot a thick fallen branch the size or a club. The boon lets me pick it up easily and swing it at the bear's head. The bear rears, roars, and flicks the branch from my hands. It flies into the trees, causing a shrill of squeals from annoyed birds and squirrels.

The bear's massive paw swats at me. I duck and kick sweep its legs. It crashes onto its backside, shaking the ground. I smile, but my smile flees at the bear's enraged roar.

The mammoth beast squirms, rolls back onto all fours, and charges again. When it's almost on top of me, I side kick at its nose—the soft spot for most animals.

Shrill screams explode past my lips. The bear's long claws slice across my leg before my foot connects. As I tumble to the ground. My Shen Breath quickly sooths and heals the wounds. But the Pang Bear slashes and slices my shoulders, ribs, and arms. Fiery pain stings harder and deeper.

The warmth of the Shen Breath engulfs me. It's all that keeps me alive. The bear paws and claws me over and over like I'm no more than a rag doll.

When the bear stops mauling me, I lay limp on a carpet of moss and leaves. Although Shen Breath's pulsing heat continues to heal me, I can't move. My strength has fled. Hot saliva drops from the bear's fangs on my cheek as it hovers over me. Rage lights the bear's eyes. It's hot, fish-tainted breath blows against my face in non-stop pants. I close my eyes, waiting for it to finish me with a snap of its powerful jaws and sharp teeth.

But the snap doesn't come. The hot of its breath vanishes. Its fur brushes across my stomach and legs as it turns. I gasp and jerk in pain as one of its hind paws steps on my leg, crushing bone as it walks away. The Shen Breath works on healing that too, but healing comes painfully slow.

No more swirling Shen Breath remains in the clearing. Either I it used up in my healing or the warming sun burned it up like a morning fog. My few Shen Breath reserves are all I have left to heal me. My eyes turn toward the Pang Bear, lumbering toward the spot where I hid Ling. It hasn't found her yet, but the bear continues to sniff the air, searching for her.

Near the bear, one last patch of Shen Breath swirls about leaves and flowers. I crawl toward it, growing a little stronger with every inch I draw closer to the bear. My broken bone and most of my wounds heal by the time my reserves vanish. I'm still tired, but I have enough strength to get to my feet.

While the bear continues to search for Ling, I walk toward it without a sound. Five paces away from the beast, the last of the clearing's Shen Breath flows toward me. I stop, letting it renew my strength. I hope it's enough. Before the last wisp seeps into my flesh, the bear rushes forward. A yelp from Ling tells me she's been found.

I race toward the bear. It crouches over Ling. It lunges. I leap onto its back, wrap my arm around its neck, and squeeze hard. The bear shakes and swats at me. I hold on tight and out of reach of its claws. I squeeze and squeeze. Please, Tiānqì Shen! Give me enough strength to make it faint before it can shake me loose.

The bear jerks and dances in wild motions, trying to buck me off. Ling cries and sobs nearby. Every few moments I get a glimpse of her log, but the bear moves so fast I never have a chance to see if she's still there. My grip weakens as my strength starts to fade. My boon is almost gone, but the bear is no closer to going down. Its shakes grow fiercer. It roars louder with more anger.

"Meilin! Meilin!"

Cai? What is he doing here? Ling continues to squeal and sobs. Other shouts sound—male and female voices I don't recognize. Hands clap. Drums pound. Sticks clack. I keep squeezing. Please fall Master Bear.

When the last of the boon fades, I still squeeze until I fall. Claws slash my back. My arms. My stomach. I scream in agony.

Shouts surge around me as black dots flash before my eyes. I struggle to stay conscious, but all is dark. No! I have to save Ling. I have to save her. But I can't move. I tense for another slash of claws, but it doesn't come. It doesn't matter. The Chi of life drains from me. My fight ends. I can do no more.

Garbled shouts and noise surround me. I try to open my eyes, but all I see are images in my mind of Ling sobbing behind her log. I failed her. The images shift to Lian huddled in chains aboard the Imperial Warship. I failed her too. Who will rescue her now? Cai, perhaps? I should have told him about Tiānqì Shen's gift. If he is Shen-Blessed, he'll need her boon to save Lian. Why did I have to be so selfish and proud? Keeping it to myself could be Lian's doom.

My last thoughts turn to Mama. I wish I had had the chance to tell her goodbye. I wonder about Father. Would he mourn my death if he knew? Or would he be happy to be rid of me for good? I will never know.

Chapter 21
Chao Cai – Thorny revelations

"Does a threshold of intelligence, power, or popularity exist where when reached one can displace the Creators' known truths with one's own beliefs?."
- Pan Ru: Essays on the Mysteries

Are you crazy?" I want to shout as Meilin hangs onto the back of a raging Pang Bear, but dread grips me. Other than my trembling from heel to hair, I can't speak or move. Blood covers her grays that hang on her in tattered shreds. Blood covers Meilin. How is she still alive? I've never seen a Pang Bear before. It's massive, larger than I ever imagined. How in the Two's name can Meilin hang on? While she always excelled at most Fei Chi forms, she lacked power in skills that required strength.

Amazement replaces some of the anger and worry I felt when I discovered she had gone ashore alone, but only a little. Why did she go so far from the boat? Everyone knows how dangerous Gudai's deep can be. But Meilin is not like everyone. She never has been.

Tell her to be silent and she sings. Punish her and she smiles. Always the defiant one. I couldn't help but smile at her courage, but every village elder felt it his personal duty to rein her in and teach her full respect. She would submit to their correction and thrashings with bowed head and submission, but her shoulders never drooped and cries for mercy never came. When the beatings ended, she acted as if she had received the greatest gift in the world. Meilin faces life with smiling courage.

How can you not admire that kind of spirit? Was Lian right? Did I more than just admire Meilin? No, Lian just wanted to feel better about trying to rid herself of me. Sure, I admired and cared for Meilin, but Lian always had my heart. At least, she once did. Today, I'm not sure where my heart is. But that doesn't matter now. What matters is Meilin is in danger.

Finding Meilin riding piggyback on a Pang Bear shouldn't surprise me. But why is she doing it? It doesn't make sense even for Meilin. She's daring, but not witless. She's probably the most quick-witted girl in all of Ning. I hate to admit it, probably even more so than Lian. Meilin knows better. You stay clear of Pang Bears, not dance with them.

No more than ten paces away, a small, tousled mop of black hair framing fear-filled eyes pops up from behind a log. The little girl bites her bottom lip and trembles as she watches Meilin ride the bear. Oh, I see. For all the respect I have for the village elders, I doubt any, except maybe Master Jin, would risk their lives for a young stranger. But for Meilin the choice is natural. For all her faults, she stands above others in ways many refuse to see.

I want to rush to the little girl, but that would only draw the bear's attention and undo Meilin's efforts. There has to be something I can do. I have no weapon. Even if I did, attacking the bear would do little good.

"Meilin! Meilin!" I shout.

The bear swings its head in my direction. My muscles freeze. It stares down at me with fierce hunger. Now that I have its attention, I don't want it. Still, I step toward it and wave my hands and shout louder. The bear steps toward me but stops and turns to one side and the other as other shouts join mine.

Near the young girl, dozens of armed warriors dressed in forest greens step past the fringe of trees and brush into the open, hollering and screaming at the bear. They bang their spears, rocks, and bows and arrows. The bear roars in angers. As it does, Meilin loses her grip and slides off its back.

Before Meilin hits the ground, the bear spins and slashes with one clawed paw and then the other. The Pang Bear hovers over her as she crumbles lifeless onto a mound of moss and leaves, its teeth bared and claws ready to strike again.

"No!" I shout, charging toward it. I yell with all my strength as I run. I have no chance against the bear, but it doesn't matter. Before I'm even close, the chorus of shouts from the armed warriors rise louder as they also charge. Rocks pelt the bear from every direction. In rising anger, its eyes move across the field of charging warriors. It bellows one last roar before turning about and speeding away from the clearing on all fours.

When I reach Meilin, I have to fight the urge to sick up. Blood and guts have been part of my daily life since I was old enough to wield a filet knife. But this is different. This is someone—someone I know. Someone, who no matter how much she drives me crazy, I do care about. Blood colors every bit of skin not covered by her blood-soaked shredded rags. Much of it is dried and caked with dirt and leaves, but still, too much of it flows freely from her torso like tiny crimson rivers.

My insides twist. Why didn't I do more to help her? Why didn't I charge the bear sooner? If it had attacked me, Meilin would be fine. This is my fault. I should be the one dying not her.

Kneeling at her side, I pull off my tunic and tear it along the side seams. Her eyes stay closed. Her body remains limp. I wrap my tunic tight around her back and front like a large bandage. My chest tightens. I blink hard to push back tears.

"No!" I say. "You can't die."

Something inside me breaks. I don't understand the churn of emotions. It was hard enough to lose Lian, I can't bear to lose Meilin too.

Blood soaks my makeshift bandage. Even if it's slowing the bleeding, it won't be enough. Meilin needs more help soon or she'll die. Her chest barely rises with her slow, short breathes.

Ignoring Meilin and me, the armed warriors huddle close around the little girl. A brawny man with strands of tattoos wrapping around the length of both his arms sets down his spear to pick up the girl and hug her close. Tears dot his cheek as he strokes her short hair and whispers in her ear. After a few moments, the little girl smiles and giggles.

When a shorter member of the group with similar arm tattoos reaches for the girl, I realize with surprise that it's a woman with sheared short hair. While only a few have tattoos, men and women make up the whole armed group.

I've heard rumors of warrior women in Yemaren and beyond, but not within Huyan's borders. Innate Honor forbids women warriors. But these people openly defy the decrees of the Lord Emperor, Chosen of Heaven. I'm not sure what Huyan law says about women with tattoos, but I know the village elders back home would frown on that too. It doesn't matter. I need their help.

"Please!" I call, stepping toward them. "My friend is dying. She needs a healer."

Their grips tighten on their weapons as they look toward me. Their grim and fierce expressions present a stark contrast to the string of purple orchids they each wear around their necks. It would be an embarrassment for a men in Ning to wear flowers in public. But this isn't Ning.

The woman holding the young girl looks at Meilin, and eyes me from heel to hair as if considering a difficult decision. The little girl taps the woman's cheek, grins, points at Meilin, and shouts, "Meilin!"

"Yes," I say. "Meilin is my friend. She needs help. Do you have a healer?"

"Meilin! Meilin!" the girl says with excitement.

The woman frowns but sets the girl down and steps toward us. The tattooed man grabs the woman by the elbow, stopping her. She shakes her arm free and in a stern voice speaks to him in some dialect of the deep I've never heard. I make out the words, "honor" and "life", but that's all. My eyes widen when the man steps back and bows low toward the woman, a symbol of great respect. I've never seen any man do that before.

The woman hurries to Meilin and kneels at her side. My nose twitches as the strong peppery scent from her string of orchids tickles my nose. I fight hard to hold back a sneeze.

Ignoring my discomfort, the woman lifts my makeshift bandage to study Meilin's wounds. She shakes her head and makes clicking noises with her tongue. Even though she's a woman likely in her late twenties or early thirties, her diamond-shaped face exudes the command and confidence of a village elder. While she doesn't appear to be the group's leader, she has earned their respect and honor to a degree unheard of for any woman in Huyan, except perhaps for women of royalty.

"Jades' shade, so much blood," she says. "This girl should be dead."

"Can you help her?"

She raises her eyebrows as she looks at me. "If I try, she might die."

"If you don't, she will die. Please help her."

She takes a deep breath and exhales. "I am Liu Fen. You should know the name of the one who takes the life of your true heart."

I open my mouth to tell Fen that Meilin is not my true heart, but I stop myself. Saving Meilin's life is all that is important now.

"Please, do what you can," I say.

Fen nods, reaches into a pouch at her waist, and pulls out a handful of bright purple powder. My nose twitches further at its sharp smell. It's the same peppery smell as her orchid necklace, but nastier and more pungent. She lifts Meilin's bandage and sprinkles generous amounts of the powder into Meilin's open wounds. Meilin's body jerks and tenses as the first bits of powder touch.

Fen pauses and looks up at me as if to make sure she wants me to continue. "She will know much pain, but it should slow the bleeding."

I nod my head for Fen to continue. I twinge as Meilin's body convulses at each touch of the powder. It probably does her little good, but I take Meilin's hand in mine, hoping to provide some comfort to her. Her hand is hot to the touch and sweat streams from her forehead. But that's much better than if she were cold and lifeless.

Moments after the last bit of purple powder has been applied, Meilin's body relaxes. Her chest rises slowly with shallow breathing, but most of the bleeding looks as if it has stopped.

After Fen readjusts and tightens the bandage, she gives me a stern look. "Her wounds will reopen if not stitched. Can you use a needle and thread?"

I nod. Whether from a slip of a fillet knife, or tangling with an eel or aggressive catfish, most fishermen have suffered enough bites and gashes to cause them to keep a sewing kit on their boat and learn how to use it. I'm confident I can stitch Meilin's wounds without too much trouble. My biggest concern is getting her to back to the boat without the wounds reopening.

I consider asking for help, but before I can another man and woman from the group kneel beside Meilin and move her onto a makeshift stretcher made from two spears and the man's tunic.

"No!" Fen shouts, grabbing and holding down one of the spears before the couple can lift Meilin up.

The couple stops and look toward an older man with a graying ponytail. He stands a few paces away with a somber face and his arms folded across his chest. Fen jumps to her feet and storms toward the man. I'm not sure why Fen is so angry. I'm happy that they're willing to help.

In her dialect, Fen shouts at the man. Once again, I make out the words, "honor" and "life", as well as "wrong" and something that sounds a lot like "goat-headed stupidity." As Fen continues to yell at him, he remains silent with a smug smile. When she finally ends her tirade, she turns to walk back toward me, but is stopped by an armed couple who step in her path.

With a scowl, she looks back at the gray-haired man, but makes no further attempt to approach me. After two clicks of the tongue from the gray-haired man, the couple prod Fen with their spears and usher her away out of the clearing. The tattooed warrior who first held the young girl and tried to stop Fen from helping Meilin, shakes his head with a grimace. He whispers something into the young girl's ear, picks her up in his arms, and follows Fen and her guards into the thick of the trees.

Once they disappear from sight, the gray-haired man grins and struts toward me. I stand to face him, but before I can ask him what upset Fen, he says, "I am Gu Zan. Do forgive my niece. Oft-times she leaves her manners behind. She would refuse the hospitality you and your companion deserve. We are a recluse, yet honorable people. Your companion needs further care. Let us guide you to our village where she can be stitched, and you both can be fed and rested."

The offer of food and rest sound tempting. Meilin can use the rest, but she would be furious if we wasted time having her recover in a village in Gudai's deep when she can rest just as well on the boat once I have her stitched up. There are only five days until Lian's marriage to the emperor. With three days of travel left to reach Quanli, any delay could make us too late to rescue Lian.

"Thank you for your kindness," I say with a bow. "Your healer has done much already to help my friend. I can finish seeing to the wounds myself. We have no desire to trouble you further. But if you're willing, I would welcome help carrying my friend to our boat."

Zan's smile widens. He clasps his hands, rocking them in front of his chest. "No," he says. "We will care for you and your friend. It is not a trouble. It is not a request. It is a command."

He clicks his tongue twice, turns on his heels, and walks away into the forest. Before I can stop the couple from lifting Meilin on the stretcher, the remaining warriors surround me with their spears leveled and bows drawn.

Chapter 22
Qiu Meilin– Too Many Secrets

"While the Two's hundred or so Shen children have definitely been imbued with powers, it cannot be assumed they are the only entities that the first Mother and first Father have raised to god status."

- Pan Ru: Essays on the Mysteries

The tingling and sting of my wounds drive me crazy. It feels like a dozen xudupedes dancing and biting their way across my throbbing back and stomach. All I want to do is scratch at them, which might be why my wrists and ankles have been lashed tight to the corners of a raised, narrow bamboo table. It's a healer's table, much like the one that Ho Cu would use back home to treat cuts, scrapes, and broken bones.

The bamboo walled room looks much like the room Cu uses to care for Ning's villagers. It has two old wooden stools, a wooden storage rack with bandages and small towels on one shelf, porcelain basins and mixing pots on another. Two other shelves have cinnamon twigs, bamboo leaves, dried peels, dried flowers, licorice roots, ginger roots and bunch of other herbs, roots, and flowers I don't recognize.

Above the closed door, a Shen Breath lantern hangs, broken and empty. But in the far corner of the room another lantern hangs from a hook in the wall. Its swirling tendrils call to me, inviting me to come closer so it can finish healing my stomach and back wounds. I pull at the binds that hold my wrist. I need that Shen Breath. After what the Pang Bear did to me, I'm lucky to be alive.

How much time has passed? Faint light shines through the room's open window, suggesting thick shade from the forest canopy or that it's almost evening. Have I lost too much time to save Lian from marrying the emperor? Am I in Ling's village? A large pine branch in front of the only window blocks most of the outside view.

"Hello!" I call. "Anyone there?"

The creak of wood sounds outside my door, followed by departing foot falls.

"Hello!" I cry again, but I hear only the whistle of birds and the click and buzz of insects.

I tug at the ropes around my wrists, but cringe at the spike of pain in my stomach the movement causes. Even if I could free myself of the ropes, my wounds wouldn't let me go far. Will someone eventually untie my bounds? Or am I actually a prisoner? That would not be pleasant news. What about Ling? Did she get away? Maybe that's why I'm tied up. If Ling got hurt, maybe her parents blamed me. If so, why care for my wounds? Why not leave me as an afternoon snack for Gudai's hungry predators?

Hurried footfalls approach followed by the quick opening of the door. A short-haired woman rushes in, the door slamming behind her. She wears a tunic and trousers the same dark shade of green as what Ling wore and what I wear now. I don't know where my old grays are, but I'm thankful for the new clothes. After my encounter with the Pang Bear, I'm certain there was little left of my grays except for blood and shredded rags.

The short-haired woman's commanding eyes look me up and down as she hurries toward me. She stops abruptly when our eyes meet. For a brief moment, her lips purse. Dimples form on her angled cheekbones and pointy chin. She takes a deep breath and exhales, her face showing relief and relaxing into a wide smile.

"Jade's shade, I'm glad you are doing well," she says. "I worried for you."

She takes slow measured steps toward me until she stands by my side. That's when I first notice the tattoos on both her arms. I have heard of warriors having simple skin markings before, but not women. And these are so elaborate. Interlacing strands of different characters start at her wrists and wrap around her forearms and elbows, continuing beneath the sleeves of her tunic.

I don't recognize many of the tattooed characters, but many are also paired with the Mother stroke. They're similar to the pairing of the wind character and the lone Mother stroke in my gift mark.

"Please forgive the bindings, my young Pangze Wu." Her smile flattens as she touches the rope that holds one of my wrists. "This should not be, but I can do nothing for it."

She lifts my tunic and pulls back the bandages on my torso. She makes a clicking noise with her tongue as she examines my wounds. "You are a mystery young lady," she says as she lowers my tunic. "You survive a Pang Bear attack that you should not. Some of your wounds have mysteriously healed, others have not. Why is that so?"

My eyes meet hers. Such intensity in those eyes. It's hard not to recoil from her penetrating gaze. Does she know about my boon from Tiānqì Shen? Does she know it's forbidden? What will she to do me if she does? Is that why I'm tied up?

"Do not fear me, Pangze Wu." Her soft voice comforts me. "I am Liu Fen. You saved my little Ling. You have my life bond. I could never hurt you."

"Then why have you tied me up? Why don't you free me?"

Fen steeples her fingers beneath her chin and frowns. "I have pled your case to the Shouling, but they have decided you are a threat."

I pull hard at my bounds, but recoil at the sting of pain that shoots through my back and stomach. "I saved your daughter! How does that make me a threat?"

Fen shakes her head. "Your true heart saw the Shared Honor of our warriors—the Shared Honor of our clan. Outsiders cannot know. The Shouling think the danger is too great. We would not survive the emperor's wrath. But I believe you would keep our secret."

I don't hear anything after she says, "True heart." I laugh. I don't have a true heart. Who is she talking about? She can't mean Cai. Then I blush, remembering how he held me after my encounter with the Jianzha Jiang. I didn't want to leave the warmth of his embrace. I shake the thought from my mind. Lian and he are meant to be.

"Is Cai here? Where is he?"

Fen nods. "He is safe. He worries for you though." Fen smiles, a hint of mischief in her grin. "But I wonder if he really need worry."

Fen turns and walks toward the lantern swirling full of Shen Breath. She lifts it off the hook and eyes me with suspicion. "When our warriors carried you in, the lantern above the door burst. At first, I thought nothing of it. Lanterns wax old and Chi escapes their hold. But at that moment you gasped and breathed steady, where your breath before had been faint and fitful. When I looked at your wounds, they did not seem so bad as when I first treated them. Why do you think that is so?"

My lips tighten. I'm not sure what Fen is up to, but I can't help but worry.

Fen holds the Shen Breath lantern out toward me. Its song grows loud in my ears. Its colorful tendrils push against the walls of the lantern in my direction. Even as her eyes move between me and the lantern, Fen doesn't notice the tendrils reaching out to me. At least if she does, she doesn't say.

She takes a slow, short step toward me, watching me. Watching the lantern. She steps again. With each step the song grows louder, and the tendrils push harder against the lantern wall. Then, the lantern bursts.

Fen jerks in surprise. The stream of colored mists rushes toward me and fills me with warmth and healing. She lifts my tunic and bandages, clicking her tongue as she watches my wounds heal. Only a few heartbeats pass before the healing uses up all the Shen Breath. A few tender spots remain on my stomach, but other than that I feel great.

"Amazing," she says. "So strong in the Blood of the Two. I had guessed as much when I saw you fight the Pang Bear. But to see your wounds disappear before my eyes is remarkable."

My lips tighten. What will she do with my secret? I tense as she pulls a knife from a sheath at her waist and holds it over my stomach.

"Be calm," she says. "You are safe, little Pangze Wu. But you have no need of your stitches further. If you hold still, I will remove them."

I tense as her knife hovers over me, but say "I am Meilin. Why do you keep calling me Pangze Wu?"

Fen laughs. "Because you are one who dances with the Pang Bear, of course. A fitting title, don't you think?"

A slight smile raises the corners of my mouth, helping me relax as she cuts away my bandages. I feel the tickle of threads being pulled from the skin on my stomach and back where the bear's claws left deep gashes. When she finishes pulling out the stitches, she wraps new bandages around my torso.

I give her a questioning look. "The bandages will make others think you are still weak from your injuries," she says. "They do not need to see how your wounds have healed."

"So, you will keep my secret about how I healed?"

Fen smiles a sad smile. "Jade's shade, who would I tell? You have secrets the emperor must not know. We have secrets the emperor must not know also."

"What secrets do you have? You spoke of Shared Honor? What did you mean by that?"

Fen blinks slowly. "You will see soon enough." Fen lays the blade of her knife atop the rope holding one of my ankles down. "Can I trust that you will not attack me if I release you?"

I stare at the knife and the way Fen grips it. She holds it like a warrior—one not afraid to fight. Even with my Fei Chi training I don't know that I would be a match against Fen without my boon. I nod my head in agreement.

"You must also promise not to escape." She winks at me and then whispers, "At least, not till the right time."

I nod, but what does she mean till the right time? She cuts the ropes from my hands and feet. I stretch and rise slowly to sitting position.

She whispers again, "Over a week ago we met a young one like you. He too did our clan a great service. But once again the Shouling feared he would reveal our secrets to the emperor. But this one was a mighty warrior. All our warriors combined could not make him stay."

How am I not a mighty warrior? I fought and survived a Pang Bear. I fought and survived the Jianzha Jiang. I even survived my encounter with the Imperial Army. I doubt she meant it as an insult, but I still feel slighted.

"Thank the Jade, we know some of the gifts that can come to those with the Blood of the Two, but not like him. Not like you. Not in the ways of Shen. Even though a few of us have traces of the Blood of the Two, the Chi of the mist does not heal us. It does not stay with us as it did with this man, as it does with you."

Fen reaches into her belt pouch and pulls out a necklace stringed with a few dozen coin-like ceramic discs. She drops the necklace onto my lap. As I turn them over in my hands, my fingers run along the raised character strokes on the different discs. None have the wind symbol, but the characters on the discs still remind me of my gift mark. The different symbols on these discs are paired with the Father stroke instead of the Mother stroke.

Thirty-five discs. Thirty-five different gift mark symbols. Do these all represent different gifts from different Shen? How many gifts do the Shen have to offer? How many does Tiānqì Shen have? Did she give me more than one? If not, why not? I shake my head. If the owner of this necklace actually has everyone one of the gifts on these discs, no wonder he overpowered Fen's warriors.

As I look at closer, I realize each disc has traces of dried ink on the raised symbols. Genius! Ink stamps. Instead of having to draw a gift mark when needed, the discs can stamp on the mark instead.

Fen inclines her head toward the necklace. "These discs belonged to the young warrior. Do you know what they are for?"

I nod.

"You keep them, then," she says. "Put them to good use."

I shake my head and hold the necklace up to return it to Fen. "Thank you, but no. It doesn't work that way. These would do me no good."

Fen smiles but makes no move to take the necklace. In an even quieter whisper, she says. "After your escape, maybe you will find their owner. You can return them to him. I am sure he will be happy to have them back."

I finger the Weight symbol on one of the discs, wondering what gift it might bestow. "I doubt my path will cross this man's. Even if it did, how would I know him?"

Fen laughs. "Your paths might be closer than you think. And you will know him by his markings—make right the wrongs. Also, he goes by the name Fan Wei."

I stare at her confused, but she gives no further explanation. Instead, she flicks her hand toward the necklace and whispers, "Put it on under your tunic. The others must not know you have it."

Once I slip the necklace on, she nods, but gives me a look of warning. "Pangze Wu, you must not let the others see how well you have healed. Understood?"

I nod and Fen steps back toward the door and bangs on it three times. "Ju! Yong!" she shouts. "The girl is ready."

With spears raised, a tall lean woman and a broad-shouldered man march in. Both have the look of warriors, but unlike Fen, neither bear tattoos on their arms.

"Ju, I can do nothing more for this girl," Fen says to the lady warrior. "Take her to her quarters to finish her recovery."

Ju gives a slight bow to Fen, as does the man named Yong. Both warriors gesture with their spears for me to head toward the door. Following Fen's advice, I feign a grimace of pain as I slide off the table and step gingerly toward the door. I limp between them single file, the woman in front and the man behind. They say nothing to me, but their scowls and tight grips on their spears tell me what will happen if I do anything to upset them.

A fit of sneezes takes me the moment I step out the door. Twisting vines of purple orchids hang from the edges of the building rooftop, giving off a powerful scent of pepper. Once I get my sneezing under control, my eyes go wide.

We stand on a bamboo walkway more than twenty feet off the ground. A village of houses, shops, walkways, and plazas surround us nestled high atop the branches of the neighboring pines and oaks. Young and old move along a network of bamboo spans and rope bridges that weave through the trees and interconnect different sections of the tree village.

A diminishing amount of sunlight filters through the canopy, announcing evening's approach. A few candles and lamps already shine above the thresholds of some of the tree houses and buildings, but most have yet to be lit.

With the point of Yong's spear in my back and following Ju's march, they lead me to a hanging bridge that connects to another tree with buildings and bamboo walkways built into its branches. Strung with thick ropes and lengths of bamboo poles, it spans sixty feet or more across open air. When I step on the bridge it swings sideways, almost causing me to lose my balance.

Clutching its rope rails, I keep from falling, but stop in place, not wanting to venture further onto the swinging bridge. It takes two prods of the spear to my back before I dare go any further. The bridge continues to swing with each step, but if I'm careful with my foot placement I don't teeter nearly as much.

As we cross the bridge, I see that several trees have multiple levels of ringed walkways and buildings built at different heights within the trees' branches and around their trunks. A mix of rope ladders and spiral bamboo stairways connect the different levels. While every tree has either a hanging rope bridge or bamboo span to connect it to other trees, there's not necessarily a bridge on every level of every tree. But they're all connected with an amazing mishmash of different bridges, ropes, walkways, and ladders.

I keep my pace slow and uneven, doing my best to convince the warriors that I still suffer from my wounds. I often stop to fight off more sneezing fits. The pungent purple orchids grow in abundance on creeping vines, twisting, and intertwining all along the bridges and walkways. They infest nearly all the tree branches. With such an annoying scent, why don't the villagers work to keep the orchids from flourishing?

"How can you stand their smell?" I ask, pointing to the orchids. "They're awful."

Ju scowls at me over her shoulder. "A curse to one, blesses another. Beast Bane is a cherished gift of protection from Mother Jade and the Two."

I shrug as Ju leads me up a bamboo staircase that spirals upward through the gnarled and twisting branches of a massive oak tree. The tree has to be at least four or five hundred years old.

Without looking back at me, Ju continues, "Since our ancestors first built Mu Cun, the Beast Bane has kept our people safe. Where the purple orchid grows, the Jade Leopard and the Pang Bear do not go. Their noses are even more sensitive than a Mangzi Yangzi like you."

"Mangzi Yangzi? What's that?"

Yong laughs behind me. Ju glances over her shoulder. A snide smile spreads across her face. "Mangzi Yangzi means outsider, as well as one who blindly follows a fool."

She means it as an insult, but I smile anyway. "I don't think anyone has ever called me a blind follower of the emperor, if that is what you mean."

Ju scowls, skepticism clear in her glance. "You say that, thinking you can trick us into trusting you. We are not easily deceived."

Despite the spear tip poking my back, I laugh. "You're not easily pleased either. I save one of your little ones and in thanks you make me a prisoner. Is that how you repay those who risk their life for you? Does that seem right to you? Or do you simply follow orders without questioning them? Maybe it's not me who is the real Mangzi Yangzi here. What do you think?"

Ju narrows her eyes for a moment, but her expression softens to an uncertain frown. She turns around and heads back up the spiral stairway without another word.

Silence follows as Ju and Yong lead me through the Mu Cun tree village. The further we go, the higher up we climb until we're more than one hundred feet above the forest floor. As we travel the maze of interconnecting walkways and bridges, I notice a maze of bamboo pipe works running above and alongside the walkways. The pipes connect to several large water cisterns built high in the trees and run down to individual homes, buildings, and community water basins below.

The pipes also connect to massive garden boxes built atop many of the bamboo plazas to grow vegetable and herbs. Like back home, lanterns full of glowing Shen Breath stand at the head of every row and all along the edge of the plazas with the hope that their Chi will help produce a healthy crop.

I jerk to a stop, with Yong's spear tip almost stabbing me. I don't believe it. In the gardens, men and women work, talk, and laugh together as if equals. The same is true of all the work activity within the Mu Cun tree village. On the porches of the houses, parents and their children work together, whether it's preparing ramie fibers for weaving, grinding meal into flour, cooking, sewing, cleaning, or whatever.

At some houses a lone woman might work alone, while her husband entertains himself by playing a game with his children, playing a musical instrument, painting pictures, or some other activity. But at just as many houses a man might work alone, while the woman plays or entertains herself.

It's amazingly beautiful! But scary too. What would the emperor do if he saw men and women treating each other as equals? Simple. He would destroy the entire village. No wonder the village's Shouling council worried that she or Cai would expose the secret of the Mu Cun people's Shared Honor—a clear affront to Innate Honor and imperial law.

Yong prods me his spear tip to get moving and cross a walkway that spans above one of the garden plazas.

"Your Shared Honor is beautiful," I say as I continue to watch the men and women treat each other with mutual respect. "I've never seen anything like it before."

Ju tilts her head to the side and gives me another look of distrust.

I smile. "You have no reason to believe me, but I promise, I would tell no one what I have seen here. It is too wonderful to let anyone destroy."

Ju doesn't smile, but the look of distrust fades and she bows slightly to me before, turning her back and continuing to lead me across the span.

The forest grows darker as we continue across more bridges, along different walkways, and up stairways and rope ladders. We rise higher and higher within the canopy of trees. The more the light fades, the louder the sound of crickets and other nighttime creatures rise. Little by little the villagers light torches positioned at different points along the walkways and bridges. Lamps shine in front of nearly every tree house now too.

All these pinpoints of light weaving and rising through the trees remind me of the Geng Sheng Festivals in Ning. On the one night of the year when Dìyī star shined brightly between the full moons of Shi and San we would feast and dance all night long. When the last dance ended, we would light floating lanterns and watch them rise in the sky—just as Dìyī Shen rose in brilliance to return to live with the Two after his death, victory, and rebirth after the Great War.

But our festival lights don't match the beauty and awe of these thousands of burning dots of fire that float and sway in the air below. Yong prods me again with his spear when I take too long admiring the show of lights.

Not long after, we come to a stop where the walkway ends at a tall narrow wall made of bamboo poles. Ju unties the ends of two lines of rope wrapped around tree branches that connect to the top of the wall.

Oh, it's not a wall after all. It's a thirty-foot long drawbridge. Ju slowly lets the lines of rope slip through her hands until the bridge lowers and its far end falls in place at the edge of a circular walkway that surrounds a small bamboo shack.

Ju prods me to cross the bridge and raises the drawbridge when I reach the far side. The villagers built the shack and walkway like a floating island on cutoff top of a massive tree. With the bridge raised, reaching any nearby trees or walkways has become impossible. I'm cut off from the rest of the village.

"Welcome to our new prison home." I jump at the sound of Cai's voice.

He stands in the entryway of the simple bamboo shelter with a smile on his face and worry in his eyes. "You might as well come inside and make yourself comfortable. We're going to be here awhile."

Chapter 23
Qiu Meilin– Fatal Reveals

"The first oaths that Xiang Hu made to Guāng Shen contained a promise to teach others of the Shen. To keep those oaths, he felt impelled to build shrines to the Shen all across Huyan, which created a rather large problem for him."
- Hidden Scrolls of Quingping: Study in Oath Criticalities

A small table, two woven mats, a water basin, a burning candle, and a chamber pot. Those are the only furnishings inside the shelter. That's okay since there's barely room for anything else. The fact that the Mu Cun villagers don't plan to starve us to death is a happy thought. I sit on the floor at the table eating peapods and some dried meat that I don't recognize. There are a few red wolfberries too, but Wearing a new tunic in the same dark green as my new clothes and that of the tree villagers Cai sits on his mat in silence as I eat. I'm okay with the silence since I'm not sure what to say to him. I feel bad I got him in this mess. Still, I'm glad he's here. Is that selfish of me? Probably. Regardless, I have to somehow figure out how we're going to escape.

I'm too distracted to think. I feel Cai's eyes on me and sense he wants to ask me something but doesn't. But when I glance at him, his eyes are on the bamboo floor. But when I take the last bite of the unknown meat, Cai breaks the silence.

"I'm happy you survived." He pauses, but adds with a grin, "I've never seen anyone ever dance with a Pang Bear before."

I chuckle. "Well, you wouldn't dance with me, so what choice did I have?"

Cai laughs. I laugh with him, but then Cai's expression turns serious. "You shouldn't be here."

"Well, they really haven't given me a choice," I say with a smile. "But don't worry. I don't plan on staying here long."

Cai shakes his head. "That's not what I mean. You shouldn't be alive. All the blood. Your gashes from the bear. No one could survive that. What's going on Meilin? What aren't you telling me?"

Oh no! This is it. My smile disappears. I need to tell him. But how? I know so little about the Shen's gift to begin with. But what worries me more is how do I explain it without telling him I violated one of the most serious tenants of Innate Honor by praying in a shrine. What will he do if I tell him? By imperial law, he would have the right, perhaps even the duty, to execute me. I don't think that thought would even cross Cai's mind, but I still fear his response. Will he feel the need to punish me somehow? What will he think of me? Will it end our friendship? I can't risk that.

I give him a weak smile and ignore his question. "Enough talk. We need to find a way to get out of here."

I rise from my mat and step outside the shelter. I walk to the edge of the walkway with my toes hanging over. In spite of the many lamps lit along all the levels of Mu Cun's canopy village, I can't see the forest floor through the darkness. But it must be a drop of at least a hundred fifty feet or more. I take a step back. Though the display of lights is beautiful, looking straight down makes me dizzy.

Enough light reaches our height that I can make out the bamboo walkways and the branches of the different neighboring trees. A properly aimed jump could land me on one of the walkways or houses below, perhaps even on a tree branch, but not without breaking several bones. If I had any Chi left from the Shen Breath I might survive, but it's gone. Even if I wait until the next midnight rain, no Shen Breath will rise this high. It never floats more than 10 or so feet off the ground before transforming back to regular mist. I have to find another way to escape.

What did Fen mean when she said, "Don't escape until the right time." Is she planning something? Why didn't she tell me right out what she had in mind?

I hear the creak of the bamboo walkway. Cai steps beside me. He stands so close it almost makes me shiver. I want to lean against him, have him hold me in his arms. No! Why am I thinking like that? That would be a betrayal to Lian. Or would it? She made her choice when she went to the village square instead of into hiding. She made that choice again when she ran away when I tried to save her.

Stop it! It doesn't matter. Cai's heart is with her anyway.

"You didn't answer my question," he says. "How did you survive the Pang Bear?"

I keep my gaze to my feet. I don't dare look into his kind face or caring eyes. My emotions might get the best of me. Still, I have to tell him. Maybe I can do it without telling him I entered the shrine. I at least have to try.

"When you came back to Ning, why didn't you visit Lian?" I ask, still keeping my gaze from him. "If she had known you were alive, she wouldn't have let them take her away."

Cai laughs. "Meilin, you do not know your sister."

I cock my head to the side and give him a questioning glance. "What does that mean?"

Cai shakes his head. "It doesn't matter. What does is, that I couldn't go to her. The Shashyao hunted me. If I went to your home, I could have put your whole family in danger."

That might be, but there had to be a way he could let Lian know he still lived without endangering her. I sit on the edge of the walkway and dangle my legs over the edge. My stomach tightens when I think how far I'll fall with the slightest nudge. Cai sits next to me, his arm almost brush against my shoulder. My stomach tightens further. I force myself to look at Cai even though his eyes make it harder to keep my focus on telling him about Tiānqì Shen's gift.

"Instead, you went to the shrine. Why?"

Cai raises his eyebrows. "How do you know that?"

I force a light-hearted smile. "It doesn't matter. Why were you there? What did you promise Tiānqì Shen? What did you ask her in return?"

Cai tilts his head to the side. Wrinkles crease his forehead. He frowns and his eyebrows furrow as he studies me. "Why do you want to know about my prayers? That's kind of personal, don't you think?"

I bite my bottom lip and give him an uneasy smile. "Yeah, but you did make a promise of some kind, right?"

"Meilin, you still haven't answered my question. How did you survive the Pang Bear?"

I drum my fingers on top of my legs. Cai doesn't make this easy. "I'm trying," I say with an edge to my voice. "But it would help if you would first answer my questions. Did you make a promise to Tiānqì Shen in exchange for help from her?"

Cai rolls his eyes and raises his hand, palms up. "Yes, I did. What does it matter?"

"After your prayer, did you hear Shen Breath sing to you? Did the few strands of mist remaining in the shrine stream to you in all their brilliant colors? Did your skin tingle as the mists flowed into you, filling you with amazing warmth? Did you feel more powerful than ever before? Do you still feel that power, but it's somehow out of reach?"

The wide-eyed stare Cai gives me would make me laugh if it wasn't for the fact that he might kill me once I tell him my secret. "How do you know all that?" he says. "I was alone in the shrine."

Breathe in. Breathe out. Smile. Everything will be okay. I hope.

"There is a lot about this that I don't know," I say, trying to stay calm. "Some might say you are strong in the Blood of the Two. I think having the Blood of the Two allows you to receive gifts of power from the Shen. That's why the Shashyao wanted you dead. The emperor doesn't want anyone but himself to get gifts of power from the Shen. But when you asked Tiānqì Shen for help and made an oath to her, she gave you such a gift to help you keep your oath. A gift you have not yet learned how to access. That's what happened to you in the shrine. You became Shen-Blessed, something only lawful for the emperor to become."

Cai's gaze intensifies, making me uneasy. Has he guessed that I'm Shen-Blessed too? I clasp my fingers on my lap to stop their fidgeting. I want to scoot away from him, but I might accidently scoot off the edge of the walkway. Instead, I try to relax and smile at him like I found a stash of hazelnut cookies and was offering to share them with him.

He finally shifts his gaze from mine, lifting it up toward the forest canopy where in an angry flurry of bright green feathers a pair of parakeets circle, peck, and tweet at each other in the dark of night. I don't think Cai even notices the parakeets. His thoughts look far away.

"It doesn't make any sense." His gaze is still lost somewhere in the canopy above. "I've prayed hundreds of times in the shrine before, making promises to Tiānqì Shen if she would grant me help. But nothing like this has ever happened before. Why now?"

It might be the biggest mistake of my life. In fact, it might end my life—or worse, end my friendship with Cai—but I decide to tell him. "That same day before you received your gift, I received a gift from Tiānqì Shen too. I think they might be related somehow."

Cai turns his gaze toward me. "How could you receive a gift from…" He stops and his eyebrows arch as his expression changes to shock and maybe a twinge of worry. His mouth opens to speak, but no words escape his lips.

"I was desperate," I say, answering his unspoken questions. "I know it's forbidden, but I also knew Lian was in danger. I had to help her. So, I asked Tiānqì Shen for a gift, and she gave me a kind of power. That's how I survived the Pang Bear."

I wait for some form of chastisement or disappointment to burst from Cai's mouth, but he just blinks a few times. His eyebrows furrow and he stares at me in silence. After several moments, his expression relaxes. He moves his gaze from me to stare down at the forest floor far below. His shoulders sag, and in a sad whisper he says, "You went in the shrine?"

I drop my gaze, no longer daring to look at him. "Yes. I went into the shrine." My voice is soft, but not apologetic. "I didn't have a choice. I had to save Lian."

Out of the corner of my eyes I see him shake his head. I imagine the corners of his mouth drooping in an unpleasant frown.

"You always have a choice," he whispers. "It's wrong. You shouldn't have done that."

Part of me wants to be angry at Cai for not understanding, but why should he? Innate Honor isn't only imperial law, it's the way of life. No one else would understand why I had to do it, so why should Cai. But that doesn't mean I can't try to help him understand.

"Letting harm come to Lian wasn't a choice." I pause. Breath in. Breath out. Courage. Say what needs to be said. "Innate Honor is wrong."

Cai gasps, but before he can shush me, I continue with emotion and confidence energizing my voice, "Tiānqì Shen is a woman. Many of the Shen are women. All equal to the male Shen. The First Mother and First Father revere each other as equal partners, joying in their strengths and differences. Why should it be any different for their mortal children? Do the Two love their mortal daughters any less than their sons?"

I look up to meet his gaze, waiting for his response. Turmoil. Uncertainty. Worry. All cloud his eyes. He places his hand on my knee. "Meilin, careful. Your words will kill you."

I laugh, shaking my head. "The Shashyao are already trying to kill me. Speaking the truth won't make my situation any worse. I don't care about that. I don't care about Innate Honor. I care about saving Lian. Besides, if it was really wrong for me to enter Tiānqì Shen's shrine, she wouldn't have given me a gift, would she?"

Cai looks up at me, pensive, as if thousands of unsettling thoughts churn behind his eyes. His eyelids droop and the sadness in his expression deepens. "You're right. She wouldn't have, but I don't like the harm you've brought to yourself. Now the Shashyao won't stop hunting you until you're dead."

Strange. I thought Cai would be outraged at me for defiling the shrine, but there's not a hint of anger in his voice or eyes—only genuine concern.

My smile thins. "My life no longer matters. I can't ever return home. I defied my father and brought shame to him and our family name. All that matters is saving Lian."

Cai shakes his head. "You're wrong. Your life matters too. Keeping you alive is as important as saving Lian. To do that, I need to know more about this gift. Can you tell me how it works?"

I recount to Cai my fight with the shrine guard and how the Chi from Shen Breath powered the boon to strengthen me and heal my wounds. I tell him about how I used the Wind gift mark to summon a wind that almost allowed me to get Lian free from the imperial soldiers. I explain that using the boon has to be somehow tied to keeping the oath that I made to Tiānqì Shen, otherwise I can't access its power.

When I finish, Cai doesn't question anything I say. He simply says, "Since that morning in the shrine, I have seen the gift mark several times in my mind. Except it was different. The Father stroke was paired with the wind symbol. Do you think I have the same gift as you?"

I shrug. "I'm not sure. I think there are many kinds of gifts from different Shen."

Cai looks past me toward the tree with the drawbridge and the closest walkway. "Shen Breath still burns within me from when I was in the shrine," he says. "Do you think I could use the power of its Chi to help us escape? I could try to jump to the walkway."

When he moves to stand, I stop him with a hand to his knee. "It's at least a thirty-foot jump. You can't risk it. You've never used your gift before. You don't know what you can or can't do. You don't even know how much Chi you have within you. If you miss, the fall is much more than a hundred feet. Gift or no gift, you won't survive that."

He stares down at my hand on his knee, and I quickly pull it back. "Sorry," I say.

A kind smile plays on Cai's lips, and he shakes his head. "I do not understand you, Qiu Meilin. Since this voyage began, I haven't always been as kind to you as I should. You should be happy to be rid of me if my attempt fails. Why try to stop me?"

I roll my eyes and smile. Perhaps Cai is more witless than I thought. "Lian would be furious with me if she learned you were alive only to find that I let you act the fool and kill yourself in trying to help us escape."

Cai raises an eyebrow slightly. A look of either disappointment or confusion shows in his eyes. "Do you care if I die?"

I bite my bottom lip and I lower my gaze immediately. No matter how hard I try to stop them, my cheeks blush red. I laugh to try to chase away the embarrassment, but stop abruptly when I realize he might think I'm laughing at him. "Why would you ask such a goat-headed thing?" I say with lighthearted chastisement. "I don't want anyone to die, especially Lian's true heart."

Cai laughs loud. “I am not Lian’s true heart. She ended our relationship months before I left for the army.”

“What?” My eyes widen. “That can’t be true. You spent every free hour together, right up until the day you left.”

Cai smirks. “I spent every day following her around trying to convince her not to give up on us, but she wouldn’t listen.”

“I don’t believe that. She always talked about how she loved you.”

“She wants to be more than a fisherman’s wife.”

I purse my lips. I can see Lian wanting more than the life she would have in Ning. Still, I’m certain she deeply loved Cai. Would she turn her back on that love if she thought she could escape Ning for a better life? I’m sure I would, but I doubt the emperor’s palace offers a better life for any woman.

But what if Lian doesn’t feel that way? What if being a Wife Divine is what Lian wanted all along? When did Father tell her about his dream of her becoming the emperor’s wife? Was it around the same time that she tried to end her relationship with Cai? Why hadn’t Lian told me any of this?

I shake my head. Why would she? She knew I would try to talk her out of it. She knows how I feel about the emperor. She would roll her eyes every time I spouted off about how he treats his wives like slaves, locking them in his dungeons until he has need of them.

What if I’m wrong and Father is right? What if I’m trying to rob Lian of the one thing that will bring her the happiness she wants? No. The blood and cries for help in my dream all warned of the danger to Lian. And I’m not certain I believe she would really choose life as a Wife Divine over a life with Cai. No matter her thinking, I can’t abandon her to the danger that awaits her in the palace in Quanli. I have to save her. We have to save her.

I place my hand on Cai's and squeeze it. "I'm sorry about Lian. I didn't know. But we'll escape this place. And when we save Lian, maybe things will still work out for you two, but not if you…"

Cai rises to his feet and runs across the walkway.

"No! Stop!" I shout, but he doesn't listen. Like a fool, he sprints toward the edge and leaps into the air. My fingers dig into bamboo as I watch him soar toward the landing of the raised drawbridge. It's amazing. It's like he's flying. Still, he's barely half the distance when my heart clutches. He's not going to make it.

Chapter 24
Chao Cai – Near flying

"Witless! What more can I say?"
- Chao Cai Personal History

It's amazing. I've never felt such power and strength before. The Chi surges and flows within me with burning power. I feel invincible. Reaching the drawbridge should be no problem. But with a few steps to go before leaping from the platform the surge of power wanes. It's too late. Running faster than I'd ever run before, I can't stop in time. So, I leap.

What a wonderful feeling. It's like flying. I've never jumped so far in my life. My arms and hands outstretched before me, at first, I think I might actually make it to the drawbridge. That hope vanishes quickly. It's too far. I'm falling.

I'm still not sure what I was trying to prove. That I still want to save Lian? That I want to rescue Meilin? That I'm not a coward? It doesn't matter. In any case, I'm a witless fool.

Far below the drawbridge platform I crash headfirst into a tangle of pine branches. Needles scrape my face and arms. Branches give way beneath my weight. Falling and slipping, needles scratch and scrape at me from every direction. Frantic, my fingers grasp and reach for a hold. Needles and branches slip through my hands. I flip and tumble through limb after limb. Like thrashing rods, branches slap and beat my chest, head, and back.

Crack! I come to a sudden stop, landing sideways on a thick branch. A fan of needles whips against my face. My arm twists underneath me.

Sharp pain spikes as bone snaps. I wince at the pain. I want to grab it with my other hand and hold it against my body to try to lessen the excruciating torture, but that hand is desperately wrapped around a neighboring branch to keep me from falling further.

Darkness lies beneath. Open air. I can't even see the forest floor. If I lose my grip, I doubt I'll be lucky enough to have another branch stop my fall. If could scoot to the trunk I could climb down the twenty or so feet down to a walkway connected to the lower branches of this tree. But I can't move. Any shift of my arm or body ignites a paralyzing stabbing sensation in my arm.

With the pain, dizziness sets in. I clench to fight it off. If I lose consciousness, I'll fall for sure. I've never felt so helpless and miserable in my life. I mumble a prayer to the Two and Tiānqì Shen. But I doubt even a miracle from the gods can save me now.

Chapter 25
Qiu Meilin –Agony

"Agreed! Nothing." – Meilin
- Chao Cai Personal History margin note

I want to scream at Cai for being such a goat-headed fool, but I don't want to alert the Mu Cun villagers to his escape attempt. Thanks to the Two he didn't fall to the forest floor, but I can tell he's in trouble. He makes no effort to move to the safety of the tree's trunk. And he looks like he's struggling to stay on his branch. He must be hurt. I have to help him, but how.

Without any Shen Breath inside me, it's too far to jump to his branch. My chances of making it to the drawbridge are even smaller. I'm lost as to what to do. I think about Fen's comment about waiting till the right time. Is she planning on helping us escape? Will she be here soon? Can she help Cai? It doesn't matter. I have no way of knowing if or when she might come. Cai can't hang onto his branch much longer. I have to figure out something fast.

I stare down below. A few lights on the walkways and bridges still burn, but many have been doused for the night as village activity has lessened. Most of the villagers have retired to their homes. With less light it's easier to spot the lanterns of Shen Breath lining the edges of the platforms where the villagers grow their crops. If I could reach those lanterns, rescuing Cai would be easy. But the closest plaza is at least a 40-foot drop straight down. I'd never survive. Unless…

I race inside our little shack and grab a leftover wolfberry. With a gentle pinch, I squeeze out its bright red juice and use it to draw the

Wind gift mark on my palm. It takes three more berries to complete the mark on both my palms. I take a deep breath and hurry back outside.

With my toes hanging over the edge of the walkway, I stare down at Cai. He's still clinging onto the branch in desperation. I shift my gaze to the crop platform directly below me. My eyes follow the line of Shen Breath lanterns glowing along the platform edge. Most of the lanterns are spaced a few paces apart, but at the platform corners there are three lanterns within a single pace of each other. That might be what I need.

A wave of dizziness sets in when I look past the crop platform toward the forest floor below. I squeeze shut my eyes to fight off the tremor of shakiness that starts. This is crazy. But I have to do it. I can't let Cai fall.

After a few calming breaths the shakes subside a bit, but I'm still a bit light-headed. I can do this. I open my eyes slowly. I focus on the corner of the platform. With a deep a breath, I crouch with knees bent, push off on the edge of the walkway, and dive toward the glowing lanterns.

My eyes widen and my lips tighten forcing back the scream rising up my throat. Wind blasts my face as I hurtle downward. I fall much faster toward the platform then I imagined. If I aim right, I'll dive right past the lanterns toward the forest floor. If I'm off I'll smack headfirst onto the bamboo platform, dying instantly before any of the Shen Breath's Chi can rescue me.

But my aim isn't off. I hear the pop of at least two lanterns. The warmth of Shen Breath flows into me as I fall past the edge of the platform—but only for a moment. I pray it's enough. With my palms facing downward and my arms locked straight at my elbows, I will Chi-powered wind to blast from the gift marks on my hands.

With a jolt, I jerk back and fly upward. Too late I realize that with my back to the crop platform I can't see where I'm going. I try to turn to get a better view and spot the edge of the platform. It's a body's length above me. In that moment the little bit of Shen Breath I gathered in my pass-by gets used up.

The blasts of air from my palms die. But momentum carries me a little higher. My arms stretch upward, and I reach for the curved bamboo edge of the platform. My momentum falters. I stretch as high as I can, but I fall. My hands grasp and scrabble frantically at the bamboo edge. My fingers squeeze and grip at it until I gain a secure hold.

My legs dangle in the air more than a hundred feet above the forest floor. If I lose my grip, there's a chance I might land on a walkway span or other platform before I hit bottom, but that will likely mean I'll just fall to my death sooner. If I do fall, who will save Cai? Who will save Lian? I grit my teeth. I can't fall.

Even though I've always been good at climbing the trees of Gudai near our home, I've never done a single pull-up in my entire life. That's what I have to do to get myself up and over onto the platform. And I have to do it without a speck of Shen Breath to help me.

"Come on, Meilin!" I whisper to myself. "No heart, no honor."

With a smile on my lips, I focus every bit of natural strength I have into my arms and hands. I clench the curved bamboo. My arms strain to haul me up. Nothing happens. I strain harder, kicking my feet beneath me to propel myself upward. I rise a little, but barely. My muscles are tiring fast. I can't hang on much longer. With a primeval grunt and one last burst of focused effort, I kick and pull in frantic desperation with every speck of strength I have.

My muscles burn with pain, but I rise slow and sure. When my head rises above the bamboo floor, I work my elbows over the ledge and with a combination crawl and full body wiggle I pull myself completely onto the bamboo plaza. I want to flop down and lay there till I recover my strength, but Cai needs my help now. He can't hold on forever. Two's hope, he hasn't already fallen.

Worn out, I crawl toward the other lanterns still shimmering with Shen Breath. It takes every speck of willpower and focused determination I have to slither across the bamboo floor. I exhale in happy relief at the pop of the closest lantern. Its Shen Breath flows toward me, renewing my strength and filling me with power.

I hurry to my feet and move toward the next lantern and another and another, capturing their Chi until I'm overflowing with surging force and energy. Looking up to the pine tree branches above where Cai clings for life, I will wind to gust from my palms and propel me toward him. I fly upward but struggle to stay in control, swerving and veering in every direction. It takes a lot of focused effort and several attempts to gain a measure of control of the wind before I manage to get and stay on course.

Cai's eyes widen when I crash onto a pine branch beside him. The expression of surprise only lasts a moment. His face tightens and his entire body tenses in distress as the tree jolts from my not so graceful landing. One arm hangs limp at his side with an unnatural bend to it. Broken.

I fight back the temptation to shout, "You should have listened to me!" Instead, I smile and say, "Gales and hails. You're a mess!"

To avoid being poked by its pine needles, my fingers wrap around the limb above me for balance. The pine tree sways as I step closer to Cai. His body tenses again. He inhales a sharp intake of breath. His eyes pinch shut, tears welling in the corners. Red colors his face. His tightened lips tremble before breathing out a strained whisper, "Stop! Please stop!"

I halt midstride, clenching my hold on the branch above even tighter. My heart aches looking at the pain written across his face. I gently lower my foot, trying not to move the tree.

"Cai, to get you out of this tree I have to come closer. Okay?"

He breathes slow and deep, pinches his eyes closed even more, braces himself with a tighter grip with his good hand, and nods. I move slow and careful, but spasms of pain still ripple across his body.

"Sorry," I say. "One more step and I'll be beside you, alright?"

He nods again, but he trembles in anticipation. The wrinkles across his forehead stretch and crease in taut lines of suffering.

Shaking and clenching, he groans through pursed lips when I take the last step. Now what do I do? If those few careful steps caused him so much pain, how much worse will it be if I try to lift him and fly him to safety? I can't do that to him. But I can't leave him either.

I look back down at the lanterns of Shen Breath glowing atop the crop platform. I should have grabbed one to use to heal Cai. I could fly back down to get one. No. If I use my Wind gift to fly back down, the sway from the tree will put Cai in even more pain. Besides, as soon as I use any of my Chi the lantern will likely burst to replenish it, leaving me with an empty lantern by the time I return. There has to be another way.

Feeling the warmth of my boon pulsing inside makes me wish I could simply give Cai some of my Chi. I'm sure I took in more than enough to heal him. Unlike a seal on a Shen Breath lantern, there's no stopper to remove to let out the Chi already inside me.

Or is there? I remember the fight I had with the shrine guard. The sword slice across my arm. The pain. The blood. The Shen Breath. What if... Could it work? It's crazy, but I have to try. It would be easier if I had my sharpening knife, but it's in my shoulder bag back on the boat. I have to find another way.

Squeezing a clump of pine needles in my hand, I twist and tug at a small limb from one of the branches above me. The soft and flexible nature of the limb makes it hard to break, but it eventually twists off. Unfortunately, the ends of the broken limb are too smooth. While Cai continues to grimace and bite back his suffering, I have to twist off two more limbs before I break one with jagged enough edges.

"You have to brave it out a little longer," I say with an encouraging smile. "With the Two's help, you'll be feeling better soon... I hope."

I close my eyes a moment and take a deep breath. Once I open them, I cringe as I dig the jagged end of the broken branch into my forearm. Blood bubbles from the crude line that I cut into my flesh. Shen Breath streams in shimmering wisps from the fresh gash. Some of it works on healing my wound, but most of it flows toward Cai.

Immediate relief shows on his face as his body absorbs the Shen Breath and begins to heal him. But it's short-lived. My wound heals after a short moment, cutting Cai off from the stream of mist needed to heal his much more serious wounds.

I take another deep breath and tear my flesh again with the jagged branch. The Chi inside me lessens the pain of the wound, but it still stings enough to cause my own tears to well and make me want to scream. But this time I don't let the wound heal. In a slow, measured, and extremely painful manner I keep tearing the flesh along my arm so the Chi can't completely heal my wound and so the stream of Shen Breath will continue to flow from me to Cai.

My heart races. My breath quickens. My boon drains faster and faster. The pain in my arm rises. My eyes close to fend off the dizziness that sets in as the expulsion of Chi outpaces its ability to heal me.

"Stop! Enough!" A firm hand grabs my wounded arm, and another pulls back my branch-wielding hand.

My eyes fly open. Cai's holding me, keeping me from inflicting anymore damage to my arm. Blood, but no Shen Breath, streams from the gash. The wound burns with pain. My boon is completely used up and I feel exhausted.

"What were you thinking?" He snaps at me. "Look what you've done to your arm!"

Without looking up at him, I snap back, "I was thinking you were a goat-headed fool for breaking your arm. And if I didn't save you, who would?"

"No, that's not what I mean." His voice softer now. "Why would you hurt yourself to heal me?"

I lift my eyes and his dark eyes stare at me with deep intensity. His head is at a slight sideways tilt. The expression of pain and suffering has left his face, replaced with a visage that I can't quite decipher. Anger? Confusion? Gratitude? Affection? Maybe a mix of some or all.

His grip on my arm and hand loosens, but he doesn't let go. His fingers feel warm. Pleasant. I don't want him to let go. My skin tingles with exhilaration. I feel guilty for feeling this way. I want him to hold me. Be close to him. In my mind, he belongs to Lian. Am I betraying her even though he's told me she no longer cares for him?

My eyes widen as he lowers his gaze and bows his head toward me. Whether it's a sign of his own shame or respect for me, I've never known any man in Ning to show such humility or reverence to a woman.

"I'm sorry," he whispers. "You were right. I should have listened to you. I'm a witless fool. Please forgive me."

Another surprise? No man apologizes to a woman. It's not necessarily part of Innate Honor. It's just not done. I don't how to respond. So, I ignore his words for now.

"We have to get out of this tree and get out of here before the Mu Cun guards find us."

"No," Cai say, lowering his eyes toward my bleeding arm. "We first need to take care of you."

I swallow hard. Blood drips from the jagged wound, much of it smeared on all my skin and staining my new clothes. The sight makes me sick. But the feeling only lasts a moment. The need to act takes over.

Cai lets go of me and grips the bottom of his tunic as if to rip it in shreds for a bandage. A vague image pops in my mind of him doing that same thing once before, hovering over me and caring for me. Did that happen? I don't remember it. Where did that memory come from?

I place my hands on his before he can tear his new tunic. "No. There's no need." I reach under my own tunic, remove the bandages Fen had recently wrapped around my torso, and hand them to Cai. "Use these. They'll work better."

Cai's hands are firm, yet gentle as he wraps the bandage around my arm. The urge to lean in and snuggle against him grows as he binds my wound. Instead, I lose myself in the sincere kindness and concern his eyes. When he finishes bandaging my arm, our eyes meet, and his fingers continue to rest on my arm. We both smile but say nothing. My gaze lowers to his lips for a moment—lips I so desperately want to kiss. Does he feel the same? I look back up at his eyes. Is that longing or uncertainty I see. I feel dizzy, not certain if it's from blood loss or looking into those deep, beautiful eyes.

I want to shout, "Kiss me you goat-headed fool!" But we just continue to share a gaze. Silence and inaction eventually make the moment grow awkward.

"We better go," I mumble, cursing myself for not being brave enough to make the first move.

He nods his head and lets go of my arm. I curse myself again, acknowledging that I'm actually the goat-headed fool for passing up the perfect moment.

We scoot along our branches over and through pine needles toward the center of the tree. The needles catch on our clothes and scratch our skin. But other than that, it's easy to make our way along the tree's thick branches. Once at the trunk, we climb down branch after branch. I'm tired and out of breath by the time we step down onto one of the many bamboo walkways that spans the trees of Mu Cun.

"Where now?" Cai whispers.

The question takes me by surprise. Is he asking me to take the lead? What is going on with Cai? I like it, but I'm not used to it.

"We need to find another crop platform," I say, adjusting the blood-soaked bandage on my arm. "My arm needs more Shen Breath. And the way you're careful with your arm means you're not quite done healing either."

Staying in the shadows as much as possible, we move with as much stealth as we can through the maze of walkways and swinging suspension bridges. Only a few lamps burn among the tree houses and community buildings we pass. The nighttime whistles, clicks, and buzzes of the forest cover up the sound of our steps, but we're still careful as we walk. It's late enough that no Mu Cun villagers are out and about, but we have no desire to accidentally run into one.

We only have to backtrack a few times and try different routes before we reach a crop plaza lined with Shen Breath lanterns. Before we can move toward their healing power, footfalls sound behind us, approaching fast. We freeze. There's no time to hide.

I consider making a run for one of the Shen Breath lanterns. If I can get to their healing and strength, I can fight our way free. No. I don't have the strength. I'm exhausted and dizzy from so much blood loss. I can barely walk and stand without toppling over.

Cai takes my hand in his and gives it a slight squeeze. Its warmth brings me comfort, but as our eyes meet, his gaze confirms to me that he's in no condition to rescue us either. I squeeze his hand back and clench the fist of my other hand. We were so close to getting free.

As one, we turn to meet our captor. With a heavy spear pointed in our direction, a large muscular man with tattooed arms steps toward us. It's hard to see his face clearly in the night's shadows, but his grim expression is plain to see. His grip tightens on his spear and his eyes narrow as our gazes meet.

I expect to him to shout an alarm to alert other Mu Cun warriors of our escape, but his mouth remains closed in a thin frown. He stops a few paces away, close enough to skewer us with his spear if we try to get away.

With a broad smile I say, "Lovely night for a walk, isn't it?"

The warrior's lips tighten, but he says nothing. No command to be quiet. Not even an order to head back to our prison hut high in the trees. He stands in grim silence, staring and watching us. It's almost as if he's waiting for something. Maybe he doesn't know we're prisoners.

Still grinning, I gesture in the direction of the garden boxes behind us. "We were admiring your crops. Do you mind if we take a closer look?"

He scowls—a definite no. He jabs his spear in the air in front of us. I lean back and blink as the tip of the spearhead comes within a hand span of my chin. I want to grab its shaft and yank it out of his hands, but I keep my stupidity in check—a little.

"This is silly," I say, trying to sound nonchalant. "We've done nothing wrong. If you leave us alone, we'll be on our way."

One side of his mouth rises in a crooked smile. "You have fire, little one, but your haste has been most inconvenient."

Before I can ask him what he's talking about, footfalls sound behind him. A short, lean spear-bearing warrior stomps into view from the shadows. It's Fen. She knits her eyebrows close together and stretches her mouth into a thin scowl.

"Jade's shade, I told you to wait!" It's a whisper, but the force of her voice makes me flinch and step back. "We've been looking all over for you. You're lucky we found you before others did."

My smile wilts, but before I mouth a "sorry", her eyes fall on the blood-soaked bandage on my arm.

She shakes her head. "Pangze Wu, what foolery did you do? Never mind. We've wasted enough time. Come on!"

She marches toward the Shen Breath lanterns glowing among the crops, beckoning us to follow. It takes six lanterns to heal my gash and fill me to overflowing with the warmth and power of their Chi. Cai only needs five.

Once we fully recover, Fen presents Cai and me each with a flowered necklace strung with the pungent purple orchids—Beast Bane. Though I'm not overly fond of the bad smelling gift, I take it with a smile and a thank you. I slip it over my head onto my neck, trying hard not to crinkle my nose at the smell.

Cai stares at the necklace offered him like it's a pit viper, not moving a hand to accept the gift. I'm tempted to elbow him for his bad manners, but Fen eliminates the need.

"Your pride will kill you," Fen says with an edge to her voice. "It is at great peril that Bo and I plan to lead you to your boat through dark of Gudai in its most dangerous hour. The Beast Bane will keep most creatures away. But if you refuse to wear it, your scent will float on the breeze inviting all of Gudai to feast upon your Mangzi Yangzi flesh. What do you choose?"

A sheepish grimace turns down the corners of Cai's mouth as his eyes move from Fen to the necklace. His nose crinkles as he takes it from her hand and pulls it over his head. Looking as stern as ever, she nods in approval. Without another word, she and Bo turn on their heels and walk into the darkness. Cai and I exchange a quick glance and hurry after them, anxious to be free of the Mu Cun tree village and back on our boat, headed toward Quanli, the City of Heaven, capital of Huyan.

Part 3

Chapter 26
Qiu Lian – Luxurious Misery

"Tis nothing to speak a lie. Tis everything to live with it."
- Notions from a Royal Peasant

Divine One, perhaps you would enjoy roast pheasant in plum sauce. Or if you desire, I could bring you a skewer of shrimp with a platter of peaches, mangoes, and tangerines."

I want to scream at the servant girl to get her face off the floor and stop kowtowing. But I fear if Lord Zheng hears of it, he will beat her with a thrashing rod for displeasing me. I can't bear to have anyone else suffer because of my mistakes.

"No thank you, Chan. I really am not hungry. Please, I would just like to be alone."

"You must eat Divine One. Lord Emperor Xiang, Chosen of Heaven will not be happy if you wither away from lack of nourishment."

Her voice quivers. I can't see her face, but I sense she's fighting back tears of terror. I am such a witless fool. Of course, she's terrified. Lord Zheng has no desire to present the emperor a frail malnourished Wife Divine to be. The servants' job is to plump me up, so I look as desirable as possible. If I refuse to eat, Chan and the others will pay the price. My attempt to punish myself with starvation, punishes the servants. How did I get into this mess?

"Forgive me, Chan. You are right. Some peaches and mangoes would be nice."

"And skewered shrimp?" The hopeful, almost pleading anticipation in her voice tells me she won't completely escape punishment if I only eat the fruit.

I sigh, giving in. "Yes, shrimp would be nice too. Thank you."

She practically skips out of the room, having won a major victory. I want to cry, but my tear ducts have long dried out. Once I entered the sedan back at the village square and the silk curtains closed, the tears flowed without restraint. I try to muffle my sobs. I don't need the imperial servants knowing my distress. If Lord Zheng knew of my tears I now wonder if perhaps he had beaten the sedan bearers too. Such a mixed-up world I've stepped into.

No one here could ever understand why I'm not thrilled to become a Wife Divine. It brings immense honor to my family. The bride price the emperor bestowed upon Father made him rich. And the wealth would not stop there. Father would immediately have become a village elder. No, not just village elder, an elder of the highest degree.

He will never have to work another day of his life. Every month he'll receive a stipend from the village taxes. But he will likely never have to spend a single zhu of it. Out of honor to Father, most of the villagers will gift him nearly anything he needs or desires for the rest of his life. He will forever be wealthy in coin and honor. At least Father received what he wanted.

In a twisted, horribly soul-wrenching way, I received what I wanted too—to be free of Ning. Free, but forever tortured by guilt and hopelessly alone. When Father told me of his dream, I knew it was my chance to escape. Of course, being chosen as a Wife Divine was only to be the first step in my master plan.

Next step, servants would wait on me, bring me whatever I wanted and do whatever I desired of them. With riches at my disposal, I simply would choose the right moment before the marriage ceremony to slip away forever into some remote land that the emperor neither cared for nor thought about.

Last step, when Cai finished his military term, I would have sent for him to join me. Life would be perfect. At least, that was how it was supposed to have worked out, until I sent Cai to his death.

I should have told him the truth. But I thought it too dangerous. It would have made him party to my treason. If anyone found out, he'd be executed. And what if the emperor discovered Cai loved me or I loved Cai? To what lengths would the emperor's jealously drive him? Prison for Cai? Torture? Execution? I thought I was so smart, all the lies I told Cai so he would be safe, so he wouldn't worry about me, and so he would enlist early for military service.

But if I had let him wait to serve, he would still be alive. I'm such a witless fool. I might as well have been the one to pierce his heart with a sword. I killed him.

The day the messenger came with news of Cai's death, my plans changed from one of freedom to one of eternal torment. I deserve the life of torture that Meilin believes comes with being a Wife Divine. That's why I kept to the plan, that and how it would bless and honor my family.

But I've seen no hint of dungeons and torture. Even the sedan chair spoke of luxuries to come. A bronze pitcher full of spice wine and a platter of sweet lychee fruit left inside the sedan for me to enjoy. I left them untouched. Once onboard the boat, servants have come non-stop, bowing and offering me enough meats and fruit to feed all of Ning for a month. I don't want any of it. The smells and sight of it bring waves of sorrow and guilt that make me nauseous.

I see now that even if Cai had lived, my plan had too many flaws to ever work. The biggest flaw being that I can't go anywhere on my own. They won't even let me walk anywhere alone on the ship, except inside my room. I must either be carried in my new sedan or remain in my room. No common eyes are allowed to view the future Wife Divine. I was a witless fool to think I could easily slip away undetected.

I long to be thrown in prison for what I've done to Cai, to our promised life together. I miss him so much. That is at least some punishment, but not nearly enough. Feathered silk pillows, cushioned chairs of cherry wood, and beautiful screen paintings adorn every space. It even has a small window that lets me look out onto the Pangbo River and watch the passing landscape. I fear more extravagant luxuries to come once we reach the palace.

And the clothes. For any other woman it would be paradise. A never-ending supply of elegant silks of purple and red. A myriad of designs with breathtaking florals. The silk feels wonderful on my skin, racking my soul to even greater heights of guilt. I want to tear them to shreds, but they'll just bring me more clothes, shaming me further. Oh, I hope Meilin is right, that they will lock me in a rat-infested dungeon and bolt the door for eternity.

Without a knock or request to enter, the door to my room opens. Lord Zheng strides in, his gold-cuffed purple robes flourishing as he walks. The wings on the side of his square hat flap up and down. Coupled with his thin, pointed nose, he resembles a raven on the prowl.

Halfway across the room he stops abruptly and bows with hand in fist as if he just remembered proper protocol for approaching someone of my new station. Wives Divine are elevated above the precepts of Innate Honor. All must show the emperor's wives deep respect. Still, Zheng barely bows. Perhaps that is expected. Zheng is a high lord, second only to Lord Emperor Xiang Hu, Chosen of Heaven.

I know little of imperial politics or code of conduct, so I'm not sure if the honor of a Wife Divine outshines a High Lord's honor or not. In Lord Zheng's case I doubt it matters. He feigns to treat me with respect.

Uncaring disdain fills his eyes when he looks at me. At least his perception of me is honest. I'm little more than a worthless peasant girl.

"Wonderful news, Divine One. We will dock in the Dragon Port of Quanli within the hour. You must be anxious to see the City of Heaven and your new home in the palace."

His shrill voice annoys me, but not as much as the insincerity of his words. Lord Zheng cares nothing for what I might want. His visits always concern what he needs or wants me to do.

I smile, hoping it's as noticeably insincere as his words. "Of course, honorable Lord Zheng, the anticipation makes me breathless. But surely you have not graced me with your appearance to solely hear the extent of my yearnings. How may I honor your presence?"

Lord Zheng clears his throat and forces a smile. I cover my mouth trying not to laugh at the fact that his smile is more insincere than my own.

"Divine One, the moment we arrive at the dock an imperial carriage will be ready to convey you to the palace. The ride takes a little under an hour. Before then, I am certain you will want to waste no time making yourself presentable enough to meet Lord Emperor Xiang Hu, Chosen of Heaven in case he deigns to admit you to his presence. Of course, we would not want to keep the carriage waiting if by the Two's disfavor you happen to not be ready upon our arrival. Do you not agree?"

I want to scowl at the man, but my fake smile only flinches a trace. He has insulted the way I look, my punctuality, and my importance in the eyes of the emperor. And it would not surprise me if he's more concerned about getting me ready quickly rather than how the Lord Emperor thinks I look. I'm simply a burden that he hopes to be rid of as soon as possible.

"Why of course, Lord Zheng. I will make myself presentable without delay. That is if you will please excuse yourself with all speed."

Lord Zheng turns on his heels after the briefest of bows. I plop back on my bed and blow out a long sigh the moment he's gone. If anyone deserves fifty blows with a thick thrashing rod, it's Lord Zheng. Once we reach the palace, I hope to be rid of him too.

After my anger settles, I sit up and ring the bell at my nightstand. Barely a second passes before Chan enters in with a hurried shuffle and several kowtows.

"Yes, Divine One, how may I honor you?"

I give Chan a real smile. I like the sweet young girl and appreciate her kindness. I hope she'll continue to be with me when we reach the palace.

"Lord Zheng doesn't find my appearance acceptable for meeting the Lord Emperor, Chosen of Heaven. Can you help me change that?"

A wide grin spreads across her face. "It will be my extreme pleasure, Divine One. I will gather the others. We have much work to do and so little time."

I laugh aloud. In her eager sincerity Chan inadvertently insulted me nearly as deep as Lord Zheng. Worry fills her eyes as she realizes the offensive nature of her words.

I laugh again. "Yes, Chan you are right. We do have much to do. Go and hurry back with the others. We surely do not have enough time, but I'm certain you will do your best."

Chapter 27
Fan Wei – A Dancing Heart

"Advanced preparation is key. Know weaknesses. Know strengths. Identify potential allies and assets. Devise multiple execution strategies. Prepare retreat venues. Remain undetected."

- Hidden Scrolls of Quingping: Practices of Engagement

Sweat-soaked, my black tunic and trousers cling to my skin beneath the borrowed armor of the Red Phoenix Guard. Its scarlet-painted chainmail drapes from my shoulders down to my knees. Even with the shade of the River Gate watchtower's roof shading, the spring sun slow cooks me to death. How do they survive in these uniforms when summer comes?

But it's not all bad. At least I'm not back at the slave camps dehydrating to an even slower and more tortuous death digging up salt or some precious ore. For now, I'm free and life is good.

Oh, and my helmet has this glorious neck guard of scarlet fabric that lets the breeze cool the back of my head and sides. That's worth at least a cheek-to-cheek smile. I only wish the fabric reached further around the sides of my face. I don't need people spotting the red birth markings that make the left side of my face so pleasant to behold. True, the markings add to my already handsome appeal, but it also raises too many undesirable questions.

I grin at the four tied up and gagged guards sleeping at my feet. They had too many questions. Like, "Hey, how did you get up here?" "Where did you come from?" "Wow, can you teach me that awesome whip kick?" Okay, they didn't ask that last one, but they probably would have if they were still conscious. But for city guards, they really are quite nice, letting me borrow one of their uniforms while they sleep off the beating I gave them.

From their post on the River Gate's main watch tower, I have a spectacular view of the seaport in front and the capital's more than one hundred city wards behind me. The square-shaped, self-contained, and walled communities spread out for at least two leagues in all directions like a massive chessboard. The ward's walls and gates rise at least four times my height, making it easy for guards to secure each ward at a gong's notice.

Fed by the Pangbo river, eight canals run in straight lines provide the almost two million citizens fresh drinking and irrigation water. At more than three hundred paces wide, the Imperial Highway cuts through the middle of all of Quanli's wards, starting at the River Gate and ending at the Dragon Palace at the city's far side.

Moving between wards between sunset and sunrise can be near impossible unless you're me. The past week I've looked for clues in a dozen of the city's most affluent wards, snooping about opulent mansions, spacious temples, and even modest monasteries.

I even spent a few afternoons in the palace gardens disguised as an Imperial Gardener hoping to hear a morsel of gossip or slip of confidences that might provide answers.

Chatter and excitement about the pending arrival of the new Wife Divine has filled most of that gossip. That leaves me no closer to discovering the hiding place of the Most Holy Wife, the beloved empress of all. But it hasn't been a complete loss. I squeezed in time to sculpt an ordinary ficus tree into the likeness of our not-so-beloved emperor being eaten alive by a Pang Bear—a truly magnificent work of art.

Today I hope answers will surface outside the city on the riverfront. From my watchtower, I can see every boat and ship that docks, as well as anyone wanting to enter the city's main gate. But right now, I only care about one ship—the Imperial Warship conveying the new Wife Divine.

Officials made no secret that she would arrive today. No wonder a drunken stupor plagues most of Quanli with both commoners and elite indulging in an abundance of rice wine and pathetic dancing. Even when the crowds' celebrations have grown rowdy, the Red Phoenix Guard has only occasionally subdued the people's joyful outbursts. That laxed behavior runs counter to the city guards' regular tight-fisted, violence hungry reputation.

Deafening applause and a roar of cheers rise from the crowded riverfront when the Imperial Warship sails into view with its dragonhead prow. The extravagant warship looks more like a floating palace. It has a three-story tower in the back and relatively modest two-story tower in front. A giant fan-shaped sail rises high between the two towers. Another large sail rises behind the back tower, and another rises in front of the forward tower.

As the ship comes closer, sailors raise the sails so the oarsmen can better guide the great warship into the Imperial Dock. Creating a clear path from the docks to the River Gate, about one thousand Gold Dragon Guards—the emperor's personal security force, stand at attention in their black, steel-plated leather chest and skirt armor, gold capes, and shimmering helmets with yellow plumes.

Brandishing thick thrashing rods, crossbows, and swords, the Gold Dragon Guard keeps the crowds back as a purple-robed imperial official rides a big black horse down the gangplank. Blue-robed servants and a score of armored soldiers follow close behind on foot. Cheers and shouts swell when servants heft a lavish sedan chair down the gangplank. Purple silk curtains conceal the future Wife Divine from view, the emperor's newest naïve pawn.

The crowd silences when the sedan stops by a lavish two-wheeled carriage decorated with red feathered plumes, purple curtains, gold trim and a red sandalwood roof shaped like an umbrella.

The servants position the side of the sedan so the future Wife Divine can move into carriage without being seen. By tradition, if a commoner sees the Wife Divine before the wedding ceremony, the Two's disfavor will be summoned. How absurd. The emperor summoned the Two's disfavor long ago with his foul treatment of the empress and the thousands of Wives Divine he has married over the centuries. That's just one of the wrongs I plan to right.

A head pops up above the sedan through its silk curtains. A collective gasp moves through the crowd of onlookers. Tense silence follows.

"Wonderful!" I whisper, grinning. The future Wife Divine reveals herself to the world, dooming all of Huyan with a curse from the Two. I want to laugh. What could be better? If only I believed in such superstitions.

Servants and soldiers stop around her like statues. With a prayer to Yanlì Shen I tap into my Farsight and get a close-up view of their expressions of fear and horror. My eyes move to the future Wife Divine. My breath stops. My heart swells. Euphoric dizziness spins through my head. She's dazzling.

Kind smiling lips. Cheeks curved to graceful perfection. Skin smooth as silk. Adorable little nose. And behind those exquisite dark eyes, light gleams. I've never before viewed such a magnificently bewitching sight.

"Mother of Light! Love seize me."

I take a deep breath and exhale. Her eyes move across the crowd of stunned soldiers and citizens. Then, her gaze moves upwards, stops on me, and she smiles. A huge grin spreads across my face. Okay, her eyes didn't really stop on me, and she was already smiling, but I can dream.

One of the guards tied at my feet stirs and mumbles something through the gag in his mouth. With a firm grip on the hilt of my sword I arch an eyebrow and give him my sternest look.

"Hush your jabbering!" I order. "I'm falling in love and you're ruining the moment."

The guard only quiets when I pull out my sword a hand span from its sheath. By then the gaze of the future Wife Divine has moved on and her servants have recovered from their shock. They rush toward her in an uproar of chattering and bowing. In moments her divine beauty vanishes from view into the confines of her imperial carriage, but not before one last smile and wave. Both of which I'm certain she aimed at me.

The carriage conveys the glorious future Wife Divine through the River Gate and up the Imperial Highway amid a procession of the nearly one thousand Gold Dragon Guards. I watch them until their nearly out of view and then tap into my Return gift.

In an instant I appear several hundred paces away to the top of a five-story temple in one of the wards that borders the Imperial Highway. Sitting, my legs straddle one of the wing-tipped corners of the temple roof. As the carriage and parade of guards move along the highway not too far beneath me, I reach beneath the roof and touch the paper sides of one of the Shen Breath lanterns hanging there. Its music sings to me and its Chi pulses warmth into my fingers, spreading beneath my flesh throughout my body.

Earlier in the week I painted several Return marks throughout Quanli to make traveling the capital faster and easier. I only need to remember what all the different places look like and make sure the Return mark on my chest hasn't faded. A mistake with either one and I could end up in the wrong part of the city.

To make sure neither happens, I choose locations that have Shen Breath lanterns within easy reach and I regularly re-ink my Return mark.

My hand instinctively goes to my chest where my necklace of discs used to hang. Nothing. I feel naked without them. But my gift mark discs are lost to me. I haven't had time to make new ones. Until then, I'll have to continue drawing them by hand instead of quickly stamping them on.

As the procession of carriage and soldiers continues to distance itself from my watchful gaze, I travel to yet another vantage point overlooking the highway. From rooftops to towers to other balconies and to even a few lofty trees, I follow their course using Return mark after Return mark until I find myself sitting in the crook of a grand chestnut tree.

A fat crow caws at me for intruding on its roost. My smile fades. Not at the incessant crow, but because the carriage and procession rolls through the palace gates. I expected this would be their destination, but I had hoped that perhaps they would take the future Wife Divine to some secluded manor where they secretly hide all the other Wives Divine and the Most Holy Wife. Of course, how would it be secret if a multitude of servants and Gold Dragon Guard members knew its location?

It makes sense they would keep the future Wife Divine somewhere in the palace at least until the marriage. Even though moving through the palace grounds is not easy, I'll have to keep a close watch on her until the ceremony. Once it's over she'll disappear to wherever the other Wives Divine have been hidden. If I'm lucky, she'll lead me to the empress too. If not, I'll need a new plan.

Maybe by then Suyin will show herself. It's been two days since I first sensed her presence in the city. I'm not certain I can trust her, but I may have no other choice if my path to the oath fails. We seek the same end, but I fear my sister's paths take her where no Deliverer should travel.

My lips push out in a deep frown when the gates to the palace close behind the future Wife Divine's procession. I wonder when, if ever, I'll be able to behold again her divine beauty. Not likely, but I can dream.

Still, I hope my path to fulfilling my Deliverer's oath includes stopping the marriage of this new Wife Divine.

It would be a true shame to have such rare loveliness wasted on Emperor Hu, Despised of Heaven. If she could just meet me, I'm sure her heart would dance for me too.

Chapter 28
Lord Emperor Xiang Hu – Visions of Destruction

"What kind of sheepherder will I be? One that flees when the Pang Bear attacks or one that carries to safety the lambs that cannot protect themselves."

- Personal Meditations of Xiang Hu

Neither day, nor night. Slivers of gold and scarlet blaze a thin line above the horizon and reflect upon the great river's end. The fire of sunset softens into cloudy streaks of deep blues and purples in the sky above and the rippling water below. Directly above, like lovers in the darkening sky, the moons San and Shi meet, merging nearly into one as the glowing emerald of San passes in front of the brilliant lavender of Shi until only Shi's glowing edges encircling San can be seen.

Head up and eyes focused straight ahead, I walk along the grassy shore toward the glowing horizon. My grip tightens on the gems on my Zhangchi's hilt. Silence reigns except for the rumble of river and a slow thumping drum beat far in the distance. Chains rattle somewhere deep beneath my feet and the thick grass and moist soil. That's how it always begins—with evening twilight, the thump of a drum, and the rattling of chains.

"I do not fear you!" I shout at the sky. "Thanks to your brothers and sisters, my gifts are many. You cannot overcome."

Cruel laughter rises on the wind. The voice of Xié Shen taunts back in a whisper that shakes the air. "Really? You will need to gain more gifts than you can imagine if you ever hope to stop my favored ones from rising. And when they rise, they will free my greatest creation and wreak destruction throughout all of Dashi."

I raise Zhangchi high above my head, the rays of the setting sun shimmer like fire upon its silver blade. "Your favored have no chance!" I shout back. "I have seen to that. Heaven has chosen me as its protector. I alone wield their blessings. Neither you, your followers, nor any of your abominations shall rise to conquer."

The wind howls with Xié Shen's laughter. "Your pride blinds you. You cannot stop what you do not see. Even so, look! Behold what awaits you unless you bow to me—beast maker, oath breaker, shadow lord, god slayer, true ruler of Dashi."

The chains rattle louder and louder. The ground trembles and quakes beneath my feet. Sprays of rock, dirt, and grass fly up from the shore in all directions. A loud crack shakes the air as the ground splits, opening into a bottomless chasm.

Cold shafts of darkness fly upward from the pit, suffocating any life they touch. Flowing through a series of Fei Chi forms, I slash and parry Zhangchi against the dark shafts that streak toward me, destroying them with the blade's kiss.

A thunderous roar booms as an all-black winged demon dragon rises from the pit with broken chains dangling from its limbs. It dives toward me, spewing shafts of darkness in my direction. Slicing Zhangchi upward, back and forth, my blade's touch extinguishes the shafts from existence.

With another roar, the demon dragon swoops over me and upward. With a tilt of its wings, it turns northward, flying upstream above the shimmering Pangbo. Death, destruction, and wails of misery follow in its wake as it speeds away, spitting darkness in all its path, extinguishing the last of the evening's rays.

From deep within the pit, Xié Shen's laughter rises like a great whirlwind. "The future is set," Xié Shen howls. "My favored ones still live. My servant will rise. You cannot stop me. Dashi will soon be mine and I will be free."

Xié Shen's voice fades. The demon dragon disappears. The vision of darkening twilight vanishes. The touch of the morning sun on my face stirs me from my sleep and the night's dream. A cold shiver envelopes me despite my bed's layers of blankets.

The dream has not changed much over the past three hundred years, but this one had a greater sense of immediacy and foreboding. And Xié Shen's voice, I might have imagined it, but it rang with greater confidence and surety. Could the demon god be right? Have I failed despite all I've done to stop the dream from coming true?

Icy shivers grip me, but I still throw off my covers, hurry to my closet, and in a chaotic rush pull on my clothes.

Soon after, I sit on the silk cushions of the Dragon Throne. A servant pops a kumquat into my mouth as Wu Kang, my Imperial Commandant, enters the Imperial Throne Room. Head up, but gaze on my feet, he walks toward me under the intense stare of the Gold Dragon Guard lining both sides of the long corridor. Kang kneels at the steps to the Dragon Throne and kowtows three times. As proper, on the final kowtow he keeps his face to the floor, waiting for me to address him.

"Hear my orders, Kang. Before the setting of today's sun, I must have reports from every squad of Shashyao on their efforts."

Kang nods as much as one can with their nose to floor. "As the Chosen of Heaven commands, it will be done."

No objections. No cries of, "Impossible!" I'm not certain that brings me comfort. Kang knows disobedience brings shame, while failure only brings death. His family's honor guarantees he will do all he can to obey my command—even if he believes my orders are impossible. It doesn't matter if we don't have enough flash towers, messengers, or time to comply. He will not refuse me. At times I wish my leaders were more concerned with truth than fear of shame.

"How else might your unworthy servant honor thee, Chosen of Heaven?"

I force back a sigh. I cannot show worry or fear. But in truth, no matter how far I've expanded Huyan's borders, it might not be enough. Too much of Dashi is beyond my reach. Xié Shen's favored ones could be anywhere. But perhaps the dream's vision gives a clue—the location where the demon dragon rises from the depths of Kaioda's prison.

Still, I hesitate. Perhaps I should go there myself, hunt these favored ones and deal with them on my own. No. I have no way of knowing if that's where they'll really be or when they will act. They could show up anywhere at any time. I can't leave the affairs of the kingdom on an uncertain guess. Besides, I have tomorrow's wedding ceremony to attend.

"Before nightfall I want three squads of Shashyao hunting the shores of the Pangbo inside the Quingping province. That will remain their post until I command otherwise. No defiled found must be allowed to live. Understood?"

Kang nods again without looking up. "As the Chosen of Heaven commands, Kang obeys."

"Very well. See to it."

Kang's devout obedience usually comforts me, but not today. As he marches away, Xié Shen's words haunt me. "The future is set. You cannot stop me. Dashi will soon be mine and I will be free."

Chapter 29
Qiu Lian – Friend or Assassin?

"As a tenet of Light, healing does not represent the traditional usage of the word. It has more to do with healing or elevating one's inner soul or personal Chi through constant improvement and refinement to one's spiritual, physical, and emotional natures."
- Pan Ru: Essays on the Tenets of Light

Elegant yet minimalistic—that's the nature of my new room. Panels of aloes wood cover the walls, filling the room with its pleasing dark, resinous aroma. Fancy rugs with beautiful floral designs and woody landscapes decorate and cushion the floor. The furnishings include a sleeping mat, two chairs with cushions, a small table decorated with a vase of peonies, and a beautiful screen painting of the mountaintop marriage of Dìyī Shen and Guāng Shen. My favorite is the ground-floor balcony that looks out to the Imperial Gardens. But of course, I haven't yet had time to enjoy anything more than a few moments view of its stunning trees and flowers.

I never dreamed that becoming royalty would be so much work. Yes, Chan and the other servants still pamper me, dressing me in silk dresses and trying to fatten me up with exotic meats and fruits. I even had a hot bath scented with frankincense and sandalwood.

But since arriving yesterday most of my hours and minutes have been spent with tutor after tutor. I've been drilled on the proper way to prepare, pour, smell, hold, and drink tea. I've been tutored on how to pleasantly laugh with my mouth covered, to glide as I walk, and to bow to the Lord Emperor Chosen of Heaven without ever making eye contact.

Suffering through my private lessons with Lord Zheng has been the worst. He reminds me of an angry badger. Not just because of his long triangular face, long thin nose, and the constant scowl of his beady eyes, but he squeals in a high pitch when I make the smallest of mistakes practicing my marriage vows. The ceremony is two days away. How can I stand being in his presence for that long?

"You imbecilic child!" he screeches. "Your promises of loyalty to the Lord Emperor are for the public ceremony only. Only recite the oaths to Zhì Shen during the private ceremony you must, and you must do it exactly as I instructed. Now try again!"

The veins on his forehead swell. Bright red colors his face. His cheeks bulge to bursting. Let him think I'm a fool. The torture he inflicts on himself when I pretend to forget or mix up a line makes me smile.

But I can only endure a little of Zheng. To end the torture, I recite every vow and oath perfectly. Zheng huffs and mutters curses as he stomps from the room.

I sigh as the door closes behind him. I want to curl up on my sleeping mat for a nap, but no doubt another tutor will quickly interrupt my rest. My eyes turn to the gardens as a warm spring breeze brushes against my open balcony door. The air fills with the scent of peonies and pine. What if…

I hurry to the balcony before another tutor can arrive. I climb over the rail and step down into the gardens. Freedom. I can't stop grinning. The scents of all the different flowers and blossoms delight my nose. I run down a winding cobblestone path under an archway of white and pink blossoming apricot trees, and past curved rows of pink, purple, and white azaleas.

Shen Breath lanterns hang waist high from hooked poles along the path every few paces. Their swirling-colored mists adds an ethereal ambience to the already spectacular gardens. I have always loved to watch the way the colored vapors glow, dance and spin.

Narrow unpaved foot paths lead away from the cobbles every so often toward small, yet elegant shrine pavilions. Most share a similar two-tiered roof pagoda style built with rich cherry wood, trimmed in gold, and supported by six sturdy columns. Roses or peonies encircle most shrines. Chrysanthemums, asters, bamboo, cherry trees, or apricot trees surround others.

A beautiful statue of its patron Shen fronts each shrine. I'm tempted to get a closer look, but a Gold Dragon Guard stands sentry at each shrine. No matter my high station, the guards would not treat me kindly if I ventured too close.

The cobblestone path takes me through a grove of yellow blossomed cinnamon trees, arched trellises of wisterias, and curves toward a shimmering lake. The path intersects with other paths that cut through colorful fields of peonies or lead to other shrine pavilions.

My path leads me near the lake beneath the shade of a few flowering magnolias and clusters of manicured ficus. I sit on a bench under a pavilion that's almost as elaborate as a Shen shrine.

Like a collection of living artwork, shrubs and trees sculpted into various caricatures and scenes rise up in random spots among the peonies and near the shore. A horned dragon snakes its way across the field. Stampeding horses rise from a bubbling surf. Fei Chi masters hold deadly poses. Children skip and dance in a circle. A sleeping panda curls up on a low branch. Quails march in a straight line. Elephants, bears, wolves, leopards and more come to life in different sculpted stances and poses.

"The circle of hippos is my personal favorite."

The deep, yet lighthearted voice startles me. I almost fall off my bench. A few paces away, a gardener in peasant grays and a big bamboo hat kneels near the pavilion digging weeds out of a crescent shaped bed of purple peonies. He's so close. How did I not notice him earlier? I follow his gaze to the hippos and grin. The pine tree sculpture shows a man with a remarkable resemblance to Lord Zheng dangling by his belt on the bottom tooth of a mama hippo above the hungry mouths of three baby hippos.

"Do you think I got his sneer quite right," The gardener asks, exaggerating a tone of seriousness. "I wanted to capture the majestic essence of his perpetual surliness?"

I giggle, barely covering my mouth. Did the gardener notice? Probably not. His big bamboo hat covers all but his chin. Besides, he's a commoner. Even a glance in my direction could get him in trouble with Zheng. Except for my servants, no common eyes are to see the future Wife Divine until after the wedding. I despise that rule.

I twist my head side to side looking in all directions to make sure no one else is within hearing distance. In an excited hush I say, "I love it. Did you do all of the sculptures?"

The gardener laughs a loud, yet pleasant laugh. "I am not so blessed, your most beautiful Divine One. I am new to the gardens. This is only my second work of art. I would show you my first, but one of the other Imperial Gardeners chopped it down."

"What? Why would they do such a thing?"

A soft chuckle rumbles from underneath his hat. "Definitely jealously. My depiction of Emperor Hu was incomparably exquisite. Combine that with the show of indigestion from the bear eating him and you have a rare masterpiece."

He can't be serious. The slightest mockery of Lord Emperor Xiang Hu, Chosen of Heaven could be cause for execution. I suddenly feel uncomfortable. Am I endangering myself by talking to this man?

"Who are you?"

The gardener bows low into the peonies. I still can't see his face, but I imagine flower petals must be tickling his nose. "No one of importance.

Only a simple gardener. But blessed Divine One, I would be honored to serve you in any way that might please you."

Strange. Why would a gardener offer to serve me? He must know I have servants falling over themselves to please me. Besides, the palace has strict orders that servants serve, cooks cook, and gardeners garden. Failure to perform one's assigned duties or deviate from them could bring swift punishment from a thrashing rod or worse.

"That is kind of you master gardener, but I am already well cared for by my servants. Thank you."

He rises from his bow, but his hat still shields his face. His efforts to avoid looking at me far exceed that of other commoners in the palace. Most show respect by keeping their gaze low or away, but when they think no one is looking they usually try to steal a glance at me. It's not surprising. It's only every few dozen years or so when a new Wife Divine comes to the palace.

"Of course, but do your servants bring you fresh orchids for your heavenly hair?"

Without looking up, he lifts up his palm before me, presenting the most vibrant blue orchids I have ever seen. Before I can wonder where the orchids came from, since I've yet to see a single orchid in the garden, his other hand lifts a beautiful arrangement of pink and scarlet roses. Where did those come from?

"Or perhaps a fresh bouquet might please your lovely eyes and divine nose."

For one who tries hard not to look at me, how does he know if my eyes are lovely or my nose divine? If it wasn't suicidal on his part, I might think he's flirting. He acts extremely strange for a gardener.

What if he's not really a gardener? What if he's a spy for the emperor, testing my faithfulness? Or maybe a Yemaren spy? Or even an assassin? By the Two, what was I thinking? I never should have left my room.

In a rush, I rise from the bench, gather the folds of my silk dress, and hurry from the pavilion.

"Wait!" The man's tone is anxious, but kind. Once again, he bows his face low in the peonies, his hands flat on the ground. The blue orchid and bouquet of roses have disappeared. "Forgive my words and actions if they have made you uncomfortable. I have no desire to worry you, only please you."

I stop on the path. Although eight or so paces separate me from the man, I have the sudden sense that such little distance would not keep me safe if he wanted to hurt me. The slight movements of his lean figure have a grace reminiscent of a Fei Chi master.

"You are not an Imperial Gardener," I say, trying to sound firm and confident. "Tell me the truth of who you are, or I will sound an alarm and you will meet a swift death."

Even as the words flow from my mouth, I realize how hollow they must sound. If he is a Fei Chi master, he could dispatch me before I have a chance to scream. Besides, this is a man who delights in sculpting trees to mock the emperor and one of his highest officials. Either he doesn't fear death, has the confidence to handle any threat from the emperor's guards, or is simply an insane fool.

Honoring me with a fist in hand salute, the man lifts his head from the peonies while keeping his face hidden beneath the forward tilt of his hat. "You are as perceptive as you are enchanting, beloved Divine One. You are right. Though I do pride myself in my sublime talent as a gardener, I am not in the emperor's employ. Like you, I am a stranger here. As to who I am, I have been called many things in my life, most of which are not so pleasant. But to you, I hope you might call me friend."

I cross my arms across my chest, my patience thinning. "That is no answer. Show me your face and tell me the truth of who you are."

The man chuckles pleasantly. "Thank you Divine One. I welcome the honor to introduce myself to you."

He starts to rise to his feet and lift his hat to reveal his face, but before he can a young woman's frantic voice calls from behind me, "Divine One, there you are!"

I turn to see Chan running down the stone path toward me. In one hand she holds the folds of her blue servant robe, in the other a purple veil. "Thanks to the Two I found you. You must put this on at once."

Chan had warned me earlier that I must always wear the veil if I ever leave my room, to further ensure that no common eyes behold my face before the marriage. I scowl at the veil and then at her, but take it, attach its combs into my hair, and drop the veil over my face.

"Now, you must hurry," she continues. "Your tutors have waited most patiently, but I fear if you don't return at once, they will inform Lord Zheng of your absence. Believe me, Divine One, that would not be good for any of us."

My heart softens at the fear in Chan's eyes. I see it's not only for her and her friends, but for me as well. I give her a slight bow and a grateful smile. "Thank you, Chan. My apologies. One more moment, and then I will come at once."

I turn back toward the gardener, anxious to see his face and learn his name, but he has vanished.

Chapter 30
Qiu Lian – Quanli, City of Heaven

"Hope sails emotion's swells.
Joy skims passion's thrill.
Fear churns worry's knells.
Grit holds victor's will."
- Private Journal of Qiu Meilin

A wet morning breeze blows through the open windows, chilling me in the shelter's shade. Cai kneels on the boat's bamboo floor outside the shelter adjusting a rope on our sail. I love that sail! After escaping the Mu Cun tree village, we spent one more day taking turns steer poling through Gudai's deep. Three days ago, we reached the Pangbo. If the wind blew in our favor we could set the sail, snuggle in the shelter's back, and steer the boat with the long stern oar. Sublime bliss.

Nothing in my life has felt as wonderful as melting into the warmth of Cai's arms. I imagine how much more wonderful it would be to kiss his perfect lips. But Cai seems content to simply hold me close when we have the chance. I'm not sure if it's some noble commitment to honor or if part of his heart still beats for Lian.

Regardless, I haven't had the courage to push things any further. Sometimes I think it might still be a betrayal to Lian even though she broke Cai's heart. But mostly I wonder what Cai really feels for me. I want to ask him, but what if I don't like his answer? Everything is good right now. I don't want to upset it.

Of course, Snubby would love to see an upset. Snuggle time with Cai has meant less time Snubby gets to sit in my lap and get his furry head stroked. At first, he squeals and chatters for attention, wildly waving his arms. But after a few minutes of being ignored, he shakes his head while sticking out his tongue at us, then stomps away to sit on the roof to pout and pester Peck.

But it hasn't been non-stop snuggles. We still take turns switching between sleeping and steering so we don't lose any time getting to Quanli. Every morning, we go ashore and venture a little way into Gudai to collect berries, nuts, mushrooms, and an assortment of edible flowers and roots. Most days Cai spends some time fishing with Peck. Occasionally we'll exchange greetings with others travelling the river.

Using some of the money Master Jin gave me, we even bought some new peasant grays from a passing river merchant. We feared the green tunics and trousers the Mu Cun villagers gave us might direct unwanted attention to us once we reach Quanli.

And I carved my own wooden stamp for the Wind gift mark. It's not too bad for my first successful wood carving— "successful" being the key word. It took six previous failed attempts and some tutoring from Cai to get the disc mostly round and the markings right. But this one turned out well. Cai carved a version with the Father stroke for himself.

As proud as I am of my handiwork, the single wooden disc hanging on the new necklace around my neck looks meager compared to the many ceramic discs on the necklace Fen gave me. Does its owner really have that many gifts from the Shen? If so, he truly must be mighty. Does the emperor know that such a warrior exists? Do the Shashyao hunt him, too? Do the Shashyao still hunt Cai and me, or have they moved on to other prey?

"Meilin! Come here! You must see this." The excitement in Cai's voice pulls me from my thoughts. I tie the stern paddle in place and scramble on hands and knees out of the shelter into the open air.

This section of the Pangbo runs from west to east. On the south side of the river, a thick mix of Gudai's oaks, willows, and bamboo trees rise in vibrant strokes of green. On the north side, farmland stretches for leagues behind us. Thousands, maybe hundreds of thousands of workers, tend the fields. While the endless fields of crops are impressive, I'm not certain I understand the excitement in Cai's voice. But then I look further downriver and see the city walls.

At the far edge of the farmlands the lifeless gray walls rise in abrupt contrast to the deep greens of the fields. Almost a hundred paces back from the river, the front wall stretches along the river further than I can see. As far as I can tell it could go on and on alongside the Pangbo until it empties into the Great Sea where the lavender moon Shi has started her slow rise after her normal one-day absence.

The city's side wall goes on forever too, running south to north beside the never-ending rows of fields, perhaps only stopping at the foot of the mist shrouded Wu Meng mountains several leagues in the distance.

As our boat sails closer I see glimpses of ornate temples and mansions rising behind the walls. Their green and red rooftops majestically sweep heavenward at the corners. Atop the towering city walls red-armored soldiers pace back and forth behind protective parapets. Stone watchtowers rise up high against the backside of the walls every fifty paces or so. Why do they need so many soldiers or watchtowers? Who could possibly be so witless as to try to break through or climb over those massive walls?

Me, I guess. Well, I'm not really going to break through or climb over the walls. I'm going to walk through the front gate, somehow get past all of the emperor's guards, and rescue Lian. No problem.

But I never imagined anything so enormous, so fortified, as Quanli. With the wedding only a day away, how can I hope to find Lian in there, let alone rescue her? Somehow, we'll have to.

Hordes of commoners in their peasant grays fill the highway that passes in front of the city wall. A few dressed in purples, greens, reds, and blues move within the press of people, indicating various ranks of officials, scholars, soldiers, and servants. Most of the throng make their way on foot, while a few travel on donkeys, water buffaloes, and even carriages.

The river way is almost as crowded as the highway. It becomes even more crowded the closer we get to the city gate. Small fishing boats similar to ours are abundant. Merchant ships and cargo transports also move up and down the river.

We reach the common docks near the city's River Gate in little under an hour. The stink of rotten fish and rancid sweat is pervasive. The common docks' network of fifty or more long bamboo walkways jut out into the water, hosting thousands of moored fishing boats and small merchant boats.

Rough looking dock workers bustle about the walkways wearing little more than ragged trousers and broad bamboo hats as they adjust mooring ropes, fix fishing nets, check on boats, and perform other tasks. The bamboo planks of the dock's walkways have grayed and frayed with age and overuse. As have most of the dock workers.

As our boat glides in alongside the common dock, a tall ancient looking man with a long gray scraggly beard hobbles quickly to our boat. He reeks of rice wine and the stench of the unbathed. When he plants his dirty foot and long yellowed toenails on top of the mooring post to keep us from tying off our boat, I'm tempted to push him into the water. I want to get off the boat. I'm also desperate to spare my nose of his awful smell.

With a proud tug, he straightens the tattered blue coat he wears over his bare chest and squints at us with a one-eye-closed defiant stare. "One copper zhu to dock." His voice sounds as gravelly as it is surly. "If you can't pay, you can't dock."

He grunts and lifts his foot off the docking post when I hand him a copper zhu from my bag. After a close examination of the zhu, the man tucks it in a bag hanging from his trousers.

Scratching the side of his nose with one hand and his belly with the other, he gives us a crooked smile. The dock lurches and water slaps up in a spray onto us and against the side of the dock as we step off our boat onto the walkway.

"One more zhu for every day you dock," the worker says with a chuckle as we walk past. "If you can't pay, we keep your boat until you can."

I want to protest the high fee, but Cai whispers, "Don't. If you haggle, he'll charge us more. He can charge whatever he wants. This is the only place we can dock safely within a league."

I scowl at the man, but keep my mouth shut. But after we walk out of hearing distance, I huff, "It's robbery. There should be a law against that."

Cai laughs. "Imperial Law that lets them do it. The more they charge, the more the Imperial Ministry collects from them in taxes. Both are happy with the arrangement."

I shake my head and bite my tongue but keep on walking. After we leave the common docks and several minutes of pressing through crowds headed toward the city's River Gate entrance, we pass the Imperial Docks and their broad and brightly painted green walkways, fancy roofed pavilions, and fine dressed dock workers. Everything about the Imperials Docks makes it clear it's reserved for ships and floating mansions belonging only to those with bulging bags of gold zhu's.

My chest tightens and I suddenly stop. "Lian's here," I breathe out in a hurried breath.

Tied off with dozens of arm-thick mooring ropes, the Imperial Warship that sailed off with Lian now floats in the section of the

Imperial Docks closest to the River Gate. Of course, I knew she would be here, but seeing the towering ship here in Quanli makes it more real. The emperor has her.

The crowds bump and jostle me from behind, forcing me to move on and turn my gaze from the ship to the city's entrance through the heavily guarded River Gate. Anxiousness builds inside me. We have to hurry. Who knows what tortures Lian might be going through? We can't waste any time. We have to get into the city and find her.

Nervousness mixes with my anxiousness as our place in the crowded lines of people moves closer to the city gates. Will the Red Phoenix Guard know who we are and why we're here? Did Lord Zheng suspect I would follow them here and tell all the city soldiers to watch for me? It sounds crazy, but he could have. He will not easily forget me since I stole his horse and nearly escaped with Lian.

At the gate, one of the soldiers in red armor stops us without looking up from his tattered logbook. "Names and place of origin?"

Cai squeezes my arm hard when I open my mouth to respond, reminding me that it's his place as the man to answer, not mine. I bow and tighten my lips closed, trying not to let it bother me. No matter how much I want to change how things are, I will never be able to if I never take the chance. Still, Cai is right. Now is not the time. So, I force myself to relax and smile, and let Cai answer.

"Ren Sheng and Ren Lu from Wu Chu," Cai says, uttering the fake names with ease.

The guard never looks up from his logbook as he records the answer and asks, "Purpose in the city?"

I wince as Cai fakes excitement in his reply. "Holy marriage of the new Wife Divine."

The soldier grunts. From the conversations all around us, that's why more than half the people have come to the city, bringing more crowds and more work for the gate guards.

Sounding bored and annoyed, the guard repeats the same instructions he has given to everyone else who has entered the city. "City and ward gates close at sunset. Twenty blows from a thrashing rod to any found on the Imperial Highway or outside their ward after the drumbeats of curfew sound. Fifty blows for attempts to scale city and ward walls at any time. Eighty blows to any who enter a city canal."

Relief replaces nervousness when the guard finally waves us through the gate. Once inside the city, the crowds spread a little. Even though the massive road is three hundred paces wide, the road's middle is nearly empty, reserved for travel of imperial officials, nobles, and aristocrats. Commoners travelling from the city gate toward the palace must use a narrow strip twenty-five paces wide on the east side of the highway, while another twenty-five-pace strip on the west side is for commoner traffic heading away from the palace.

Giant willows line the highway, making me feel like I'm walking along a never-ending forested plaza rather than a wide thoroughfare. Every so often the highway intersects with much smaller side roads that lead to the city's different neighborhoods, or wards as the gate guard called them.

Roasted chestnuts, ginger, tangerine peel, and the smells of other foods and spices waft through the air as we pass the different wards. Cai eyes with interest the roads leading to these neighborhoods as we pass them. It's only been a few hours since we ate. Is Cai seriously wanting to eat now? We're finally in Quanli and Lian is likely somewhere within the palace grounds. I want to get there as soon as possible. Right now, food is only a distraction.

When we come to one of the wider roads leading to a ward, the stench of manure, pig slop, and other animal odors hit hard. I plug my nose and quicken my pace to hurry past it. Cai's fingers wrap around the inside of my elbow and jerk me back to a stop.

"Gales! What are you…"

Before I finish, he pulls on my arm again to drag me down the road to the ward. "The East Market is over there. We should go buy something."

Surprise and annoyance take me at Cai's order and rough treatment. This is how other men act, not Cai. What is wrong with him?

Annoyance almost gets the best of me as I consider giving him a quick elbow jab to the ribs. But I stop when I notice Cai's expression. Concern. Nervousness. Not for me, but something else. Something behind us on the Imperial Highway.

I turn to look over my shoulder, but Cai stops me with a slight shake of his head. "Someone follows us," he whispers. "The East Market might be our best chance to lose them."

My stomach tightens. Who could be following us? No. I don't really want to know, but no matter how hard I try I can't push the likely answers from my mind. None of them are pleasant, but some are definitely worse than others.

Pigeons coo at us from above as we pass beneath the shade of giant willows toward the market. Two Red Phoenix Guards at the ward's gate look up from their hushed laughter and whispers to glance at us. But as we pass, they return to their private conversation without a word to us.

The stink and sound of animals amplifies once inside the market. Grunts and squeals sound from stalls full of pigs lining each side of the lane. A round, heavy-set man in mud-stained grays greets us with a toothless smile and a bow. With a thick spike he strikes a small set of chimes he holds above his head, sounding out a simple melody. To the ting of the chimes, he croaks out in song the most dreadful poem I have ever heard.

Pink flesh belly big
Young sow fertile pig
Low pay value best
Home take joyful jig

We force a smile at him as we push through the crowds to hurry past, only to come into hearing range of another vendor standing near his penned-up pigs, treating marketgoers with his own melodic chime tinging and awful off-key poetry singing. I smile, certain that the poetry can't get worse.

But the further we venture into the market, the chimes and songs create a painful cacophony with all the different vendors trying to out-sing their neighbors as they boast of the questionable virtues of their sows and hogs.

We quicken our pace not only to distance ourselves from our followers, but to get away from the pig vendors' dreadful noise. Even the pigs sound miserable, bellowing and grunting a discordant chorus.

Before we reach the end of the pig lane and near the goat market, we hear the strum of a pipa ahead. And more singing and more awful poetry. Cai and I exchange pained smiles. Our path through the market will not be a pleasant one.

Then, the chimes and music behind us goes quiet in a jumbled, disjointed wave. The crowds hush into panicked whispers. Over my shoulder, I search for the cause among the throng of people. I see little more than the heads and shoulders of the people.

Then, where we first entered the market, the crowd parts in a frantic frenzy as if a mad water buffalo bullied its way through the crowd. But it's not a water buffalo. Through breaks in the crowd, I see the red and gold demon-wolf masks and black robes and armor of two Shashyao.

Chapter 31
Qiu Meilin – Weaponless

"Zhangchi literally means the ability to wield Chi as a weapon. In terms of bladesmithing it's an amazing work of art, but in a master's hand it can be fatal against even the most gifted Shen Blessed."
- Hidden Scrolls of Quingping: Practices of Engagement

Shashyao!" I breathe out in an urgent whisper. Cai and I leap into a run. We shove and bump our way through the crowds. Curses follow us. We race past the scowls of the pipa playing goat vendors. Some silence their poetry singing so they can add their own curses to the chorus of others, which is actually a great blessing since I would much rather hear a goat vendor curse than sing.

When we reach the end of the goat stalls, we sprint up a lane lined with penned up water buffalos. One grunts when I bump its cage. Angering a caged water buffalo is never a good idea. But I have bigger worries at the moment. How in the name of the Two did the Shashyao find us so easily? Right now, it doesn't matter. If they catch us there will be no mercy. The slice of their swords will be sharp, swift, and fatal.

People start to move out of our way, making it easier to race down the lane past the stalls of other water buffalos. Before long, the boom of barrel drums greet us as we enter the slave lane. Thousands of slaves sit in weary silence, chained and caged. Only layers of filth and ragged strips of cloth cover their skin. The sight sickens me.

I want to open their cages to set them free. But each slaver has several armed guards keeping vigilant watch over their valuable wares. With my boon and Wind gift I might be able to overpower them, but I would unlikely manage to actually free any of the slaves before the Shashyao caught up to us.

Still, as I hurry past, I can't keep my gaze from the sickening sight of these chained people. Many are from Yemaren with tan skin and husky, block-shaped bodies. Others have the pinkish hue of skin common to the tall and gangly Menshk people of the south and the heavy-set Hari people of the west. Only a few cages hold females.

The slave sellers ignore us as they sing of their slaves' remarkable strength and talents. Past the slavers, we try to lose the Shashyao by continually changing direction and turning down different paths within the market. We weave through crowd after crowd, past vendors of leather works, apothecary supplies, porcelain goods, silks, and ramie cloth. No matter how fast we go or how many turns we make, excited gasps and panicked screams draw closer, alerting us to the fast-approaching Shashyao.

Smells of roast pork, oyster sauce dumplings, garlic chicken, and other savory and sweet scents rise up when we enter the restaurant district. Unlike the ordered rows of the other lanes, this area has an open courtyard. A wide cobblestone lane lined with red and purple flowers runs through its middle. A large grassy area lies on the right side of the lane with the far edges shaded by giant chestnut trees and the long stone wall that marks the ward's border.

Pear trees bloom with bright white blossoms and plum trees blossom in vibrant pinks in several places amid the grass. Families, couples, and even a few ministry workers eat at tables, on benches, and on the grass.

On the lane's left side, food vendors cook and sell food under colorful awnings. Herb and vegetable gardens grow near a few stalls. Like a gridwork, every fifty paces small lanes run between the different stalls from the main cobbled lane to other food stalls and other sections of the market ward.

The vendors do not sing here, but it has its own music. The clang of pots, jingle of coins, bartering and laughter, shouts for food and shuffle of steaming bowls full rice, vegetables, meat soup and dumplings.

"Ginger pepper partridge?"

A young boy steps in front of me and shoves a spice-covered cooked bird on a stick into my face. It smells delicious, but even without its head and feathers it reminds me too much of the pigeons strutting about the market. Before I can tell the boy no, his mouth drops open, his eyes fly wide, he drops the roasted bird at my feet, and runs away.

A hush grips the market, but only for moment. Plates clang. Chairs and tables upturn. The thump and thud of rapid foot falls race around the market.

"Shashyao! Shashyao!" sounds in frenzied whispers. Customers and vendors stampede in different directions. Even the pigeons flutter and flee in a chorus of coos. In a panicked instant, all of the lane's exits clog with men, women, and children deserting the eatery in a hysterical rush.

Together, Cai and I turn to face the Shashyao. The evil smiles of their demon-wolf masks dare us to run. But we have nowhere to go. The crowds of fleeing people block our only escapes. Their steel blades hum as the Fei Chi assassins unsheathe their swords in a quick, fluid motion. Their blades glow as if immersed in a halo of Shen Breath.

Zhangchi. Demon slayers. Fabled names of the Shashyao swords. They are said to be able to slice through diamonds and make the Shashyao invincible. Although the wooden training swords I often used to practice Fei Chi sword forms with would do little to protect me, holding one now would still bring me some comfort. Zhangchi or not, facing a Fei Chi sword master with empty hands is certain death.

"By the Two, we've done nothing wrong," I say. "Please, leave us be."

In near unison, both assassins take a smooth, deliberate step toward us, slicing the air in front of us. The Chi of their swords sings to the boon swelling inside me, tugging at it and beckoning it to break free of my feeble flesh and join the power of Zhangchi.

Those swords sucked the Shen Breath from the lanterns near our village crops back home. Can they steal my own Shen Breath? Instinct whispers to me that even the softest touch of one of those blades will leave me powerless. Both Cai and I step back off the cobbled lane onto the dirt near a small herb garden.

"Defilers of the gods," rasps the one facing me. "By the Two, your hearts will bleed rivers before we finish here."

When teaching the forms Master Jin would often say, "Let patient defense be your friend." He would then add with a playful smile, "A hasty fool attacks too quick. But a dead fool attacks too slow." I might be a fool, but I have no intention of being a dead one.

With one hand outstretched in front of me and the other raised behind my head, I crouch into the dragon stance. To my side I see Cai crouch and spread his hands outward in the stance of the phoenix. My stomach tightens, roiling with guilt and fear for Cai's life. He can't possibly survive the Shashyao unless he uses his gift from Tiānqì Shen. Too many times we cuddled when I should have encouraged him to try his gift. If he uses it now, this will be his first attempt. Maybe he'll be fine, but I can't take that chance.

Before his attacker advances further, I leap in front of Cai, summon the Chi inside me, open my hands, and blast the Shashyao with a fist of wind. The assassin flies back and away. The backlash of the force causes me to stumble backwards into Cai and into a basket overflowing with cabbages. I really need to get better at handling that backlash.

I untangle from Cai and the cabbages and jump to my feet. The other Shashyao advances. He slices Zhangchi down toward me faster than any Fei Chi master I've ever seen. Shen Breath pulses inside me, speeding my agility to twist away from the attack. My hand shoots toward his wrist to disarm him. He spins away and completely around, slicing Zhangchi sideways toward the back of my waist.

I drop into the splits, lean forward, and duck under the blade. It whistles above the back of my neck. In one motion, I plant my palms on the ground and spin my front leg back to sweep his legs. The Shashyao leaps clear, twists in the air, and slices Zhangchi toward me as he falls. The sword cuts into the dirt and a lone cabbage as I roll out of reach.

Only a moment before the masked assassin has his sword out and ready, I'm on my feet in the dragon stance again. The Shashyao slides his feet across the dirt toward me. My heart races at his slow approach.

"Killing me is wrong," I say, between rapid breaths. From the corner of my eyes, I try to spot Cai. I haven't seen him since we untangled. Where is he? I could use his help.

"You are an abomination!" The Shashyao snaps as he moves closer. "You need to pay the price for your sins."

"What sin? That I'm a girl and I prayed in a Shen shrine?"

"With your corruption, you have desecrated their holy dwelling place. For this you must be destroyed."

The Shashyao holds his sword steady with his slow approach. I back away. I can't beat him on my own or unarmed. I need a weapon. A staff. Chair. Or even some pots and pans. Something to give me more of a chance.

Like a flash of light, the Shashyao lunges. The tip of Zhangchi races for my heart. I jump back and up. At the same time, I face my palms toward the Shashyao and unleash a blast of wind. As I hoped, I fly several paces backwards out of reach. The Shashyao stumbles backward too. His sword flies from his hand, landing near an open fire where a pair of chickens roast on a spit.

Using a burst of wind from my palms, I fly toward his sword. But I'm too slow. The Shashyao retrieves his sword while I'm still paces away.

I land by the fire and grab the wooden handle of the iron roasting spit. In defiance, I fling the sizzling chickens off the spit toward the Shashyao. He laughs, sidestepping the cooked birds. I raise the iron spit before me as if it's a magnificent blade.

The Shashyao laughs louder. "You are not only an abomination, you are a fool. Your defiance is futile. Accept your punishment and die with what little honor you still have."

Through his demon-wolf mask, his eyes follow mine as we circle each other, waiting for an opening.

"You say I have little honor, yet you hunt me down simply because I prayed to Tiānqì Shen. Where is the honor in that? Tiānqì Shen is a woman. Tell me, does her own presence there defile her own shrine? If not, why would my presence defile it? That makes no sense."

"She is Shen! You are a lower than the worms and filthier still. Your very breath defiles and disgraces all around you."

"Because I'm a girl or because I'm a girl that sought the Shen's help?"

"Both!"

"If I'm so miserably wretched, why would Tiānqì Shen bestow a boon upon me?"

He growls, slicing Zhangchi at me. I sidestep and parry. The clang of Zhangchi on my iron roasting spit fills me with relief. Perhaps, Zhangchi can't slice diamonds in half after all, let alone a simple iron roasting spit.

"Blasphemer. You steal a gift from the gods and dare claim it was freely given. Every moment you breathe is an affront to the Shen. Your death cannot come too swift."

I continue to circle, adjusting the angle of my weapon to match that of Zhangchi. "I'm a blasphemous thief? Amazing! If I'm so wicked, why would Tiānqì Shen take the time to talk to me?"

The Shashyao pauses. The steel in his eyes softens, but only a moment. His body tenses and the grip on his sword tightens.

"Lying witch!" he spews. "The Shen speak only to Lord Emperor Xiang Hu, Chosen of Heaven."

"And what do the Shen tell the emperor? To slaughter innocent women simply because they want to pray?"

"No woman is innocent. You are all fallen!"

"Says the emperor. What about the men you slaughter at his command simply because they have Blood of the Two?"

"We kill only those who have demon blood flowing in their veins."

"Interesting," I say adjusting my grip on the iron spit. "Does that mean you plan on killing the emperor too? Test his blood. You might be surprised to find it's the same as those you say have demon blood,"

The Shashyao howls in rage and strikes in a flurry of slashes, pushing me back toward a row of stalls where noodles hang to dry. I parry the attacks best I can, but if not for the strength and speed granted from my boon, I could not withstand the power and pace of his strikes. But with his fury, his discipline falters. His strikes grow sloppy. The balance in his stance wavers.

I fake a misstep, stumbling backward. When the Shashyao rages forward to take advantage, I spin from his attack and stab the tip of the iron spit into the back side of his lower ribs. The Shashyao screams. His skin sizzles as the still hot iron point pierces his flesh.

Before I completely withdraw my weapon, the Shashyao turns and swings his sword in a wild sweep. Unable to parry, I jump back out of the way, but not far enough. The tip of Zhangchi nicks my cheek. It's only a brief sting of pain, but the touch of the sword's enchanted steel pulls the surging strength of the Chi inside me. My boon vanishes.

Exhausted and weak, I collapse on my back into long strands of noodles hanging between drying posts. The roasting spit falls from the Shashyao's side and clangs onto the cobbles as he steps toward me. As he hovers over me, his mask hides his mouth from view, but I see the gloating smile in his eyes behind the peep holes.

He presses the tip of Zhangchi against my heart and in a voice full of mockery and scorn asks, "Tell me, when Tiānqì Shen spoke to you, did she tell you how pitifully you would die beneath my blade?"

"No!" I say with a defiant scowl. "She told me to always keep my oath to her."

A scoffing grunt sounds behind his demon-wolf mask. "And what oath is that?"

My gaze hardens as I glare up at him. With steady firmness I answer, "To do all I can to save my sister. Tell me, mighty warrior, slayer of so-called demons, what oaths do you make and keep? To save lives or destroy them? Do you truly believe your oaths bring you honor? Spare me or slay me, but I will die knowing the honor of the oath I keep. Can you say the same?"

The Shashyao hesitates. His grip on Zhangchi relaxes and its tip rises a finger-width from my heart. A hint of uncertainty shows in his eyes, but it's only a brief moment before anger takes its place.

"You will die, but not with honor." His grip on Zhangchi tightens and once again pushes the tip of his sword against my heart.

Chapter 32
Chao Cai – Flowers, Fruit, and Fish Oil

"While some petitioners might have no understanding or expectation of receiving a gift, when an oath is made with a plea for help, the Shen might still elect to grant the gift. For such petitioners it can be a struggle to learn how to use a gift, that is if they ever even recognize its receipt."

- Hidden Scrolls of Quingping: Study in Oath Criticalities

What is Meilin thinking? She leaps between me and the Shashyao, putting herself in danger. Before I can try to save her, she flies backwards into me like a boulder shot from a siege engine. We tumble and tangle in a heap. I land on my back, hitting my head hard on the ground. My vision blurs and my thoughts go fuzzy. It takes a few moments for me to think clearly and remember what's going on. The Shashyao.

I leap to my feet and almost faint from getting up too my fast. Once I'm steady and the dizziness passes, I spot Meilin. She faces the armed Shashyao with an iron roasting spit from one of the stall's fire pits. At least she managed to find some kind of weapon.

Kicking cabbages and an empty basket out of my way, I rush to help her. I have no weapon as I hurry down the cobble stone path. No weapon except my gift from Tiānqì Shen. I focus on my oath to the Shen goddess and summon the Shen Breath inside me. The strength and energy of its Chi flares beneath my flesh and through my veins. That's when I see the other Shashyao racing with sword raised toward his companion and Meilin circling each other.

He's closer to them than me, but I run to try to intercept him. My legs carry me faster than I've ever believed possible. Still, I'm too far away. He'll get to them before I can. And together, the two Shashyao will easily cut Meilin to the ground.

My fingers rub the palms of my hands where yesterday I stamped the Wind gift mark. The symbols warm my palms, anxious to unleash their power. Meilin told me when she uses her gift it's like blasting a torrent of wind from her palms. The force is so strong she has to brace herself to keep it from knocking her backwards. I can't take time to stop to brace myself. Running full speed toward the second Shashyao, I aim the inked marks on my palms at him and summon Tiānqì Shen's gift.

My palms burn with energy, but no wind—not even a breeze—bursts from my hands. At first, I think I must have done something wrong, but then I see the rising plume of plum blossoms and red and purple petals rush toward me. Amid the blossoms and flowers, a squawking chicken, bits of paper, and a sword-flailing Shashyao fly through the air toward me.

I dive out the way of the wind-flying Shashyao only to be hit in the face with a shower of petals and an angry chicken. The Shashyao flies over me and lands on a table covered with fried lizards on a stick.

I leap to my feet and grab a pole support from one of the stalls' awnings. It might not be as good as a Shashyao sword, but in the right hands a staff can be deadly. Master Jin complimented me more than once on my own expertise.

Still lying on the table among a scrambled collection of fried lizards, I push the end of my pole hard against the Shashyao's throat before he even has a chance to lift his head. He gasps for air and his eyes widen beneath his mask. I'm not certain if this is one of the Shashyao that slaughtered my army friends and has been hunting me ever since, but I have no reason to believe he's not.

His sword is gone. My eyes leave his for a moment to search for it, but I can't see it. When he shifts his body a bit on the table, I push the staff harder against his throat. The Shen Breath still pulses strong and hot inside me. Shashyao are dangerous, but this one is not hurting me or anyone else until I get some answers.

"How many of you still hunt me?"

No answer. I push the staff even deeper into the flesh of his throat and shout, "You murdered my friends. Their innocent blood will stain your soul with eternal shame. Ending your life will bring me no remorse. Give me a reason to let you live a bit longer."

"Just the two of us hunt you for now," He answers in a choked whisper. "But others know of your escape. They know of the girl's abomination too. Kill me and they will rise up and hunt you down as well."

"How did you find us so easily? What magic led you to us so fast?"

The Shashyao laughs. "No magic. It only takes a zhu or two to get even your closest friends to betray you, especially when they think you are already dead. It is no secret that before you left for the army that you were in love with the future Wife Divine. And everyone knows that the Wife Divine's sister, the abomination you travel with, tried to stop the Imperial Army from taking the future Wife Divine to the capital. Where else in your hopelessness would you go to try to get her back? We simply had to wait at the city gates and watch for your arrival."

I feel like a witless fool. The Shashyao makes it sound like my and Meilin's plans were obvious. Maybe they were to these Shashyao, but what do others really know? Do they know what Meilin and I look like? Could these Shashyao possibly have had time to give other Shashyao much information about us? If so, why aren't there more here to help them? Perhaps these two thought they wouldn't need any help. Or maybe this one simply lies about what others might know.

If I let him live, he will tell others about Meilin and me. He will continue to hunt us down. And next time, he will bring more Shashyao to make sure they finish us. Even with my short time in the Imperial Army I have never killed anyone. I have no desire to change that now, but what choice do I have?

My thoughts distract me enough that without realizing it I relax my grip and how hard I push the pole tip against the Shashyao's throat. He moves so fast that before I retighten my grip, he grabs the pole, twists it out of my hands, and swings it at my head. I duck under the strike and sweep kick the table legs. Two of the legs break, sending the Shashyao and a pile of fried lizards to the ground.

Too late I realize that his sword slides off the table with him. He had been lying on it. He grabs the sword before I have a chance. He rolls to his feet quickly moving into the Fei Chi sword form of Dragonfly Dances. In tight back and forth sweeping motions, his blade slices toward me at unbelievable speed.

With my Shen Breath powered boon, I barely evade his attacks. I manage to grab the awning pole again and try to parry his strikes, but one slice from his blade cuts the pole in half. I parry with the two halves, but he quickly cuts those down, leaving them worthless as weapons.

I spin and dance out of reach of his blade, moving back and in between the different market stalls. I throw eggplant, winter melons, and baskets of dumplings at him. I knock over tables of skewered vegetables and meats to block his advances. No matter what I do or where I duck or retreat, the Shashyao's blade follows. He's relentless.

I think about summoning my Wind gift again. I might be able to use it to knock him off balance or even crash him into a stall or tree. But I worry that I might accidentally fly his sword from his hand into my heart. Not a pleasant idea. I also feel the power of my boon decreasing as use it to keep out of reach of his sword slices, thrusts, and chops. I have no idea how much longer the Shen Breath will sustain me. If I'm to survive,

I have to beat the Shashyao fast.

The heat of an open fire warms my legs. In between sidesteps and crouches to dodge the slash of his sword, I glance at the fire pit for a weapon. No roasting spit, but a fat fish fries in the sizzling oil of a large iron skillet.

I roll to the ground to avoid a slice from the Shashyao swords and rise to my knee with the pan's wooden handle in my grip, I fling the pan's oil and fish into his face. He howls, but only for a moment. His mask and armor protect him from most of the hot oil, causing him temporary discomfort, but fueling his anger.

He attacks, slices, and lunges with renewed effort and increased passion. If not for the small amount of Shen Breath I have left and the frying pan to deflect the ferocity of his attacks, I would be dead already. His attacks push me backward through the stalls onto the cobble stone path. Hopelessness grows within me. My Shen Breath fades, and I have no better weapon than the frying pan to parry his attacks.

I can only hope the Shashyao will make a mistake or grow tired soon. Neither of which seem likely. Prayers to Tiānqì Shen and the Two fill my mind. Please honor me with your help, lest my oaths and life soon be doomed.

Chapter 33
Qiu Meilin – No Mercy

"Bitter wind blasts wretched flailing fall.
Deathly arms rise near-dead flesh to maul.
Humble lips scream divine rescue I plead.
Soft limbs embrace, no need after all."
- Private Journal of Qiu Meilin

My heart pounds hard and fast beneath Zhangchi's sharp point. The grip on the Shashyao's sword hilt is so tense that his arm trembles. I have little hope that my words convinced him to spare me. No mercy shows in his eyes. Yet I still live. What is he thinking? What is he waiting for?

Except for the distant sounds of the city and a few shuffles and bumps somewhere among the food stalls, an eerie silence holds the market courtyard. I lay in a long, tangled clump of wet noodles between two drying posts. I have no strength left to fight the Shashyao. I fear even my slightest movement might prompt him to plunge Zhangchi into my heart. I debate speaking to him again. My words might send him into an even greater rage than before.

"Why don't you help me?" I want to shout to Tiānqì Shen. But my oaths to her and her gifts to me are not a guarantee of protection. Tiānqì Shen said herself it's not enough to ask, I must act. I must do my part. But what if I do all I can, and my actions aren't enough? Will she step in to save me? What of the Two? Will they help me? Aren't all the people of Dashi their creations? Do they ever take sides? Or do they simply leave it to the whims of their children the Shen to decide when they will or will not give gifts? How far will the Shen or the Two go to help us keep our oaths?

There's so much I don't understand. But when the Shashyao finally decides to finish me, none of it will matter. My thoughts go to Lian. Will she even know I tried to save her? Will she even care?

A screeching squeal interrupts my thoughts. A blur of orange leaps from a stall awning onto the Shashyao's face. Snubby squeals again. His legs wrap around the assassin's neck, belly pushes against his mask, and his fingers pull the man's topknot.

I inhale deep as Zhangchi presses harder against my chest before clanging harmless to the ground. The Shashyao curses and in a frenzy tries to pull Snubby off his face. As tired as I am, I roll to the side as fast as I am able, which is quite slow, and grab Zhangchi's black hilt.

As my fingers wrap around the paired lines of rubies and emeralds embedded in the blade's handle, my exhaustion vanishes. Chi flows into me like Shen Breath bursting from a thousand lanterns, giving me back my strength and replenishing my boon. It's like the sword's blade draws and stores Chi from other sources into itself and then through the handle gifts the Chi for its wielder to draw upon it as needed.

But it's much more than that. The strength and agility I feel is significantly greater than what I have felt when my boon has been at full strength in the past. The Shen Breath stored within the sword has not only refueled my gift from Tiānqì Shen, but it has magnified it.

That adds to the questions that have bothered me since I first fought the Shashyao. Are they Shen-Blessed? If so, why does Emperor Hu let them live, while he specifically uses them to hunt down and kill other Shen-Blessed. If they are not, how can their strength and speed match that of a Shen-Blessed?

I don't think they are Shen-Blessed, since I doubt Emperor Hu would allow them to live if they were. But the sword must grant the Chi's power to any who wield it—Shen-Blessed or not. And for Shen-Blessed, it doubles their power. It's the only thing that makes sense. But I still can't help wondering why Hu allows anyone but himself to have access to so much power. Unless he thinks it's needed in order to wipe out what he feels is a greater threat—letting Shen-Blessed live.

The howls and squeals from Snubby grow more animated as the Shashyao tries to get him off his face. With one final curse, the man finally manages to pull Snubby off and throw him to the ground. Snubby rolls across the cobbles, pops onto his feet with little trouble, scurries over to me, climbs up my back, and perches on my shoulder.

With a high pitch laugh, Snubby bounces up and down, and wags his fingers in the direction of the Shashyao as if saying, "Ha! Ha! I win! You lose!"

The Shashyao tenses when he realizes I hold Zhangchi. I wonder how long the power of the Chi he gained from the sword will last now that it's no longer in his grasp. It doesn't matter. I'm confident I will have no problem handling him now.

The Shashyao keeps his gaze on me as he drops to his knees. "Make my death quick," he says. "I welcome the honors of Heaven that await me for trying to cleanse this world of abominations such as you."

"You don't know much about pleading for mercy, do you?" I say with a laugh.

He spits on the ground. "Xie spawn! Defiler of the gods! I would never lower myself to beg anything of you. End me and be done with it."

I shake my head. "I meant what I said before. My oaths to Tiānqì Shen are about saving lives, not ending them. Don't misunderstand. For all the murders I'm sure you have committed in the emperor's name, I would feel little guilt in ending your life. But I don't need your blood on my hands."

Behind his mask, hate fills his eyes. "You are a fool! If you let me live, you will never know peace. I will hunt you down till Heaven calls me home."

"You don't know much about Heaven either, do you? When your time comes, I'm confident the call won't be coming from there."

The Shashyao stiffens further. "You…"

I'm done listening and talking to him. He crumbles to the ground as I land a quick snap kick to the side of his head. I lay my hand on his chest to make sure his chest still lifts and lowers with his breath. It was a forceful kick, but not as forceful and hard as I wanted. Still, he should lay unconscious for a while.

Snubby chatters at me as I lay Zhangchi on the ground and hurry to undo the straps on the Shashyao that hold the sword's scabbard on his back. I'm keeping Zhangchi. I might need its help to rescue Lian. After some effort, I strap the scabbard on my back and sheathe Zhangchi safely in place.

I scoop Snubby into my arms and stroke the fur behind his ears. "Thank you, little friend. You saved me once again."

A shout of pain and anger sounds from across the courtyard. It takes a few moments to spot the source. About hundred paces away on the cobblestone path, Cai tries to hold off the other Shashyao's flurry of sword slices and thrusts with nothing more than a large metal pan. Considering the mismatch Cai is doing okay, but from the sag in his posture and the uncertainty in his step, he's tiring. He won't last long.

"Stay here," I tell Snubby as I set the cuddly ball of fur on the ground. "Cai needs help."

Snubby whimpers. I smile at the pouty face the monkey always makes when I turn my attention from him to Cai. After a glance at my palms to make sure my Wind gift marks haven't faded too much, I tap into my boon. Wind blasts from my palms, flying me across the courtyard toward Cai and the Shashyao.

The distance seems so far as I watch Cai's parries grow weaker and weaker. Cai drops to his knees and barely rolls out of reach of a downward slash. He rises onto one knee holding the pan with two hands, but it's not enough to keep the Zhangchi blade of the Shashyao at bay. The pan drops from Cai's hand as the sword slices a large gash in his shoulder.

Whatever Shen Breath Cai had left, the touch of that blade stole it from him. The Shashyao laughs. Cai is now defenseless. Drawing even more on the Chi of my own boon, I push a magnificent gale of wind from my palms. Accelerating faster than a fish hawk diving for its prey, I steer toward the Shashyao and slam into him.

The whoosh of air punched from his lungs and the crack of ribs breaking fills my ears as my shoulder drives into the Shashyao's side. His sword clangs to the ground and he continues to twist and flop through the air even after I stop flying. He crashes back first onto a barrel of ale, breaking its slats, spilling its liquid, and smashing the cask to the ground. The man moans and lies motionless except for a slight shudder from one of his boots.

I turn to Cai. Holding his bleeding shoulder, he lays curled on the ground pale skinned and heaving and gasping for air. I search the area for the Shashyao's sword, knowing a touch of its handle will heal Cai and restore his strength, but I can't see it anywhere. Frustrated at its disappearance, I kneel beside Cai and lift him to his knees, I hug him close and place his hands on the hilt of the Zhangchi sheathed on my back.

Color returns to his skin. His breathing slows to normal. The flow of blood from his shoulder stops and the wound heals. His body warms and I can feel strength return to his muscles. The warmth of his breath brushes across my cheek as his eyes open to meet my gaze.

"Hello." He smiles, glances down at my lips, back up at my eyes, and wraps his arms around my back holding me even closer. "Why didn't you tell me this is how you rescue people? I would have let the Shashyao find us a long time ago."

My heart pounds and I can't help but smile. As I do, he moves his lips closer to mine. But before they touch, shouts and the thump of several boots on cobblestones sound behind me. Cai pulls back and frowns as he looks over my shoulder.

"The Red Phoenix Guard," he says. "We have to go."

Chapter 34
Qiu Lian – Truths Unveiled

"Floral floor, aloes walls, and a painting so fine.
Oh, lovely palace prison, chamber cell divine.
Endless tutor torture lessons deathly dull to learn.
Flee. Escape. Garden refuge calls, before you lose your mind."
- A lotus leaf

Beside a bright blue lotus flower on an almost perfectly round green lotus leaf, the elegantly stroked characters of the poem stare up at me. The lotus flower and leaf lay neatly on the little table in front of my peony vase by my purple veil. Where did the flower and leaf come from?

Neither the lotus flower nor leaf were there when I woke this morning. They weren't there after my breakfast of fried squid and cinnamon jellyfish. Neither were they there after my tutor sessions on chopstick etiquette, no-teeth smiles, and how to cup my hand when waving to crowds. They definitely weren't there when Lord Zheng tested my memory on my wedding vows. Nor after Zheng stormed from the room after I sipped from the practice wedding chalice and accidentally burped extra loud.

Right after Zheng left, I stopped at the table to smell the peonies on my way to the balcony to admire the gardens. No lotus flower or poem bearing leaf then. But as my eyes followed the cobblestone path winding beneath the white and pink apricot blossoms, a light tap sounded behind me. When I turned, no one was there. But the lotus flower and leaf could clearly be seen.

My fingers trace the edge of the leaf as I read the poem again. An invitation? I smile at the thought. No matter how much I deserve the torture my lessons bring, I want a break. Besides, with the wedding happening tomorrow who knows if I'll ever have any time to myself again?

I hide the leaf poem under my sleeping mat and tuck the lotus flower in the vase among the peonies. I grab my veil off the table and put it on before I head to the balcony and climb out. The vivid colors and floral scents of the gardens breathe new life into me. I love it here. Birds sing. Little creatures chatter. Insects buzz and chirp. Everything is so alive. Even the longing for Cai and pang of guilt for his death that often haunts me softens here. As much I can never forgive myself for what I did to Cai, he would want me to enjoy these gardens. He was sentimental that way.

As I approach the pavilion, the garden's crystal lake shimmers beneath the afternoon sun. Along the shore red, pink, peach, yellow, white, and purple peonies dip and bow with the breeze. The hedge and tree sculptures of dragons, horses, wolves, and other creatures nearby bring a smile to my lips. The smile dips a little when I see that stumps are all that remain of the sculpture of Zheng hanging from a hippo's tooth.

I try not to frown when my searching fails to spot the gardener anywhere. I thought for sure he would be waiting here for me. But what if the poem invitation wasn't actually from him? What if someone was trying to lure me away from the safety of my room? My stomach sickens with more worry as dozens of "what if's" run through my mind.

Coming here was a bad idea. I turn my back on the pavilion, gather the folds of my dress in my hand, and hurry up the cobbled lane back toward my room. After only a few steps I halt. The folds of my dress drop from my hand and my eyes widen. I can't believe what I see.

In between two flowering magnolias surrounded by a circle of golden rose bushes a new sculpture stands. Impossible. Yesterday only roses grew in the circle. Today a mix of boxwood, yew and spruce grow shaped into the most amazing garden sculpture I have ever seen. Sculpted in hedge and tree, a beautiful young woman dressed in flowing robes stands high on a pedestal encircled by the sun, moons, stars, and lightning. Beneath her feet a majestic crane, fierce dragon, fiery phoenix, noble horse, and mighty tiger kneel around her. With outstretched arms she holds a scepter in one hand and a heart in the other.

I step closer. My eyes narrow as I study the statue's face. Its oval shape, point of the chin, soft smile, curve of the cheek, slope of the nose, and arch of the eyebrows seem familiar. They remind me of Meilin a little, but not quite. Or maybe Mother. No. I lean in closer and gasp. It can't be. In our little bronze mirror at home or on the river's surface, I've only seen my reflection a few times and never a clear look, but I think the young woman in the statue is meant to be me.

"Do you like it, Divine One?" The deep voice of the gardener startles me but makes me smile too. "I wanted to capture the essence of your ethereal beauty. What do you think?"

With his bamboo hat tilted low to cover his face, the gardener leans against the trunk of a flowering magnolia near the statue. He wasn't there a moment ago but is now. How does he suddenly appear and disappear like that.

"Are you daft? You've made me look like a goddess!"

The gardener bows his head and puts a fist to his chest. "My apologies, Divine One. My art displeases you. Do not worry. I will remove it at once."

Putting his back to me, he turns toward the garden display. He lifts a hand above his head, palm toward the statue as though with a wave he might be able to make it all disappear. The thought is comical. But when I think about how he suddenly appears and disappears, maybe it's not.

"Wait!" I step toward him and grab his forearm to stop him. I release it immediately and step back tense and awkward. I shouldn't have touched him. Innate Honor doesn't allow women to show such aggression toward a man. Even if the restrictions of Innate Honor no longer apply to me, it's probably not proper for a future Wife Divine to condescend to touch someone so far beneath her station. The irony of the opposing prohibitions is perplexing. But no matter what view you take, touching him in that manner is completely inappropriate.

"Please leave it be," I say, trying to settle my thoughts and emotions. "I love it. But what if it makes the emperor jealous? He could have you executed."

The gardener chuckles, turning toward me, but with his face still blocked by the tip of his hat. "Yes, I suppose. But I doubt any harm will come of it. People will simply think it depicts one of the Shen, Divine One. Rightfully so, since you are so heavenly."

My eyes narrow, peering at him through my veil. "How do you even know what I look like? Laying eyes on the face of a future Wife Divine before her marriage is forbidden."

The gardener falls to his knees and bows nose to the cobbles. "Forgive me, Divine One." Delight fills his voice, leaving no hint of real remorse. "Yesterday, in the gardens you did not wear your veil. Neither did you at the riverfront. So, I peeked… Multiple times. You are so divine. How could I resist?"

I blush at his flattery and smile at the jovial way that he speaks. It puts me at ease and makes me want to listen to whatever he has to say.

"Tell me your name and why you make so much effort to conceal your own face."

He keeps his face down but lifts his forehead a fist-width above the cobbles. "Divine One, so you might never question the truth of who I am, I have been named many things in my life. Son. Brother. Kin. Cast-off. Slave. Master. Shen-cursed. Shen-Blessed. Xie-spawn. Xie-foe. Traitor. Warrior. Assassin. Deliverer. And most recently gardener. But from my mother's womb I was named Fan Wei."

I worry a moment at the mention of assassin, but if he meant me harm why would he tell me he was assassin?

When I remain silent, he continues, "I prefer Fan Wei, or simply Wei, but call me what you wish, Divine One, and I shall be honored… Except, perhaps Son. That might prove awkward."

I cover my mouth to hide a giggle, even though my veil already covers it. "Fan Wei, please show me your face."

"As you desire." He rises from his bow with his hat tipped back, but his eyes lowered to keep them from my already veiled face.

The sight startles me, but I have the composure not to gasp. Big red character markings cover his cheek and forehead on the left side of his face. Make right the wrongs. That's what the characters says, but what does it mean? What wrongs need to be righted? And why would anyone tattoo such an obscure phrase on their face? But as I stare longer at the markings, I notice the characters' splotchy edges and unevenness of their coloring. It's not a tattoo. It's a birthmark. How could that be?

Shen-cursed. He said that was a name he had been called. Is this some kind of curse from the Shen? What could he have done to be so cursed? Or was it a curse placed on his parents before his birth? Or is it a curse at all? Am I making a hasty judgment?

"I see you are enraptured by my alluring eyes and charming smile," he says with a kind chuckle. "My enchanting looks always have that affect."

I blush, embarrassed that in my stare I only noticed the red markings on his face. "Please forgive me. I didn't mean to be insensitive."

He laughs a lighthearted laugh. "No need to apologize," he teases. Even a heavenly beauty as yourself must find it difficult to pull your gaze from such a pleasing visage as mine."

I force myself to look beyond the birthmark at his eyes, nose, lips, cheeks, and chin. If not for the red markings, he would be quite an attractive young man. He's probably only a year or so older than myself.

Taking my gaze off him, I walk past him, past the rose bushes, past the sculpted dragon, and up to the sculpture of me. Standing on the leafy pedestal, the statue's slippered feet are level with my shoulders. My fingers run over the fine, dense leaves. It's so beautiful and realistic. But how could he prune and shape it overnight? The bigger question is, why did he do it?

I sense Wei only a few paces behind me. "For a gardener, you are quite bold in your speech and actions," I say. "Don't you worry that someone might wonder about your overly friendly overtures to the future Wife Divine?"

Wei clears his throat. "I have only been a gardener for a few days. I didn't know friendly overtures from gardeners were forbidden. I'll have to read the rulebook sometime."

I laugh but stop abruptly when Wei appears in front of me. How does he do that? His face is no more than two fists width away from me. The warmth of his breath pushes against my veil.

I step back. Not that I'm afraid of him, but I'm a bit flustered and nervous. I might say or do the wrong thing. But why am I worried about that. I'm a future Wife Divine. A simple gardener shouldn't make me nervous. Especially one with such kind eyes and a kind smile?

"I've only been a future Wife Divine for a few days," I say, looking away from his eyes. He's right. They really are alluring. "Still, I'm pretty sure any overtures between a gardener and myself would be considered too friendly."

A grin spreads across his face, and he steps away. He pulls a pair of gardening shears from a pouch hooked onto his belt and starts to trim a few leaves on the phoenix sculpture. Without looking up from his work he asks in a jovial tone, "You think I'm too friendly? I apologize. I thought being trapped in your room with tutors and lords all day, you might welcome a friend."

I'm glad my veil hides my smile. Being out of my room, talking to Wei has been a wonderful escape. Still, I'm not sure it's appropriate for a Wife Divine to talk so freely with a gardener—well at least someone pretending to be a gardener. It's not that I care what people think. It's just that, even though I have no desire to be the emperor's bride, I'm still promised to him. Are these visits a form of disloyalty? Worse, could they be considered treason? Not that Wei cares, but if anyone knew, it could still put him in serious danger.

"I welcome friendship," I say. "But I wonder what else I might be welcoming."

Wei stops pruning for a moment and looks up at me with a big grin. "Ah, there are so many ways to answer that, don't you think?"

I shake my head with a pinched smile. "Can't you ever be serious?"

He grins wider. "More serious than you can imagine, but that's not fun. Life is meant to be enjoyed."

"Wei, tell the truth. Why are you here? Why do you pretend to be a gardener? Why did you sculpture me into the tree? Why did you invite me here? Why do you risk your life paying so much attention to me?"

"So many why's." His eyes narrow and he pushes out his bottom lip as if in deep thought. He looks straight at me as if he can see through my veil. "I seek what I cannot have and look for what is hid."

I fold my arms across my chest. "Thay's no answer. That's a riddle."

Wei grins again as if he won a contest, then returns to pruning the phoenix with his shears. "All the great philosophers answer questions with riddles. It makes them appear wise."

I step toward him and snatch the shears out of his hands. "You're a philosopher now too? Well, wise one, stop with the riddles or watch me walk away. Is that what you want?"

"No." Wei frowns and bows deep. His expression turns serious. "Forgive me, Divine One. I meant no displeasure. The last thing I want is to be absent from your divine presence. If it pleases you, let me answer the best I can."

I grin. Now maybe I'll get to the bottom of what he's up to. I hand back his shears. "Yes, it does please me. But no more riddles."

Wei clears his throat. "I will trust you, Divine One. But know this, if you tell anyone what I say, it could cost me my life."

He puts his shears away, sits cross-legged on the garden floor, and looks up at me. "Many generations ago, one of my ancestors was enslaved by the emperor against the wishes of Ling Yuan, the Divine Lady Empress. Since that time my ancestor's descendants, my people, have lived and suffered as slaves, working the quarries near Quingping. I escaped the quarries to come to Quanli to ask the Divine Lady Empress if she would petition the emperor to free our people."

My eyebrows arch. "I'm surprised. That actually sounds like an honorable pursuit."

The corners of Wei's mouth turn up in an amused smile. "I don't believe that is a compliment."

I shrug. "Think what you think, but I'm also confused. If you seek the Empress, why are you in the gardens posing as a gardener?"

His grin shifts to a guilty frown. He looks down. His fingers pull at a weed in front of his lap. "The whereabouts of the Empress is a guarded secret. The emperor has people executed just for asking about her."

I laugh. "You can't be serious. He wouldn't do such a thing."

Wei looks up and his frown thins. "He would and he has. Over the past three centuries my people have sent more than fifty others like me seeking the Empress, in hopes that she could soften his heart to free our people. By the emperor's orders, all were killed or severely injured for simply trying to find her."

I shake my head. This sounds like a tale Meilin would tell. But what motivation would Wei have to lie to me? It makes no sense. "That doesn't explain why you're here posing as a gardener."

His guilty frown returns. "The answer shames me. I will lose honor in your eyes if I tell you."

He can't see it through the veil, but I hope he can feel the stern look I give him. "You will lose honor in my eyes if you do not tell me."

A hint of a smile returns to his lips. "Divine One, please believe me. When I first saw you on the waterfront, my heart sang with joy at the sight of you. Though I knew you were promised to the emperor, I hoped for the chance to meet you, to get to know you. But no matter what my heart feels, my duty to my people requires that I watch and follow you. For the path of the future Wife Divine might lead to the Most Holy Wife, Divine Lady Empress. And that path might lead to the freedom of my people."

"I see." A laugh escapes my lips. "Your overtures weren't friendly after all. You're just stalking and spying on me on behalf of your people. Wow, that makes me feel much better."

Wei frowns, looking quite uncomfortable. "Believe me, Divine One I do wish to be friends...or more. But I must honor my duty too."

My lips tighten. "And your sculpture and flattery, are those to get me to help you? What do you really want, Fan Wei?"

Wei's frown deepens as he lowers his eyes. "This is not an easy position for me to be in, Divine One. You have every right to be angry with me. But my overtures have been sincere and from my heart. If not for the honor of my people, I would ask you to escape these gardens with me and run away to some far-off paradise beyond the emperor's reach. I would give you my heart and take you wherever your heart desires."

I hold back a pained laugh. His words wrench my heart and turn my stomach upside down. He offers what I wanted for Cai and myself. A dream I destroyed with my own deceits and lies. What lies and deceits does Wei now offer me? "You barely know me, yet you speak of giving me your heart. Don't play games with me master gardener, master deceiver."

"No games." His voice is soft, meek. He looks up at me with unassuming eyes that beg me to believe him. "In the little time I have known you, I have seen what goodness and beauty lay in your heart. I'm confident the longer I know you, the more goodness and beauty I will see."

I clench my toes inside my slippered feet. A trick I taught myself when I was much younger and needed to control my temper without exhibiting any outward frustration. It became quite useful in letting Father believe I was his dutiful daughter even when his actions angered me deeply.

"Pretty words," I say, thinking of how Father often expressed his love to me while at the same time expressing his excitement at selling me off as the emperor's bride. "Where does your heart really live? With your people or your supposed feelings for me? What if marrying the emperor brought upon me a life of torture and unbearable imprisonment? Would you free me from that life if it kept you from finding the empress?"

Wei doesn't flinch at my words. Face and voice calm, he answers, "My people—several thousands of men, women, children—suffer torture, slave labor, and unbearable imprisonment every day of their lives from birth to death. I know this much about your heart. You would not want me to put any hardships you might face above the agony and hardship of so many others. Yet, I confess, it would be a hard choice for me, but I would choose my people. Still, I would do all I could to free you too. I would do that, even if the thought and sight of you did not make my heart dance and sing with longing."

The anger inside me melts. I take a deep breath and exhale. My toes unclench. I know men who spew words about honor as an excuse for doing what they please, when they please. I know others who speak little of honor but live it to some degree or another. But if Wei's words match how he really lives, I have never known someone with such honor as he.

"Your answer shames me," I say, lowering my head. "Please forgive me. I should not have asked such a selfish question. Nor would I ask you to do such a horrific thing as I suggested. You are right. You must save your people. How can I help you?"

Wei rises from his sitting position onto his knees. "Give me your ear."

"What?" I tilt my head, certain I didn't hear Wei correctly.

Wei pulls from his pouch a black ink stick and a small grinding stone. He spits in the grinding stone and grinds a small amount of black ink on it. He pulls a bamboo pen from his pouch and dips its tip into the ink.

"Kneel beside me and let me see your ear," he says.

I don't move. I stare at him and his bamboo pen. "Why? What are you going to do?"

Wei grins a patient grin. "There is little you can do to help me find the Divine Lady Empress other than marry Emperor Hu and follow the path you are given. But if you allow me, I have a way to find you no matter where they take you. Even if you do not lead me to the Divine Lady Empress, I can come rescue you if you're in danger."

His grin turns mischievous, and he adds, "Or I can also rescue you if you're simply bored and miss my friendly overtures."

Behind my veil a pinched smile forms as I continue to stare at Wei. I still don't understand what he's going to do. Can I trust him? I want to. And I do want him to come find me again, regardless of whether I really need rescuing or not.

I kneel beside him. "Will it hurt?"

He chuckles. "No but it may tickle. If it does, try to hold still. It will be hard drawing small enough so none of your servants or even the emperor notices the characters."

He pushes the flap of my ear forward, and I try hard not to jerk as the wet tip of his pen glides across the skin behind my ear.

With a laugh in his voice, he says as he writes, "No matter what your mother taught you, try not to wash behind your ear. Don't let your servants either. If the ink washes away or fades, I will not be able to rescue you no matter how great my heart desires."

When he finishes writing, he cleans off his pen and grinding stone with a cloth and puts them all back into his pouch. "One more thing," he says, his expression turning somber. "After the public marriage ceremony, there will be a private ceremony where you will make oaths to one of the Shen."

I nod my head. "Yes, to Zhì Shen."

"Really? Interesting. Anyway, after you make your oaths, do not drink from the wedding chalice the emperor offers you. Only pretend to drink from it. It will be drugged. So, pretend to fall asleep also."

I'm glad the veil hides the worried look on my face, but I can't help saying, "Okay. Any other lifesaving tips I should know before marrying the most powerful and dangerous man on all of Dashi?"

Wei grins. "Stay alive. I will see you again.. Trust me."

His words warm me. I know I deserve whatever torture awaits me, but deep down I want Wei to rescue me. Is that okay? How much punishment must I take to pay for my crime? Cai paid with his life. Must I do so as well? Oh, how I wish I could change the past. I'm not sure what I would have done different, other than I would not have lied to Cai.

Wei's fingers wrap around my own, pulling me from my thoughts. Before I can react, he bows forward and kisses the back of my hand. The warmth inside me grows even after his lips rise from my flesh.

"May the Two watch over you, Divine One, till our gaze joins again." He looks up at me, smiles a wide grin, and vanishes from sight.

Chapter 35
Qiu Meilin – The Rod's Sting

"The truth behind the legend of Shi and San is not pleasant. The Shen couple betrayed the Two and sided with Xié Shen during the Great Shen War, committing horrific acts of murder and violence."
- Pan Ru: Early histories of Dashi

The sweet scent of cherry blossoms floats on the air and crickets chirp all around us. Cai and I hide in the dark shadows of cherry trees near the palace walls. Clouds darken the night skies, but more light shines than I would like. Low to the west, the emerald glow of the moon San peeks through streaks of clouds. Not too many hours past twilight, San and Shi embrace high in the sky above. After, San hurries toward setting, anxious to reach and embrace Shi again in two more twilights. Shi takes her time in her descent, as swirling mists encircle her lavender gleam, shining higher and brighter in the western sky.

Every dozen paces or so along the stone-paved highway that runs near the palace walls, lanterns glow—some red-papered lit by candles and some clear-papered gleaming with multi-colored streams of Shen Breath. A silhouetted Red Phoenix Guard walks the highway toward us. He whistles a tune that only the crudest of men sing.

Cai and I hold still and silent. Snubby chatters with other snub-nose monkeys in the lofty branches of nearby oaks. As much as I appreciate Snubby saving me before, I worry that he might get Cai and me caught. The drums of curfew sounded long ago. If the guard spots us, our punishment will be more than a beating from a thrashing rod.

If needed, we have our boons from Tiānqì Shen to help us. I also have Zhangchi hidden in a bamboo carrying tube strapped to my back. But I'd rather not risk the attention a fight might bring. We've already spent the whole day avoiding soldiers by hiding in a warehouse full of human and animal waste waiting to be used for fertilizer. The stench was bad enough to drive away any soldiers that might have considered looking for us there.

Although outside now, we still need to stay out of view. Our plan is simple. Get inside the palace walls without being noticed, search for Lian until we find her, and bring her home. I'm crazy enough to believe it might work.

"You ready?" I ask Cai after the whistling soldier passes and disappears in the darkness.

He nods, steps close to me, and wraps his arms around my waist in a tight embrace. I can barely breathe. While I like being close to Cai, there's nothing romantic about this hug. With my palms facing downward, I use my Wind gift to fly us over the wall and onto a large expanse of manicured grass on the other side.

The palace outer courtyard is astonishingly beautiful. Hundreds of lanterns illuminate it with a heavenly glow, lighting the different cobblestone paths that wind through its wide expanse of grass and ornate gardens. The courtyard is at least as big as all of Ning valley. More lanterns light the paved thoroughfare running from the front gate to the gate that leads to the inner courtyard.

The outer courtyard has only two buildings—lavish, two-story banquet halls. One on each side of the courtyard thoroughfare, the massive structures loom on the far side of the courtyard near the inner wall—the wall that separates the outer courtyard from the inner courtyard.

It's in the outer courtyard where the emperor hosts galas, feasts, and celebrations for thousands of lords, nobles, and aristocrats. No doubt the marriage ceremony for him and Lian will be held here too.

We stay away from the lighted paths and run in the shadows across the courtyard's grass and flowers toward the inner wall. I tap into my boon to increase my speed and quiet my breathing. Every once in a while, I skirt close to a Shen Breath lantern to make sure my reserves stay full.

A few Gold Dragon Guards patrol the paths and thoroughfare, but we stop and crouch in the shadows whenever they come close. We also stop every time we hear voices from the guards above who walk and keep watch from the ramparts atop the courtyard's side wall.

Once at the inner wall, Cai embraces me tight again and we fly over into the inner courtyard. We land on the grass between two willow trees. No gardens or illuminated paths greet us. Large willows and locust trees run along the inner courtyard wall. A connected cluster of several one-story houses take up most of the space in this section of the courtyard. Red-papered lanterns glow on some of the houses' front porches, but no lights shine inside the homes.

Cai nods toward the houses, "Do you think she's in one of those?"

I shake my head. "Too plain. Probably servants' quarters. She'll be further in. Some place more extravagant."

We creep alongside the shadows and trees of the inner wall to circle around the houses and to get closer to the palace. We stop about a hundred paces away from the inner court gate and the thoroughfare that runs up the middle of the courtyard toward the palace. Lanterns light the thoroughfare. If we get any closer, we'll be easy to spot. Leaving the shadow of the trees, we hurry across an open grassy stretch that runs between the servants' quarters and the length of the thoroughfare.

Even though it's an open area, it's in the shadows far enough away from the lanterns on either side of us so the darkness can conceal us. But the closer we get to the center of the courtyard, the darkness lessens. Several hundred white and black-papered candle lanterns and an extravagant temple to the Two light the middle of the courtyard. As we circle the temple, its lights push away the shadows that conceal us.

We angle further away from the temple and thoroughfare closer to the servants' quarters. Still, a pair of Gold Dragon Guards stroll right in front of our path. We drop to the grass and hold our breath. Please, by the Two, don't let them see us. The guards laugh and exchange a joke that I can't hear, and walk away without noticing us.

We circle around to the back of the servants' quarters and step into a garden lit by gold, red, and Shen Breath lanterns. Beautiful! Blossoming apricot, cherry, and plum trees. Flowering magnolias. Bamboo. Peonies. Roses. Azaleas. Chrysanthemums. A small pond. Streams and bridges. Curving paths of marble.

"It's past curfew! What are you two doing outside the servant quarters?"

I bump into Cai as I spin around to face the voice. Three Gold Dragon Guards stare us down. A deep scowl stretches across the face of the lead guard. The other two smile wickedly. The lead guard pulls from his belt a thrashing rod as thick as my thumb and as long as my arm.

"Answer me! Or do you want to double the twenty strikes you've already earned?"

Cai and I could handle these three, but others would hear or notice in such a well-lit area. Before long we'd be facing a battalion of Gold Dragon Guards. I decide on a different strategy.

I shine a demure smile and cuddle close to Cai, wrapping my arms across his waist. "Sorry, great one," I say in a meek, innocent tone. "We are new to Quanli and the palace. We arrived today to serve Lord Emperor Xiang Hu, Chosen of Heaven in his wedding to the new Wife Divine. We only wanted to enjoy the beautiful gardens for a moment. We did not know of the curfew. Please forgive our indiscretion."

The soldier's scowl deepens. "You're here to work, not dally in the emperor's gardens." His eyes move from me to Cai. "Do you always let your woman speak for you? Have you no honor?"

Cai bows his head and puts a fist to his heart. "I am not worthy to speak in the presence of such a great solider as yourself. I had hoped the honeyed voice of my true heart might honor you better than mine."

"You're right. You're not worthy. You're worms! And since you let your woman speak for you, she can take your punishment too." The soldier raises the thrashing rod high above his head. "Kneel woman!"

Cai tenses and starts toward the guard. I shake my head and touch his arm to hold him back. His lips tighten. The soldier laughs. I remove the bamboo carrying tube concealing Zhangchi and hand it to Cai before I kneel down to take my strikes.

"This is wrong," Cai says. "Punish me, not her."

The guard clears his throat with a wet guttural sound before spitting to the side. "Now you've earned your woman forty strikes. Be silent, or I'll double it again."

Cai steps back. His body tenses. His lips flatten as thin as paper. He wants to fight, but that will make things worse. I shake my head again, warning him not to do anything witless. Then I lower my head to submit to my punishment.

I clench back a scream as the rod whips against my back. I'm tempted to call upon my boon to lessen the pain, but the guard needs to see me truly suffering. He needs to see the wounds he leaves on my back. Once he's satisfied with how he's tortured me, he'll leave us alone and go away. Anything short of that could upset him more and raise his suspicions.

I clench again and my body shakes at the sting of a second and third strike. Welts rise on my skin. Six strikes in a row without pause. I lean forward, my arms folded tight across my chest to brace for the next hits. The soldier waits this time, making the anticipation worse. The welts on my back throb deeper and deeper. I jerk as two more strikes come, tearing through my tunic onto bare skin.

Strike after strike comes. I lose count. No matter how hard I try to hold back tears, they streak down my cheeks. Still, I grin through the pain as more strikes come. They sting harder, sharper, and deeper. I shudder and groan with every strike. Welts burn and throb across my back. I sob and lay flat on the grass as more strikes sting.

My fingers dig into the ground and pull at the blades. My body writhes in agony. I want to send it all away. I can with a simple thought to will my boon, but I won't. The guard has to see me suffer or he'll not leave us alone.

Strike. Sting. Throb. Strike. Sting. Throb. The rhythm of misery. When the strikes stop, the stinging and throbbing grow worse. I'm too weak to scream. I convulse and whimper on the ground like a dying dog.

"Now get back to the servant's quarter," the soldier commands. "If I see you out again tonight, you'll both get worse than the thrashing rod. Go on. Go!"

Cai's arms slip under me as he lifts and cradles me close. I clench. The throbs and pains burn and sting harder as he moves. A stinging jolt burns across my back with every step he takes.

"Heal yourself," he whispers with a sob in his voice. "They're gone now. It's safe."

No. I have to be sure. "Inside." Is all I say. Cai must understand because he doesn't ask me again until I hear his feet clop on the bamboo floor of the servants' quarters.

I don't wait. I will the boon to heal me. Relief doesn't come as fast as I want, but it does come. The stings dull. The throbbing fades. But even when the pain leaves, the shaking, sobs, and flood of tears continue.

Cai sits beside me and holds me closer, comforting me. Calming me. "I'm so sorry," he whispers. "So sorry."

I want to tell him it's okay, but I can't form the words. So, I sink into his hug and try to forget. Try to push out the memory, the suffering, and the fear. Darkness and silence surround me, except for the sound of Cai's soft breath. That's all I need, to hear and feel him close as I try to calm down and eventually slip off to sleep.

Chapter 36
Fan Wei – Love or Honor?

"Downy chicks peep and cheep, Oh, blissful unaware.
Wicked fiends slash, bombard, quite a fatal terror.
Mother wings shroud, safeguard. Razor beak screams beware!
Lone peep shrieks far from reach. Oh, puzzle gravely unfair.
Stay? Go? Help most or one? Who can love forswear?"

- Fan Wei scribblings

My gardener sandals clop on the polished stone of the grand steps leading up to the Imperial Gallery. Moonlight from the lavender and emerald spheres of Shi and San gleams on the sweeping gold-tiled roof of the magnificent building. The majestic structure glows with its bright gold-papered lanterns illuminating polished stone walls and the series of red-streaked marble columns that line the entrance.

Only a few building in Quanli have marble pillars and polished stone walls. Most others were built with common stone, brick, rammed dirt or wood. No one questions why the emperor chose to use such extravagant building materials for such a public building. Then again, no one questions the emperor about anything.

Opulence fills the interior of the Imperial Gallery. The fragrance of cinnamon incense floats through the air. Light from hundreds of oil-burning porcelain lamps shine and flicker on the red-streaked marble floors, but it's the artwork on display that makes the gallery so rich in its splendor. Although the emperor pretends it's simply a treasury of his favorite pieces of art, my cousins and I know better. Hu built the Imperial Gallery to honor the Divine Lady Empress, Most Holy Wife, or Mu Po, as the cousins affectionately call her. Few realize it, but all the art in the gallery tells snippets of her life history, a shrine to the emperor's memories of the wife he betrayed.

A full-size copper statue of Guāng Shen, the Goddess of radiance greets just inside the entryway. Ruby stars, emerald and lavender moons, and citrine suns glisten on her veil and pinned up hair.

Beneath the gallery's vaulted ceiling, I venture further in past full-size screen paintings, statues, and statuettes of the Shen. Except for an occasional glance, soldiers do not guard the gallery. The emperor says it's his gift to the people, welcoming all to enjoy its works of arts freely and without fear. Of course, anyone who damages or steals any piece of its art will face extreme retribution. To avoid the appearance of suspicion, few actually visit gallery.

I sit cross-legged in the gallery's center facing a large wall mural of the Two breathing rainbow streams of Chi into Dashi's first mortals. My eyes move among the many other screen painted masterpieces that surround me.

The emperor's Danwang summer palace atop a daffodil covered knoll overlooking a shimmering lake. A young couple climbing the highest branches of a giant blooming cherry tree. Butterflies swerving through an overgrown jungle. A lone walnut tree shading a humble country cottage. Sheep ambling down a grassy hill toward a glistening creek.

Several statues and paintings portray exquisite renditions of the red phoenix in different poses and settings. Jade carvings Porcelain figurines and vases. Embroidered wall hangings with floral designs.

Since first coming to Quanli, the Imperial Gallery has been my favorite place to visit. At times, I think Mu Po speaks to my thoughts, guiding me. Or perhaps, those are divine thoughts from the Two. No matter, a peace exists here. May the Two grant me the inspiration I need this night.

With my eyes fixed on the mural of the Two, I whisper, "First Mother and Father, you set me on this path, but I need your help. I must find Mu Po, but I cannot bear to put my divine Lian in danger. How I wish I could steal her away from this dreadful place and flee to some foreign land far from the emperor's reach."

I pause, listening for the Two to nudge my thoughts. "Yes, I know. I have my duty to my people and to you. Still, would it be wrong for you to let me do my duty and be with the one I love?"

Silence answers me, but chastisement stirs in my mind. Still, I laugh. "Yes, perhaps I am a fool to speak of love about someone I barely know. But I have sensed her Chi. She is strong and pure. Her eyes shine with the glorious brilliance of a virtuous soul. I do not want to lose her, and I fear the fate she will face once her marriage to the emperor is complete."

I continue to gaze at the mural as I wait for the Two's inspiration. My mind wanders, wondering why artists always depict the Two with such an ample girth. Don't artists know that it takes more than truth and honor to stand in the Light? You must first have the health and strength to reach the Light. Of course, what do artists really know about the Two and seeking the Light? For that matter, what do I really know? Even among the cousins, stories passed from mother to child over the generations no doubt stray from the truth dab by dab.

Frustration tightens my chest. Inspiration from the Two doesn't come. Why will they not speak to me? Why won't Mu Po speak to me? Have I angered them by doubting my duty?

I take a deep breath to push down the pinpricks of anger, but my whisper still raises a notch. "How can I stand in the Light if honoring my people and duty require me to allow danger to befall one I love? Is this how you would have me to seek the Light? Where is the honor in this?"

More silence follows. Not even a nudge of inspiration enters my thoughts. I exhale a long, deep sigh. I do not like to admit it, but sometimes standing in the Light requires learning how to meekly submit to the source of that Light. Meekness in any form has never been one of my strengths. Regardless, with hand in fist respect and my legs still crossed, I bow my head until my nose almost touches the floor.

"Beloved Two, please forgive my insolence. I will honor my errand and duty to you and my people without condition. As you wish, I will do."

I sigh and raise my head but stop halfway up. "Even so, if you can find it in your mercy to help me find the Divine Lady Empress and save my most sweet Lian, my gratitude would burst to grand and glorious overflowing."

When I completely raise my head, a peace settles in my mind and heart. The softest of thoughts whispers in my mind, "Do not worry, divine son. What happens will happen."

A wide smile creeps up the corners of my mouth. The words themselves bring little comfort, but a peace touches my heart and gives me a glimmer of hope. Even though the Two's promises do not always unfold as desired or expected, the Two do care for their children. If they tell me not to worry, I will move forward with the hope that all will be well.

I have only a flash of time to enjoy the Two's peace before echoing footfalls on the gallery's marble floors disrupt the moment.

"It wasn't there this morning, but tonight it was," says an agitated whisper that pierces the silence of the gallery. "Why didn't the servants who brought it to his room bring it here? This is not an errand for grade one servants."

Another more subdued and cautious voice cuts in, "Tan Na, our honor is to serve the Chosen of Heaven, not to question his command. If you do not rein your tongue, you might find your head in a basket and your stump in a box."

"I am..." The voice goes quiet when the two blue-robed servants carrying a folded-up screen painting step into view and see me. Their bodies tense. Their mouths tighten into thin-lined frowns. Even though I'm dressed as a simple gardener, both know their words could mean their death if I repeat them to another.

I rise to my feet and spread my arms out to the men with a friendly grin stretched across my face. "Friends, you startled me. I was so deep in my mediations that I did not hear you speak. Were you perhaps addressing me? If so, how might a lowly gardener as I assist such esteemed servants as yourselves?"

The servants relax and the lead one nods at me, flashing a brief smile of gratitude at me. My words have had the desired effect to ease his worries.

"Honorable gardener, please forgive our intrusion. We did not mean to startle you. We will finish our task and be on our way."

They both smile and bow toward me, as they hurry past me. Being careful with the work of art, they set up the screen painting between a statuette of Luxíng Shen and a painting of the scholar Pan Ru on a meadowed knoll teaching a group of young children. The moment they finish the task, the servants hurry away, wanting to be far from me in the hopes I will soon forget their treacherous words.

I step toward the painting, wondering what new piece of history in the Divine Lady Empress' life it depicts. It shows a young warrior with sword in hand, scaling the forbidden heights of Mount Qiangu toward a hidden cleft high atop the mountain where a golden dragon and red phoenix guard the tree of life. At the foot of the mountain, a beautiful princess awaits the return of her champion.

I grin, knowing the true rendition of this story. Sitting on Mama's lap as a child, I've heard many times the tale of how long before they became emperor and empress, Hu stole a peach from the Tree of Life to heal Yuan from rose fever, and ultimately grant her and himself immortality.

As I admire the beautiful strokes and colors of the work of art, I notice the similarities between the painting and my current situation.

"By the Two's mercy," I whisper. "Lian, I pray your wait for my rescue will only be brief and that neither you nor I truly have need to worry."

Part 4

Chapter 37
Qiu Lian – Tears and Fears

"Uncertainty can't beat us if we move forward with the best possible decision, prayer, and unyielding work."
- Notions from a Royal Peasant

Chan and the other servants wake me to the laughing whistle of a flock of thrush sounds outside my window. It's hours before sunrise, but neither the servants nor the laughing thrush care. I can barely keep my eyes open. Thanks to the Two I really don't need my eyes open since the servants do all the work to get me ready for the wedding festivities.

They bathe me in sandalwood scented hot water. Red and yellow rose petals float on the water's surface. As they scrub me down, I watch to make sure they keep their sweet-smelling soaps and steaming wash cloths away from my ears. I have no idea what Wei drew behind my ear, but I want to see him again. I don't want whatever he painted behind there coming off.

After they towel me down, they dress me in silk undergarments and an elegant bright jade wedding dress. Embroidered designs of chrysanthemums and lilies interlink across my fitted bodice and up over my shoulders. Gold long-tailed dragons decorate my wide draping sleeves. Red trim lines my high collar and swooping hem that swooshes above the jade silk slippers on my feet. Embroidered in gold, each slipper has the slanting cross strokes for the symbol of the Two. But attached to the bottom of each slipper is a hard, thick wooden sloping block that makes them terribly uncomfortable to wear.

Chan powders my face white with rice flour, brushes my eyebrows with a dark dye, pastes a gold-plated plum blossom on my forehead, accentuates my dimples with dove-shaped flakes of jade, colors my cheeks with rouge, and paints my lips with a bright vermilion balm. The makeup process alone takes well over two hours.

While Chan applies my makeup, I sit across from her in my cushioned chair and the other two servants work on my hair. They arrange my dark tresses in a complex braided updo. Red chopsticks with gold designs hold the braids in place. As the finishing touch, they place a phoenix bridal headdress on the front of my hair. Dotted with rubies, the headdress' fine gold wires link together in intricate feather-like patterns. On each side of my face, five braided gold chains representing tail feathers drape and jingle from the headdress in varying lengths down to my jaw line, bodice, and in between. Down my forehead five teardrop rubies dangle above my eyebrows on the end of five fine gold link chains.

When the servants finish, they hang a sheer bright red silk veil in front of my face that drapes down past my shoulders. It's beautiful, but it makes me think all that time spent putting on makeup was a waste. I'll be wearing the veil most of the day. I'm not sure anyone else but my servants will even see my face today.

By tradition the veil stays on until the bridegroom removes it in the bridal chamber. I'm not even certain that will happen. I've yet to meet the emperor and he's not interested in meeting me. That makes me wonder what will happen after the wedding ceremony, especially given Wei's warning to not drink from the wedding chalice.

"Your escorts will be here soon," Chan tells me after the other servants bow to me and leave. "You have a long day ahead of you, Divine One. I will leave you, so you may rest."

Chan bows and starts to rise from her chair. I touch her arm. "Chan, I do not wish to be alone." She stops half-crouched above her seat, uncertainty on her face. "Will you please stay with me a little longer?"

Chan sits back down but appears uncomfortable. The sounds of the whistling thrush and calls of other birds float in from my balcony window as we sit in silence. A slight warm breeze brushes through the room bringing in the mixed scents of the garden's many flowers and blossoming trees.

Looking more and more distressed, Chan breaks the silence. "How may I serve you, Divine One?"

I smile at her, hoping to put her at ease. "Chan, you have already served me well this day and all the days past. You have more than served me. You have been a friend to me. For that I thank you. Now I simply wish to have your company a bit longer right now."

A weak smile turns up the corners of her lips, but the uncertainty remains. Actually, it's more like fear than uncertainty. What could she possibly be afraid of? I'm the one getting married.

My chair squeaks as I lean forward to place my hand on her knee. "Chan, what is the matter? You're upset. Have I offended you in some way?"

She gasps. Her eyes go wide in a panic. "No, No, Divine One! You could never offend me. You have treated me with great kindness well above my station. Well above what I could ever hope to deserve."

I gently squeeze her knee. "Then what is bothering you so? Please tell me."

The look of fear returns. Her hands begin to tremble. She squeezes them tight, but they continue to shake. I place my hand on hers to help her settle down, but her trembling grows stronger. "Chan, what is the matter? Please tell me."

A blue jay lands on the balcony rail of my window and starts to squawk and chatter. I want to yell at it to go away, to stop bothering us with so much noise so Chan can speak. Chan lowers her head as the jay keeps squawking. But before she does, I see tears well up in her eyes and stream down her cheek.

"Chan, I am your friend. You have nothing to fear from me. What are you afraid of? Please, tell me. Maybe I can help."

Chan shakes her lowered head. I rise from my chair and wrap my arms around her. Her body shudders. Why won't she tell me what's wrong? What could she be afraid of? Me? Zheng? Something else?

"It will be okay, Chan," I say. "Whatever has you worried, I will take care of it."

But my words and embrace do nothing to calm her. Muffled sobs escape her lips and her body trembles even more. I feel helpless. Everything I say or do makes Chan feel worse.

Before I say another word, the heavy thud of several boots pulls my attention to my chamber door. Four Gold Dragon Guards stand at the entry, stern expressions steel their faces. They look majestic and intimidating in their black leather armor with its shining silver plates. Not even the yellow plumes poking up from their helmets soften their menacing appearance.

"Divine One, I am Captain Bai Zan, the leader of your personal guard detail," says the one at the front. "Lord Emperor Xiang Hu, Chosen of Heaven has charged us with your safety and protection, or our lives."

I want to laugh. It's my fourth day in the palace and only now is the emperor concerned with my safety. It's probably because with the wedding procession today I'll be paraded publicly outside the palace. Maybe the emperor thinks as long as I'm in the palace walls I don't need protection. If he does, he obviously doesn't know how easily Wei was able to leave messages for me and visit me. I'm glad he doesn't.

Captain Bai clears his throat and continues, "Divine One, if it pleases you, we will now escort you to your wedding sedan."

The firm tone in his voice tells me it really doesn't matter if it pleases me or not. He has orders and that means it's time to go right now.

I squeeze Chan with one last hug and smile at her. "All will be well, Chan. You will see."

As I let her go, Chan looks up at my veiled face. Tears cover her cheeks. Fear still reigns in her eyes. "I will miss you, Divine One. I will truly miss you."

My eyebrows wrinkle together. Why will she miss me? Where is she going? I had assumed she would continue to serve me after the wedding. Won't she? I would think a Wife Divine needs servants as much, or even more so than a future Wife Divine. But as I stare into her eyes one last time, I realize her fear is not for her. Her fear is for me.

Why? What will happen to me after the wedding? Is Wei right that they will drug me? Was Meilin right about the emperor locking up his wives in some squalid dungeon?

"Divine One, the procession waits," Captain Bai says with urgency. "If it pleases you, we must leave now."

I want to ask Chan what she knows of my future, but it's too late. I nod at the captain and give Chan one last smile before I follow the soldiers out. As we walk, thousands of possibilities of what truly awaits swarm my mind, none of them pleasant. I push down the thoughts, but my mind works overtime to figure out ways to prevent all the different calamities from happening.

I'm finally able to lessen my anxiety and slow down the constant stream into my mind of all the different misfortunes that might come my way by remembering that I should at least be safe until the wedding ceremony ends. So, why not try to enjoy all the festivities until then. Besides, what else can I do?

When we reach the procession sedan it makes me think they've built a mobile shrine. Elaborate gold designs trim its red posts, chair, drapes, and corner peaked roof. Unlike my other sedan, the drapes are pulled back so all the crowds along Quanli's imperial highway can get a glimpse of the emperor's newest bride. Two of my new personal guards walk on each side of me as four servants in blue robes and black round felt hats carry me in the sedan. They move at a fast and steady pace from the inner courtyard through the outer courtyard until we reach the main palace gate.

A deafening cheer rises when they open the palace gates. A chorus of music swells with deep booming drums and a clear, bright melody of hundreds of suonas playing. Standing in neat endless columns, members of both the Gold Dragon Guard and Red Phoenix Guard stand at attention in the middle of the Imperial Highway in ordered rows. The rows are at least two hundred paces wide. The columns stretch down the highway farther than I can see. There must be thousands, maybe a hundred thousand soldiers.

What little room that is left on the sides of the Imperial Highway is filled with crowds of citizens, young and old, and rich and poor. Many wave banners bearing a red phoenix, the symbol for immortality and the Mother or female half of the Two. Sometimes the red phoenix is also used to honor Divine Lady Empress Ling Yuan as well as the emperor's Divine Wives. My body tingles at the sights and sounds of it all. I've never seen anything like it before

As my sedan bearers and personal guard escort march through the palace gates, the mass of Gold Dragon Guard and Red Phoenix Guard parts in a wave on both sides to allow us to move up the middle through them. More cheers from the crowds swell as we move through the row of guards down the Imperial Highway.

When we reach what must be the middle of all the columns of soldiers they begin to march with us. The shouts and cheers of the crowd surge louder and continue to sound as the imperial procession moves through the heart of the capital city. Remembering what my tutors taught me, I raise a cupped hand and wave at all the crowds. They wave their phoenix banners back at me and shout louder.

It's strange being the focus of so much attention. Being loved by so many strangers. The feeling is false. Their excitement of having a new Wife Divine might be real, but it has nothing to do with who I am. They don't know me. They don't know what I look like—except for the few who glimpsed me on the waterfront when I first arrived.

If harm comes to me after the wedding, none of them will know. None will care. Well, one might.

Crowds press the edges of the Imperial Highway to get a better look at me as the procession of music and marching soldiers go by. Once in a while on a temple rooftop, a mansion balcony, or even the branches of a towering chestnut tree I see a lone figure.

Every time the figure appears, he's dressed in simple grays and a wide brim bamboo hat tipped forward to obscure his face. Even if the hat wasn't tipped forward, from this distance I wouldn't be able to clearly see the face. But I don't need to. I'm certain it's Wei.

It brings me comfort that he's watching over me. No matter the dangers that the wedding might bring, I'm anxious for it to come. Not to be with the emperor, but because soon after I will see Wei again. And if nothing else does, that will bring a smile to my face.

Chapter 38
Qiu Meilin – Defiance

"For we who suffer, sometimes patience is all we have."
- History of the Descendants: Volume 11, Page 301

I'm a witless goat-headed fool with snails for brains. How could I let myself sleep all night? I wasted the best chance we had to rescue Lian before the festivities began. I should have used my boon to take care of those guards. But no, I thought it better to endure the forty strikes from a thrashing rod. I knew the boon would heal the physical pain, but I had no idea how emotionally and mentally tiring the suffering would be on me.

"Girl! Stop daydreaming! Do I need to beat you with a thrashing rod to get my oysters?"

I tense at the mention of a thrashing rod but relax when I realize it's only the sauce matron. With her beefy hands on her wide hips, she taps her foot impatiently and scowls at me with an intensity that could raise the dread of Xié Shen into even the fiercest of warriors. Even though it's against imperial law for any female to wield a thrashing rod, I wouldn't be surprised if the sauce matron has one hidden in the deep pockets of her apron.

I offer the matron a weak smile and bow my head. "Sorry matron. I will go at once."

I put my bucket yoke on my shoulders and hurry away before she has a chance to inflict any punishment on me. Since sunrise I've been her beast of burden, hauling buckets of water, garlic, onions, ginger, sesame oil, soybeans, and anything else you might use to make all the different sauces for the wedding banquet's ten-course lunch.

The emperor has a little less than two thousand servants whose sole responsibility is to prepare food. Hundreds more servants were brought into to help prepare for the wedding banquet. Once we found some blue servant robes to wear, Cai and I blended in fine. None of the chefs or cooking matrons know me or Cai, but without us saying a word they put us to work—me as errand girl for the boss of all the sauce and Cai gutting an endless supply of carp, catfish, and shad for the fish chef.

The vast lawns of the courtyard bustle with activity of so many servants making final preparations for the banquet. It's been that way all morning. Scents from the cooking fires and ovens waft through the courtyard, twisting and mingling the smells of roasted pork, duck, deep fried crab legs, baked lobster, stir fry prawns, snow peas, steamed rolls, braised abalone, steamed fish, scallions, ginger, onions, garlic, soy, and a dozen different sauces.

Tables line the courtyard in neat rows, all decorated with gold silk tablecloths, red silk napkins, copper goblets and platters, and small Shen Breath lanterns. Thousands of dragon and phoenix banners wave in the breeze from tall posts across the courtyard.

The tables sit empty for now as the more than twenty thousand banquet guests crowd the edges of the thoroughfare, chattering in loud anticipation for the future Wife Divine and her procession to arrive through the front gate. The pounding of drums and high pitch chorus of suonas grow louder as her procession draws nearer and nearer.

I leave the sounds of the courtyard as I enter one of the massive indoor banquet halls and make my way down multiple flights of stairs past two levels of cellars into the palace ice pits. Huge blocks of ice line the walls of the vast chamber. Streams of mists form with every breath I exhale. Bumps rise on my arms, and I shiver as I fill my buckets from one of many barrels filled with oysters shipped in from the eastern coasts of Huyan.

When I emerge from the cellar and banquet hall, I feel divine as noon sun warms my face and clothes feels. By the time I return to the sauce matron, my shoulders ache from the weight of the buckets of oysters. A deafening cheer rises from the crowds. It startles me and I nearly drop one of the buckets on the matron's foot.

"Holy eel muck!" the sauce matron curses. "Fool girl, watch what you're doing, or I'll have you beaten and locked away."

I contemplate how a quick heel kick planted on her plump backside would silence her ill-tempered scolding, but instead I smile, bow politely, and offer a meek apology.

"Please forgive my unworthiness, most esteemed matron. I will endeavor to be less clumsy."

"Humph!" Her scowl remains as stern as ever. "I need those oysters shucked and boiling before the Divine One's sedan arrives. Do that and I might overlook how worthless you really are."

"Of course, matron!" I force a smile. "Right away, matron!"

I heft the bucket yoke back onto my shoulders and from the corner of my eye I watch as dancers dressed in bright jade robes prance, sway, and leap past the front gates. They parade a long gold dragon made of cloth and bamboo high above their heads. As I hurry away, I watch the dragon move up and down and side to side along the thoroughfare. Firecrackers explode in front of the dragon dancers, causing a cheer to rise amid the crowds. When I reach the preparation tables crowded in the corner between the banquet hall and the west wall of the palace, the drum beating and suona playing musicians march into the courtyard. Firecrackers continue to explode, and the crowds continue to cheer.

The sauce matron will be checking on me soon. So, I pull my gaze from the parade, grab an oyster knife, and begin shucking the oysters' meat from their shells. I stopped counting how many buckets of oysters I've hauled, shucked, and boiled well over a dozen trips ago. I'll be more than pleased if I never see, smell, or feel the slime of another oyster again after today.

In between the shucking of each oyster, I peak at the parade's progress. The dragon dancers have moved off the main thoroughfare onto the side road that leads to the west gate where they continue to sway and dance in place. The musicians file off in the other direction, onto the side road that leads to the east gate.

Lian must be near. Columns of Gold Dragon Guard march through the palace main gate onto the thoroughfare. The Red Phoenix Guard also marched in the procession, but by strict imperial rule they would not be allowed inside the courtyard since their duty is to protect the city while the Gold Dragon Guard is to protect the emperor and the palace.

As the Gold Dragon Guard enters the palace, they split formation. Most turn to the right or left, marching on the grass alongside the interior of palace courtyard walls, not stopping until they almost completely surround the courtyard. The remaining soldiers march up the main thoroughfare and the side roads until both sides of all the lanes are lined five-deep with members of the Gold Dragon Guard.

Once all the soldiers are in place, the dragon dancers stop dancing. The musicians stop playing. The chatter and rumble of the crowd roll to a quiet in a receding wave. Once silence permeates the courtyard, a servant on a knee-high raised platform in front of the inner gate pounds the gong three times.

All eyes turn to the platform in anticipation. Shen Breath lanterns line the front and back edges. Front and center on the platform rest two luxurious chairs of dark wood. An elaborate golden dragon's head and wings have been carved into the largest chair. The other chair has a red silk cushion and a beautiful phoenix carved into its backrest.

The servant strikes the gong three more times. The moment the sound fades, the emperor suddenly appears on the platform in bright yellow silk robes. How did he do that? Is it a gift from the Shen?

He stands with a broad grin in front of the dragon chair, holding his arms out to the crowd in welcome. For a three-hundred-year-old man, he's quite handsome. He doesn't look a day over twenty-five, which is still too ancient for my tastes no matter how attractive he might be.

Still, my admiration of his good looks makes me slow to notice that everyone else in the courtyard, except for the Gold Dragon Guard, has dropped to their knees and lowered their heads to kowtow to the great Lord Emperor Xiang Hu, Chosen of Heaven. Before too many notice, I drop to the ground and kowtow three times in unison with the multitude. When the emperor lowers his outstretched arms, the crowds rise.

"Honored guests," Emperor Hu says in a soft, but somehow easily heard voice. "With the blessings of the Two we celebrate this auspicious occasion. Please join me in welcoming your new Wife Divine, Qiu Lian, daughter of Qiu Feng, an elder of the highest degree in the village of Ning."

Emperor Hu waves a hand toward the front gate. A cheering roar rises from the crowd. Musicians beat their drums and play their suonas. Escorted by four Gold Dragon Guards and borne by four blue-robed servants, an opulent sedan of red and gold passes through the palace gates. Dressed in a glorious bright jade silk dress trimmed in elaborate gold and red, the new Wife Divine sits stiff and uncomfortable on the sedan's cushioned seat. A majestic gold phoenix headdress rests on top of her head and a red bridal veil covers her face. I wish it wasn't, but I know it's Lian.

More firecrackers explode as the sedan progresses up the thoroughfare. Hundreds of pigeons rise along the lane in a great fluttering wave as handlers release them from cages. All around the courtyard, guests send thousands of red floating lanterns skyward. Everyone cheers and smiles, except me. My chest tightens. My stomach sickens.

How can they be happy? Why don't they ask what fate their cherished Wife Divine faces? Don't they wonder the whereabouts of the other hundred Wives Divine? What about the Most Holy Wife, Divine Lady Empress Ling Yuan? Where is she? Are they afraid to ask or do they just not care?

When the sedan reaches the platform by the inner gate, Lian stands and steps onto the platform. The servants with the sedan move out of sight. Her escort of Dragon Guards marches to the platform and stand in rigid attention. The emperor motions for Lian to sit in the phoenix throne, but he never even glances at her.

The emperor stretches out his arms again. "Beloved citizens, I must leave to care for some imperial duties, but I will return soon for the glorious wedding ceremony. Until then, enjoy the banquet and feel free to pay your respects to your new Wife Divine."

The emperor vanishes. Another cheer rises from the crowd. The music from the drums and suonas swells louder. Most of the twenty thousand guests crowd their way to the tables to enjoy the ten-course banquet that has been prepared for them, but a few hundred or so fight against the flow toward the platform to greet Lian.

I shake my head. Most care little for the new Wife Divine. What they've waited for is the extravagant, ten-course banquet of exotic food and drink the emperor has gifted them.

I have yet to finish shucking all the oysters, but I have to act now. I search the preparation table where Cai has spent most of the morning gutting fish. There's no sign of him. I can't wait. While the sauce matron chastises a few other servants, I leave my oysters.

My plan is simple. When I reach the platform, I'll grab Lian and use my gift to fly her over the palace walls. Her Gold Dragon Guard escorts won't have time to react before we're out of reach. Not even archers would dare shoot at us for fear of injuring their new Wife Divine. My biggest worry had been the emperor. Even if half the tales of his powers and abilities are true, I would have little chance to defy him with my single gift from Tiānqì Shen. But in his absence, I have little to fear.

I head toward the platform, fighting my way through the press of guests still trying to find a place at a table. When I reach the line of people waiting to honor Lian, about fifty people stand ahead of me. High lady aristocrats. Nobles. Scholars. A few soldiers, including a Shashyao. Those in line give the Shashyao—slayer of the defiled—plenty of space.

I shudder. Could it be the same Shashyao Cai and I fought in the market? If so, will he recognize me? What will I do then? As I look at the sheathed Zhangchi sword strapped to his back I wish I had my Zhangchi. This morning, I hid it in a cluster of golden chrysanthemums in the gardens near the servant quarters. Even if I carried it in the bamboo tube case, it would draw too much attention. The sauce matron would likely have confiscated it from me. But now I wish I had taken that chance.

The Shashyao stands in line a few places ahead of me, but ignores me. With his back to me, he focuses only on Lian. Odd. Why is he here? Why would he want to honor the Wife Divine. I never imagined the Shashyao as people with real emotions. Why does this one care about the new Wife Divine?

As the line moves, he steps with the fluid grace and agility of a Fei Chi master. Yet, something seems off in the way he stands and moves. What is it? Should I be concerned?

When the Shashyao reaches the platform, he kneels and kowtows three times to Lian. As did many before him, he lays a yellow lily at her slippered feet. But as he does, he pushes something against the wooden heel of her slipper with his fingers. He does it in such a quick, stealthy manner I doubt anyone else noticed.

I crane my neck to see what he did, but it's not until after the next two people in line move forward to honor Lian that I'm close enough to see the small characters ink stamped on her slipper's heel. The symbols for a cart and walking, meaning transport or deliver, and the Mother stroke of the Two symbol.

A gift mark? Why would a Shashyao stamp a gift mark on Lian's slipper? What does that particular one do? And why stamp one paired with the Mother stroke instead of the Father stroke? None of it makes sense.

Thick fingers wrap around my elbow and yank me backward. I almost stumble to the ground.

"Get back to work, fool girl! My oysters still need shucking and boiling."

The sauce matron's grip tightens as I try to right myself and keep my place in line. Her scowl is fierce, but I don't care. I won't let her foul my plans.

"Release my arm, most revered matron," I say in a calm, yet confident tone. "It would sadden me deeply to see harm come to you for disobeying a sacred command from Lord Emperor Xiang Hu, Chosen of Heaven."

Her grip loosens, her scowl softens, and wariness shows in her eyes, but her voice is as harsh as ever. "What harm? What are you talking about?"

I smile, my eyes burning with hard determination. "Lord Emperor Xiang Hu, Chosen of Heaven invited all to pay their respects to the new Wife Divine. Would you dare defy that invitation?"

Her fat lips turn down in a sneer, but more uncertainty clouds her eyes. "You are a lowly servant, lower than the worms beneath my feet. He did not mean you!"

My smile twists upwards with confidence and I hold my gaze firm on her. "He invited all. Do you dare challenge the words of the Chosen of Heaven? Would you like the Gold Dragon Guard to enforce his command and punish your rebellious acts?"

The sauce matron's eyes dart toward the four members of the Gold Dragon Guard standing near the raised platform. Her face pales, but only for a moment. Her deep scowl and venomous gaze returns. "Pay your respects to the Wife Divine, but when you're done report back to me and discover what punishment I inflict on those who fail to show respect due me."

She releases my arm and storms away. My grin widens as I turn back toward the platform and realize there is only one person left between me and Lian. I wiggle my fingers and take a deep breath. I made it. Lian will soon be safe and free once again

Chapter 39
Qiu Lian – Weighing the Costs

"One who feeds the rich, honors himself. One who feeds the hungry, honors life."

- Notions from a Royal Peasant

I have never expected or sought praise and honor from others. Women don't do that in a world where Innate Honor rules. But I admit, I like the way it feels to have wedding guests line up to greet me. High ladies, soldiers, and even a few imperial ministers and scholars take turns kowtowing before me and laying lilies at my feet. What a strange, yet wonderful thing.

Their words humble me and stir feelings of love for these strangers. "The Two bless you!" "May you always know peace and joy!" "The breaths lift you!" "May the Two watch over you!" And even, "We love you, Divine One!"

These people who don't know me. How can they care so much for me? They seem sincere. Even the soldiers look at me with expressions of hope and affection.

The only exception might be the Shashyao in his all-black leather armor and terrifying demon-wolf mask. I try not tremble as he steps forward. Despite my efforts to stay in control, my fingers twitch a few times. I've heard the tales of their slaughter of those who blaspheme the Two and the Shen, but I've never seen a Shashyao in person before. I never really believed that they existed.

He says nothing. The dark eyes behind his mask stare at me with no emotion, no love, and no joy. Some say the Shashyao have no souls. I almost believe that's true. Still, the Shashyao kowtows before me in respect and lays a lily at my feet. Still, I can't help twitch and close my eyes for a brief moment as his gloved hands reach so close to me. I fear that at any moment he'll draw the sword strapped to his back and slice me in half for whatever sins he might think I've committed.

When he rises and walks away, relief washes over me. He moves away through the crowds with urgency and disappears from sight. But as quick as that relief leaves, I tense as a new worry hits me.

One of the head servants, a hefty looking lady with a merciless scowl, storms toward the front of the line of those greeting me. She grabs the elbow of a young servant girl in line and scolds her like a farmer chastising a dog that ate all of his prize chickens. The young servant girl is Meilin.

Part of me wants to leap from the podium to smother her with hugs. Another part wants to scold her for putting herself in danger. I know why she's here. To rescue me. Doesn't that girl ever give up? For all of Meilin's goat-headed, foolish ideas I have to admit she's determined and resourceful. It's amazing enough that she somehow traveled all the way to Quanli from Ning, but it's a whole other level of stunning that she managed to get inside the palace courtyard disguised as a servant.

Why does she think she has any chance of rescuing me in the middle of the palace surrounded by several thousand of the Gold Dragon Guard. Still, she almost managed to kidnap me out from under a battalion of imperial soldiers back in Ning. She must have some crazy plan to rescue me again. And no matter how crazy it might be, with Meilin's cunning she might just be able to succeed.

My toes clench again. Although part of me wants Meilin to try to free me, I can't let that happen. There's too much at stake. She means well, but she doesn't understand the costs. Even though I deserve whatever horrors the emperor has in store for me, it's no longer about that. If I don't marry the emperor, I might rob Wei of his best chance to find the empress and free his people.

Meilin might leave me alone if I could explain it to her, but she won't give me the chance. Her "act now, ask later" attitude has put her in thick trouble plenty of times in the past. She won't act any different now. I have to stop her before she has a chance.

Chapter 40
Qiu Meilin – Traps

"I have no problem with patience. People that make me wait are the problem."
- Private Journal of Qiu Meilin

As the lady in front of me finishes her kowtows and greetings to Lian, I rehearse my plan in my mind. Keep my head down. Walk slow and deliberate to the platform. Kowtow three times as expected. When I rise, jump onto the platform, wrap Lian in a tight hug, and use my gift to fly us away. It's simple.

After the lady places a lily at Lian's feet and walks away, I move forward. I force myself to not hurry. I can't afford to draw attention to myself. Nervous excitement builds inside me the closer I get. Three paces away from the platform, strong hands grab my elbows and lift me off my feet.

"Wait! What are you doing?" Two of Lian's personal guard hold me, while at least twenty other members of the Gold Dragon Guard follow behind as they carry me away from Lian. "You can't do this! I want to honor the new Wife Divine. Lord Emperor Xiang Hu invited all to honor her. That includes me!"

The guards' grips tighten, but they don't answer. They march me around to the back of the platform, through the inner gate, and into the inner courtyard. With a quick tap into my boon, I could easily overcome the two soldiers holding me. I might even be able to get past the other guards to Lian, but I'm unarmed. With so many armed soldiers, too many swords will bar the path between me and my sister.

I could use my Wind gift to blast a clear path to Lian, but it's as likely to blast Lian and harm her. Besides, I'm certain Lian had the guards stop me. Why can't she see the danger she's in? How can I save her if she won't let me?

I sigh. Once again, Lian's stubbornness has ruined my best chance to rescue her. I stop resisting the guards, knowing that will make things worse. I'll let them lock me up somewhere and use my boon to escape later to rescue Lian. That will give me time to come up with a plan to take Lian by surprise. Or maybe I need to wait until after Lian's marriage when they lock her up with all the other Wives Divine. After a little torture and suffering maybe she'll finally see I'm trying to help her.

No. I recall the visions of blood and screams from my dream. There will be much more than a little torture and suffering. People will die. If I wait too long, Lian will die. Once I escape, I have to find the best chance to save Lian before she can stop me and before any harm comes to her.

The soldiers march me through the gates into the Gold Dragon Guard barrack compound. The smell of horses, sweat, hay, and manure sour my nose as we pass the stables and onto the barrack's large grassy compound. Plain one-story wooden living quarters line the compound on three of its sides.

On the grass, thousands of soldiers move through the different Fei Chi forms, duel with swords, march with halberds, shoot bows and arrows, and practice other forms of combat. The sight of all the soldiers makes me realize that escaping might be harder than I thought.

Once again, I wish I had Zhangchi with me. The increased power and the almost endless supply of Shen Breath it provides would make escape so much easier. I'm tempted to simply break free now and attempt to fly to safety. But any one of those archers could bring me down with ease. I need to be patient and figure out an escape that won't cost me my life.

A moment later I realize my mistake. The soldiers stop in the middle of the compound near an iron grate in the ground. About the size of a shield, the grate has five bars as thick as my arms, three large hinges on one side, and a large sliding bolt on the other side to secure it closed. With considerable effort, one soldier slides the bolt free of the locking mechanism. It takes two other soldiers working together to open the grate, revealing a dark hole below.

Without warning, the soldiers drop me in the hole. It's not a far drop, but I stumble hard on the floor below. Stone walls, ceiling, and floor surround me. The underground cell is more cramped than my room back in Ning. I hurry to my feet and jump toward the hole above. It's at least twice my height above, which is not a problem with my boon, but I'm too late.

The grate slams closed with a loud clang, bashing hard against my up-reached hands, and knocking me down to the ground. The grate's vibrations shake the floor and all around me. I keep my ears covered at the high pitch scrape and squeak of the grate's security bolt being slid back into its locked position.

"You can't leave me here!" I shout up through the hole. The truth is the Gold Dragon Guard can likely do whatever they want to me without repercussions.

The thin shafts of light that shine through the grates, do little to chase away the dark shadows that grip the hole. How long do they plan to leave me here? Did Lian know the soldiers would take me.

"Gales and hail," I curse as I fumble in the darkness and accidently kick a small metal pot. I cringe at the splash and slosh that follows, realizing that I emptied a used chamber pot on the floor. I back away from it and sit in a far corner, but I can't escape the putrid smell.

I try to push down the panic and the feeling of the close walls and shadows squeezing in all around me. I cross my arms tight across my chest to try to stop my trembling, but it does me little good.

"I'll be okay," I whisper to myself. "I need to stay calm and be patient. I have my boon. Getting out of here won't be a problem."

But I have little faith in my words. The boon gives me great strength, but I'm almost sure it won't be enough to jump up and push open the locked grate. I'm trapped.

Chapter 41
Lord Emperor Xiang Hu – Sacrifices

"It's not that the Shen condone evil use of their gifts. It seems they are bound by the oaths they accept and the true intent of the oath maker."
- Hidden Scrolls of Quingping: Study in Oath Criticalities

Situated on the northwest borders of Huyan, the province of Quingping is for the most part a remote and barren wasteland. Few of my people live here. Why would they want to? Except for a few spots along the Pangbo, none of the land can be easily farmed. Most of the produce from the few existing farms either goes to my armies protecting the northern borders or to my slaves who mine the salt, copper, and iron in the nearby quarries.

Still, a few tiny villages dot Quingping where the Pangbo flows near. Wang Qing was one such village. No bamboo groves stand here, but it has a single hazelnut tree, a couple plum trees in blossom, a small rice field, and furrowed fields showing early green shoots of peas, turnips, barley, and some other vegetables.

An eerie silence hangs over the village, broken only by the mournful croaks of a cormorant. With wings spread wide, the large black bird perches on the deck of the village's lone fishing boat. The small craft bobs in the Pangbo's shallows against the strain of the current and its land anchor staked on the shore. The fisherman lies face-first in the mud near the anchor. His lifeless fingers lay a hand span away from the anchor knots he hoped to loosen before the Shashyao ended his life.

Hollowness squeezes my chest. The bodies of the village's other eighty-nine men, women, and children lay strewn about in Wang Qing's fields, shops, and mud-brick homes. Surrounded by Wang Qing's bloodied lifeless, the lone Shashyao responsible for the massacre kneels in a kowtow at my feet. My gloved hand clenches the hilt of Zhangchi sheathed at my waist.

"Did all these fallen have the Blood of the Two? Did you test any before you slew them?" The scorn in my voice is genuine, but most of it is directed to myself. This was not the order I gave my Shashyao, but the guilt is still on me. I wouldn't have admitted it at the time, but I expected this outcome. I wasn't surprised when this same scene played out in the last three Quingping villages I visited in the past few hours. I'm not surprised now. I'm angry.

The Shashyao have done far worse at my command. I have done worse. As much as I despise the bloodshed, it has all been necessary to keep the powers of Xié Shen from rising.

"Lord Emperor, Chosen of Heaven, there was no time to test their blood," The Shashyao's face still a finger's width above the ground. "At the sight of me, they all began to flee. I felt it prudent to take their lives to ensure I honored your order to let no defiled live. I serve at thy will and at thy command. If I have not done honor in your sight, please take my own life in recompense."

"No, you have done well." The harshness in my voice has left, replaced by sorrow and self-loathing.

The other Shashyao in the other massacred villages all had similar responses. It unsettles me that so many innocents must fall to stop such a great evil from rising. But many more will fall if Xié Shen and his servants are unleashed. My dreams have told me as much. Sacrifices must be made to keep my oaths to the Shen to protect all the people of Huyan. "Rise. You have done honor to yourself and to your family. You have done honor to me. Go. Continue the search for the defiled. I have a few more villages to visit."

The Shashyao rises to his feet, gives me a palm in fist salute and a slight bow, and hurries away to kill more innocent people in my name.

Hopefully, some of those killed will not be so innocent. Hopefully, they will find and destroy all the favored ones of Xié Shen before the demon lord can use them to unleash his demon dragon and ultimately free him and all his followers from the depths of Kaioda. My dream cannot come true. Xié Shen must be stopped.

Chapter 42
Chao Cai – Pleas for Help

"We know of at least 111 honorable Shen, but who's to say there aren't more?"

- Hidden Scrolls of Quingping: Study in the gifts of the Shen

With the smell of fish all around, memories of home engulf me. Every day since I could walk, Father would take me on our little boat onto the Pangbo. Father taught me how to read the river's current, judge the winds, and use the sails. He trained me how to fish with a net, line, and spear. He taught me how to train cormorants to be faithful fish hunters for their masters. I was fifteen when I first started training Peck, my favorite bird of all.

And of course, Father taught me my least favorite task as a fisherman—how to use a knife to quickly and neatly gut and fillet a fish. That's what I've done most of the day today. Somewhere after the thousandth fish, I stopped counting how many I had cleaned and filleted.

Both Meilin and I have been so busy we've had little time to say more than a few words to each other since we first woke this morning. Even if we had time, our tasks for the wedding preparations have kept us apart. It's been strange not being able to be with her and joke with her. There's a strength and comfort that comes to me whenever Meilin and I are together. It's not something I've felt before, not even with Lian.

I loved being with Lian, but it was different. Lian was a challenge. If I'm honest, Meilin's an even greater challenge. Trying to figure out what she's going to do next is impossible. What is she thinking and why? What makes Meilin happy? What makes Meilin angry? What makes her sad? When do I offer help? When do I stay out of Meilin's way? When do I talk? When do I hold her and listen, or let there be silence? How can I make her happy? And why does Meilin even like someone as simple as me?

The challenge with Lian was different. She was exciting, but she was always an enigma, a puzzle to be solved. Honor and propriety always mattered to Lian, yet you could sense at times that she was at odds with what society expected of her. She never would say much, but her quiet confidence demanded the respect of others. She was often serious and thoughtful, but once in a while she would transform into a playful tease. And Lian always had high aspirations to do great things for people throughout the kingdom of Huyan, yet so often she would talk about disappearing to a remote part of Dashi where she could live a simple life of peace and solitude.

As I look back, it was the thought of being with Lian that was exciting. Being with someone who would someday do great and wonderful things. Even though Lian and I had fun together, I could sense she always held back a part of herself. Perhaps, that was the greatest enigma about Lian, trying to figure out who she really was and what she really wanted from me and from life.

As the cheers thunder as her sedan bearers march her through the palace gates, my heart jumps and old emotions begin to stir. Memories surface of how some evenings as the sun began to set, we would sneak away and sit on the dock together, dangling our bare feet in the shallows of the Pangbo to watch fish jump above the water to snag buzzing insects for dinner.

In her soft, yet serious voice she would ask the most perplexing questions. How many fish are in the Pangbo? Enough to feed all of Dashi? Why do the fish stay in the Pangbo? Why don't they swim to the Great Seas in the east where fishermen will leave them alone? Who really owns the Pangbo? Emperor Hu claims it, but if much of it flows from the snowpack of Yemaren's Great Khasheeq Mountains, why don't the Yemaren own it? Or maybe it belongs to Tiānqì Shen, who blesses us with rain and snow. Perhaps, the Two claim it as creators of all Dashi?

I could never answer her questions, but she often got my mind thinking in ways I had never thought before. What is she thinking now as she sits on her platform, raised above the most important people in Huyan kingdom? Does she see the marriage to the emperor as a chance to change the world? Does she understand the danger she's in? Does she still believe I'm dead? Does she miss me? Did she ever miss me? Did she ever love me? None of that really matters now. What matters is that somehow, Meilin and I need to rescue her from whatever the emperor has planned for her.

The afternoon hours pass too fast. Meilin and I never have a chance to make our plans for how to free Lian. Once all the fish are cleaned and filleted, I spend the afternoon to near evening hefting baskets of fish guts and muck from the courtyard privy sheds and taking them to the compost piles in the palace gardens near the northeast end of the inner courtyard.

Passing through a small, little known service gate in the inner wall that leads from the outer courtyard to the inner courtyard, I carry my twelfth load of fish guts and privy muck in my shoulder-yoke. Rolled up cinnamon leaves shoved up my nostrils help me tolerate the putrid smell coming from my muck baskets, but it's not enough.

From all the trips that I and the other servants have made to the garden compost piles this afternoon, have worn a path in the grass from the service gates to the paved inner courtyard's thoroughfare. When I almost reach the thoroughfare, about two dozen armed Gold Dragon Guards march through the inner gate into the inner courtyard. Two of the guards drag Meilin by her elbows.

What has she done? She was supposed to wait to act until we decided together on a rescue plan. They're about twenty paces ahead of me when I step onto thoroughfare. They don't notice me. It's amazing how carrying baskets of fish guts and privy muck from a shoulder-yoke can make you invisible. I hurry my pace to get a little closer, but not too close. I don't want the smell of my load to make them take too much notice of me, or worse, encourage them to chase me away.

They march Meilin to the barrack compound of the Gold Dragon Guard. I stop at the entrance, watching them carry her across the courtyard. They pass other soldiers doing combat drills. The soldiers with Meilin stop in the center of the compound. Their backs are to me. What are they doing?

A deafening clang sounds and Meilin shouts, "You can't leave me here!"

All but one guard march back toward me, but Meilin is gone. The lone remaining soldier kneels on the grass pushing something that screeches and scrapes as it moves.

A holding pit. I make a mental note of its whereabouts in case there's more than one. Even with the Chi from the Shen Breath flowing inside me, I don't know if I can get Meilin out of there. To take on a whole courtyard of Gold Dragon Guards, I need a plan.

"Worm!" A broad, hulky officer storms toward me and shouts, "Get that stinking muck out of here!"

I jerk to attention, almost spilling the contents of my baskets on his boots. I bow meekly toward the soldier and hurry away toward the muck shed in the northeast garden. I don't want a fight right now. I need to think of how to rescue Meilin. Once she's safe, we can worry about saving Lian together.

On my way to the muck shed, I pass a number of Shen shrines, and the seed of a plan starts to form in my mind. After I reach the muck shed and empty my buckets, I ditch my shoulder-yoke and hurry toward the shrine of Chéng Huáng Shen, the god of protection.

Amid a small orchard of plum trees in blossom, the green-roofed pavilion has a small moat surrounding it that can be easily stepped across. Spotted carp of black, white, and gold swim the moat's shallow waters. Lilies grow on both sides of the moat's banks. On the other side of the moat, a knee-high wall surrounds the pavilion. A lone member of the Gold Dragon Guard sits on the wall, guarding the pavilion's entrance.

The soldier's gaze narrows as he eyes me. "What do you want, worm? Don't you have work to do?"

I bow toward the soldier and give him a hand in fist salute. "Please excuse my intrusion, esteemed warrior of the Gold Dragon Guard. I simply wish to pay my respects to Chéng Huáng Shen."

The soldier laughs, a scowl clear on his face. "The shrines are only for Lord Emperor Xiang Hu, Chosen of Heaven."

I bow again. "My apologies. I did not know." I keep my head bowed, not only to show respect to the guard, but to give me time to think of a different tact.

"Scat, you muck wreaking worm." The soldier rises to his feet with his hand firmly gripping the hilt of his sword. "Your filthy stench sicks me up. Get, before I run you through."

Focusing on my oath to Tiānqì Shen, I call upon the Chi stirring inside me. In a blur of speed, I leap across the moat and in mid-air I plant my foot hard against the soldier's chest. The force of my strike knocks him over the low wall where he lands hard on his back on a patch of grass, falling unconscious.

I drag him by his boots into the pavilion. After a quick bath in the moat to wash all traces of muck and its stink off myself, I put on the soldier's uniform, black leather armor, and gold cape. I gag the guard and bind his ankles and wrists with strips of cloth that I rip off from my servant robes.

At the back of the pavilion stands a marble statue that uses rectangular stones of different sizes to depict the thick arms, legs, and torso of Chéng Huáng Shen. On his round head sits a crown shaped like a city wall with five guard towers, a city gate, and a surrounding moat. I kneel before the statue and kowtow three times, and place on the altar a catfish filet that I had been hoping to eat since before lunch but hadn't yet had time. With a fist in hand salute, I bow my head and close my eyes.

"Chéng Huáng Shen, I am a simple man of little worth in this world, yet I beg your help. My life is in danger. Those I love are in danger. My only wish is to help them and preserve them. By the Two, I pray thou wilt help me do so. All thanks to you and the Two."

I open my eyes and raise my head. My offered prayer was almost the exact prayer I offered in Tiānqì Shen's shrine, but I can't tell if it's been accepted by Chéng Huáng Shen. I look at the Shen Breath lantern glowing on the floor beside me. It glows bright, but not any brighter than usual. The Shen Breath sings its beautiful melody, but it's no louder or different than when I first heard it sing in Tiānqì Shen's shrine. Should I expect something different? I don't know.

As I reach toward the Shen Breath lantern, its tendrils bend toward my fingers, but no more so than usual. When I touch the lantern, its Chi flows into me, but only enough to replenish what I used to knock out the Gold Dragon Guard manning the entrance to the shrine. I don't feel any different.

My stomach growls as I stare down at the catfish fillet on the altar tray. I hope I didn't waste my only chance at lunch or dinner. I rise to my feet, shaking my head. How do I find out if Chéng Huáng Shen granted me a gift or not?

Stepping over the still unconscious and bound soldier, I walk out of the shrine. I stop on the porch and study the characters painted in yellow across the dark wood of the shrine's crossbeam. Chéng Huáng Shen's name is written across the top. Beneath those are the symbols for pit, wall, moat, hide, and shield.

Tiānqì Shen's shrine also had symbols painted on its crossbeams beneath the weather goddess' name, but for wind, mists, storm, lightning, and sunshine. Before I even stepped out of Tiānqì Shen's shrine, the symbol for wind paired with the Father stroke filled my mind. I ignored it best I could, but I had a strange, yet persistent compulsion to draw the symbols somewhere, anywhere on my skin. Right now, no such thoughts or compulsions regarding any of the symbols on the crossbeam of Chéng Huáng Shen's shrine haunt my mind.

Did my plea for a gift from the god of protection fail? Why? Was my offering not good enough? Was my oath lacking or not sincere enough? What did I do wrong?

"Frustrating, isn't it?"

The voice startles me. I spin around to see who's there while I hurry to unsheathe the sword at my belt. I expect to find a member of the Gold Dragon Guard, but all I see is a gardener pruning the branches of one of the nearby plum trees. He smiles, but the sight of red splotchy symbols marring the left side of his face startle me further.

"Why is a quarry slave in Quanli pretending to be a gardener?" I blurt. Near Quingping, my regiment encountered many quarry slaves with those markings. We had strict instructions to kill any who wander outside the quarry zone. But he's none of my concern now.

The fake gardener laughs. "Why is a pretend Gold Dragon Guard breaking imperial law by trying to get a boon from Chéng Huáng Shen?"

I slide my sword back in its scabbard and give the gardener a forced smile. I could threaten him to silence. But he somehow knows I'm a fake and could sound an alarm. I don't need that right now.

He watches me as I step over the shrine's low wall and leap over the moat. The gardener continues to grin as I step onto the cobbled path and hurry past his plum tree.

"Friend, it takes a brave man to defy an emperor," the gardener whispers loudly. "But it does little good if you forget the rule, women first."

What? I stop and look back at the man. Women first? Is the gardener's neck itching for the executioner's blade? Those words are blasphemy to every tenet of Innate Honor. I have no love for those tenets, but I'd like to keep my head on my neck for the time being. With a quick shake of my head, I hurry away toward the gardens near the servant quarters.

A trace of the setting sun can be seen above the horizon when I reach the gardens and unearth Zhangchi from beneath a clump of gold chrysanthemums. In a rush, I strap Zhangchi's scabbard to my back and hurry to the barracks, working out an outrageous plan to rescue Meilin.

Chapter 43
Qiu Meilin – Desperation

"I've always believed if you try hard enough you can find a reason to smile. I might have been wrong."

- Private Journal of Qiu Meilin

Keep going! I can do this!" I mutter. But inside I know I'm a goat-headed fool. I dangle high above the pit floor with a chamber pot in one hand and my other hand grasping the grate's bars. That's the easy part. Doing much more than dangling is what's difficult.

Earlier, I had tried using my boon to spread the bars far enough apart to allow me to squeeze through. But I could barely budge them. The next several attempts after that, I squeezed one arm through the bars to reach the locking bolt. But the bolt angles awkwardly so I can't get the leverage to slide it free no matter how much Chi I called upon.

Now dangling by one hand, I use the chamber pot in my other hand to scrape away bits of the concrete ceiling next to the grate. Concrete dust falls on my face and gets in my eyes, but I do my best to ignore it. My hope is to scrape enough away that the ceiling will weaken and allow the grate to break free and fall. But I've been scraping for more than thirty minutes, and I've scraped away less than a finger's width of concrete. Worse, my Shen Breath ran out more than five minutes ago. Not only have my scraping efforts worsened, but my arm muscles burn with pain and fatigue. I can't hang on much longer.

I should have risked an archer's arrow earlier and flown away while I had the chance. I could be trapped in this foul hole forever. Stop thinking like that. I'll get out of here. There has to be a way.

My arms burn with pain. I try to switch hands, but as I do the chamber pot slips from my hands. It disappears in the dark shadows and clangs on the pit floor. Gales! I really am a goat head.

Still dangling by one hand, but without the chamber pot, I use my fingernails to scrape at the concrete. The sound and feel of it makes me shiver and hurts my ears, but I have to get out of here. I scrape until my fingernails wear down to the flesh of my fingertips. Tears well in the corners of my eyes at the burning pain in my arm holding the grate. I fight to hold on, but my muscles give in.

I crash to the ground in an exhausted heap. I lie there limp. I don't want to move. I just want to rest for a moment or two. But I have to escape. I have to rescue Lian, whether she wants rescuing or not.

Breathing heavily, I rise to my hands and knees and crawl in the dark feeling for the chamber pot. Once in hand, I crawl to one of the concrete walls and start scraping again. This time to scrape steps and hand holds up the wall to the grate.

Scraping away enough concrete for a single foothold takes at least an hour. It's progress, but I have to stop. My fingers hurt and shake so much I can no longer hold onto the chamber pot.

Kneeling on the cold, hard ground I tilt my head back, stare up at the dark sky above the grate, and yell, "Let me out! Let me out of here!"

No one answers. But what else can I do? So, I shout and scream until my throat hurt. I keep screaming. No one can probably hear me, but I scream anyway.

"Quiet down there!" a harsh voice yells from above.

I open my mouth to yell again, but a shower of cold water drenches me from above. The icy water silences me. Shivering, I wrap my arms tight around myself and crumble to the floor. My drenched robes cling to me as I curl up into a fetal position.

"Let me out," I whisper, fighting back the sobs that rise in my throat. "Please, please. Let me out."

Chapter 44
Qiu Lian – The Marriage

"Other than her pentad of gifts that includes Learn, Solve, Decide, Detect, and Remember, we haven't learned enough about Zhì Shen to construct a shrine for her yet."

- Hidden Scrolls of Quingping: Study in the gifts of the Shen

A full catfish, a lobster tail, a couple crab legs, three prawns, and a slice of roast pork sit on a porcelain platter on a tray beside me. My stomach growls and aches with hunger. I haven't eaten since before sunrise, and sunset is less than an hour away. The platter of food is mine. I'm just not allowed to eat it. It's for later, when the emperor and I have the private ceremony.

Watching the emperor's guests eat, drink, laugh, and dance for so many hours is unbearable. Watching them gorge themselves while I try to look regal is horrible, especially since my empty stomach stings for want of food. At least my veil covers my face, so I don't have to smile and pretend to be happy for all of Huyan's elite as they feast.

But it's not just the hunger. The mass of people and noise overwhelm me. I want to run away and find a place to be alone. The peacefulness of the gardens would be so delightful right now, as would Wei's company.

I've searched for him in the crowds and even on the ramparts of courtyard walls, but it's hard to see clearly through the veil, especially when looking at a distance. He could be out there, but I've not had a single glimpse of him. By the Two, I hope he is here somewhere and that he will still come for me.

What if Wei doesn't come? Will the emperor throw me in a dungeon and torture me like in Meilin's stories? If so, what will happen to Meilin?

Will my guards release her after the wedding ceremony as I asked, or have I condemned her to a life of imprisonment? I wish I had thought of that possibility sooner.

I have to stop worrying so much. Wei will come and rescue me from any harm the emperor might intend against me. And when he comes, I'll make sure he sees that Meilin is freed too.

My body shakes. I almost jump out of my chair when the gong sounds. Its vibrations thunder so close to me. The crowd goes silent almost in an instant. All eyes turn toward me. No, not toward me, toward Emperor Hu. He suddenly reappears on the platform standing in front of his throne.

I rise to my feet, facing forward, but watching him from the corner of my eyes. He smiles wide, but it's contrasted by a grim, sorrowful look in his eyes.

"My beloved people." His voice is soft, yet powerful. "By the Two's favor, I trust you have enjoyed the festivities of this day."

A loud cheer rises from the crowds, augmented with hand clapping and banging of copper goblets. When the crowd quiets, Emperor Hu gestures toward me with his hand and continues, "The time has come for this faithful daughter of Huyan to become your newest Wife Divine."

Cheers erupt again. I frown. Why does he call me their Wife Divine and not his Wife Divine? He's the one marrying me, not the people.

As the cheers die down, servants carry a fine-crafted sandalwood altar table up the platform steps and set it a few paces in front of me and the emperor. In the lattice work of the table's surface the right slanting curved Mother stroke and the left slanting curved Father stroke of the Two symbol repeat in a connected series, making an intricate pattern. Carved in cherry wood, a plump statuette of the Mother riding a fiery phoenix sits on the right side of the table. On the left is a gold leaf plump statuette of the Father riding a coiled sinewy dragon.

Between the emperor and me, another servant places a tray on the table with two white porcelain teapots and two teacups glazed in blue with a blossoming peach tree on each one. Following my tutors' instructions of the past few days, once the servant walks away, I kneel in front of the Two's altar table and kowtow three times. Emperor Hu kneels and kowtows as well. I rise when he rises and doing my best to match his movements, I pick up my teapot, pour a small amount of tea into my cup, and raise the cup above my head. The Emperor does the same.

In unison, we say, "Thanks to the Two, Mother and Father of all creations and all that is good."

At the same time, we upturn our cups and pour the tea onto the lattice work of the altar table, mine in front of the statuette of the Mother and the emperor in front of the statuette of the Father. We each take three steps back and as we do servants carry away the altar table, slowly promenading down the steps of the platform.

Once they leave, another set of servants step up onto the platform and set a different altar table in front of us. This one is also made of sandalwood with a plain lattice work surface made of circles. Instead of having statuettes of the Two, miniature carvings of all one hundred eleven of the honorable Shen line the edges of the table.

After kowtowing in unison three times before the altar, the emperor and I rise in unison, pour tea into our cups, raise the cups above our heads, and say, "Thanks to the beloved Shen, the honorable children of the Two, for their bounteous gifts and watchful protection."

As before, we upturn our cups and pour the tea onto the lattice work of the altar table. Emperor Hu and I stare in silence at each other as servants take away the Shen altar table. The crowds in the courtyard grow quieter. Their gazes lock unto us, waiting in anticipation for the emperor to do what in any other circumstance would be unthinkable. My toes clench and my chest tightens as he kneels on the ground and kowtows toward me three times. With his face still to the floor, I kneel and kowtow three times toward him.

The hush remains as we rise. We pour tea into our cups and offer it to the other. We say no words, but I drink his and he drinks mine. When we set our cups down onto the tray, a deafening roar rises from the courtyard. It's so loud I want to cover my ears, but I have to stand still and regal beside the emperor facing the crowd. The public portion of the marriage ceremony is complete. One last private task remains before our marriage can become official and in force—the removal of the veil.

While the crowd still cheers, the emperor and I walk side by side down the platform steps. The cheers grow like rumbling thunder when we turn our backs on the crowd to walk through the inner gate into the inner courtyard. Likely they believe the emperor is leading me to his royal chambers in the palace to remove my veil and consummate the marriage. But I assume that will be later. Right now, we're going to the shrine of Zhì Shen for a private ceremony that, according to Lord Zheng, few know about.

We only take a few steps before servants hand each of us a basket. Mine holds the uneaten food from my banquet platter. I assume the emperor's has food inside his too. If few know about the private ceremony, I wonder if the servants think the emperor and I are going on a picnic. I also wonder why we walk instead of taking a sedan or carriage.

We walk in silence along the smooth stone path that leads through courtyard lawns and gardens. We pass between the servant quarters and imperial barracks. On the one side of the courtyard, the servant quarters stand still and quiet. On the other side, clangs and shouts of dueling and form practice echo from the barracks.

When we reach the temple of the Two with its majestic rising tower and multi-tiered roof, the emperor pauses and opens his mouth as if to say something. But then he closes his mouth and continues walking in silence.

The emperor slows his pace as we pass the noble housing, guest rooms and the palace proper. When we step onto the cobbled paths of the northeast gardens, the scents and beauty of blossoming trees and flowers surround us, and the emperor's expression relaxes.

"Tell me of your life, Qiu Lian." The emperor's voice startles me. What do I say? Before I can pull my thoughts together, he adds. "You were born and raised in the village of Ning? Is that right?"

When I nod, he smiles. "Tell me what it was like growing up there and about your family."

I hesitate at first, but then begin to tell him of our small home on the side of the hill that overlooks our little valley near the Pangbo river and Gudai forest. I talk of how Mama and I would spend each day caring for the house, cooking meals, harvesting the village silk, preparing ramie stalks for weaving, and if time allowed painting pictures. I tell how Father tends our crop of soybeans, peas, and cabbage, as well as takes his turn working the village rice fields.

I don't mention Meilin, for fear he might have heard of how she stole Lord Zheng's horse to try to rescue me. I also don't mention Cai. It still hurts to talk or think of him. Also, I don't how the emperor would react if he knew I once hoped to marry someone else. And I definitely keep silent about Wei.

The emperor's tone is light and carefree as he asks about friends and village traditions. He even laughs when I tell him how Master Jin would scold us when as little children we would play Dragon's Tail in the shrine gardens. But his voice turns serious when he asks how well the soldiers guard the shrine pavilion's entrance. My response satisfies him as the lightness in his voice returns and he asks more about my life.

The sun is near setting when we reach the shrine of Zhì Shen. The emperor immediately stops talking and the smile on his face disappears, replaced with grim determination. With a wave of his hand, he dismisses the Gold Dragon Guard stationed at the entrance.

As I watch the guard walk away, I shrink back as my eyes fall on another Gold Dragon Guard hurrying away from another shrine close by. The soldier's back is to me, but his posture and the way he walks reminds me of Cai. My heart tightens as the guilt and emotions crash and surge within me. The loss of Cai still hurts deep. I can never forgive myself for what I did.

It doesn't matter that the lies I told were to protect him. Those lies sent him off to war and to his death thinking that I never really loved him. My attempts to punish myself have done little to soften the grief and guilt. Rather, I've betrayed his memory by the luxury I've enjoyed these past few days in the palace. The only really peace I've felt is the time I've spent with Wei, but that feels like another betrayal.

"Qiu Lian, are you well?" The emperor's voice brings me back to the present, stirring up more anxiety for what I'm about to do.

"I am fine, Lord Emperor, Chosen of Heaven." My voice trembles as I speak. Deep emotions still thrash hard inside me. "Please forgive me, I am a little nervous."

A kind grin rises on the emperor's face. "I understand, but you need not worry. All will be well. You will see."

He sounds so sincere and kind, it makes me question the dangers that both Meilin and Wei warned me about.

The emperor continues toward the shrine pavilion, which stands on an island in the middle of a small pond covered with lotus flowers. The colors of the setting sun shimmer on the shrine's blue wing-tipped tile roof. A short footbridge arches from the cobbles of the garden path over the pond to the shrine's stone porch. Painted in yellow across the pavilion's rosewood crossbeam are the three-character symbols for the wisdom goddess' name—a straight arrow and a gateway leading to daylight. Painted beneath those are five more symbols for learn, solve, decide, detect, and remember.

The planks of the footbridge creak as I follow the emperor across. I stop on the shrine's stone porch even though the emperor beckons me to follow him inside. Lord Zheng told me I must enter the shrine for the private ceremony, but I also know it's against Innate Honor and imperial law for any women to enter a shrine, punishable by immediate execution. I wonder if this might be a test of some sort.

I remember Meilin's stories of how the emperor tortures his wives. Once I enter the shrine will my disobedience of imperial law give him cause to inflict some horrific torture against me? The thought is ridiculous. The emperor can choose to do what he wants regardless of whether or not I obey imperial law.

I step inside, the wood soles of my slippers clop loudly on the porcelain tiles. At the end of the corridor stands a gold statue of Zhì Shen. She wears a plain, long flowing robe. A crown encircled with several large eyes made of rubies holds up her hair. A necklace of golden ears hangs from her neck. In one hand she holds a wide scroll as her scepter. Above her other hand floats the world of Dashi orbited by the sun, moons, and stars.

I follow the emperor down a short corridor lined with glowing Shen Breath lanterns. I pass a painting on the wall of the great scholar Pan Ru sitting on a boulder atop a high mountain. Next to him, Zhì Shen reposes on a floating cloud. She whispers in his ear as he writes on a long flowing scroll.

The emperor stops when he comes within three paces of her statue. I stop beside him. In unison we drop to our knees and kowtow toward Zhì Shen. We rise, take a step, kneel, and kowtow three more times. One more time we rise, step forward, kneel, and kowtow three last times. At last, we kneel side by side in front of Zhì Shen's statue at the altar tray with rosewood trimmed edges and white lattice work surface.

The ceremony begins with me making the oaths, but I don't move or say a word. I tense to keep from trembling as Wei's caution and Meilin's stories roll through my mind. My toes fully clench. The silence of the shrine adds to my nervousness. When Emperor Hu draws his sword from his sheath, my nervousness boils up inside until I feel like I will explode. I want to scream. Instead, I clench my toes even tighter, reminding myself that the sword is part of the ceremony.

I relax a little when with a soft clink, Emperor Hu places his sword in front of him on the porcelain floor. I continue to kneel, nervous to break the silence. With his face forward and eyes fixed on Zhì Shen, the emperor clears his throat, urging me to do my part.

I let out a long breath to calm myself and reach into the basket of food the servant gave me earlier. My hand hovers between a slice of pork and crab legs, trying to remember if Lord Zheng ever mentioned what food I should choose first. When the emperor clears his throat again, I hurriedly grab the pork. In my haste, it slips from my fingers, but I catch it before it hits the ground. The emperor says nothing—not a throat clear or even a twitch. Either he didn't notice or he's being very patient with me.

Taking another deep breath, I place the pork slice on the lattice surface of the altar. A tiny speck of pork sticks to my fingers. I'm so hungry, I'm tempted to lick it off, but I think better of it and simply wipe it on top of the altar to make sure Zhì Shen receives my complete offering—nothing held back.

Still, I cringe as I watch juices from the pork drip through the altar tray lattice down into the drain beneath it. I would give an eye and an ear to catch a few of those drops on my fingers and lick them clean. Instead,

I bow my head, close my eyes, make a fist in hand salute pressed against my chest, and utter the words of the oath.

"Most honorable, high and holy Zhì Shen." My voice trembles a bit, but I try to bring it under control as I continue. "Huyan kingdom and all of Dashi need thy help and protection. By the Two's favor and at your will, I pray that thou wilt grant me of your gifts. If it so be granted, I swear by the Two and your holy altar that I will use your gifts in service of Huyan and Dashi. All thanks to you and the Two."

I open my eyes, raise my head, and turn toward the Shen Breath lantern on the floor beside me. I blink my eyes. Strange. The mists of the lantern glow with a deep brilliance I've never noticed before. Their swirling tendrils twist and stretch toward me like they want to escape the lantern and come to me.

As part of the ceremony, I reach toward the lantern and touch its side with the tip of my finger. The mists burn brighter. The side of the lantern bulges. Its tendrils streak toward my finger. A powerful warmth and strength flows into my finger and spreads beneath my skin throughout my body with a glorious euphoria burning within me. I must be imagining, but I hear singing, like a heavenly voice oohing and aahing in a beautiful melody. I want to sing with it. I want to rise to my feet and shout for joy at the indescribable overwhelming sensations I feel.

Lord Zheng warned me to only touch the lantern for a moment, but he didn't tell me of the wondrous surge of life, energy, and music that the Shen Breath would bring. I want to feel and hear it forever. But a glance from the emperor urges me to obey. I grin. Even when I pull my finger from the lantern, the euphoric feeling continues to dance and burn inside me.

But like a blast of freezing water drenching a raging fire, the warmth and surging power are gone the instant the emperor touches his sword blade flat against the back of my saluting hands. Cold, hollowness chills my insides.

"No! Give it back!" I want to shout, but I hold my tongue. Tears form in the corners of my eyes at the loss. How could something so wonderful disappear in such a quick instant? The melody of the Shen Breath still calls me, but rather than comforting me, it's a grim reminder of the glorious feeling that was so abruptly robbed from me. With my veil hiding all my facial expressions, the emperor gives no indication that he notices my distress.

As if nothing happened, he lays his sword back in its place in front of him. He pulls a few prawns from the basket at his side and lays them on the altar. Without a word or hesitation, he bows his head, closes his eyes, makes a hand in fist salute, and recites the words of the oath exactly as I did.

Once he finishes the oath, he removes a glove from one of his hands and touches a Shen Breath lantern at his side. The mists bend and glow at his touch, but the emperor makes no indication that he feels the wonderful feelings that I felt. Not even a hint of a grin changes the somber expression on his face. His finger lingers on the lantern only a moment as if nothing spectacular happened at all.

I stare at the sword lying on the floor in front of him, expecting him to pick it up and lay its blade against his flesh, but he makes no effort to do so. Instead, he clears his throat and nods toward me to once again to continue with the ceremony.

I muffle a sigh as I reach into the basket and pull out a lobster tail. My stomach growls as I lay it on the altar. I try to forget my hunger as I bow my head and close my eyes. I make a fist in hand salute and repeat the oath. Once the words are said, the Shen Breath sings a new melody, harmonizing with the first melody it sang. It's so beautiful, almost hypnotic.

This time I don't hesitate. I touch the Shen Breath lantern, and the exhilarating warmth and power overwhelms. I want to feel it forever, but as soon as I pull away my finger, the emperor's blades touches my hands, and the sensation vanishes once again.

With my part done, the emperor once again places an offering of food on the altar, bows, shuts his eyes, recites the oath, and touches the lantern. Each taking our turns, we perform the oath ceremony a total of five times. By the time we finish, the up and down spikes of exhilaration and depressing emptiness, emotionally exhaust me. Only the songs of the Shen Breath bring me relief, now harmonizing like a five-part chorus.

"Well done," Emperor Hu says as he pulls his glove back on his hand and re-sheathes his sword at his belt. "Now, to seal our vows with a toast to Zhì Shen and her gifts of wisdom."

He pulls from the basket two copper chalices and a bronze wine container. The sweet aroma of rice wine with a hint of honey wafts through the air. He pours the amber colored liquid into the chalices, filling them each almost halfway and setting them both on the altar tray. He gestures for me to take one.

That's strange. The emperor has shown me very few courtesies today, let alone since I've arrived in the palace. Why give me a choice or courtesy now? Wei warned me not to drink the wine. Is the emperor worried I might refuse to drink? Is this his way of trying to put me at ease, to make sure any suspicions I might have are swept away so I will drink?

If the wine is poisoned, surely it will poison the emperor too. Or will it? He's immortal, isn't he? Will poisoned wine hurt him? If not, both chalices of wine could be poisoned. I tend to over think things. Is that what I'm doing now? The real question is, who do I trust more, the emperor or Wei? Definitely Wei.

So, I take the chalice closest to me and lift it in the air. Emperor Hu picks up the other chalice and raises it toward mine in toast.

"To Zhì Shen," he says. "May her gifts bless all of Dashi."

"To Zhì Shen," I repeat.

I watch as the emperor puts the chalice to his lips and drinks. When he nods at me to do the same, I take the chalice beneath my veil, put it to my lips, and pretend to drink. When I set it back down on the tray, the emperor's gaze lowers to the chalice still half full of wine.

He laughs. "You must take more than a sip. Zhì Shen may take offense if you don't drink it all."

I wince. How am I going to do this?

I take up the chalice again and lift it to my lips beneath my veil. I take a light breath and drink, but don't swallow. My cheeks bulge as they fill with wine. Thanks to my veil, the emperor can't see my bulging cheeks.

I tightened my lips closed as I pull the chalice away. I grimace as I see a little bit of wine still swirling at the bottom of the chalice. I'm scared I can't fit anymore in my mouth without it bursting out. But I have to try.

With an intent focus on breathing through my nose and not my mouth, I put the chalice to my lips again, tip the bottom of the chalice all the way up, and sip in the remaining bit of wine into my mouth. My cheeks bulge as far as they possibly can. Still, it takes a lot of effort to not spew it all out.

The emperor smiles when I set the chalice back down and he sees my chalice is empty. His gaze moves back to me, but he doesn't say anything. I kneel in silence, primarily because I can't talk with a mouthful of wine, but also because Lord Zheng never told me what would happen after the Zhì Shen oath ceremony.

The emperor continues to watch me intently. As the moments pass, his smile droops and anxiousness begins to show in the corner of his eyes. A similar anxiousness sounds in his voice as he asks, "How are you feeling? Are you okay?"

I can't answer, but I have to do something. Hoping I'm convincing, I sway my head and shoulders side to side as if dizzy. I lean forward, placing my hands on the porcelain tile floor as if to keep me up. As graceful as I can, I crumble to the ground, laying my head on the altar tray. My cheek squishes against the wet juices of the pork slice, its savory smell tantalizing my nose.

"Very good," The emperor says. Through the veil I watch him rise to his feet and walk toward the pavilion entrance. As his footfalls echo on the porcelain tile, I let the wine dribble out my lips through the altar tray lattice work down to the drain below.

When I hear the emperor call to the shrine guard to return to his post at the shrine entrance, I lift my cheek off the pork slice and with my teeth rip off a small piece and chew. It tastes divine. It's so soft it almost melts in my mouth. I want to savor it, eating as slow as possible, but at the sound of the emperor's returning footfalls I hurry to finish chewing. I desperately want to take another bite or two, but I can't risk it.

The emperor kneels beside me, putting his mouth near my ear. What is he going to do? Fighting the urge to tense, I try to remain still and relaxed.

"Do not fear, Qiu Lian," he whispers. "You will be well taken care of. Still, with the Two's favor I pray that when the next life comes you will forgive me for the life I robbed you of."

It grows harder not to tense up as I expect him to draw his sword and end my life. Instead, he encircles me with his arms, lifting my head off the altar tray and my upper body off the floor. I close my eyes as he stares down at me. I don't think he can see through the veil, but with his face so close to mine I want to be sure.

"What is this?" Anger burns in the emperor's voice. He loosens his embrace, only to clench my upper arms tight and shake me hard. "Who put this mark behind your ear? Who is the defiled one that did this? A servant? Lord Zheng? Someone else? One of Xié Shen's favored? Tell me now! I demand it!"

I keep quiet. It takes all my effort to stay limp and relaxed as if sleeping. If he believes I'm sleeping, he'll know I can't answer. He has to believe I'm drugged and knocked out.

"It doesn't matter. Their ploy will not work." The sharpness remains in his voice, but he's in more control now. "If I have to kill Lord Zheng and all your servants, I will discover who is behind this treachery."

I cringe inside. I feel no pity if Lord Zheng dies, but I can't bear for the emperor to kill Chan. But there's nothing I can do. If I tell the emperor the truth, he will hunt down Wei and kill him. That would be even worse. The emperor will likely kill me too. I stay quiet and continue to fake sleep.

I hear the guttural sound of spitting, followed by the emperor rubbing the tips of his wet fingers hard behind my ear. My heart aches with hollowness. The mark Wei placed there will be gone now. Now, he won't be able to rescue me or find the empress to save his people.

The emperor's grip on my arms loosens and he wraps his arms around me once again. "Sleep on, young one. You will still serve Huyan and Dashi well. None of the defiled ones, nor any of Xié Shen's favored, will succeed at bringing their master to power. I will see to that."

The emperor stands, holding me in his arms. I feel him tense for a moment and a breeze swirls around me as dizziness washes over me. The air around me changes in an instant. It's thinner, with a biting chill to it.

"Rest, Qiu Lian," The emperor whispers, as he sets me down on a soft surface. "Continue your sleep. Someone will come soon to take care of you. And do not worry, I will check on you often. Goodbye for now."

Air rustles around me, and then it stills. I slowly open my eyes and peer through my veil. The emperor is gone. I sit up on a plain narrow bed of pillows in a room as large as the village square back home in Ning.

Large, white animal furs cover the walls. Dimly lit by a few oil lamps spread throughout, the room doesn't have a single window. In neat rows all around me are one hundred beds—all similar to mine. On each bed sleeps a woman. Covered in thick white fur blankets from toe to chin, each woman has a red bridal veil covering her face. I have found the emperor's Wives Divine!

Chapter 45
Chao Cai – Burning Chaos

"I consider myself a logical person, but you wouldn't know it by some of my witless schemes."
- Chao Cai Personal History

Sparring and form practice has ended for the day, giving into a more relaxed atmosphere among the soldiers in the barracks compound. Even though the sun has set, glowing bonfires, lamps, and torches light the compound well. The marriage banquet has ended, crowding the compound with five times as many soldiers as before. Every few minutes, more soldiers return from banquet duty and stream into the grassy compound. Many retire to their rooms. Others huddle around the hundred or so small bonfires that burn in front of barrack housing that runs along the sides and back wall of the compound.

Dressed in my stolen uniform, I join one of the groups marching into the compound. I pass the warmth and crackle of several bonfires where soldiers laugh, tell stories, and share jugs of wine. Others play cards and dice beneath the light of torches or oil lamps. A few walk or sit by themselves in the shadows, but never too far from the burning fires.

Far from the light of the fires and lamps, only a few torches stuck in the ground chase at the shadows covering the center of the compound where Meilin is imprisoned. Several guards patrol both the compound edges and its center where the holding pits lay. Keeping my eyes on the patrols, I slip away from the group of soldiers and move closer to the center of the compound and its holding pits. To avoid suspicion, I stay within the light of the fires and the sounds of the soldiers as I go.

Moving as close to the center's shadows as I dare, I stop beside a wooden rack that holds several dozen flags bearing the symbol of the emperor and his personal army—the gold dragon on a sky of blue. My gaze moves over the iron grates covering the holding pits. The grates lay in three neat rows of five, each grate spaced about ten paces apart.

I think I know which iron grate covers the entrance to Meilin's pit, but the patrols guarding the area will make it difficult to get her out. A quick signal of alarm from any one of them would alert the several thousand guards in the compound. In a few heartbeats, I would be surrounded. Even with Zhangchi and my boon, I can't fight off that many soldiers at once. I hope my distraction works.

"You don't belong here." A large officer with a fat nose and a pear-shaped head steps out of the shadows. He scowls down at me with his thick bushy eyebrows. I tense. Does he recognize me as the muck-hauling servant he yelled at an hour or so ago? "You're not on pit patrol! Back to the fires with the others or to your barrack. Get! Unless you're hungry for a taste of my thrashing rod!"

His hand goes to the rod hanging from his belt. I give him a quick bow and hurry closer to the fires. I join a crowd watching a few soldiers playing dice beneath the glow of flickering torches. I look back over my shoulder at the officer to see if he's still watching me. His attention has moved on as he marches toward a different soldier off by himself in the shadows of another part of the compound.

I move from the group of dice players to one of the bonfires to get a better view of the more than twenty housing units that line this side of the compound. Each unit has been built like a one-story grand house with brown rammed dirt walls, white lattice work windows, a red-tile roof peaked at the corners, and five golden doors spread across the front of the grand house. The doors lead to separate sub-units that all share the same roof and share a wall with their neighboring sub-units. A small alley about five paces wide separates each grand house, leaving room for a row of privy sheds for the use of those who live in the housing units.

I step a few paces back from the bonfire to be more in the shadows and to give myself a little room to run if my plan goes wrong. I've only used my Wind gift once before. I'm not even sure if I can do what I have in mind. If I mess this up, the fire and the group of men around it will become my shield. That might be enough of a distraction, but I'd prefer the intended distraction to happen further away if possible.

Thinking on my oath to Tiānqì Shen, I place one hand on the hilt of Zhangchi to draw upon its extra power. I turn the palm of my other hand, facing it toward one of the privy sheds between the grand houses. The Wind gift mark on my palm burns with warmth as I call upon its power.

Nothing happens—at least at first. Dirt and rock start to rise in a swirl around the privy shed. The shed begins to teeter back and forth. I use the wind to lift the shed in the air and guide it toward me. Instead, the shed teeters until it tumbles forward and plops on the ground with a loud crash.

Silence hits the closest bonfires. The men jerk their heads toward the noise. Several jump to attention with swords drawn. Hoots and hollers of laughter erupt when they see it's a tipped over privy shed. But the laughter drops to a low rumble when the big officer with the bushy eyebrows and fat nose storms over to see what happened.

He turns his back on the tipped over privy and scowls at the men huddled around the nearby fires. "You think this funny?" he raises his thrashing rod above his head and shouts. "Tell me who did this, or by the floods I'll have you all thrashed till your skin's raw."

The men lower their heads and turn their gaze away. Their eyes burn with a mix of anger and contempt. But none say a word. Not even a grumble. I lower my gaze and slump so the men standing in front of me block the officer's view of me. I keep the palm of my free hand pointed at the tipped over privy and drop the hand to my side so it's less conspicuous. I draw on more Chi and focus harder on the gift inside me.

"This is your last chance!" the officer yells. "Speak up now and I might spare your skin."

Heads lift around the fire. Those sitting, stand. Those standing, stand taller. Their gaze focuses not on the officer, but on rock and muck that swirls in the wind around the privy shed. Eyes go wide as the shed shakes and rises a finger's width off the ground. All of the sudden, it flies toward them like a massive arrow.

"Run!" soldiers shout as they sprint in different directions.

I join them, not wanting to be plowed down by the flying privy shed. Still, waving his thrashing rod over his head, the officer's leg gets clipped from behind. He spins and falls on his back in trail of muck. Guiding the flying shed with my hand, it continues forward until I close my fist and it crashes into the bonfire.

The shed wood explodes in towering blue flames, spewing smoke, bits of muck, and an awful stench. The flames consume the shed quickly, and once they do its sludge and sewage spill out to snuff out most of the bonfire. Without getting to close to the smoldering stench, soldiers rush about in chaotic curiosity and excitement to try to figure out what happened.

Before the shock of what happened has a chance to wear off, I use my Wind gift to fly another privy shed into another bonfire. Soldiers yell and scatter to get out of its path. It too erupts in an exploding burst of flames before its internal muck smothers it down to stinking embers.

Amid the scattering chaos, I continue to send more and more privy sheds into other bonfires. More fiery messes. More explosions. More scattering and shouting soldiers. Chaos rises as soldiers rush from the other sides of the compound to investigate. Guards on patrol sprint over to see what's going on. The surprise and shock among the soldiers gradually change to humor and curiosity. Soldiers laugh, yell, and jostle each other for a better view of the fiery muck, creating even more tumult and pandemonium.

With the chaos still in full force, I slip away to the holding pits in the center of the compound. With so many of bonfires out, the shadows conceal me more, but they also make it harder for me to tell which holding pit contains Meilin.

I press my face against the bars of one of the grates and shout, "Meilin!" No answer. It's too dark below to see if she's there. I move to the next grate and call for her again. Still, no answer.

As I kneel at the next grate, strong fingers wrap around my arm and jerk me up. In his muck-stained uniform, grime streaking down his face, and anger flaring in his eyes, the bushy eyebrow officer lifts me off the ground like I'm a rag doll. Moonlight glints off the long blade of steel raised in his other hand.

"Time to die, worm!"

I don't have time to draw Zhangchi as his blade slices toward me. Aided by my boon, my open palm slams against his wrist. His strike stops mid-swing. My fingers clamp hard around his wrist. His eyes widen and he yelps in pain as I twist his wrist back and down.

As his swords falls from his hand, I break free my other arm from his grip and plant a palm strike beneath his chin. His head jerks back and I spin low to sweep kick his legs out from under him. As he falls, I draw Zhangchi, gaining even more strength and power from its Chi. He back thumps hard on the grass. His eyes close. His body goes limp, but his chest continues to rise and fall with breath.

I re-sheathe Zhangchi and hurry back to the grate and peer down into its darkness. "Meilin! Are you down there?"

"Cai?" Her voice trembles with a tired, anxiousness. "Is that you?"

"Don't worry," I call back. "I'm going to get you out of there."

The heavy locking bolt doesn't move easy, but with help from my Chi, it eventually slides, screeching and squeaking as it clears the locking mechanism. The grate's heavy bars make it hard to lift. After several tries and getting in the right position, I finally manage to raise it, turn it on its hinges, and flop it over onto the grass with a thump.

"The grate's open!" I call, sticking my head down into the hole. "Can you jump out or do you need help?"

Her response comes in a weak whisper that I barely hear. "My Chi is spent. Please, help."

As I ponder the hole's depth and try to think of the best way to get her out, the image of Meilin slowly comes into view at the bottom of the pit. The sparkle of her eyes. The sheen of her dark hair. The blue of her servant robes as she lay, curled up on the dirt floor below. At first, I think my eyes have simply adjusted more to the dark. But then I notice the shadows moving on the pit floor below and hear the snap and crackle of fire behind me.

I lift my head up and look around. "Hails!" I'm surrounded. Flickering flames light the grim faces of more soldiers than I can count. There's too many too fight. So, I do the most logical thing I can think of. I jump into the holding pit with Meilin.

Chapter 46
Qiu Meilin – Dance of Death

"I've heard brilliance often disguises itself in witlessness." – Meilin
- Chao Cai Personal History margin note

Exhausted and shivering in my drenched robes, hearing Cai's voice gives me hope. Still, I can barely lift my head to look up at him. Through night's shadows, his warm eyes peer down at me from the pit opening above.

In barely a whisper, my voice trembles. "Please help."

A halo of warm light flickers above him, illuminating the edges of his pulled-back hair with a glow. Torchlight. Something is wrong. My heart pounds in my chest. What's happening?

With a thump, Cai drops into the pit and lands beside me.

"What are you…"

"Shhh!" he says, kneeling beside me and putting a finger to my lips. "You're going to get us out of here."

I recognize the scabbard for Zhangchi as he slips it off his back. He lays the sheathed sword beside me, gently takes my wrist, and places my fingers on the hilt of the sword. Shen Breath flows from the hilt's gems into my fingers and throughout my body.

Its warmth chases away the cold and exhaustion, fueling me with energy and new life. My grip tightens on the hilt as Shen Breath continues to flow inside me and strengthen me. Within a few heartbeats, my body has taken in all the Shen Breath it can. I hand the sheathed sword back to Cai.

"I need both my hands," I say. "Wrap one arm tight around my waist. Wield Zhangchi with the other to make sure no one tries to stop us."

Cai nods. With my palms facing down, I focus on the Wind gift marks that I inked on earlier. Above, the heads of soldiers peer down at us from the pit's opening, wondering why Cai jumped in.

Cai's arm tightens around my waist, holding me close. His other hand raises unsheathed Zhangchi high with its tip pointed straight up. Calling on the Shen Breath's Chi, wind blasts from my palms, shooting me and Cai upward. The soldiers gasp. Their heads back out of our way as we fly up through the opening. Angry shouts follow us, but they quickly fade as we fly out of sight over the barrack walls.

Most of my Shen Breath is depleted by the time I land us in the shadows of a peach tree in the northeast gardens. Lighting the nearby cobblestone paths, alternating gold and red-papered lanterns flicker and hang from poles that look like half-size shepherd crooks. On about every tenth pole, a Shen Breath lantern hangs with its swirling and glowing rainbow-colored mist. Watching their heavenly glow amid the garden's peaceful beauty helps stop my trembling and chase away the panic and anxiety still entrenched in my thoughts.

I sit on a large decorative boulder surrounded by pink and purple peonies trying to catch my breath. Cai sets the sheathed Zhangchi on the ground and sits next to me, wrapping his arms around my shoulders. Closing my eyes, I relax in his embrace and rest my head against his chest. I could stay here forever.

I savor breathing in the fresh blossom-scented air and listening to the soft coo of doves, a few buzzing insects, and an occasional bird chirp. I drink in the freedom of the openness of the vast starlight sky above— a welcome contrast to the horrid confines of the pit. I couldn't have been trapped in there for more than an hour or two, but it felt like a never-ending nightmare.

"Thanks for rescuing me," I whisper.

A quiet laugh escapes Cai's lips. "From the person who never needs rescuing, especially from a man."

I grin, snuggling closer to him., "Yeah, well, I felt bad for you," I whisper. "After saving you so many times, I thought you might need a turn feeling useful. Did it work?"

"Not really." Cai chuckles. "Remember, I'm the one who jumped in the pit to escape a bunch of angry soldiers. I only brought you Zhangchi. You're the one who got us out."

My grin widens. "Oh yeah, I forgot. Well, maybe next time I'll give you a turn to really save me so you can feel more useful. How about that?"

Cai shakes his head. "No, I'm fine with you doing all the saving, as long as you don't do anything crazy and get yourself hurt in the process. What happened anyway? Why did the soldiers take you?"

My lips thin in a tight line and I explain what happened. Cai listens with sorrow clouding his eyes. I can't tell if tears fills his eyes, but he pulls me tighter in his embrace.

Cai sighs. "She'll be gone by now," he whispers. "No one ever sees the Wives Divine once the wedding celebrations end."

I slip out of Cai's embrace, stand, and begin to pace. I didn't come all the way to the City of Heaven just to lose Lian. We have to figure out a way to find her and save her.

As I pace, my gaze falls on a shrine across the cobbled path rising above a trellised bramble of berry bushes. Several gold-papered lanterns hang beneath the shrine's blue tiled roof, lighting its rosewood walls, posts, and crossbeams. Big gold symbols painted across the threshold name the shrine's god—Luxíng Shen, the god of journeys. Beneath his name five other sets of symbols have been painted representing Step, Leap, Return, Transport, and Track.

The fourth one—Transport—the symbol set containing a cart and walking foot holds my attention. Paired with the Mother stroke, it's the same symbol that the Shashyao stamped on Lian's slipper.

I still don't understand why a Shashyao would use a gift mark. Could the Shashyao actually be Shen-Blessed. No Shen Blessed hunting Shen Blessed makes no sense. Besides, when the Shashyao ran through the fields in Ning, Shen Breath from the crop lanterns didn't flow to the black clad warriors. It flowed to their swords. But if they're not Shen-Blessed, why put the mark on Lian's slipper? I'm missing an important clue, but I can't figure out what.

A sudden chill makes me shiver and a wave of dizziness makes me drop to my knees. I bow my head low and close my eyes to fight off the dizziness. As I do, my mind fills with a vision of one hundred small squares of red silk. They float down through the air like falling leaves on a breezy autumn day. Amid the falling silk squares moves a lone Shashyao. He spins like a graceful dancer, slicing his sword through each silk square. A high-pitch scream pierces the silence and blood splatters in the air with every slice.

When not a single square of red silk remains, a river of blood floods the ground, coursing around a pair of jade-colored slippers—Lian's slippers. Like a brilliant beacon on a dark, moonless night, the Transport gift mark shimmers on the side of one of the slipper's wooden sole.

"Meilin! Are you okay?" Cai's strong fingers grip my shoulder, shaking me gently.

I blink several times as his voice pulls me from the vision. The jade slippers and river of blood vanishes as the lantern-lit shrine and gardens come back into view. I pull my arms tight across my chest to fight off the shivers—not so much from the slight breeze in the air, but from the vision's disturbing images.

"Something terrible is about to happen," I say. "We have to find Lian, now."

The wrinkles of concern on Cai's face mirror my own. He holds my gaze, looking long and deep into my eyes. After a long pause, he asks, "Okay, where do we look? For all we know, she's not even on the palace grounds anymore."

My eyebrows furrow and my forefingers tap my elbows in rapid succession. "I have an idea," I stop my finger-tapping. "But first, we're going to need to find some leftovers from the wedding feast."

Chapter 47
Qiu Lian – The Search

"Freedom can be complicated. Is it okay to take one person's freedom in the name of protecting another's?"
- Notions from a Royal Peasant

Like the sound of a hundred miniature bellows breathing in and breathing out, the soft sniffs, snuffles, and whistles of sleeping women surround me. Ten rows of tens beds per row. What is this place?

I've never seen so many beds and so many people sleeping in a single room before. With so many in one room, I would expect the stench of muck, sweat, and filth to overwhelm me. While a slight undercurrent of stink exists, it's almost completely smothered by the aromas of peppermint, honey locust, peach blossom, ginseng, plant ash, and burning hemp oil from the lamps lighting the dim room.

Folding my arms tight across my chest to fight off the chill in the air, I slide off my bed to explore. My wooden-soled slippers clomp loudly on the tile floor. I expect the sudden noise to wake the women, but none of them stir from their sleep. Not wanting to draw attention to any who might be in nearby rooms, I remove my slippers and welcome the warmth from the heated tiles beneath my feet.

I step to the bed of the one sleeping closest to me. Similar to the white furs hanging on the large room's walls, a thick white fur blanket covers all but the woman's head. Like all the other women sleeping in the room, a red bridal veil covers her face too. The veil rises and falls above her lips with the rhythm of her soft snores and breathing.

I place my hand on her shoulder and shake her gently. "Hello! Where are we?"

She doesn't wake. The rhythm of her breathing doesn't change. "Wake up." I say, shaking her harder. "Can you hear me?"

She continues to sleep. That's when I notice the small bamboo tube poking out from under her veil connected to a series of other tubes that bend and run up to a porcelain basin on top of a tall, narrow shelf beside her bed. I raise her veil to reveal the face of an aged lady with deep wrinkles and loose gray hair. The end of the tube pokes into her mouth.

I look around and each woman in the room has been connected to a similar series of tubes. I've never seen anything like these bamboo tubes before, but I guess that's what's keeping the women asleep. How long have they all been here? Have they slept the entire time since the day of their marriage to the emperor?

As I look at their red veils, I realize their marriage to the emperor was never completed. He never removed their wedding veils. But married or not, why would he keep them all here sleeping? Whatever his reason, it's not right.

I lean over and yank the tube out of the old lady's mouth and swing it to the side of her bed. Small drops of milky liquid drip off the end of the tube onto the floor. I expect the woman to wake up immediately, but she keeps sleeping. If the liquid contains some kind of drug, it must take time to wear off.

"Who are you?" I whisper, not really expecting an answer. "What dreams did you have before the emperor stole your life from you?"

No matter how much I might deserve it, I will not allow the emperor to do to me whatever he is doing to these women. I pull my veil off my face and drop it on the floor by my jade slippers. It's a small act of defiance, but a liberating one. Now, it's time to liberate these other Wives Divine too.

Moving from bed to bed, I remove the tubes from their mouths. Each time I peer beneath a veil, I hope it will reveal the face of Ling Yuan, the Divine Lady Empress and Most Holy Wife. If legends of her immortality are true, her face would still look as young and as glorious as depicted in the paintings of her and the emperor that hang in the market square of nearly every village and city throughout Huyan kingdom.

But disappointment sinks within me at each bedside. Most of the Wives Divine are middle-aged to wrinkled and gray. A few have younger faces, but none that resemble the Lady Empress. She's not here. A deep ache tugs at my heart and twists my stomach. Wei was certain that if he found the Wives Divine, he would also find the Lady Empress. But he was wrong. How will he save his people?

Wait. The emperor wouldn't stick the Divine Empress in a crowded room with all the Wives Divine. She would certainly get her own room. In my bare feet, I run across the warm tiles to the only doorway in the chamber. It leads to a narrow hallway also with furs covering its walls. It has five doors, two on each side and one at the end. The first door leads to a storage room full of several baskets of sweet and pungent herbs, dozens of porcelain bottles, and a few large barrels.

The next room has a table and two chairs in its center. Some large wooden bowls, porcelain cups, an assortment of porcelain basins, several chopsticks and a few ladles lay strewn across the table. The third room looks like a woodworking shop with an axe, knives, files, clamps, a worktable, and several lengths of bamboo and other wood stacked on the floor or leaning against the walls. Stacks of fur blankets, a few fur coats, and some fur boots fill the fourth room. When I open the door at the end of the hall, flakes of snow swirl in on a biting blast of wind from the frigid outside night air.

Gales and hails! I shut the door to the cold and snow as fear tightens my chest. I'm not in the palace anymore. I'm not even in Quanli. Where is this place? And how am I going to find my way back home, let alone find the empress?

Maybe there are other buildings or homes nearby where I might find help. I rush back to the room with the furs and pull on one of the coats and boots. I also grab one of the oil-burning lamps from the large room.

Tiny snowflakes and frosty air brush against my face once I step outside. Atop a snow-covered mountain, several snow-laden pines and sheer craggy mountain walls rise up at my sides and behind me. Except for a beat-up coal shed, no other buildings or shelters stand nearby the building sheltering the Wives Divine. Less than twenty paces ahead, a steep snow-covered ravine drops in front of me, towering pines fronting its craggy rock walls.

Several hundred paces down the ravine I see a pin prick of light burn in the night amid the light snowfall. Where there's light, there are people. Perhaps, I'll find the Lady Empress down there. If not, the people there can at least tell me where I am and maybe help me get the other Wives Divine to safety.

Although the trail down the ravine is steep, the snow is packed down into steps, making the hike not too difficult. My fur boots still sink a little in the fresh snow and I have to be careful not to slip, but I'm able to keep a good downhill pace. The return trip uphill might not be so easy. Most of all I'm glad the fur coat and boots keep most of the chill off. But with every step, the cold works its way deeper into my bones.

Chilling wind blasts flakes of snow against my face as I plod my way down the snow-steeped ravine. A whining howl pierces my ears. At first, I think it's only the wind, but I tense when I spot a pair of yellow glowing eyes peering down at me from between the boughs of pines on the snow ledges atop the ravine walls.

Even though it's almost twice the size of a Jade Leopard, when it's solid, the white silhouette of the giant Frost Cat's body is hard to distinguish from snow. Once our eyes meet, its body loses its shape as its melds with the snow. My only chance is to run.

It follows me from the ledge above, its eyes moving swift through snowbanks like two yellow marbles skimming the surface. I kick up puffs of snow with every hurried step as I race down the ravine's snowy steps. I have to reach the building below before the Frost Cat changes back to solid form and attacks. I'm safe as long as it stays in snow form.

The white furs on the building's walls and the one I'm wearing should have hinted to me that Frost Cats haunt these mountains. Why didn't I look for a weapon before braving the snow? But even with a weapon, I have little chance if the Frost Cat attacks.

I know all the Fei Chi forms, but I'm not a fighter. For me, the forms are about self-mastery, control, peace, opening myself to Chi, and finding harmony with the Two. Being able to hold the Cypress Bends and shutting out all the noise of the world for one hundred heartbeats will do me little good with a Frost Cat bearing down on me.

I'm sweating beneath my coat while my fingers and face are numb as I rush down the snowy steps. Despite their savage nature, Frost Cats are opportunistic predators. They avoid prolonged fights since they prefer their snow form and tire fast when solid. Their solid form is also when they're most vulnerable since it's the only time they're susceptible to physical weapons.

No matter how hungry it might be, it will wait to attack when it has the biggest advantage. Staying ahead of it might be enough to keep it at bay. But the slightest stumble will bring the giant cat on me in an instance.

With that thought fresh on my mind, my foot slips and I flop on my back. I flail my arms and legs, scrambling to get back to my feet. The howling whine of the giant cat pulls my gaze to the top of ravine wall. Now in solid form, it leaps from the ledge down toward me.

In a panic I roll down the snow. The Frost Cat howls after me. Its paws pound the snow behind me. I'm surprised it hasn't shifted back to snow form for speed and to conserve energy. Either the snowpack on the stepped ravine isn't deep enough, or the jagged pattern of rock or wood steps beneath the surface interfere too much with its ability to flow within the snow.

The pounding of paw stops and a swoosh of snow signals that it's found a nice blanket of snow to the side of the steps. I stop rolling and hurry to my feet, bounding down two snowy steps at a time. Its yellow eyes track me as it streaks down the snow beside me.

Not far ahead of me the ravine ends at the porch of a simple monastery built of wood. I just need to reach the porch. Ten more paces and I'll be there. The yellow eyes race down the side of the ravine past me. With a thundering roar, the Frost Cat rises from the snow in solid form, leaps in front of my path, and crouches on its hind legs.

I scream, the shrill of my voice hurting my ears. The cat shakes his head and howls as if in pain. I scream again and charge, waving my arms and screaming shrill and loud. The cat winces and howls, but leaps toward me. At that moment I dive beneath it, collecting a face full of snow as it leaps over me.

It roars, but doesn't look back. I jump to my feet and race for the porch. I feel the wind of its swiping paw as I stumble onto the wood platform. It roars and howls again, frustrated that I made it to solid ground. Panting and trying to calm my racing heart, I sigh in relief as I lie safely on the porch. No matter how vulnerable I might be, the Frost Cat won't leave the safety of the snow.

Nestled against a rugged mountain wall on one side, the monastery sits on a ledge barely big enough to serve as its foundation, overlooking a sheer thousand-foot drop. I smile when I see the symbols above the monastery threshold. They indicate it belongs to the Shuang order, a religious sect that honors the Two by its members dedicating their lives to the service of others.

The monks and nuns of some of its factions build shrines throughout Huyan. Others run orphanages or care for the sick. Many live in isolation, spending their days writing poetry, creating paintings, or transcribing ancient texts about the Two and the Shen

Stepping onto the porch beneath the shelter of the roof's eaves, I knock hard on the monastery's oversized door. Hanging on a post beside me, a burning oil lamp swings back and forth with the breeze. Even though its warmth is slight, it feels good to stand next to it as I wait.

Several heartbeats pass, yet no one answers. Could they be asleep? It's only a few hours past sunset, but perhaps mountain people go to bed early. Or maybe living in such a remote area, they don't get many visitors and an unexpected knock on their door might go unnoticed.

Tired of waiting, the door creaks on it heavy hinges as I push it open and step onto a rough wood floor inside a small vestibule. The door creaks again as I close it behind me, shutting out the night's cold air. A burning lamp hangs from a hook in the ceiling above, giving light and a little warmth to the cramped entry room. Thick white furs surround me; one on the door behind, two on the side walls, and one hanging in front of me as a partition separating the entry from the rest of the monastery.

"Hello!" I call, not sure if I should venture past the fur partition without being invited. "Anyone here?"

No one answers. I pull back the fur partition and step into a large room. Thick furs cover its walls too. At the room's center a glowing coal burning stove warms the room, its flue rising up high to the lofty ceiling. Incense burns in canters strewn about the floor, filling the air with the fragrance of lavender and cinnamon. A flickering mix of hemp oil lamps and beeswax candles scattered about on tables and stands light the room with a warm glow.

On rustic wooden stools along the room's edges, a score of young to middle-aged nuns sit in silence. Dressed in bright green robes and matching bright green bowl-shaped hats, each has a long-braided ponytail that reaches down to or beyond their waists. Most of the nuns sit at small individual tables studying or writing on long, thick scrolls. A few sit before easels painting landscapes or floral designs. A couple of nuns glance at me, but don't acknowledge my presence before returning to their work.

"Hello," I say. "I need your help."

Some of the nuns look toward me expressionless, but turn back to their painting or writing without a word or hesitation. What is the matter with these people? I thought the Shuang were supposed to be hospitable.

"This is important," I say. "Please, up the ravine, there's a whole building full of women. They need help."

Most continue to ignore me. A few exchange concerned somber looks, but none look at me. A middle-aged nun with a pleasant face turns from her pile of scrolls toward a gray-haired nun painting a picture. The pleasant-faced nun smacks her lips together making a series of popping sounds. The older nun keeps painting, moving her brush in smooth strokes as she colors in the blue sky above of a mountain top meadow covered with lavender.

After several heartbeats the gray-haired nun sets down her brush, turns to the other nun, and starts making popping sounds too. After a few more back and forth exchanges with these popping noises, the graying nun rises from her stool, walks to the other side of the room, and pushes her way past a fur partition leading somewhere else within the monastery.

I take a deep breath, relieved that now I might get some help. "Thank you," I call to the pleasant-faced nun. "You are kind to help."

A few nuns, not much older than me, grin and make a series of squeaks and popping noises that strangely sound a little like giggling. The pleasant middle-aged nun scowls at them and makes a loud pop that silences the girls.

When the younger nuns return to their work, the middle-aged nun rises and walks toward me. She stops in front of me, tilts her head to the side and narrows her gaze as if studying me.

"Do you have a name?" I ask. "I'm called Lian."

The nun frowns and makes a single, loud pop with her lips. As she does, I see into her mouth and tense. She doesn't have a tongue. My eyes scan the entire room. Are each of these nuns, tongue-less? If so, why? What happened? I desperately want to ask, but it would be a dishonorable question. Besides none of them could give me an answer that I could understand.

Part of me wants to apologize and wrap my arms around the nun to comfort her. But her pleasant and confident expression tells me she needs no comfort. There's an enduring strength with this woman. Whatever the cause of having no tongue, it's not something that she allows to bring her down.

A creak in the wooden floorboards draws my attention back to the fur partition at the other end of the room. The gray-haired nun walks back in, followed by four stern-looking nuns dressed in fur coats and fur boots similar to the ones I'm wearing. I don't make the connection right away, but I realize my mistake in a helpless panic the moment the four nuns surround me with thick spears pointed at my gut.

Chapter 48
Qiu Meilin – New Oaths. New Problems

"Ninety-nine veils float, flutter, flee.
Ninety-nine brides sweet peaceful sleep.
One demon blade sharp fatal sting.
One crimson flood lone silence bleeds"
- Private Journal of Qiu Meilin

Cai and I kneel before the statue of Luxíng Shen, a skinny old man, with a knotted traveling staff, a wide droopy old hat, big hands, big feet, and big ears shaped like wings. I kowtow three times before the god of journeys. On the last bow, I leave my forehead pressed against the cold porcelain floor and place a lobster tail on the altar tray. The tail is one of the many banquet leftovers Cai and I pilfered on a quick trip back to the outer palace courtyard where servants were still cleaning up after the wedding festivities.

"This is a waste of time," Cai whispers. "Why won't you believe me? I already tried getting another gift at the shrine of Chéng Huáng Shen and it didn't work."

I want to ignore Cai, but I worry that Luxíng Shen might feel disrespected if we squabble during the offering. Besides, I'm not really sure this will work either. I don't want to do anything to lessen our chances.

"Cai, haven't you ever wondered why the emperor forbids women to pray in Shen shrines?"

Cai stays silent. I roll my eyes. "Tell me, what you really think. I promise, I won't be offended."

He clears his throat and answers at a slow, measured pace, "The emperor thinks women unworthy. Everyone knows that. All his edicts and laws perpetuate a cultural belief that women are inferior to men. Women should always defer to men. The man leads, the woman follows."

I chuckle. "Have you ever read any of the love ballads that the emperor wrote about Ling Yuan, the Divine Lady Empress?"

Cai doesn't answer, but I sense in him a hint of embarrassment. Few men ever admit to reading romances. "If you had, you would know how much the emperor loves the Divine Lady Empress. I believe, he might even sacrifice his life for her. How can someone profess such great love for a woman, but at the same time think her inferior or unworthy?"

"Meilin, what are you saying?"

"I'm saying, what if there's another reason? What if the emperor wants to reserve all the blessings of the Shen for himself? What if denying women certain privileges helps make sure that no man and no woman can gain the gifts of the Shen? What if not allowing women to pray in shrines provides added protection against others gaining those gifts?"

"No, that doesn't make sense," Cai answers. "If that were true, he would kill all the women Shen-Blessed. He wouldn't need to bother killing the men Shen-Blessed."

"Are you sure? What if he needed women Shen-Blessed in order to gain those gifts himself? In that case, men Shen-Blessed become a threat, while women Shen-Blessed become an ongoing necessity that he has to somehow control through laws and edicts like Innate Honor. Lian is Shen-Blessed. They tested her blood, like they tested yours. My guess is that every Wife Divine is Shen-Blessed and that's the only reason the emperor marries them—because he can't get the gifts of the Shen without them."

"What? How did you come up with that crazy notion?"

"From you," I say with a smile. "You've prayed in the shrine lots of times before, but it was only the most recent time that you received a gift from Tiānqì Shen? Why is that? What was different this last time? What if the gifts have to come in sets of two, first to a woman and then a man? Maybe you received a gift this time because earlier in the morning I prayed in the shrine and received a gift from her before you."

A long uncomfortable silence follows until Cai mumbles, "It does little good if you forget the rule, women first."

I knit my eyebrows together, not sure I heard him right. "What did you say?"

"It's something a strange gardener said to me earlier. Maybe that's what he meant. What you said."

I sigh with a grin. "Does that mean we can continue now? This porcelain floor isn't the most comfortable place to rest my forehead."

When Cai doesn't answer, I take it as a yes. I make a fist in hand salute against my chest and close my eyes.

"Wondrous, Luxíng Shen, I need your help. My sister, Lian is in great danger. There are many in Huyan who need help. I fear the emperor will use his power to do great harm to her and many others. By the Two, I will do all I can to help Lian and other innocents who might be in danger if you will grant me a gift to help them. This is my oath. All thanks to you and the Two."

I raise my head off the floor and reach out to touch a glowing Shen Breath lantern beside me. The warmth of its Chi flows into me. In addition to its soft trilling woos, the Shen Breath pounds out a new deep beat that complements the trilling melody.

I nod to Cai to take his turn. He kowtows three times and places a crab leg on the altar. With his forehead still pressed against the floor, he makes a fist in hand salute and recites his own oath.

"Luxíng Shen, I am not a great man, but I try to do good," Cai whispers. "Will you help me to do good? Lian is in danger. I fear Meilin will soon be in danger too. The world is a dangerous place. Will you help me preserve those I care about? Will you help me make the world a safer place? By the Two, I will strive to do so with your bounteous gifts if you grant them to me. All thanks to you and the Two."

When he finishes, he raises his head and touches a Shen Breath lantern beside him. As soon as he finishes, I bow, close my eyes, place another piece of food on the altar, and repeat the same oath as before. We both complete the offering and oath rites a total of five times to match the number of symbols written on the shrine threshold— Step, Leap, Return, Transport, and Track.

As we rise from our knees, Cai grins at me. "You were right. I think it worked."

I grin back. "We'll soon see."

On our way out, Cai salutes the shrine guard lying on the floor that we tied and gagged earlier in order to gain entrance to the shrine. "Thanks, soldier," Cai says with a sarcastic grin. "You've been a wonderful help."

A light rain starts to fall, adding a wet chill to the night as Cai and I hurry through the gardens. We follow the winding, lantern lit paths through rose, azalea, and peony gardens; ponds and lakes; manicured and sculpted shrubs; and groves of blossoming fruit trees. The light showers turn to a sweet-smelling pounding rain as we settle ourselves beneath the shelter of an open pavilion amid a circle of pink blossoming apricot trees.

"Now what?" Cai asks. "We have Luxíng Shen's gifts, but I'm not sure I know how to use them. Do you?"

"Of course, I do." I grin wide to hide the lie. Since making our oaths, thoughts and impressions have come to my mind about the gifts, but I'm not really sure about any of them. But Cai doesn't need to know that. "Obviously, the gift's names describe what they do."

"Obviously," Cai laughs. "So, tell me wise one, which gift helps us find Lian?"

I bite my lip, thinking. I think we need to use the Transport gift, since its mark is what the Shashyao put on her jade slipper, but I have no idea what the gift will do. Will it transport Lian to us? Will it just bring her slipper? Or will it transport us to her? If so, how do we get back to where we want to go?

"To be safe," I answer. "We might need to use multiple gifts."

I reach into my shoulder bag, happy I was able to convince Cai that we needed to take time to retrieve it from the servants' quarters on our way to get leftovers from the wedding feast. I pull out an ink stick, grinding stone, bamboo pen, and the necklace of ceramic gift mark discs that Fen had given me.

"Take this," I say, handing the necklace to Cai. "There should be disc with a Return, Step, and Transport mark. Ink and stamp the Return mark somewhere inside the pavilion. Then stamp each of the other marks on yourself above your heart. If you end up somewhere you don't want to be, the Return mark should be able to return you here."

He nods and takes the necklace, while I start grinding my ink stick. Once the ink is ready, I let Cai use some and then I kneel on the stone floor in a corner of the pavilion with my back to Cai. After using my bamboo pen to draw my own Return mark on the floor, I draw all three marks multiple times on my skin above my heart.

"Okay, let's see if we get Lian," I say, rising to my feet and stepping toward Cai.

He takes my hand when I hold it out to him. Its warmth ignites a jumble of emotions inside me. I love the feeling, but I also worry what

Lian would think if she saw us holding hands. Probably nothing. She broke up with Cai. She won't even care.

"Ready?"

Cai nods and I smile back. "Okay, let's do this." I focus on my oath to Luxíng Shen and the Transport gift mark above my heart, and then call upon the Chi of the Shen Breath inside me. Nothing happens. I focus harder. Still nothing.

"Is everything okay?" Cai asks.

"Of course, it is," I say, in a bit too snappy of a tone. "It just takes time. Now don't distract me."

Once again, I focus on my oath and the Transport gift mark. This time I also picture Lian's jade slipper with the gift mark stamped on the side of its heel as I call upon the Chi. It feels like that should work, but still nothing happens. I try two more times, but it doesn't work.

Why didn't it? I release Cai's hand and sigh. "I'm sorry, but I can't do it. It's not working."

Concern creases the wrinkles in Cai's forehead, but he doesn't say anything. On top of the helplessness I feel, a sense of urgency builds inside me. Lian needs me, but there's something more. Another danger is out there. A more imminent one that threatens more than just Lian.

Luxíng Shen, why didn't your gift work? What did I do wrong? I need to get to Lian. I need to help her. Silence. The god of journeys does not answer.

I step away from Cai and walk to a railing at the edge of the pavilion and stare out at the rain. The downpour has grown fiercer. Rivers of rainwater flood the patches of flowers and shrubs. The flooding water reminds me of the river of blood in my vision.

I close my eyes and I replay the vision in my mind, hoping if I focus hard enough on what I remember of it, I might see a clue that tells me what I need to do. The falling red squares of silk. What do they mean?

That's the problem with visions and true dreams, sorting the difference between the symbolic and the literal. It could mean both. What about the Shashyao? Literal. I'm sure of it. He brings the death. He brings the river of blood.

This isn't helping. What do I see? Where is this taking place? I focus on the surroundings. Are there walls? Landscapes? Trees? Is it inside or outside? I can't tell. Everything is a blur but the silk squares, Shashyao, blood, and Lian's jade slippers.

Wait. There's more. As I focus on the memory, I realize there's something beside the slippers. A single square of red silk. I didn't pay attention to it before because its color blended in with the blood. As I focus more on the square, I realize it's actually a veil. Lian's bridal veil. What does it mean? Does it offer any other clues to help me find Lian?

I strain to remember all the vision's details, replaying it over and over. When the end nears, and I envision the river of blood coursing around the slippers and red veil, a question pops into my mind.

Why does the blood go completely around the slipper and veil, instead of over it? Is that symbolic of something or is it literal? What could it be symbolic of? That Lian is untouched by the threat? Maybe. But if that was the only meaning, why even have the slipper and veil in the dream? Why have any reference to Lian? Because the slippers and veil are literal, and maybe they are actually there. What else is actually there?

I take in a slow deep breath and exhale long and slow to relax. I touch the Chi inside me and urge its warmth to flow to my head. I replay the vision in my mind again, but this time I push away everything symbolic to see what is left. The falling red squares are veils. Still, they're symbolic. So, I push them from my thoughts, and they're gone. The splattering of blood. Gone. The river of blood. Gone.

What remains? The Shashyao, slashing Zhangchi in a swirling dance. The jade slippers. The Transport mark on the side of one of the slippers. Lian's red veil. What else?

At first, I see nothing but whitespace. But as I focus harder and let Chi surge through my thoughts, images fill the blanks one piece at a time. A gray tile floor. Imprinted on each tile is the pattern of a lotus flower surrounded by eleven curling lotus petals. Thick white furs cover the walls of a large room. Several rows of beds fill the room. A woman sleeps on each bed—except for one. Carved into the headboard of the empty bed are the characters for a straight arrow and a gateway leading to daylight, the symbols of Zhì Shen. On the floor beside one of the legs of the empty bed are Lian's jade slippers and her red bridal veil.

With a grin, my eyes flutter open. "I know what to do."

I pull from my shoulder bag a blank paper scroll and ink sticks for the different colors I'll need. In a rush, I grind ink and mix colors. I stroke shapes and lay down colors on the paper as fast as I can. It's not a beautiful work of art, but it's an accurate representation of Lian's red veil and jade slippers, and the fur-walled room I envisioned around them.

Cai leans over me as I draw the Leap mark beside the empty bed in the painting. "What are you drawing?" he asks. "What is that place?"

"Never mind, for now," I say, blowing on the ink to help it dry. "turn your back and give me a little privacy for a moment, please."

Cai raises an eyebrow but turns away. Once he does, I draw the Leap mark above my breast amid the other gift marks already there. Instead of blowing on the ink, the thought comes to my mind to tap into the warmth of my Shen Breath to dry the ink. A whisper of a thought also guides me to focus on my oath and urge the Shen Breath to forge a link between that gift mark and the mark I drew on my painting.

"You can turn back around now," I say as I quickly clean up my inks and pens. I put away all my supplies but my grinding stone. I crumble up my painting into a small ball and place it on the stone.

Cai frowns. "What are you doing? I know that wasn't the best art I've ever seen, but why did you take the time to paint it, just to throw it away?"

"It's not art and I'm not throwing it away. I'm burning it. Do you have a fire stick?"

Cai gives me a questioning look but pulls a fire stick from the pouch on his belt and hands it to me. Crouching over my painting, I strike the stick against the grinding stone and light the crumbled painting. I cup my hands around the flames as close as I can without getting burned, trying to make sure no ashes float away on the night breeze. Once the paper burns completely, I wait for all the embers to die out and the ashes to cool. When they're cool to the touch, I carefully dump the ashes into my hand and close my fingers around them into a tight fist.

"Wrap your arms around my waist," I tell Cai, as I rise to my feet. A content grin rises on my lips as the warmth of his arms enfolds me. I'm pretty sure he only needs to hold my hand or arm to Leap with me, but this is much nicer. Besides, it's been way too many hours since we've been able to be this close.

Squeezing the ashes tight in my fist, I will my boon to warm the Leap mark on my breast and to warm the ashes in my hands. The warmth grows and spreads inside me. The ashes in my hand grow hot and when the heat is almost more than I can bear, I throw the ashes into the air. Dizziness overtakes me and I teeter to the side. Thankfully, Cai's arms stop me from toppling over.

The air around us vibrates and glows. One moment we're standing in the shelter of a garden pavilion watching a downpour of night rain, and the next, we stand beside an empty bed in a large room with fur-covered walls and rows and rows of beds filled with sleeping women. It's the same room I envisioned and painted minutes ago.

As my dizziness passes, I see a Shashyao a few paces away hovering over one of the sleeping women. He holds Zhangchi high above his head. His gloved fingers grip the blade's hilt tight, readying himself to end the sleeping woman's life.

Chapter 49
Fan Wei – Unexpected Enemy

"While casualties happen, Deliverers must seek to free, not destroy."
- Hidden Scrolls of Quingping: Practices of Engagement

Gardeners don't usually work at night. It's too easy to snip the wrong branch or prune the wrong tree when relying on what little light the moons and stars give off. But since Gold Dragon Guards know little about the intricacies of gardening, I'm not too worried. Besides, pruning plum blossoms helps me relax and stay calm. Right now, I need all the calm I can get.

It's been over an hour since Emperor Hu called the guard to return to his post at the Zhì Shen shrine pavilion. Hu could still be inside with Lian, or the emperor could have leaped himself and Lian away the moment he stepped back inside the shrine. I have to be certain they're gone before I act. If I Transport Lian too early, I lose my only chance to discover where the emperor has hidden Ling Yuan, the Divine Lady Empress, Most Holy Wife.

From this distance, I can barely see the soldier standing guard on the little island, let alone see if anyone might still be inside the shrine. I've not dared come any closer. My gardener disguise easily fools most, but as much as I despise the emperor, he is no fool. If anyone were to see me for who I really am, it would be him. Especially, if he gets a glimpse of my face.

I have to be patient. I can wait all night if needed. The hiding place of the Divine Lady Empress is not likely to change in the next few hours, let alone in the next few days or weeks.

I smile. My ability to wait always drove Suyin crazy. On those days when we would slip away from the quarries to hunt, she would always chide me for getting comfortable in the crook of a tree for a relaxing nap while she prepared to track prey.

"You lazy eel!" she would say. "Mama and the cousins will not be pleased when you come home without meat to put in the pot."

I'd laugh, tip my hat over my eyes, and fall asleep before she could think of something worse to call me. And when she'd return with a string of pheasants and rabbits, she'd wake me with a strain of curses once she saw the spotted deer I'd already gutted and cleaned while she was gone.

I'd slip down from the tree and eye her catch for the day with a smile. "Nice work, Suyin. But like I always say, wait in the right place long enough, and the best prize will come to you."

Suyin never liked that saying. Right now, I'm not sure I like it either. I've worked and waited my entire life for this moment—the moment to find the empress and free our people. That moment is so close, I can feel it. But that's not what has me anxious. I'm anxious for Lian, the sweet and beautiful Divine One.

The pang in my heart spreads and cuts deep. I'm choosing duty to my people over Lian's safety. How will I live with myself if anything happens to her? The risk I've put her in is too great. It was necessary, but I do not like it. I told Lian the truth. Too many innocent lives will be lost. Too many innocent children and families will continue to live in torture and slavery if I fail to find the Divine Lady Empress. And Lian is the only hope I have in finding her.

Still, I can't wait any longer. I tuck my pruning shears into my pouch and step onto the cobbled path toward the lotus pond where the Zhì Shen shrine sits upon its little island. With a grin, I stop and crouch near a patch of peonies along the way and pick several of the flowers until my arms hold a giant bouquet.

With a bounce in my step and the front of my hat tipped down to obscure my face, I hurry on toward the shrine. When I stop in front of the little footbridge that arches over the pond to the shrine's island, the shrine guard straightens and puts a hand on the hilt of his sword.

"What do you want gardener? It's late to be picking flowers."

I breathe in the sweet smell of the peonies, smile, bow to the guard, and hold the bouquet of flowers in front of me. "It's never too late to pick flowers for the Lord Emperor, Chosen of Heaven and his new Wife Divine. Do you not agree?"

The guard stiffens. "Who told you the Lord Emperor was here? His movements are not your business."

I laugh. "Friend, I'm a gardener. When the Lord Emperor Chosen of Heaven escorts his new Wife Divine through the flower and trees of the garden, I cannot but help notice. I mean no harm. I only wish to honor them with a bouquet of handpicked peonies. Master soldier, would you deny the emperor a wedding gift from one of his humble servants? If you prefer, you can deliver the flowers for me."

The guard scowls. "The Lord Emperor Chosen of Heaven cares nothing for a lowly gardener's worthless offering. Besides, he is no longer here. Now go away, you are wasting my time."

I feign a frown, which changes to a smile as soon as I turn and walk away from the guard. He has told me all I need to know. The emperor has already taken Lian to be with the other Wives Divine. Now to bring her back.

Once out of sight of the guard, I Return in an instant back to the open garden pavilion where I first talked with Lian. The warming caress of Shen Breath tickles through my veins as I renew my Chi with a finger's touch to one of the lanterns hanging from the shrine's crossbeams.

Still holding the bouquet of peonies as a welcome back gift for Lian, I coax my Chi to engage the Transport mark on my chest, while I picture the mated gift mark that I drew behind Lian's ear. I will the power of my boon to bring Lian to me.

Nothing happens. I try again. Still nothing. The mark on my chest burns warm, but I can't feel a hint of hers. It's as if it never existed. Did I make a mistake drawing it? No. I'm certain I got it right.

The only other explanation is that part or all of the gift mark has been wiped away. The peonies slip from my fingers and fall on the pavilion floor. Dread and terror grip me. If the emperor was the one to discover the mark, I've put Lian in terrible danger.

Even if he didn't, she's now out of my reach to save her. What will the rest of her life now be thanks to my carelessness? How will I bear living, knowing what I've done to her? How will I bear living without her? How could I be such a witless fool?

My mission to find the empress has been ruined as well. I've let down my people. Crushed their hopes. Anger at my foolishness simmers and heats to a full boil. The bitterness for the emperor's centuries of mistreatment of my people builds to fury and outrage as I add the theft of Lian's life to his endless list of misdeeds.

Perhaps, Suyin is right. Perhaps, destroying the emperor himself is the only way to end his cruel reign. But it's impossible. The emperor is too powerful. Even with our years of training and the gifts of the Shen we wield, they are nothing compared to the emperor's many gifts and powers. As clever and brilliant as Suyin is, can't she see that there's no way she can hope to defeat Hu? The advantage weighs impossibly high in his favor.

Wait. Suyin did know his advantage was too high. No wonder she refused to tell me her plan. There's only one clear way to remove that advantage. Kill all the Wives Divine. She knew I would do all I could to stop her from doing that one, unimaginably horrific thing. Suyin is pragmatic, but I never imagined she could justify committing such an atrocity.

"Sacrifices must be made," Suyin would often say. Oh Suyin, don't you know? Some types of sacrifices must never be allowed to be made.

No more patience. No more sneaking. No more sleuthing. It might be too late, but I have to act now. I have to do whatever it takes to find Lian and the other Wives Divine to save them from Suyin.

Chapter 50
Qiu Meilin – Assassin

"Although Step has the shortest range of Luxing Shen's gifts, in some respects it is the most useful and versatile with facile and minimal activation requirements, as well as low Shen Breath consumption."
- Hidden Scrolls of Quingping: Study in the gifts of the Shen

Stop!"

My shout draws the attention of the masked, black-clad Shashyao. But I don't wait to see if he heeds my command. I break free of Cai's embrace and rush toward the Shashyao. I draw Zhangchi from by back sheath and press its tips against the Shashyao's leather chest armor.

"Withdraw or I'll pierce your heart before you can blink."

"Back away girl! Unless you want to die!"

Anger laces the Shashyao's command, but his voice sounds strange. Forced. Unnatural.

I push the tip of Zhangchi harder into the leather without quite piercing it. "I won't let you kill her. I won't let you kill any of them."

The Shashyao laughs. The laugh sounds wrong too. "You can't stop me."

The Shashyao spins away faster than a blink. Before I know it, he's standing on the other side of me and the tip of his Zhangchi hovers a finger width above my nose. The other Shashyao we fought couldn't move that fast. I can't move that fast. How did he do that?

My eyes watch the point of his Zhangchi hover above my nose. What will happen if his blade touches my skin while I'm holding my own Zhangchi? Will I lose my Chi? Or will it simply be replaced by the Chi stored in my Zhangchi? Which makes me wonder, how much Shen Breath can a Zhangchi store?

"Leave her alone!" Cai calls from behind me. "We only want to keep the Wives Divine safe."

Stay put, I want to shout at Cai. I can't see him, but I hope he doesn't do anything dimwitted. Without a Zhangchi of his own, he's no match for this Shashyao. As fast as the Shashyao is, even with my boon and my Zhangchi in my hand, I'm not sure I'm a match either.

The Shashyao laughs his unnatural laugh. "I'm surprised you're the only ones the emperor employs for their protection. A little girl who doesn't know how to use her sword. And a little boy soldier barely old enough to join his army."

"That's a strange comment from someone who spends his life killing for the emperor," As the words come out, I realize it's even stranger for a Shashyao to be attempting to kill the emperor's Wives Divine. Then the pieces start to fall in place. "Who are you? You're not a Shashyao."

"Snails for brains, you really are slow." The forced, unnatural quality of the voice vanishes as the words come out in a high pitch tone.

"You're a girl! And you're Shen-Blessed! That's why you used the female version of the gift mark on Lian's slipper."

The Shashyao-disguised girl pulls back her blade a hand span from my face, Curiosity and surprise show in her eyes behind the demon-wolf mask. "What do you know of Shen-Blessed?" She snickers. "You're not the emperor's dogs! You're the ones the Shashyao hunted in that pathetic village upriver. You're both Shen-Blessed, aren't you?"

Cai steps up beside me, his sword ready. "Where is Lian? What have you done with her?"

"You mean, the new Wife Divine? Unless she's one of these sleeping princesses, I have no idea. When I arrived, all I saw of her were her slippers and veil. Now, leave me be. I have work to do."

In an instant, the Shashyao-masked girl vanishes and reappears several paces away beside another sleeping Wife Divine. As she raises her blade to strike down the Wife Divine, I tap into my boon and blast the girl with a focused surge of wind. The blast hits her in the chest, and she tumbles back against a bed behind her.

Before she can recover, I call upon my new Step gift. In an instant I'm hovering over her. With a swipe of Zhangchi, I try to knock her own sword from her hand, but she vanishes before reappearing several paces away beside another one of the wives. Cai appears beside her and locks his sword with hers before she can strike the sleeping wife. With a quick twist of her Zhangchi, she disarms Cai and elbows him in the face, knocking him backward.

I send another stream of wind at her, but she disappears and reappears somewhere else before it hits. I Step to a spot behind her and wrap my arms around her, my sword arm squeezing tight around her waist and my free hand grabbing the wrist of her sword hand.

"What's the matter with you?" I say into her ear. "They're innocent women. They have done nothing wrong, except follow the commands of the emperor. Why do you want them dead?"

She tries to break free of my grip, but in strength we're evenly matched. "They have to die. It's the only way to bring down the emperor and free my people."

I sense the girl tap into her Step gift and in a blink we Step to another place in the room. Once again, she tries to break free of my hold, hoping perhaps the sudden move would catch me off guard, but I still hold her tight.

"How does killing innocent women bring down the emperor?"

"You naïve whiffet. You don't understand how Shen's gifts work, do you? It's simple. Kill the emperor's oath mates and he loses his gifts and power. He will be no stronger than you or I. Then he can be killed."

"He's immortal! He can't be killed."

The Shashyao-masked girl laughs. "You have felt the power of Zhangchi, the demon slayer, designed to kill all Shen-Blessed. Do you really think the emperor in a gift-less state can withstand its destructive power?"

The girl Steps again. Somehow, we're now upside down with our feet planted on the ceiling. I flail my arms, letting go of her. And as soon as I do, I fall and crash to the floor.

The girl laughs from above. In a quick, fluid movement she lets herself fall toward me. She flips upright onto her feet before she touches ground.

She slices her sword downward.

The wind of its stroke brushes my back as I roll out of its way.

I jump to my feet and block her next strike just in time.

Cai appears near me. We strike at her in unison.

She parries stroke after stroke with incredible speed and ease.

"How can you justify slaughtering innocent people," I say as we battle. "You're no better than the emperor."

"The emperor has slaughtered thousands over the centuries. Probably millions. All innocents. He kills to keep his gifts and power to himself. He has built his kingdom on the broken backs of my people—slaves he has whipped and tortured to do his bidding."

Cai and I continue to press her with attack after attack. "That doesn't give you the right to take these women's lives."

She parries our attacks with ease. "At the emperor's command, quarry guards had no right to whip my father till he died. Nor did they have the right to starve my grandmother when she grew too weak to work. Hundreds of slaves die each year to enrich the emperor. If his hundred wives die today, that and many more lives will be saved every year from this day on."

I have no answer for her words, but that doesn't make her right. I have to stop her, but I can feel my boon weakening. Zhangchi no longer strengthens me with its power nor replenishes my Chi. I've used all the Shen Breath stored within the blade. My speed and strength wanes as my own Chi fades.

In desperation, I Step one last time to try to get behind her. But I don't have enough Chi. Instead of Stepping, my body jerks and shutters, knocking me off balance. In that moment, the girl whip kicks Cai in the chest, knocks Zhangchi from my hand, and spin kicks me in the face.

It happens so fast, that I'm on the floor before I realize it. Cai lies beside me. The girl hovers over me. I have no more Chi to keep up with her. The look on Cai's face confirms his Chi is used up too.

"No more games, whiffet. No more wasted time," she says as she slices the air above us with Zhangchi. "You should have left when you could. But I can risk no more interference. First you two die, the others will follow."

Chapter 51
Fan Wei – Unbeatable

"It's not that he didn't want us. He simply feared us. That still doesn't make the abandonment right."

- History of the Descendants: Volume 1, Page 13

Little has changed in Lian's guest house since I left her the poem urging her to meet me in the gardens. The sweet smell of aloes wood from the wall panels. Floral rugs. A screen painting of Dìyī Shen and Guāng Shen's wedding. Lian's sleeping mat. A vase of now-wilting peonies atop the tiny table. Two cushioned chairs. But as expected, Lian isn't here. Neither is her servant, Chan.

Dressed in the blue robes of a palace servant myself, I wander the series of courtyards and covered walkways that connect the different guest houses where lords, nobles, and royal guests stay while visiting or working in the palace. In my search, I can't find any servants who waited on Lian during her short stay in the palace. All of them are simply gone and no one knows where they went. I'm sure the emperor knows, but I doubt the answer is a pleasant one.

Other than the emperor, the one person that I hope has answers about Lian's whereabouts is High Lord Zheng Gong. As loveable as a weasel with a barbed thistle stuck beneath its tail, it will take prodding to get Zheng to help me.

Like a servant on an urgent mission, I continue through the housing compound's covered walkways. I pass small gardens, as well as statues of dragons, cranes, phoenixes, and some of the Shen. Servants and guards hustle pass me going the other direction. Few spare me a glance. None even regard me when I occasionally stop to replenish my Chi from a few of the many Shen Breath lanterns that hang along the walkways.

That's the beauty of being disguised as a servant. You become almost as invisible as a gardener. But servant garb has one big weakness—the little blue circular cap on my head has no brim to tip forward to hide my face. That forces me to keep my head down low, so people don't notice my red birthmarks.

At Lord Zheng's guest house, four bored, yet brutish looking members of the Gold Dragon Guard stand at attention—it's actually more of a lethargic slouch. They stand in front of the porch of what looks like a lavish temple but is actually Zheng's palace residence.

In the city's most affluent ward, Zheng spends some of his nights in a luxurious estate bestowed by the emperor. The estate has a magnificent mansion, flourishing gardens, and a lake complete with swans, colorful Koi, and an opulent boathouse. But other times, when he isn't bullying servants, snickering about the incompetence of other lords, or smooching the underside of the emperor's slippers, Zheng hides away in this lush palace guest house with its own private courtyard.

Before the guards can give me more than a feeble glance, I kowtow a few paces from their spit-shined boots. "Most stuporous and ignoble warriors of the realm, I have an urgent missive for his supreme obtuseness, High Lord Zheng."

Puzzled looks cloud the guards' faces at my words. The lead guard straightens his shoulders, but he looks as bewildered as the others. I grin at the ground. When faced with an enemy of superior numbers, confusion can be your greatest ally. Not that I really need any extra help in taking care of these oafs, but if I sufficiently fluster them, they might let me in without a fight. If not, that's okay. One of my secret pleasures in life is to humiliate bullies without them realizing it.

"What did you say?" asks the guard.

"My kind flaccid sentinel, your torpidity exceeds that of the most illustrious loons. I said, I have imminent tidings for your most ignominious master. I must enter at once."

The guard raises his eyebrows and exchanges a glance with the other three, hoping that one of them might understand what I'm talking about. When they shrug, the guard scowls at me and grips the thrashing rod at his belt. "I don't have time for you worm. Tell me clearly what you want with High Lord Zheng before you wear down my patience."

I raise my face from the ground and give them a friendly smile. Their gaze narrows at the sight of the markings on my face. "Friends, I have no desire to hurt you. So, I'm hoping you will simply let me in so I can have a little chat with High Lord Weasel Face. What do you say?"

"You dare such disrespect?" the lead guard growls. All four draw their swords. Anger tightens their expressions.

"You're right. That was bad of me. I can see how that might offend weasels. Sorry. I'll be more respectful next time."

In a brutal fury, the lead guard swings his sword. I Step and in an instant I'm on the porch behind the guards. Before they can blink, I use Quicken to take their swords and throw all but one point-first into the walkway ceiling out of their reach. But that high burst of speed quickly uses all my Shen Breath. Relying on my own normal awesomeness, I drop low into the Fei Chi Phoenix stance and sweep kick the feet out from under the two closest guards.

Pointing the tip of my newly obtained sword at the downed guards, I give a wry smile to the other two, "Good friends, would you please be so kind as to tie your toppled companions' hands and feet with their belts."

"You will pay for your disrespect, worm," growls the lead guard as he kneels with the other to do as I command. "Only a fool challenges the Gold Dragon Guard."

A cheerful laugh passes my lips. "Oh yes, I am a fool. But you give yourself too much credit. You aren't much of a challenge."

The guard spits at me, which I catch with the side of my blade. I grin down at him and wipe the spittle off the sword onto the shoulder of his uniform. "I do appreciate the help with the spit-shine. Now I can see my charming face in the sword's reflection. You really are so thoughtful."

When they finish tying up the two guards, I force the lead guard to bind up his companion. Then using the butt of my hilt, I knock out the lead guard with a blow to the back of his head. After he crumbles to the ground, I tie him up too. I replenish my Chi with the touch of a few nearby Shen Breath lanterns and push open the thick purple door to Zheng's house.

Dressed in a flamboyant purple robe with gold cuffs and collars, Zheng sits on a mat on the floor painting a picture of a lone magpie roosting on the branch of a blossoming peach tree. Surprisingly, the painting is quite stunning. I never imagined Zheng to be one with such artistic talent.

On the walls hang other paintings; misty mountains, flowering meadows, and a lone cypress on a tall peak. From the ceiling to the floor painted in thick black symbols on one of the walls run a few verses from Pan Ru's epic poem on the battle between Dìyī Shen and Xié Shen. No chairs are in the room. Yet, several silk cushions dot the floor. On the far side stands a fine crafted rosewood table covered with several scrolls. Amid the scrolls, a bamboo cricket cage sits on the table with a lone cricket inside chirping his song.

"Did I not say I do not want to be disturbed?" Zheng's voice is a high pitch squeal that sounds similar to the noise cats make when fighting. He doesn't bother to glance up as he continues brushing ink across his painting. "If you addle-brained sloths can't obey simple orders, I'll have you beaten and replaced before morning."

“Don’t be too hard on them,” I say. “They did try to keep me out.”

Zheng sneers as he looks up. His eyes move from the tip of the sword hovering a hand span from his pointed nose to my eyes and then to the markings on my face. “You are far from home, slave. You are a fool if you traveled all the way from the quarries just to try to kill me.”

“I have no desire to kill you my less than honorable high lord, but I won’t hesitate to hurt you if you do not tell me what I want to know.”

A wicked grin spreads across Zheng’s face before he looks back down at his painting and adds a few strokes of pink on the blossoms above the magpie’s head. “You should not threaten a man with a sword if you do not plan to use it.”

I lay the flat of the blade against Zheng’s cheek. “Do not worry. You will feel the cut of my sword, if you do not tell me where the emperor hides his Wives Divine.”

A grating laugh bursts past Zheng’s mouth. “You are more witless than I thought. Even if I knew, I would not reveal such secrets to a worm as yourself.”

Zheng winces as I turn the blade. Its edge nicks his cheek. A thin line of red rises on his skin. “I am a desperate man, high lord. Do not try my patience. Tell me what you know, and I will let you return to your painting with nothing more than that scratch.”

Zheng grins again, as he lifts his brush off the paper and wipes the ink off its bristle hairs. Faster than I think possible for the middle-aged lord, he grabs my wrist with his free hand and with the other thrusts the sharp-pointed end of the brush toward my heart like a dagger.

Even if I wasn’t strengthened by my Shen Breath’s Chi, Zheng’s strike would not have been fast enough. I slap away his striking hand and with a front kick I whip the ball of my foot into his face. He tumbles backward, squealing like a hurt pig. He curls up on the floor whining as blood seeps between the fingers covering his nose.

The caged cricket continues to chirp its happy song as I stride toward Zheng. Hovering over him, I rest my sword tip on his chest. "Zheng, I don't have time for this. Tell me what you know of the Wives Divine's hiding place, and I'll let you be."

"He can't tell you, because he doesn't know." Coming from behind me, the voice is low and commanding.

I spin to face the emperor. He stands in the doorway in his silk, bright yellow wedding robe. The scowl on his face turns to a smirk as his eyes fall upon the red markings on the left side of my face. "After so many failed attempts on my life, do the slaves of Quingping now send their Deliverers to maim and torture my high lord? I have not seen such cowardice in a long while. Or perhaps you are just warming up before you try to turn your sword on me, is that it?"

I grin, swaggering as I step toward the emperor. I keep my grip firm on the hilt of my sword. "There are those who would like to see me kill you Ye Ye, but I would rather talk."

The emperor scowls again, but deeper and more threatening. He places one of his gloved hands on his hip and the other on the hilt of his sheathed sword. The hilt looks like that of any other sword, but no doubt it's a Zhangchi. But if so, why wear the gloves? Doesn't the flesh of his fingers need to touch the hilt in order to gain access to the fabled sword's power?

"What would you talk of slave? How you have defiled the shrines of the Shen and disobeyed imperial law, the law of the Chosen of Heaven?"

I laugh. "I have done nothing more than you have, as is my right as one whose veins flow with the Blood of the Two. This you know and this you should respect."

The emperor's fingers flex around the hilt of his sword as he snarls. "I should kill you for your insolence."

My smile wilts to a frown. "Would you really kill me, Ye Ye?"

"Do not call me that!" the emperor snaps. "You are not my blood."

I shake my head. True sadness pulls at my heart. "Oh, Ye Ye. Does denying the truth bring you honor? Does it shield you from the shame of abandoning us? For enslaving us? For torturing your own?"

"I have done what was needed to protect Huyan, to protect all of Dashi. At least I have let your kind live, you should be thankful for that!"

"Thankful?" Laughter stumbles out my mouth laced with anger, both a stark contrast to the tears forming in the corner of my eyes. "Does Divine Lady Empress, your Most Holy Wife Ling Yuan feel thankful for what you have done, Ye Ye? Where is she? Why don't we ask her how she feels about the nation of slaves you created in the name of honor and Dashi's protection?"

The emperor clenches the gloved hand on his hip and glares at me. But the glare only lasts a few heartbeats before his smirk returns with a bitter laugh. "It was you, wasn't it? You put the Transport mark on my new Wife Divine, didn't you? Did you think she would lead you to the Divine Lady Empress? Clever. But you will never know now, will you."

Although, it's foolhardy, I level the tip of my sword at the emperor's chest. "Tell me where you've hidden the new Divine One, the one called Lian, and I will not harm you."

My own words surprise me. I meant to ask about the Divine Lady Empress' whereabouts, not Lian's. The emperor's eyebrows furrow and he cocks his head to the side, giving me a curious look before a taunting grin tips up the corners of his mouth.

"Intriguing," he says with no attempt to conceal the mirth in his voice. "Why the special interest in my new Wife Divine?"

My lips tighten. Suyin would often tease me about how I always had something to say on every subject, saying that I loved to hear my own voice. But for the first time since I can remember, I'm baffled in how to respond. Confessing my feelings for Lian might put her in greater danger, but I can't deny them either. Besides, it's the Divine Lady Empress I need to worry about. I need her to save my people. Even so, I can't abandon Lian. I have to find her.

The emperor chuckles. Then faster than a blink, he draws Zhangchi and knocks my own sword from my hand. Just as fast, he pricks my throat with the tip of his enhanced blade. In an instant, my Chi vanishes. Only the continued whines from Zheng and the song from the caged cricket break the silence as the emperor holds my gaze with his self-satisfied grin. Several heartbeats pass before he speaks again.

"No, Deliverer, you cannot harm me." The emperor's eyes turn cold, compassionless. "Renounce your oaths and I will let you live. I will even take you back to your home in the quarries myself."

I smile, more out of habit than anything else, since I have nothing to smile about. "You cannot be rid of me so easy. You know, I will make my oaths again and return to finish what I started."

The emperor's eyes narrow. A thin frown stretches across his face. "You have a point. Where is your oath mate? Perhaps, I will kill her. Then it will not be so easy to regain your gifts, will it?"

I shake my head, feeling a small touch of pity for the self-exalted man standing before me. How can someone reach such great heights, but have so little soul and honor? "Ye Ye, she is yours too. Will you really kill your own blood?"

"I will do what I must to protect Dashi."

"Right. I forgot. The lives of women carry no value in your eyes. They have no honor on their own. They are unclean before the Shen. That's the great lie you built your kingdom on, isn't it?"

The emperor lowers his sword. "You do not understand. How could you? It is a necessity. It was the best way to keep Xié Shen's favored ones from rising up. Only by controlling who gains the gifts of the Shen can I make sure none of Xié Shen's followers gain them."

I laugh. "That's pig swill and you know it. It's simply an easy way to keep all power to yourself, so no one can stand against you."

"Enough!" the emperor's voice booms. "I have no need to explain my actions to an honor-less slave. Renounce your oaths or this ends now."

I frown. "Ye Ye, you know I cannot do that. I'm a Deliverer. I have sworn to give my life to free my people, which I will do happily if needed. But no one needs to die. Take me to the Divine Lady Empress. Let us talk. I'm sure we can work things out together. What do you say?"

"No. That will not do."

The thin frown on the emperor's face remains still while in a quick thrust he jams the cold steel of Zhangchi through the center of my chest. Dizziness and shock take me as he pulls out the cold blade. Everything goes dark and I crumble to the ground.

Chapter 52
Qiu Meilin – Point of Death

"Brief mentions of "Two's Power" in ancient texts indicates it's a specific aspect of the overall power of the Two, distinct from gifts offered by the Shen. Little more is known other than random speculation."

- Pan Ru: Essays on the Mysteries

Lying on my back, I feel Cai's warmth beside me. The girl disguised in the black armored leather of the Shashyao hovers over us with Zhangchi poised to strike. Beyond the room's fur-covered walls sounds the whistle and roar of a wind rising in its rage. Other noises begin to fill the room. Ones I hadn't noticed while Cai and I battled the girl wearing the demon-wolf mask.

The light breathing and snores of the sleeping women has changed to moans, mutters, and murmurs. The women are waking. Behind her mask, the anxiousness in the girl's eyes shows she realizes the same thing. In response, her grip on Zhangchi tightens as she slices down to finish us off.

Fearing for Cai, I roll toward him to shield him from her blade. Mid-roll, our hands and bodies meet as Cai rolls to shield me too. Our fingers instinctively intertwine and like a fiery explosion of Shen Breath, an exhilarating warmth of Chi flares within me. More strength, speed, and agility than I have ever felt before surges inside, even more than I have felt with Zhangchi in my hands.

Still, I'm too late. The blade has already fallen. As if time has slowed, I can see Zhangchi a pinky's width above my arms and Cai's arms. Even with this new surge of Chi I can't move fast enough to move either one of us out of the blade's way. And I'm certain, once the blade touches my flesh, the Chi blazing inside me will vanish.

But Zhangchi's blade never touches my flesh. It stops, staying that same pinky width away as if an invisible shield blocks its progress.

The masked girl's eyes widen. "Two's power," she mutters, stepping back. "I've never…"

Before she can finish her sentence, I leap to my feet, grab her wrist, and twist it until Zhangchi drops from her hand, clanging on the tile floor. I grab her other wrist too. No matter how hard she struggles she can't break free. Cai stands beside me with Chi emanating from his countenance.

"You don't understand!" Fierce determination lines the girl's voice. "They have to die. It's the only way to stop the emperor. The only way!"

I squeeze the girl's wrists tighter. "No one is going to die today, except for you if you make any more attempts to harm these women. Understood?"

"Fools! You witless fools!"

In an instant, she vanishes. But just as fast, she reappears a step away, reaching for her fallen Zhangchi. I move faster, picking up her Zhangchi as well as my own. Bursting with Chi and a Zhangchi in each hand, I cross the blades close to her neck. "One more attempt and I do to you what you planned for each of them. Leave now and I will spare you."

More anger fills her voice. "You witless whiffet. Time will come when you will grieve your foolishness of this night. Watch your shadow. For from this day forward, I will avenge the sufferings of my people against both you and the emperor."

Before I can respond, she disappears again. This time she does not reappear. I let out a deep breath, relieved she's finally gone.

"Take this," I say, handing Cai the girl's Zhangchi and sheathing my own.

Before we have a chance to ask each other about the mysterious resurgence of Chi, a woman dressed in a jade wedding gown steps toward me from one of the nearby beds and places her wrinkled hand on my arm. Her red veil hangs to the side of her face, revealing gray unloosed hair and a wrinkled face dotted with age spots. Haunting confusion fills her eyes. Tears wet her gaunt cheeks.

"What happened?" Fear laces her scratchy voice. "My hands, they're so old. How? Can you change me back?"

The fear and pleading in her eyes and voice breaks my heart. What happened to her? What does she remember? Has she slept here in this room since the day of her marriage to the emperor? As I stare at her thinning gray hair and her frail wrinkled flesh, I try to imagine what it would be like to fall asleep young and beautiful, only to wake as an old woman with the feeling that no time has passed.

Across the room the murmurs and mutterings rise to a loud commotion of confused, angry, and fearful chatter as the ninety-nine women dressed in jade wedding gowns and red veils drooping to the side try to make sense of the changes in their appearance, as well as try to figure out where they are. I try to talk to each one, asking what they remember and explaining what I think happened. In every case, the last thing each one remembers is drinking a toast to one of the Shen while kneeling in a shrine beside the emperor, right after having made vows to that Shen.

Most struggle to believe that the emperor actually drugged them and left them sleeping in this room for all these years. How could he do such an awful thing? Moments before their marriage, he treated each one with such gentle kindness. Some insist that Cai or I must have kidnapped them. It's not until a few of the other wives, who happened to wake earlier and witnessed our defense of all of them, speak up in our behalf and convince them that we were trying to help them.

After I explain as much as I know about their situation, which isn't much, I pull Cai aside to talk in private. "We can't leave them here, but we can't stay either. We have to find Lian."

Worry shows on his face. "She's not in the building. I checked. There are only a few other rooms and she's not in any of them. A blizzard rages outside. We're on some forsaken mountain top. I couldn't see any other buildings, but with all the snow and darkness I can't be sure."

It doesn't make any sense. The slippers Lian wore are here, but she's not. Did the emperor bring her, but then take her back to the palace? Why would he do that? Could she have wandered off somewhere? No, she would have been drugged like the other wives. Did someone else take her? Maybe. I don't know. There has to be some clue here. I just need to find it.

"If Lian's here, we'll find her," I say. "But first we have to find a safe place for the wives."

"Any ideas?"

My nose scrunches up as I concentrate, trying to bring together the scattered pieces of a plan that even with the Two's help has little chance to work, but it's the only idea I have for now.

"I have an errand I need to run." One that might get me killed, but I don't tell Cai that. "You stay here with the wives until I get back. Then we'll find Lian."

"An errand? You're about to do something reckless, aren't you?"

A mischievous grin lights up my face. "Me? Reckless? Never. Now leave me alone. I need some time with my inks and brushes. I have a work of art to create."

Chapter 53
Lord Emperor Xiang Hu – Betrayal

"In the Light, morality does not flinch. In the hands of people, it bends to the whims of those with voice and power."
- Pan Ru: Essays on the Tenets of Light

The clatter of rain on my rooftop and the drums of thunder usually lull me to sleep, but not tonight. Not even the burning of extra lavender makes a difference. Midnight has come and gone, and too many disturbing thoughts race through my mind, chasing away any hope of rest.

The truth of the words from the Quingping slave still stings. He is right. My kingdom has been built upon a lie. A simple decree. A simple lie. One that became a life unto itself. It spawned oppression. Poisoned love. Twisted honor. Corrupted culture. Scourged our nation. Worst of all, it divided Yuan and me. But I made an oath. How else could I keep my oath to protect Huyan and Dashi? It was the only way. Oh, sweet Yuan, why could you not see that?

But that is not all that stings. I robbed another young girl of her life tonight. Not murder, but perhaps worse. The deceit of the marriage always troubles me. Yes, the families are well compensated, but the young girls—I steal their dreams and future without them ever knowing. Another necessary evil for a greater good. Xié Shen cannot rise. Without all the Shen's gift, I can never hope to hold him and his favored ones at bay. But if it's the right thing to do, why does it trouble me so?

"That's the burden of leadership," Zheng would often tell me. "He who leads must make and live with the weighty decisions that would crush the shoulders and souls of weaker men."

How could I get by without Zheng's wisdom and support? He has been a great strength to me for many years, helped me weather the turbulence of the kingdom. I could not find a more excellent administrator. Although, his ambitions and appetite for power can be worrisome at times. Not to mention his harsh administrative methods. But I cannot fault him. My rule and dictates have not been any less harsh. Still, I have tried to be a good and kind ruler, one that would make Yuan proud. But kindness does not quell unrest, execute justice, or win wars.

The war. How I want to make it go away. But the barbarians refuse to stop pressing our northern borders. Diplomats do me no good. The Yemaren do not listen. The slice of the blade and pierce of arrows is all they understand. But I am uncertain how much longer I can maintain and feed so many troops without raising taxes again.

My ministers argued to raise taxes long ago, but they're greedy fools, simply hoping to overflow their estates with more gold and rubies. They are blind to the tension and sparks of resentment that have already begun to ignite in some of the kingdom's outer pockets. Even here in Quanli, City of Heaven, flashes of unrest have begun to show. One more rise in taxes might be all it takes to kindle widespread rebellion.

I need to go for a walk. A stroll in the gardens would calm me, even with the downpour of rain outside. Or maybe a visit with Yuan. No. Visiting her might make the turmoil of my soul even worse. Perhaps I should call for my musicians. A soothing melody or two always brings me peace.

As I rise from bed to call my steward, the Feng Yan ring on my right hand grows uncomfortably hot.

"Dragon spit! What now?" The ring with its gold band with paired emerald and ruby settings glow with warmth. I fight to push down the anger and annoyance at the prospect of losing even more sleep, but the Shuang nuns at Shingda are disciplined. They do not light the embers of Feng Yan without good reason. Even when a Wife Divine passes in the night, they always wait till morning to alert me. Whatever the reason, it must be urgent for them to call me in the middle of the night.

After I dress, I Leap to the sanctuary in the frostbitten Shingda mountains where my Wives Divine sleep. As always, the mixed scents of peppermint, ginseng, burning hemp oil, and a variety of medicinal herbs are strong here. An uncomfortable chill hangs in the air even though I stand near the coal-burning stove that heats the sanctuary's main chamber and its tile floor.

At the sight of me, a Shuang nun dressed in a white fur coat and a bright green bowl-shaped hat steps to the low table where the steel Feng Yan tray rests. She doesn't kowtow or even acknowledge me. Nuns of the Shuang serve the Two, not emperors—not even an emperor Chosen of Heaven.

Without a sound, the nun starts shoveling the burning coal embers off the steel Feng Yan tray and dumping the embers back into the coal burning stove. Amid the embers, the linked symbols of the Binding mark and Place Touch mark on the tray glow red hot. But after only a few shovelfuls of embers have been removed, their glow dims and the warmth of my Feng Yan ring lessens.

With her job done, the nun hurries toward the chamber's entryway where other nuns of her order stand. When I look closer, I notice that three of the other nuns point the tips of their spears at a young woman in front of them. The young woman wears furs like the others, but she doesn't wear one of their bright green hats. Is this one of their own that has somehow betrayed their order?

A flame of annoyance starts to rise within me. I have no interest in their internal rules and politics. If the girl has broken one of their prescripts, they can deal with it rather than disturbing me in the middle of the night. But what if it wasn't infraction against their order? What if she did something to one of the wives?

I look toward the rows of beds. My chest tightens and stomach lurches. How did I not notice right away? I can't believe what I see. It's impossible. All the Wives Divine are gone. Small puddles pool beside their empty beds where drip by drip their feeding tubes leak their liquid meals and sedatives onto the tile floor.

Fury rises inside me as I storm toward the young woman. Zhangchi hums as I unsheathe it, ready to end this girl for her abominable crime. How dare she! At first, I think the worst, that the girl slaughtered them and dumped their bodies somewhere beneath the blankets of snow outside. But no, the wives still live. Inside, I feel each of the gifts I share with them and hear the symphony of melodies each gift causes the Shen Breath to sing.

When I reach the young nun, I point Zhangchi at her heart. "What have you done with my wives?" I can't kill her until I know where they are.

A fierce determination, not fear, shows in the girl's eyes. She even flashes a smug smile. Wait. Something about this girl seems familiar. How do I know her?

"Dearest husband, is that the proper way to greet your new bride?"

My eyes widen. I don't believe it. I haven't seen her face in person before because of the bridal veil, but Zheng showed me a drawing of her a few days ago.

"Qiu Lian? Is that you? Why? What have you done to the others? How could you betray me?"

"Betray you?" She lunges toward me, as if to beat me with her bare fists. The nuns raise their spears in front of her, barring her way. "You betrayed me and all your other so-called wives."

"So-called?" I laugh, but my eyes and face stay tight with anger. "Yes, you know the truth. I have only one true wife, the Lady Empress. I never could bring myself to remove the veils of the Wives Divine to make the marriages official. But I see you did not hesitate to sever ties with me by removing your own veil."

I step back and lower Zhangchi. "I have no desire to kill you, Qiu Lian. Tell me where the Wives Divine are and I will spare you. You can resume your sleep and no harm will come to you. I will keep secret the shame you have brought upon your family, so no harm comes to them either."

Laughter full of contempt rises from Qiu Lian's lips. "I do not know where the Wives Divine have gone. Perhaps, they walked away into the blizzard. I removed the tubes from their mouths and went to get help. When your lackey nuns brought me back here, the wives were gone."

I clench the hilt of Zhangchi, holding my anger in check. If it gets the best of me and I kill this girl, I might never discover what she has done with the Wives Divine. "My patience wanes, Qiu Lian, tell me the truth before I decide you are not worth sparing."

She smiles, shaking her head. "Truth? I told you the truth. Would you have me make up a lie to tell you? Would that please you, since you are so keen to invent so many lies of your own?"

"How dare you speak ill of your emperor! You shame yourself. You shame your family. You shame your village! Would you see them destroyed for your insolence? This is your last warning. Tell me what you have done with my wives before I strike you down and all you love."

Qiu Lian stands tall and raises her head up, sticking her nose in the air in defiance. "You shame your kingdom and all the people who trust you to watch over and protect them. You are not fit to be emperor!"

Her head jerks sideways as my gloved hand slaps her face. "You know nothing of the sacrifices I have made to protect my people. If you do not tell me where the wives are, you will endanger our people more than you can ever know. Tell me now or I will slay you where you stand! And before your blood dries, blood will flow from the hearts of your father and mother, and every living being in your pathetic little village."

Qiu Lian's mouth tightens in a thin line as she squares her shoulders and raises her head even higher. "I cannot tell you what I do not know. If you strike me down, or strike those I love down, you will shed innocent blood. For that, may the Two curse you to burn in Kaioda."

I shake my head, scowl, and raise Zhangchi's tip to her heart. "So be it."

Chapter 54
Qiu Meilin – Destroyer

"If a life in the balance has infinite worth, do many lives have more value than one?"

- Secret Musings of Wang Jin

"You had no authority to agree to such a thing!" Gu Zan shouts as he shakes his spear at his niece, Liu Fen. "You have put all of Mu Cun in grave danger!"

The click and buzz of insects, whistles of birds, distant howls, and other nighttime sounds of the deep fill in the silence as Fen scowls at her uncle. The gray-haired leader of the people of the Mu Cun tree village was not pleased to be woken from his sleep. He was even less pleased to find 99 of the emperor's Wives Divine milling about one of the bamboo-floored plazas suspended between three giant oaks in the heart of the deep. It didn't help his mood when he learned that the wives had drained every Shen Breath lantern on the platform.

It takes all my willpower not to speak up as Fen and I stand with the six-member Shouling council, surrounded by a dozen of their warriors. But after Fen agreed to allow me to Leap the wives here, she made me promise to keep quiet when it came time to convince the council and the other villagers to allow the wives to stay. Many of the Mu Cun warriors want me dead. Apparently, execution is the punishment for defying a judgment of the Shouling council, which apparently both Cai and I did when we escaped earlier.

"And do you think you have authority to send them away?" The sternness of a short gray-haired lady's voice makes Zan pause with uncertainty. She is Gu Te, a member of the Shouling council and Zan's wife. Despite her maturity, she's lithe and muscle toned. Not a single wrinkle creases her austere face or smooth skin.

"My dearest Zan, you are one of the leaders of the Shouling—not the Shouling. We pride ourselves in living a higher standard, a more honorable standard in defiance of the emperor's rule. Tell me dear husband, what value does that standard have if it causes us to shrink from our moral duty to shelter those in need of our protection, as well as refuge from the very emperor we defy?"

Zan bows to the woman, but he's not smiling. "Honorable Gu Te, what if the emperor's hunt for these women leads him to us? All we have built will be destroyed."

"Jade's shade, we have hidden behind that worry too long, using it to justify immoral actions." Te points to me without a glance. "This girl saved one of our young at peril of her life, yet we chose to imprison her on the worry of being discovered."

Zan opens his mouth to object, but Te silences him with a curt shake of her head. "I know, I agreed with that sentence. But now I feel it wrong. She and her companion escaped our prison house. Not long before that, another soul who did our village a great service escaped the decrees of a similar council judgment. I do not think it a coincidence. I think it's a warning from the Mother Jade that it's time to change our ways."

Zan throws his arms in the air, shuts his eyes, and shakes his head. "You would risk the lives of all our people on a superstitious notion?"

"Superstitious?" Te gives her husband a scolding look, warning him to watch his words. "Without the Two's blessings or that of Mother Jade, none of these could have escaped. Yet they did. And at risk of her life, she returns to ask our help. Do you dare risk the wrath of the Mother Jade by denying this girl's noble request to protect these women?"

Zan clenches the shaft of his spear tight, resisting the urge to shake it as his wife. "What would you do, invite the emperor and his demons into our very homes?"

A scornful grin rises on Te's face. "Would you send them away so they can die at an assassin's hand? Would that calm your craven worries? Or maybe you want to execute each one yourself to keep our secrets safe. Is that what you want?"

Zan furrows his eyebrows, but he doesn't answer.

Te's expression softens. She steps close to him, gripping his arms at the elbows—not harshly, but with a touch of affection. "Husband, I believe it's time for us to make a stand—a stand for those who also would defy the emperor. Show me the heart of the brave warrior I chose to marry. Show me the virtue of the moral dreamer our people chose to lead them. Stand with me. Stand with these women. Stand for what deep inside you know is right."

Zan stares back at Te in silence for several heartbeats, a disconcerting frown plain on his face. "I do not agree with what you ask. But I have never doubted your wisdom and instincts before. I will not doubt them now. Yes, I will stand with you. I support the proposal to let the wives stay."

Both Te and Fen grin at Zan's words, and I breathe out a sigh of relief. Two other Shouling council members frown and shake their heads, but the last two agree, making it a majority and sealing the decision. The council sends warriors and messengers throughout the tree village to prepare food for the Wives Divine and find housing accommodations for them. Although it's after midnight, I doubt any of them will sleep so soon after so many years of a forced sleep.

"Thank you," I tell Fen as we leave others to see to the needs of the Wives Divine. Lit only by the occasional oil lamp, we walk in the dark of night across a treacherously high bamboo span that leads from the plaza toward a less busy section of the treetop village. "I put you in a very difficult position, but you didn't hesitate to help me."

Fen puts her arm around my shoulder and gives it a squeeze. "Your cause was just. Besides, how could I ever refuse my Pangze Wu? I will never forget that you risked your life to save my little Ling. For that, you will forever have my life bond."

I grin, enjoying the warmth of her embrace and her kind words of friendship.

"What will you do now?" Fen asks. "Will you leave us?"

I nod. Cai searches for Lian at the emperor's palace. I plan to return to the place where the Wives Divine slept and continue searching for her there "My sister is still in danger. I need to find her. After I do, I will come back to visit and to check on the Wives Divine. But before I leave, with your consent, I would like to replenish my Chi from one of your Shen Breath lanterns."

Fen laughs. "I hope we can find one that is not spent. Your Wives Divine dimmed the light of more than three hundred lanterns, Shen-Blessed. I have never heard of such a thing before. It is different than our way. But now I understand how the emperor gained so much power and prevented others from doing so."

Before long we arrive at one of the village's crop platform with several Shen Breath lanterns glowing along its raised crop beds. It takes only two lanterns to top off my Chi. After another thank you to Fen and a hug goodbye, I use my Return gift to travel back to the building on the snow-topped mountain where I first found the Wives Divine.

The change from the humid jungle night air to the chill and fragrance of the fur-walled room is immediate. My heart leaps at the sight of Lian standing tall in a white fur coat less than twenty paces away. Shoulders squared, and her head raised high, she stares in defiance at the emperor hovering near her. He's armed with a Zhangchi, demon slayer sword.

"Burn in Kaioda!"

I grin. I've never heard Lian curse before, let alone to a man. And to the emperor? I want to cheer for her.

The emperor shakes his head and raises Zhangchi only a hand span away from her heart, ready to stab her. "So be it."

I'm still getting used to the gifts I received from Luxíng Shen, the god of journeys, but almost by instinct I Step to Lian's side and slam my Zhangchi against the emperor's. His sword clangs to the ground. The comical wide-eyed expression on his face almost makes me laugh. It's a mix of indignation and dazed bewilderment as if he's never been surprised before and can't believe that someone would dare do so now.

A small group of women also in white furs stand nearby wearing round bright green caps like those that nuns wear. But these women do not look like nuns. No joy or kindness shows in their eyes. Each carries a spear. One steps toward me with spear raised, but a clicking sound from one of the other nuns stops her and she retreats back into their group.

Standing more than two heads taller than me, the emperor stares down at me. His mix of bewilderment and indignation fades, replaced by a wide amused grin. He makes no move to pick up his sword. He grins at me and begins to chuckle.

"Little girl, you think yourself a warrior? You think you can strike down the Chosen of Heaven?" The emperor spreads his arms, holding the palms of his hands out to me in supplication. "Weak, foolish child, go ahead. I am at your mercy. Do you have the courage to do what you have come for? Strike me down, if you dare."

The belittling laughter in the emperor's voice stirs me to anger. The anger rages hotter and hotter as I think of all the evil he has done. Imprisoning the Wives Divine in endless sleep, robbing them of their lives and freedom. Enslaving the girl assassin's people, his guards whipping her father and starving her grandmother. Oppressing a whole nation of women with lies, smothering their rights, devaluing their worth, crushing families by turning husband against wife, father against daughter, turning my father against me, and stealing any hope that someday my father might actually express a morsel of love for me. Robbing me of Lian and moments ago intending to cut out her heart with little care or remorse.

I came to save Lian, not kill an emperor. But how many lives will be saved by his death? How many lives will his death free? Lian's? The Wives Divine? Fen and her whole village? Huyan? Mine?

Lian steps toward me. "Meilin, this isn't your fight." The nuns surround Lian, stopping her and herding her away from me with the points of their spears.

Can Lian see it in my eyes? Does she know what I'm thinking? Once again, she's trying to stop me from saving her. "I'm not going to let you die, Lian." With no more thought, I clench Zhangchi and drive it into the emperor's heart.

"No!" The shrill in Lian's voice startles me. Always so calm and in control, but not now.

Laughter booms from the emperor. No blood flows from where Zhangchi pierces his chest. I step back, releasing my hold on Zhangchi's hilt, certain I must be seeing things.

"How? Zhangchi should have stripped you of your gifts. You should be dead."

The sword's sharp edges slice gashes on the fingers of the emperor's gloves as he wraps them around the blade and pulls the sword from his stomach. "Fool girl! You think I would forge a sword and imbue it with power that could hurt me? I'm immortal. A god. I can't be slain, least of all not by a simple child as you."

I rush toward him and throw a palm heel strike to his chin. In a flash of speed and power, he back hands me across the face before my strike comes close. Even with my boon, the force of his blow knocks me to the ground. I push through the dizziness, pull myself to my feet and charge him again. Sharp pain spikes in my cheek before I move half a pace, the heel of his of foot breaking bones with a spinning hook kick. Chi warms the broken bones, healing them before I hit the ground.

Several paces away, I see his Zhangchi that I knocked to the floor earlier. I Step to it and reach, but spikes of pain from a kick to my midsection collapse me. My Chi returns my breath and strength, but the pain spikes return as he kicks me again and again.

I Step to the nuns guarding Lian to escape his kicks. That effort uses much of my Chi, but I think I have enough for one more gift. I push past the nuns' spears and grab Lian's arm. I try to use my Return gift to travel back to the palace gardens with Lian, but one of the nuns thrusts her spear through my belly.

"Meilin!" Lian screams as she pushes the nun aside and pulls the spear free.

I drop to my knees as the last of my Shen Breath streams from the wound. My Chi expires before the wound completely heals, leaving me weak and stinging with a belly full of pain.

Strong hands grab my arms beneath my shoulders and jerk me to my feet. "Are you bored of this game yet?" The emperor pulls his face close to mine. Vicious rage shows in his glare. His hot breath warms my face. "I know you now. The crazed village girl who stole Lord Zheng's horse. You tried to stop your sister from becoming my newest Wife Divine. Is that right?"

I'm tempted to stick my tongue at him, but for the first time in my life that feels a bit childish. Spitting in his face seems the next best thing, but in spite of the life and death situation Lian would never forgive me for such bad manners. So, I wrinkle my nose and furrow my eyebrows to give him my best scowl.

A thin smile spreads across the emperor's face. "Since you tried to kill me with one of my own demon slayer swords, I would wager you're also the girl who bested my Shashyao in the market skirmish the other day."

I grin. "That's right, I did."

His smile curves up higher. "Such a clever girl. I suppose you're also the one who kidnapped my Wives Divine. What did you hope to accomplish with that?"

My grin brightens. "To get them away from you. To let them live."

His smile vanishes. Anger flares in his eyes. I cringe at the stabbing pain that cuts into my stomach as he punches my spear wound. "Where are they? Tell me now, or your sister dies."

Eyes wide, I jerk my gaze toward Lian surrounded by the nuns and their sharp spears. A crushing hollowness squeezes inside my chest. What do I do? If I tell him, I condemn the wives and all the Mu Cun villagers. But if I don't, I lose Lian. I can't let her die. I can't. Worry crinkles the corners of Lian's eyes as she shakes her head.

Like a claw, the emperor's gloved fingers grab my chin and force me to look back at him. "Tell me where they are, or I'll kill you both!"

My heart breaks. I've failed Lian, but I have no choice. "No. They're safe. Out of your reach. That's all that matters."

His grip on my chin tightens. The pain spikes and I'm certain my bones will shatter. He adjusts his grip, to squeeze even harder, but as he does, the skin of his fingers warms me through the thin gashes in his gloves. In that moment, all my pain vanishes. My wound heals and strength replaces all my aches. At the same time, the emperor flinches and a flash of agony shows in his eyes. He lets go of my chin, and just as fast, the anguish disappears, replaced with wild fury.

He lifts me off the ground by the collar of my tunic and pushes his face close to mine. "That's not all that matters. If any harm comes to the Wives Divine, Huyan and all of Dashi will fall."

The crazed look on his face almost makes me worry that he might bite off my nose or an ear. I tense, trying hard not to tremble or show fear. His eyes bore into me as if he's trying to see into my thoughts.

His upper lip curls up in disgust and he drops me to the ground. "I'm in a generous mood. For now, I will let your sister live and you can go free. But in the coming hours, I will honor your family and friends with a visit. At sunrise, you are invited to join us in your village square. If my Wives Divine do not come with you, I make you this promise. Your sister will die. Your parents will die. Every mother, father, and child in Ning will die. And the shame of their deaths will haunt you through all eternity as you rot in the depths of Kaioda."

The emperor turns his back on me, walks to Lian, grabs her arm, and they both vanish. The nuns scowl before turning their backs on me and walking from the room. A few heartbeats later I hear the creak of a door, the rush of wind, and a door slamming closed before I'm left alone in silence.

Even though the emperor took my Zhangchi with him, his still lies on the floor across the room. At first, I think it's an oversight. But no, he's already proven that even with the power of Zhangchi I'm no match for him. Besides, I need Chi to go to the Wives Divine. Since the chamber has no Shen Breath lanterns, he's likely counting on Zhangchi to give me the Chi I need.

When I grab its hilt, the sword's Chi warms me once again with strength and power. But this time, I know the feeling of invincibility is a lie. There's only one invincible wielder of Chi in all of Huyan and perhaps all of Dashi.

So, what do I do? Sunrise is only hours away. Do I go to Ning to warn my family and villagers? To the palace to find Cai? To Mu Cun Village to bring the wives back to the emperor? Two's mercy, there has to be a way to stop the emperor. I just have no idea what it might be.

Part 5

Chapter 55
Chao Cai – Unexpected Ally

"The inconvenience of helping someone in-need transforms aid to divine succor."
- Pan Ru: Essays on the Tenets of Light

The sweet smell of rain-soaked trees fills the night air as I move from guest house to guest house. Pouring rains drums atop the covered walkways above me. Soaked and dripping with rainwater, my borrowed guard uniform chills my flesh. It's well past midnight, and the walks are empty except for the occasional member of the Gold Dragon Guard on patrol. None take notice of me. The cold wet of the night has few in the mood for talk or questions. They just want to make their rounds and get somewhere warm.

Hours have passed since I Returned to the palace and Meilin Leaped the Wives Divine to the Mu Cun village. Still, I'm no closer to finding Lian. I searched as much of the palace as I dare, including the holding pits in the Guard's barracks. I even searched the garden shrines, getting drenched by the rains. But I've seen no sign of Lian. My last hope is to find her in one of the royal guest houses.

My new Step gift makes it easy to pop in and out of guest houses without dealing with posted guards or bothering with doors. But more than once I Stepped too close to a table and knocked over a vase or surprised a jumpy house cat, waking and angering the house's sleeping occupants. Besides, creeping into people's houses and spying on them is not enjoyable. While hoping that I'll find Lian peacefully sleeping, I encounter too many unpleasant and unexpected sights that I simply do not want to see. There's also the raucous snoring and disgusting odors. Even the strongest perfumes and incense can't cover up the smells that emanate from houses where lazy aristocrats don't bother to bathe for weeks or clean up after feasts several days past.

Hopefully, Meilin's efforts have been better than mine, but if they have, I'm not sure how I'll find out. In our hurry, we didn't plan how to let each other know our progress. So, I search no matter how futile and distasteful it seems.

At the east end of the covered walkway, I reach the grandest of all the guest houses. It reminds me of a Shen shrine, but bigger and more elaborate. Gold paper lanterns burn bright beneath the overhang of the house's swooping, green-tiled roof. Two grim looking bronze guardian lion statues stand on each side of the porch. A garden of pink and yellow peonies and swirling topiaries front the house. The pounding rain does little to drown out the loud snores coming from two Gold Dragon Guards sleeping and sitting with their backs to the wall on each side of the house's big red door.

I touch a nearby Shen Breath lantern hanging along the walkway in preparation to Step inside the guest house. I lift the collar of my tunic and do a quick check on the gift marks stamped on my chest. I frown. Two of the three Step gift marks have completely vanished. The lines of ink on the third one have faded. I can barely make out the foot and ground characters, and the Father symbol is completely gone. From the black leather pouch hanging from my guard belt, I pull out an ink stick, along with the necklace of ceramic discs the Meilin gave me. It'll be the sixth time tonight I've had to restamp the Step gift marks.

When I finish stamping the mark and putting the necklace back in my pouch, an uneasy anxiousness tugs at my chest. Where else do I look for Lian if she's not in there? I sigh, knowing I'm out of answers.

I touch the warmth of the Shen Breath to call upon its Chi but stop when I hear a sorrowful moan beyond the end of the covered walkway. A young man with several tattoos covering his bare chest and arms sits in the pouring rain on the edge of the stone path. Partially shielding his upper torso from the rain is the flat square board of a pain yoke enclosed around his neck.

As I stare at the mix of blood and rainwater where the yoke's collar circles the man's neck and the iron shackles bind his ankles, I wonder what crime the young man committed to receive this punishment. What imperial law did he break? Or is this vengeful retribution that some lord or noble inflicted on the young man?

The man moans again as he hunches back against the stone statue he's chained to. The statue is of Chōngyù Shen, the rotund god of harvest attired in his necklace of soybeans and plums, a crown of hazelnuts on his head, and a stalk of rhubarb for a scepter. Chōngyù Shen is known as a merciful god, but those who punished this young man have shown little mercy. A bloodstained bandage is wrapped around his bare chest. And as the young man's head tilts back and slumps listless to the side, I spot bloodstains covering the whole side of his face.

Without realizing it, I walk into the rain until I hover over him. My head jerks in surprise as I realize it's not blood that stains the left side of his face. Rather, it's the splotchy red markings of a Quanli quarry slave.

It's the gardener that spoke to me earlier tonight about the rule to remember women first. The one who told me it takes a brave man to defy the emperor. Had this man defied the emperor and paid the price?

"Please. Help." His voice strains in a labored whisper. "Shen Breath. Need Shen Breath."

That's when I notice that it's not tattoos that cover his chest and arms, but dozens of different inked gift marks. "Shen-Blessed!" I mutter. "You're Shen-Blessed."

"Help. Please."

A gurgle in the back of his throat follows his whisper. Any breath he takes could be his last. He's fighting to stay alive. He shifts to the side and jerks in anguish as the needles of the pain yoke prick his flesh in someplace new. I want to help him, but I'm not sure if I should. As a Shen-Blessed, the young man's not likely a friend of the emperor. But that doesn't mean he'll be friendly to me either. With so many gift marks, I doubt I can stand against him. Right now, all that matters is finding Lian and getting back to Meilin.

"Sorry, stranger. I want to help, but I can't risk it right now. Others need me."

I turn to head back toward the last guest house, but as I do the man takes a long wheezy breath. Its death-rattle eeriness stops me before I go more than a step.

How can I let this man to die? It's not right. I have to help him. No. Helping him might stop me from helping Lian. Stop it. Am I really going to leave a man to die because I don't know what he will or won't do?

Enough! I don't have time for this. I have to save Lian. I move away in a rush.

"The Divine One… I cannot fail her."

His faint plea barely sounds over the pouring rain. Something in his words sends a cool tingling down the back of my spine. I spin back toward him and kneel in front of him with my face a fist-width away from his own.

"Who can't you fail?" I ask, doubting the possibility that pushes into my thoughts.

"I promised I would come." The whisper is ragged. Faint. "Please. Cannot break promise."

"What do you mean?" I push my nose even closer to his. "Who is the Divine One you speak of? Tell me her name?"

The man's eyes flutter and he slumps. I think I've lost him. Spittle bubbles between his lips and he whispers, "Qiu Lian. The emperor's new Wife Divine."

Chapter 56
Fan Wei – In-Between Places

"Mu Po's love for us is not in question. She fought for us but lost."
- History of the Descendants: Volume 2, Page 32

Shen Breath is such a delightful treasure. Thank the Two that they abound in so much generosity that they condescend to give mere mortals a taste of their divine power. It takes only seven lanterns full of the rainbow streaming mists from the gods to heal all my wounds. The hundreds of bloody needle pricks around my neck heal first. The hole in my chest from Ye Ye's Zhangchi takes the longest to mend.

The poke of the emperor's nasty sword would have killed me if I hadn't fallen onto a Shen Breath lantern in Zheng's front room. I'm actually a little foggy on that detail. I didn't see any Shen Breath lanterns in the room when I stepped inside. But the first thing I remember after losing consciousness is waking up facedown with my nose planted in a lantern's paper. It healed me enough to not slip down the precipice of death.

Was that Ye Ye's doing? Did he have one of Zheng's guards fetch the lantern and roll me onto it. Part of me wants to believe he didn't have the heart to kill me. That's the part that's always trying to shove soppy sentimentality into my thoughts. More likely, Ye Ye spared me only so he could inflict more torture on me. He didn't waste any time sticking me in the nearest pain yoke.

Thank the Two for my new good friend from Ning. I think Cai is his name. He rescued me from the yoke's needle pricks and the bruising of my ankle shackles. He seems a nice fellow, even if he does struggle to keep up with me as we hurry to the Imperial Gallery. Somehow, Cai is Shen-Blessed too. Although, he's an infant when it comes to using his Chi. Thank the Two again that Cai somehow had my gift mark necklace. Oh, how I have missed that treasure. What comfort it brings to have it hang around my neck once again.

And even greater thanks to the Two for sending me one who shares my desire to save my most precious Divine One. It took a bit of persuasion to convince Cai to go to the Imperial Gallery with me. But he ceded to my wishes once he confessed he had no better notion of how to proceed.

On our way to the Imperial Gallery, I draw Shen Breath from four more lanterns to bring my Chi to full swelling. As usual, when we arrive at the gallery no soldiers stand guard at its entrance. We hurry up the polished stone steps and through the entry's marble pillars. Given the time of night—rather early morning hours—it's no surprise that Cai and I are the only ones inside.

I barely spare a glance at the vast collection of statues and paintings on display as we whisk past masterpiece after masterpiece. My focus is on only one piece of art—the screen painting of the young hero scaling Mount Qiangu in search of the Tree of Life and its immortality-giving peaches.

It's a slim hope, but as the words of the servants from last night have rolled over and over in mind, a hope has risen inside me that the painting might actually hold the key to finding Mu Po, as well as my sweet Lian. That hope is that the emperor brought the painting to the empress before having it sent to the gallery, If that happened, I can Track its path back to Mu Po.

My heart races and my breathing rushes when we reach the painting. A quick touch of my Chi would calm them both, but I can't afford to squander any of its power. Taking my Track gift disc from necklace I stamp its mark twice on my chest above the multiple Leap, Step, and Return marks that I inked on by hand earlier.

The Track gift is one of the most unreliable of the Shen's gifts. For it to work, the painting will have to have to been in Mu Po's presences for at least a few days. Even then, there's no guarantee the gift will lead us to Mu Po. So many other factors affect its reliability. Did it stay in that location without moving much from one spot to another? How much time has passed since it left its last location? How many other places has it been in? How long was it in those locations? Not even the masters who schooled Suyin and I knew all the conditions that might affect how well the gift works.

There's also the risk that it will not only take us to the wrong place, but that it will take us to a place in-between. I've never quite understood the idea of in-between places, but the masters spoke of them as full of uncertainty and danger. Places where those who journey there often never return.

I glance at Cai at my side. Anxious tension shows in his eyes. I'm uncertain of his relationship with my sweet Lian. They both come from Ning. That is all I know. And he wishes to rescue her too. "Friend, are you ready?"

He nods. The anxiousness in his expression tightens a dab.

"There is a danger in what I am about to attempt. Perhaps it would be best if I went alone, and you waited my return."

"No." He shakes his head. "The danger doesn't matter. We must find Lian."

I bow my head toward him and offer him a slight grin. "Very well. Together we go."

Tapping into the warmth of my Chi, I grip Cai's forearm with my left hand and with the forefinger of my right hand I trace the symbols of the Track gift mark lightly atop the surface of the painting. Visions of the path from the Imperial Gallery to the palace proper float through my mind. Abruptly, the vision shifts with a rushing blur of colors and places. Dizziness whirls around me. I try to focus and slow down the vision, but I have had little practice in using the Track gift before. Lightness seeps into my body and I know Cai and I no longer stand in the gallery.

Colors and sights around us warp, blur, and rush past as we speed in and out of what must be the in-between places. The gift consumes my Chi at a rapid rate as we travel. I need to bring us to a stop, but I'm not certain how to focus on the desired location. If I don't so soon, it will no longer matter. We'll be lost.

Crack!

The spinning stops. A crushing pressure squeezes my body from heel to hair. Shrilling screams swirl around me. My body crashes to a jolting hard stop. My chest and face smash against a rock-hard surface. The rush of colors vanishes into darkness. Cold silence surrounds me.

Chapter 57
Lord Emperor Xiang Hu – Imperial Justice

"Being certain that one's cause is just does not create license to trample those who disagree."

- Secret Musings of Wang Jin

The wet chill from last night's rain hangs heavy and cold in the air. Dangling from hooked poles around the village square, red lanterns shimmer in the predawn darkness, casting an eerie glow on the mists floating among thick shade trees, patches of flowers, field grass, and bamboo that grow beyond the edges of the square's cobbles. Anxious for a new morning, birds whistle and chirp among the trees and atop the rooftops of the shops and market stalls. But the mood in the squalid village of Ning is anything but cheerful.

Herded by a dozen black-clad masked Shashyao, hundreds of Ning villagers tramp their way down the hillside path that winds its way between the villagers' huts and houses toward the village square. Mothers try to silence the whines and cries of babes and young children, sleepy-eyed and grumpy from being woken so early. A general grumbling among the village elders and other men rises from the procession but cuts off one by one as they draw closer to the square and lay their eyes on me dressed in my royal yellow robes. How divine I must appear, illuminated by the two gold-papered lanterns hanging above my head from the beards of the dragons that rise from the back of my travelling throne.

Like a slow rolling wave, the villagers drop to their knees and kowtow face to the ground. Confused by their parents' sudden groveling, many young ones remain standing until their parents yank them down amid a hushed buzz of "Lord Emperor!" "Chosen of Heaven!" "Emperor Xiang Hu!"

Only the first few rows of villagers kneel on the square's cobbles. Most crowd behind them, kowtow on the dirt path or strips of lawn beyond the plaza. Silence thickens until only the whistle of birds, the distant bleat of goats, and a few muffled crying babes can be heard. I let time pass, allowing the villagers to offer an ample display of reverent adulation. It's not often that such lowly peasants have the privilege to kneel in the presence of their divinely appointed protector.

When I'm satisfied with their expression of veneration, I flick my hand heavenward and command, "Rise."

Except for a few, who with a slight raise of their heads cast an uncertain glance at me, none move. I let out a long sigh of exasperation. That's the problem with adoring supplicants. Their fawning praise too often gets in the way of immediate obedience.

"Rise!" I amplify my voice, tapping into my Chi to make sure all hear and feel the force of my command. "Off your knees! I would have you see my displeasure as I speak of your dishonorable crimes."

Worry and shock sweep across the villagers' faces as they rise to their feet. They cast quick glances at their neighbors, puzzled about what misdeeds they might have committed.

"Bring out the prisoner!" I say, clapping my hands twice at two of the Shashyao standing near me.

The Shashyao bow their heads and hurry behind one of the tent stalls. Not long after, they return, dragging the girl behind them. With shackles chained to her ankles, she hobbles to keep up with the Shashyao. A pain yoke weighs down her shoulders, clamped tight around her neck. The tattered hem of her jade bridal gown drags across the cobble stones. She tries to hold her head high, fighting the weight and sharp pain the yoke's needle pricks inflict on her. Stuffed in her mouth, like a wadded-up rag, her red bridal veil silences any babbling accusation she might try to raise in her defense.

My eyes move from her, scanning the square once again for Shen Breath lanterns. The girl probably doesn't even know what it means to be Shen-Blessed, but if she happens to get infused with Shen Breath, there's a chance that neither the pain yoke nor ankle chains will keep her bound.

"Lian? Is that you?" A middle-aged man dressed in the same drab peasant grays as the others takes a half step forward. Confusion fill his eyes as he fixates on the yoked girl beside me. A pleasant looking woman trembles behind the man, fear and anguish haunt her tear-filled gaze.

"Ah, you must be her father. The shame and dishonor of your daughter's deeds should drag you down to the lowest depths of Kaioda." Disgust and anger seethe from my voice. "I paid a generous bride price for your treacherous daughter. Yet, she deserted me almost immediately after she made her vows. No doubt, she did so at your bidding. Did you think I would not seek retribution? You will repay me a hundredfold!"

The villagers' gazes shift toward Lian's father. Scorn and righteous indignation tighten the scowls on their faces. No doubt they fear my anger will overflow onto them as well. A valid fear.

The man falls to his knees and steeples his hands beneath his chin. "Most gracious Lord Emperor, Chosen of Heaven, there must be a mistake. Lian would never do such a thing."

"You call me a liar?" I draw Zhangchi. Sparks and bits of stone fly as I slam the blade down hard on the cobblestones. The crowd of villagers cringes and shrinks back. An ordinary blade would break, chip, or at least dull with the force of such a stroke, but I forged and tempered all the Zhangchi blades with more power and strength than these peasants could ever imagine. "There is no mistake! You and your villagers will pay for her crime, as well as the crimes of your other daughter."

More confusion tightens the wrinkles at the corners of the man's eyes. "You mean Meilin? What does she have to do with any of this?"

Snickers, snorts of anger, and several smug expressions accompanied by furious head nods spread among the villagers. Mutters of "Troublemaker!" "Shameful girl!" and "Xie cursed!" hum through the crowd.

The man rises to his feet and clears his throat. "I beg your forgiveness and the Two's mercy, Lord Emperor, for whatever trouble Meilin might have caused you. No matter what we have tried, she has always been an overflowing fount of discord within our home and village."

Anger darkens the eyes of the woman behind the man. Her tight-lipped scowl makes me believe it's not because of Meilin herself, but because of the man's words. What would this woman do or say if Innate Honor didn't forbid her to speak her mind in such a public forum? It also makes me wonder what my dear Yuan might say or do. With Yuan's strong spirit, she would never tolerate ill words spoken of another. A spike of guilt pinches my heart, but I push it away. Now is not the time for sentimental weakness.

My grip on Zhangchi tightens and scowl at the pathetic man before me. He kneels and steeples his hands again, bowing deep before me. "Lord Emperor, Chosen of Heaven. I know your mandates are just, but please do not lay the sins of Meilin upon the shoulders of my family and villagers. She has always been a willful child. She certainly must be behind whatever crime you feel Lian has done, for I know my eldest daughter to be loyal to the Lord Emperor, Chosen of Heaven."

Before I can shout my condemnation of Lian's treacherous acts, Lian stomps her foot, causing her chains to rattle. Through her gag, she pushes out her bottom lip in a pain-filled grimace and glares at her father. With all eyes turned to her, she shakes her head, denying her father's attempt to shift blame to her younger sister. I clench. The strength of this one's spirit is venerable. But it doesn't matter. Justice must be served. And even more important, my Wives Divine must be returned so Dashi can be protected.

"Both of your daughters will die this day! Lian for her personal treachery to me. Meilin for kidnapping my Wives Divine." A sharp gasp rises from the crowd. None say a word, not even the girls' father. Stunned expressions show on all their faces. "The question of your fate remains. If Meilin doesn't return my Wives Divine by sunrise, every soul that calls Ning home will bear the shame of her crimes and die by the blades of my Shashyao."

Color drains from the villagers' faces. Little by little, each gaze turns east to the skyline above the rocky cliffs that rise high above the far shore of the Pangbo. Tinges of light blue push upward through pink-streaked clouds into the darkness of the predawn sky. Anxious silence grips the villagers as they watch the first fingers of golden sunlight reach heavenward, announcing dawn's imminent arrival.

Time moves slowly, but eventually the tip of the sun peeks above the cliffs. Its rays touch the mists floating among the trees, flowers, and grass bordering the village square, transforming them into swirling streams of Shen Breath. The melodic harmonies of more than five hundred Shen gifts play in my mind as the Shen Breath reaches out to me. I would draw in more, but my Chi and that of my Zhangchi is already peaked.

Absorbed in the gifts' songs, I don't immediately notice the villagers focusing on something behind me. Rising from my throne, I turn to follow their gaze. Beyond the flowers and trees that grow along the village square, a haggard young girl in blue servant robes emerges from the bamboo grove near the Pangbo. She marches toward me with head high and shoulders squared, her Zhangchi drawn and ready.

Chapter 58
Qiu Meilin – Bartering for Life

"Atrocities happen. That is the price in a world where everyone has the will to choose. Great things can happen too, if we let them."
- Pan Ru: Essays on Life

Mama. Father. Master Jin. Sun Yi. Lo Jing. Magistrate Pang. And everyone else in the village stare at me with a mix of expressions as I walk through the grass toward the village square. Uncertainty. Panic. Loathing. Scorn. I'm the dishonorable daughter returned home, bringing shame to my family and villagers, as well as the emperor's wrath.

My stomach turns. My knees feel weak. What do I think I'm doing? All I wanted to do was save Lian. Now, I've endangered everyone I love and care for. I shudder. I want to run away. But I can't.

A mocking grin plays on Emperor Hu's face as our eyes meet. He stands amid a dozen Shashyao warriors. Near his throne, Lian struggles to stay on her feet, bound in a pain yoke. Beneath the yoke, her jade bridal gown hangs ragged and torn. She wears a brave face, but its intensity tells me she's in agony. Though her mouth is gagged, her eyes smile at me. Goosebumps travel up my arms and down my spine. That one look is all I need. Lian is glad I'm here. She's counting on me. I will not fail her. I will not fail my family and friends. I cannot.

Gripping Zhangchi tight in my fist, I walk with renewed determination toward Emperor Hu and the rainbow-colored mists of Shen Breath that swirl among the flowers and bushes growing along the borders of the village square.

"Where are my wives, young child?" Disdain colors Hu's voice. "I did not think you would dare risk the lives of those you love. But it's not too late. Despite your crimes and the shame you have cast upon your family and village, I will honor my word. Bring me my wives and those you love will be spared. I'm certain my Wives Divine are anxious to be safe back in my care."

I want to laugh. Does Hu really think they would be happy to return to him? Can he be so blind? They are anxious, but not to return to their sleeping prison.

I stop at the edge of the square. Streams of Shen Breath flow toward me. The warmth of their Chi strengthens me and infuses me with more power. As great as it feels, it's little compared to what the emperor can wield. I have to fight the trembling in my knees as I imagine what he might do once he realizes I have no intention of returning the wives to him. By the Two's mercy, my plan better work.

"What of your shame?" I step through the swirling wisps of Shen Breath onto the cobbles of the village square. On the outside I try to sound and look confident, but inside I'm trembling. It's so bad I have to focus not to trip on my own feet. I'm glad my favorite elm is on the other side of the village square. The last thing I need to do right now is humiliate myself by tripping on one of its raised roots.

I take slow, deliberate steps, circling around the emperor toward my fellow villagers. Their glares tell me I'm not welcome near them. Not my worry. I need to put myself between them and Hu and his assassins.

"What of your crimes?" I continue. "When you vowed to marry the Wives Divine, did you tell them they would spend the rest of their lives drugged, imprisoned in an endless sleep? You stole their freedom. You stole their will. You stole their lives. For what? So, you could pretend to be a god? How will you repay your wives of the years you robbed from their lives? How will you repay their families?"

A gruff laugh blows past Hu's lips. "The families of the Wives Divine have been generously compensated for their sacrifices. Their status in their communities has been greatly elevated, as was your father when your sister willingly promised to become one of my wives—a promise she treacherously broke."

"Willingly?" I grin, but my grip tightens on Zhangchi as I continue to move closer to the villagers. "Would Lian have made that promise if she had known she would never see her family or another living soul again? That she would never feel the sun's warmth or the touch of rain? Never walk or run? Never taste food? Never again breathe in the fragrances of Gudai after a midnight rain? Never enjoy freedom? That she would spend every minute of the rest of her life asleep on a frozen mountaintop? Would she have made such a promise if she knew all that?"

I stop ten paces away from Mama and Father. A pained smile forms on Mama's face. Father looks away, refusing to meet my gaze. Still, I see pain and confusion in his eyes.

"Look at your daughter," I say to Father. "Lian, not me. The one you love so much. Tell me, would you have accepted the bride price if you knew Lian's true fate? Is this what you agreed to, what you wanted? Is this what you dreamed for her?"

Father's gaze moves to Lian. Anger and sadness collide in his expression. I hope the anger is for the emperor, but it's likely for me. In Father's mind, I've always been the cause of everything that goes wrong.

Hu grins. "Your words almost sound noble, but the Divine Wives protect the world against a threat greater and more horrific than you could imagine. Would you really doom the entire world so a few can live in freedom? No harm comes to the wives. They sleep peacefully and are well cared for. Outside of my care they are vulnerable to the enemy. I protect them so all of Dashi can remain safe."

"You have no right to imprison them, to take away their choice and freedom!"

"Enough! I will tolerate your disrespect no more." Hu's cheeks redden as he shouts. "Bring me my wives now, else my Shashyao will strike down your family and friends this instance."

I turn back to Hu, pointing Zhangchi at him. "Does being emperor give you the right to murder innocent people? To exterminate an entire village?"

"I am Chosen of Heaven!"

"Is that how you justify all your murders? Did the heavens choose you so you could secretly slaughter any that you please?"

"Shashyao!" The emperor raises Zhangchi and gestures toward the villagers. "Kill…"

"No!" I yell, before he can issue the command. "Hear my words. If you spill any blood now, you will never learn where your Wives Divine hide."

Hu scowls but lowers his sword. My eyes turn from him to the faces of the villagers until I find Cai's father. "Chao Shui, your heart still mourns for your son, but Cai is not dead. He was with me when I left Ning. A few days ago, he told me, how at the emperor's command, the Shashyao tried to murder him and twelve of his fellow recruits. Their only crime was that the blood of the Two flows in their veins. With the help of another recruit, Cai escaped."

Chao Shui's mouth drops open. His eyes look hopeful, but uncertain. I nod. "Yes, it's true. And when you see him again, he will confirm all that I have said."

I look back at Hu. His eyes laugh as if I'm telling a fairy tale that he's certain no one else will believe. I shake my head. "Tell me, Chosen of Heaven, do you find murder and the loss of loved ones so amusing? How many other young men from Ning have dutifully gone to war to honor you and protect Huyan, only to be killed by your demon assassins? How many young army recruits from other villages have you murdered over the past three centuries? Thousands? Millions?"

Hu's lips tighten, but he says nothing.

"How many women have you murdered because they dared enter a shrine to pray to a Shen? How can you sleep after stripping every girl and woman of their dignity and self-worth, enslaving them under the cultural yoke of shame and inferiority of Innate Honor just so you can justify your murders and control the Shen's gifts? Do you really think the Two approve of you murdering and subjugating their children?"

"Silence!" The ground shakes at the sound of Hu's voice. Some of the villagers stumble and fall. "I will have your tongue cut out for your treasonous slander."

I shrug. "What you do to me doesn't matter. But know this, your Wives Divine will renounce their oaths and leave you void of all your gifts if you do not promise in the name of the Two to let them return unharmed to their homes, including Lian. You must also promise that you will spare the lives of my family and all the villagers of Ning."

A look of worry flashes across Hu's face, replaced quickly by a wry smile. "Your words tire me." His voice overflows with contempt. "You are a fool if you think I will be powerless if the wives renounce their oaths. I will still be Chosen of Heaven with the power to strike you down and any others who oppose me. And in time, the Shen will return to me every one of their gifts, but by then it might be too late for Huyan and Dashi.

"The wards that hold Xié Shen captive in Kaioda have weakened. His favored ones seek to free him. For now, all that keeps them from doing so and unleashing his vengeance on Dashi are the gifts that the Two and their children have bestowed on me. Without them, I might not be able to protect Dashi from the devastation and horrors that Xié Shen and his favored ones will hail down on the world. Is that what you want, to let Xié Shen destroy us all?"

I step toward Hu, clutching Zhangchi tight. "What I want is a promise from you that you will spare my village and free the Wives Divine." I hesitate a heartbeat or two, wondering if I dare push for more. I decide I might as well try. "You must also do away with the shame you have placed on women. You must decree they have equal standing with men throughout all of Huyan. You must abolish Innate Honor. Make these promises with a vow to the Two and you can keep your gifts."

Hu laughs. "Child, who do you think you are to make demands of your emperor? I should slice you from heel to hair until you're nothing more than a million dabs of blood and guts."

He pauses. His smile thins as his expression turns somber. "That said, I could not bear to witness the desolation that Xié Shen would inflict upon the people of Huyan and Dashi even with a brief absence of my gifts. I care more for them than you could ever know."

A glimmer of hope rises in me. Is Hu actually considering my terms? I have to force down the grin trying to rise on my face, "Promise and do as I have asked, and your gifts are yours to keep and protect Dashi with. What do you say?"

Hu arches an eyebrow and a corner of his mouth scrunches upward as his expression turns thoughtful. He lets out a sigh and relaxes his posture before sheathing his Zhangchi.

"You believe me a tyrant, but I am a merciful ruler," Hu says, resignation softening his expression further. "I'm inclined to promise as you ask. But if I do, how can I know that my Wives Divine will keep their oaths? How can I be sure that you even speak for them?"

"You will have to trust me."

Hu frowns. “No. That is not acceptable. I will make no promise until I hear from the Wives Divine themselves that they agree with the conditions you have stated.”

My lips tighten. I was afraid Hu might make this demand. But I can’t back down now. Still, I worry about the wives’ safety. They would fight to the death to keep the emperor from imprisoning them again. But I’m certain Hu won’t risk spilling their blood to take them by force. The death of any of his wives would mean the loss of several gifts. And if he employs any other tactic to enslave them, they will simply renounce their gifts.

But why am I so hesitant? I knew it might come to this. It makes sense. If I’m going to get any promises or oaths from Hu, he needs to know the wives will keep their oaths too. I have to do it. This is the only way to save Lian and the other wives. It’s the only way to save my family and the village.

Hu grips the hilt of his sword. Impatience creases the wrinkles on his face. “Well, child, what will it be? Do I get a promise from the Wives Divine or has all this been a charade? I will wait no longer.”

I swallow hard and take a quick breath. “First, release Lian and you’ll have your promise from the Wives Divine.”

Hu rolls his eyes in annoyance and shakes his head. Faster than I can blink, he draws Zhangchi and slices the gleaming blade hard down toward Lian.

“No!” My scream flies past my lips as Lian falls to the ground. I drop to my knees. I let my Zhangchi fall from my hand. How did I let this happen?

But as I look through the tears that cloud my vision, I see the pain yoke lying in shattered splinters beside Lian and the chains shackling her ankles cut in two as she tries to rise to her knees. Although weak from suffering in the pain yoke, no blood stains her robes. She lives. Hu freed her.

I rush to Lian. I cradle her in my arms and lift her off the cobbles with help from my boon. As I carry her toward Mama and Father, tears stream from my eyes. Sorrow tears for Lian's weakened stated and the pricks of blood around her neck. Joy tears that she's safe.

"All is well now, Lian," I whisper. "Everything will be okay."

"Thank you," Lian mouths back, barely able to move her lips, too tired to voice the words.

I lay Lian's weary body on the cobbles in front of Mama and Father. Father meets my gaze, tears in his eyes and a smile of gratitude on his lips. I swallow, not sure at first how to respond. With a fist in hand salute on my chest, I bow my head toward Father before I rise and return to face Emperor Hu.

"Your sister is free," Hu says as I pick up my Zhangchi off the ground. "Now when will I hear these promised guarantees from my Wives Divine?"

I take a deep breath and exhale. "You'll have your guarantee." I look past the emperor, past the tall grass growing beyond the village square toward the bamboo grove near the Pangbo. I whistle the call of the Scarlet Thrush, three quick notes dropping from high to low, followed by a long trill of the first high note.

My gaze remains fixed on the grove. Several heartbeats pass. Nothing happens. Worry tightens my throat. My grip on Zhangchi tightens too. Where are they? Did they hear my call? Maybe I didn't whistle loud enough. Should I whistle again? Did something happen to them? Could they have decided to leave?

Though the morning is still cool, beads of sweat form on the back of my neck. What will Hu do if the wives don't show? What will I do?

Several horrible scenarios flash through my mind until there's a rustling of movement near the edge of the bamboo grove.

Dressed in their jade bridal gowns and faces veiled in red, row after row of Wives Divine emerge from the grove into the field of grass. Colored streams of Shen Breath swirl around them. The rising sun angled behind them, backlights them with a heavenly glow as they march forward. I smile. It's a glorious procession.

When the last of the ninety-nine wives steps from behind the thick stalks of bamboo into the field of grass, I look back at Emperor Hu with satisfaction. He's smirking.

Oh, Why the smirk? Something must be wrong. What did I miss? Three full heartbeats pass before I get a hint. Only seven Shashyao stand near Hu. Where are the other five?

My gaze whips back toward the Wives Divine. All at once, more than twenty Shashyao rise within the tall grass to the side of the wives. It happens with such speed that I have no time to react. They raise short bamboo tubes to their lips, I can't hear the whoosh of the darts at this distance, but panic tightens my chest. One by one, every Wife Divine topples unconscious to the ground until not a single one stands.

"Thank you, child." Smugness fills Hu's voice. "You have done the people of Huyan a great service by helping me return my Wives Divine to their peaceful sleep. Still, the shame of you and your sister cannot be ignored. You, your sister, mother, father, and entire village must all die."

Chapter 59
Qiu Meilin – Stand or Die

"The greatest test of honor is what we do when all hope is lost, and we stand alone."

- Pan Ru: Essays on Life

Streaks of color from the sun continue to brighten dawn's sky. I want to scream at the Shen Breath swirling above the tall grass. Its laughing dance mocks me near to tears.

How could this happen? The wives are Shen-Blessed. They were full of Chi. How could they fall so easily to the Shashyao's drugged darts? Their Chi should have strengthened them against such an attack. Isn't that why their mountaintop prison didn't have a single Shen Breath lantern?

The more I learn, the more I realize how much I really don't know. One thing I do know. I failed the wives. I failed the villagers. I failed my family. I failed Lian.

"What now, child? No more demands of your emperor?" Hu stands in front of his throne, grinning wide. I desperately want to snap kick the grin off his face. "Your arrogance has doomed you. Will you still think your cause just as you watch all those you love die?"

My lips tighten. I want to shake my sword at the heavens and cry, "Why didn't you help me?" All of my efforts have been for nothing. I can't stand against the emperor and survive. Even if I were only facing his Shashyao, I couldn't hope to overcome so many. Still, I won't give up. There's only one thing to do.

I step forward and crouch into the dragon stance. The open palm of my free hand faces forward toward Emperor Hu. My other hand raises Zhangchi level above my head, its tip pointing at Hu's heart. "They have done nothing wrong. Let them alone."

Hu sniffs but says nothing. The seven Shashyao at his side stand as silent statues, waiting for their emperor's command to attack. A few of the twenty or so other Shashyao stand guard over the fallen Wives Divine, while the rest move toward their emperor through the grass field and swirling mists with a graceful deliberateness.

Hu rolls his eyes. "You tire me, child. Lay down your sword and let justice be served. Bring no further humiliation to yourself or shame to your family."

I clench Zhangchi tighter, and I rise on the tips of my toes. "If you seek justice, take my life and let all these others go. My life for theirs."

Hu laughs. "You overestimate your life's value. They will die. You will die. You cannot change that."

"Maybe," I say, continuing to hold the dragon stance and rising a little higher on my toes. "But I can fight. I will protect my family, my village, the Wives Divine, and any others you seek to destroy or enslave. I will fight you until my veins bleed dry. No matter what you threaten, I will stand against you."

Hu scowls and sits back onto his throne. "Then you will stand and die alone."

As one, the Shashyao turn their masked faces toward the emperor, waiting for his signal to attack. Hu grips one of the armrests of his throne with one hand and raises his other in a fist, but stops. His scowl deepens as his eyes move to the side of me.

"No. Not alone." The sound of Lian's voice at my side startles me. "I will stand or die at my sister's side."

The haggard look in Lian's gaze is gone. Strength shines in her eyes as she smiles at me. I don't know where she got it, but with the grip of a warrior she holds a sword ready to fight. Her presence comforts me, but I want to tell her to go away, to go somewhere safe. But with Emperor Hu and his Shashyao near, nowhere is safe.

Master Jin steps up on my other side in his flowing bright green priest robes. "I too, will stand or die." His kind voice gives me confidence as does the graceful way the Fei Chi Master draws his sword and slides into the leopard stance.

Father's voice almost makes me jump. He steps up beside Lian. "I will stand as well. Too long, I have been a fool. I will not lose either of my daughters again."

Goosebumps tickle the back of my shoulders and spine. A mix of regret, pride, and determination shows in his eyes. A faint smile tips up the corners of his mouth as he nods at me. I can't remember the last time Father looked at me that way. I want to hold that image of his gaze in my mind forever.

"You are all fools!" Hu shouts. He flicks his wrist at the seven Shashyao beside him. "Go! Spare none. Kill them all!"

Shashyao blades hum as all seven draw their Zhangchi and rush forward. I tap into my boon, letting the warmth of my Chi surge within me and strengthen me as I prepare for their attack. The assassins almost double us in number. Even with my boon and gifts, I don't see how we can hope to stand against so many. And it won't take much longer for the more than twenty others to join in and completely overwhelm us.

When the seven Shashyao are less than ten strides away, one near the middle spins and slices the midsection of one Shashyao on the left and then the one on the right. Gales and hail! What is going on?

In an instance, the other four Shashyao halt and pivot their attack toward their traitor. In unison, their swords swing toward the turncoat, but their blades hit air as the Shashyao vanishes.

The lone Shashyao appears near my side and says in a familiar girl's voice. "Fan Suyin, Deliverer of the Blessed, Cursed and Heiress of the Shining Lady of Peace stands with the cursed whiffet too, though I'm sure I'll regret it."

It's the voice of the Shen-Blessed girl who tried to kill the Wives Divine. I never would have expected her help, but I won't turn it away. Now with three Shen-Blessed, a Fei Chi Master, and my father, our odds against the Shashyao don't seem as grim.

Father and Lian team up together against one of the Shashyao, while Suyin, Master Jin, and myself each face off with one of the remaining three. My opponent attacks and moves with an amazing speed and grace. His blade strikes and slashes with relentless fury. But my Zhangchi and boon lets me move faster. Our blades blur. Their steel ring and clang. I have no desire to kill the masked warrior, but that's his sole intent. If I let our duel continue much longer, he'll quickly have the help of the other Shashyao to end my life.

After I brush off one of his strikes with a blade flick, I palm strike his face. His demon-wolf mask cracks in half as I smash it against his nose. In the same motion, I step into him and half-spin my back against his front. My freehand shoots down his sword arm and I grab his wrist, twisting it and crushing the bones. Zhangchi falls from his grip, clanging on the cobbles. I elbow his gut with my sword arm and stomp his toes with the heel of my foot. I complete my spin and palm strike his face again. His eyes roll back as he collapses unconscious to the ground.

A few paces away, a bloodied Shashyao lies dead where Suyin fought. One moment, she fights alongside Master Jin, and the next she steps in to help Father and Lian combat their Shashyao. With the girl's help, neither of them need me.

I pivot toward the grass field beyond the square, tensing to face the charge of the more than twenty other Shashyao. But they do not come. A battle howl erupts from behind them. Liu Fen, her husband, and six other tattooed Mu Cun warriors sprint from their hiding place in the bamboo groves toward the Shashyao.

The warriors shake their spears high above their heads as they leap and run through the lingering wisps of Shen Breath that float above the grass. They howl again and chant "Zhu Yu Bao Genggai Wo. Zhu Yu Bao Genggai Wo."

Streams of Shen Breath spin around the eight warriors. Their tattoos glow, shining brighter and brighter until from heel to hair their skin emits an ethereal glow of jade colored light.

When only a few paces separate the Shashyao and warriors, blinding green light flashes from the warriors. In an instant they transform into large Jade Leopards. The flash and transformation startles the Shashyao. In that moment, the leopards pounce and bring down eight of the Shashyao with their slashing claws and dagger-like fangs.

Before the remaining Shashyao can recover, the Jade Leopards dart and dash out of reach of the assassin's swords. The Jade Leopards circle the Shashyao, lunging and retreating to keep the assassins off balance. As soon as they isolate any of them, two or three of the leopards pounce on the lone assassin and bring him down.

The Shashyao try to stay close together to keep the beasts at bay, but as they do a Jade Leopard leaps high over the group's heads out of reach of their swords. Another one leaps over them from another side. As the Shashyao raise their gaze to follow the leaping cats, blinding lights flash around the assassins and two or three of the leopards transform back into warriors. In that moment, the warriors thrust the tips of their long spears into the hearts of unsuspecting Shashyao before immediately transforming back into Jade Leopards.

With attack after attack, the numbers of the Shashyao quickly dwindle until only three remain standing. As the last wisps of Shen Breath fade away, these last Shashyao drop their swords and fall to their knees in surrender. At that same moment, the Jade Leopards fade back into their original warrior form, surrounding the assassins with the tips of their spears.

Emperor Hu claps his hands. Laughter rumbles past his lips "Impressive, but you've only delayed your extermination."

With leisurely nonchalance, the emperor stands from his throne and removes one his leather gloves. He crouches down to pull out a weed growing between the square's cobbles. As he rises, he rolls the weed between his forefinger and thumb. He grins at me before he turns his gaze toward the Mu Cun warriors. He crumbles the weed in his hand, squeezing it tight in his fist. As he does, in a burst of growth the tall grass near the warriors swells into thick vines and surges upward.

The vines wrap around the warriors' legs, chests, and arms binding them tight. They struggle to break free of the vines' grip, but the vines are too strong. The arm tattoos on a few of the warriors glow for a moment as if they're trying to transform, but whether it's from lack of Shen Breath or something about the Chi enchanted vines, the glow of the tattoos quickly extinguishes.

"Kill them!" Hu orders the kneeling Shashyao as he pulls his glove back on his hand.

Before the three assassins can reach for their Zhangchi, I Step to within paces of them. With a blast of wind, I lift the Shashyao in the air and drop them in the middle of the Pangbo River. The splash quickly swallows their shouts for help.

Before I can cut loose the vines that hold the Mu Cun warriors, the ground starts to shake. In the square, near my family and the villagers, the cobbles vibrate with rapid intensity. Cobbles shoot up from the ground with a loud grating and explosion of dust, and fly toward my family and the villagers.

I Step back onto the square and with a sweeping motion of my hand, blast my family and villagers out of the way of the flying cobbles. But I'm not fast enough. Several of the stones hit villagers in the head, chest, and legs before I can move them to safety. One hits Lian, bloodying her face. Another slams into Father's chest.

The ground continues to shake, and Hu launches more cobbles. Before I can raise my hand to move the villagers to safety again, multiple cobbles pummel me in the back of my head, neck, and shoulders. The force of the stones knock me to the ground. I try to get up, but more stones hit me from multiple directions. Even though my Chi and that from my Zhangchi heals each crushing blow, it doesn't diminish the pain.

I manage to lift my head, searching where Lian or Father fell. I tense as a hail of cobbles flies toward Mama and the villagers. Before the stones hit their target, Suyin appears in their path. She raises both arms above her head, holding Zhangchi high in one hand and the palm of her other facing forward. The cobbles stop midair with a thump after thump, as if hitting an invisible wall before dropping harmlessly to the ground in front of Suyin.

Emperor Hu continues to send cobbles at Suyin's wall of air. The strain on Suyin's face makes me worry she won't be able to keep up her invisible wall much longer. I'm not sure how much longer I can withstand the emperor's attacks on me either. My Chi drains fast. I have to change tactics or we'll all quickly fall to the emperor.

I Step out from under Hu's barrage of cobbles back to the field of grass where the Chi enchanted vines hold the Mu Cun warriors prisoner.

With several quick slashes of Zhangchi I free Liu Fen and throw her the sword. "Free the others and go somewhere safe. This might not end well for the rest of us."

Without waiting for her response, I search through the grass until I find two Zhangchi blades dropped by the Shashyao. The warmth of their Chi flows inside me, healing me and strengthening me. Holding both swords in my hands makes me feel almost twice as strong as before. Two's mercy, I hope it's enough.

With my eyes raised heavenward, I whisper, "Tiānqì Shen, please help me know what to do." I take a deep breath and let out a long exhale, trying to push down the terror rising inside me. I take one last breath and whisper one more prayer. "It's a loon's wish, but by the Two, please help us survive."

With barely a heartbeat passing after my uttered prayer, I Step from the fields to Emperor Hu. Little more than a sword's reach separates me and his crazed, glowering eyes. Gales and hail. This has to be the most witless, goat-headed thing I've ever done.

Chapter 60
Qiu Meilin – Fatal Tactics

"As fluid as their view might seem regarding honorable intent, a few reported incidences indicate that the Shen might make exceptions to some of their fickle rules in favor of one who lives the tenets."
- Hidden Scrolls of Quingping: Study in the pertinence of the Tenets of Light

Thump after thump sounds behind me as cobblestones continue to fly into Suyin's invisible wall. Delight plays in Emperor Hu eyes as he looks down at me. "Child, haven't we already danced to this song before? You couldn't kill me with one sword. Do you really think using two against me will make a difference?"

I'm not sure what I think, but I tighten my grip on the hilt of both Zhangchi blades. I crouch into the dragon stance with one sword cocked back above my head and the other extended straight out at my chest level. I have to stop Hu from murdering my family and villagers. It's a game to him. With over five hundred gifts from the Shen, he likely has much more efficient ways of killing than hurling cobblestones. When he loses patience for the game, I doubt there will be little that I or anyone can do to stop him.

"You don't have to do this," I say as I continue to offer silent prayers to Tiānqì Shen and the Two. "If you need to punish someone, punish me. Let the others go."

His lips tighten in a thin line with one corner of his mouth rising in a smirk. "It's not that easy child. It never is. I have a world to protect. I can't risk letting you or your family and friends make that job any harder than it already is."

Hu raises the tip of his Zhangchi level with my chest. "I have already let you waste too much of my time and energy, but no more. This ends now."

In a ready stance, Hu twirls his sword tip in small, tight circles in front of me. His ability with the sword is the least of my worries. He can easily overwhelm me with all the Shen gifts at his disposal. Tiānqì Shen, guide me. Help me keep my oaths to protect Lian and those I care for.

In that moment, an image of a whirlwind forms in my mind. The Wind gift marks on my palms warm as I tap into my boon. Unlike the past, this time I don't will the wind to burst from my hands. Instinct tells me instead to use my Chi to reach out to the Chi in the air surrounding Hu and me. With my mind, I coax it to do what I want.

A tunnel of fast whirling wind speeds around us, whipping my ponytail and tugging at my blue servant robes. The wind tunnel closes into a spinning point a few arm spans above our heads. Near our feet, it races atop the ground kicking up dust and pulling in leaves and debris from around us that obscure our view of most everything outside the wind tunnel.

The wind roars in my ears, yet I still hear the thump of cobbles hitting Suyin's wall. But not for long. After a few heartbeats, the thumping stops. Is it because Hu can no longer see his targets or is there something about the Chi powered wind tunnel that prevents him from using his gifts beyond its spinning walls?

"Clever girl," Hu says. His frown thins even more. Anger wrinkles tighten across his cheeks and forehead. "But you can't trap me that easy."

I sense him tap into Chi as he tries to escape the wind tunnel by Stepping several paces away near a market tent on the other side of village square. But the wind swirling around us, pulling at our clothes and racing against our skin, creates a connection between me and Hu. It's as if we were physically touching each other. When he Steps, the wind tunnel and I Step with him.

I grin, a chuckle playing on my lips. "Apparently I can trap you."

He Steps two more times to two different places. Each time, the wind tunnel and I Step with him.

"What do you hope to accomplish girl? You can't keep this up forever."

"I don't have to keep this up forever. Just long enough for those I care about to get safely away from you."

Hu laughs. "That's not going to happen. Look for yourself."

Hu gestures toward the edge of the square. Even though the dust in the wind tunnel obscures our vision, I see the faint silhouettes of the villagers standing near the edge of the village square. None of them left. Why don't they flee? Then it hits me. Where would they go? This is their home. Besides, as long as Hu lives, no place will be safe for them. Hu is right. All I'm doing is delaying their execution. I have to stop Hu. But how?

In that moment, Hu lunges. I flick upward with one sword, deflecting his attack. I follow with a downward sweep of my other sword toward his chest. He slides my attack away with a quick parry and stab. I glide sideways out of his reach. The wind tunnel moves with me. He flows through Fei Chi sword forms with incredible speed, slicing and whipping his Zhangchi in a graceful dance of fierce movement. Powered by both my Zhangchi swords I manage to match his speed and keep the swipe and lunge of his attacks from connecting.

"Compliments to your village master. You have learned your forms well for a peasant girl."

I want to slap his smirk with the side of my blade. But my attacks never reach further than the steel of his Zhangchi. I'd curse him with the vilest insult I can think of but the only ones I know are too good for him. So, I press my attacks harder and faster against him.

We glide, twist, and spin around each other as the wind tunnel whips around us. If we come too close to its spinning walls its tendrils grab and pull at our arms and legs. Far from the slow and relaxed speed I used thousands of times on the practice lawn with Master Jin, I zip and switch through sword movement after movement. Swallows Dive and Rise. Leopard Leaps. Dragon Tail Sweeps.

Emperor Hu flows through many of the same movements and forms, plus many others. His blade slices and whips like a natural extension of his arm. Midway through Scoop the Sea's Sand, he vanishes from view. At first, I think he managed to Step from the wind tunnel, but I sense his presence in front of me through the tendrils of wind whipping around him. I even sense how and where he moves.

Using those senses, I parry and dodge his invisible blade, but not before the tip of his Zhangchi slices my shoulder. The stinging pain makes me cringe. I almost collapse at the sudden loss of my boon and strength. But the pain and loss last less than a heartbeat as the Chi from my Zhangchi blades heals and fills me with their power.

Emperor Hu reappears. A self-satisfied grin creases his face. A bead of sweat drips down his cheek. "You can't last against me," he mocks. "My gifts are endless. My skill is three centuries perfected."

I don't need the reminder. Still, the sweat on his face gives me hope. At least fighting me requires at least a little exertion on his part. He attacks again spinning, slicing, and lunging, staying visible as he moves through different forms. I keep his attacks at bay, and one of my counter slices almost contacts his chest.

When Hu suddenly vanishes again. I'm ready this time. Through the wind connection, my mind envisions his attacks and movements. I push away a downward strike of his blade, but it still slashes through the cloth of my servant robe and pierces the side of my knee. The spike of pain and loss of strength make me stumble.

"Stay down, fool girl. Accept your death with honor."

In a heartbeat, the warmth of Chi from my swords rushes back inside me. I rise in time to push back another swipe and slice of his blade. I can't last much longer. The wind tunnel and healing are draining Chi from my blades fast. Why doesn't Hu stay invisible? He could finish me off sooner. Maybe he's trying to reserve his own Chi. It's a loon's wish, but maybe he's not as confident as he acts and sounds.

As he side-sweeps Zhangchi toward my waist, I block it. While my blade locks with his, I slash my other blade at him. He stops it mid-swing, grabbing my wrist with his free hand. I push back against his strength. He keeps me in check.

While our swords tie up, I notice the smooth perfection of his gloves. No gashes mar the glove fingers. Did he change his gloves since our fight last night? Why would he do that? When I think about what happened when the flesh of his fingers touched my face, an idea comes to me. It's a bad idea. One that will surely kill me. But with the Two's luck, it might kill Hu too.

Hu vanishes again. I sense his movements with the wind, but my block still fails. The edge of his sword clips my shoulder. My body tenses at its bite. I want to scream. But in a heartbeat, relief and healing fill me. Hu reappears and I match his next attacks with a flurry of counterstrikes but fail to gain any ground on him.

Hu grins at my wasted outburst of energy. "You are a determined little ant, aren't you? It's almost a shame to have to squash you."

With the grin still fresh on his lips, I Step to a grass patch beyond the far side of the village square beneath the shade of my favorite elm. As hoped, the wind carries Emperor Hu there with me. I keep my feet firm on the uneven ground, desperate not to trip on one of the elm's raised roots. Hu is not so lucky. The sudden Step startles him. As he shifts his feet to steady himself, one of his boots catches on a root. He almost falls but catches himself.

In that flash of time, I strike with both blades. Hu laughs as neither one hits flesh. Their edges only slice off a bit of each his sleeve.

"You are a pathetic worm. Your one chance to catch me off guard and you completely miss your target."

I smile and stick my tongue out at him. His puzzled look makes me want to laugh. I let go of my Zhangchi blades and let them drop at my side. They hit the grass with a muted thump.

Hu sniffs in disdain and shakes his head. "After all that determination and effort, you finally give up?" His body relaxes, and he lowers the tip of his Zhangchi until its level with my belly. "You carry less honor and more shame than I thought."

I straighten my shoulders, raise my head, and meet his taunting eyes with a hard gaze. "I never give up. And I didn't miss."

I launch myself at Hu. My hands reach through the gashes in his sleeves and my fingers wrap tight around the flesh of his forearms. At that same moment, I pull myself toward the tip of his sword. With a hard jerk, I shove my gut against its point, forcing the cold steel to impale me, piercing my stomach and thrusting out my back.

Chapter 61
Qiu Meilin – The Cure that Kills

"True healing always comes at a cost."
- Pan Ru: Essays on the Tenets of Light

As the edges of the emperor's blade slice through my belly and out my back, streaks of pain ignite my insides like searing flames of a roaring fire that refuse to be contained. The howl of the wind tunnel silences, replaced by screams. My screams. Hu's screams. We both collapse to our knees. I can't stop trembling, but I keep my grip firm on his arms. Pain and dizziness overwhelm me. I'm going to faint.

But I don't. In a few heartbeats the searing pain vanishes.

Healing Chi flows from the warmth of the skin on Hu's arms into the tips of my fingers. My bleeding stops. Mutilated organs mend. Severed muscles and tendons rejoin. The gash in my belly and back pulls together in a smooth layer. My strength returns. I feel whole again. But only for another heartbeat or two.

When the healing stops, my body realizes the blade is still inside me. Flesh splits apart. Blood spurts. Muscles sever. My internal organs rip apart. Agonizing pain erupts inside me, shattering any dab of relief. The devastating pain tears and thrashes through me all over again to the point of near loss of consciousness until in a flash the healing relief returns.

The cycle of consuming pain followed by lifesaving relief continues over and over again. It rips me back and forth from serene calm to the brink of unbearable agony. In the moments of respite, I stop clenching and trembling long enough to see the creases of agony dig deep across

Emperor Hu's face. His face contorts, straining at the torture his gift of healing inflicts on himself. He wails for relief. But for him it never comes.

He tries to pry my fingers off his arms. But his spasms and quaking are too severe. He has too little strength or control. Since I press so close to him, there's not enough room for him to even withdraw his blade from my stomach.

"Let. Go." He utters between jerks and quivers.

I want to. Letting go would end my cycle of suffering. End the pain. End my life. Allow me to pass through the eternal veil to the realm of Peace and Light where the Two abide. But I can't. I'm not ready to rejoin my ancestors. Not yet.

During the heartbeats of relief and through clenched teeth, I answer, "Make an oath to the Two. Free the Wives Divine. No harm to my family. No harm to village. Only then will I let go."

Hu grimaces but shakes his head. "Never. Must. Protect."

How can I keep holding on? The torment and misery are too great. The flashes of healing are all that give me the hope and strength to hang on. But it also makes it worse. The rapid switch from healing bliss to excruciating anguish yanks me up and down with an unbearable ferocity through the full spectrum of pain. It never stops, cutting and boring through me heartbeat after heartbeat.

But the emperor's healing makes him suffer too. Perhaps more than me. Agony tightens his face. Fine streaks of silver slowly lighten his dark hair. Age spots dot his fast-wrinkling face. The youthful looks of the three-hundred-year-old immortal emperor peel away.

"Give up!" I say, between gasps. "Make the oath!"

The emperor's eyes close tight. His teeth clench, fighting through the torture. He can barely shake his head.

I jerk and tense as my pain spikes again. How much more can I take of this? How long can Hu last? I have to call upon every dab of emotional strength inside me to not let my resolve slip. How much resolve does the emperor have? Three centuries worth? How can I hope to survive?

Chapter 62
Lord Emperor Xiang Hu – No Surrender

"No matter how free it might seem to those who obtain it, immortality has a cost too."

- Pan Ru: Essays on the Mysteries

As the girl from Ning grabs my flesh and steals my healing gift, I feel the pierce, rip, and sting that my own blade inflicts upon her. It harrows up a rage of pain inside me that I never before thought possible. The nick and pinprick of every severed nerve and muscle. Gut wrenching spasms. Stabbing spikes. Clawing. Throbbing. Stinging. The bite and gouge of every move and wiggle of the blade's razor edge. I feel it all. Every pain and affliction she feels moves from her to me. That's the price of healing.

Healing has always exacted a painful price. No matter how I tried to guard it, now it's a weapon against me. But it will not beat me. The Two have charged me with the protection of the people of Huyan. I cannot fail them. I have sacrificed all that mattered most to me to protect my kingdom. I will not surrender now, no matter how deep and enduring the pain.

Through the haze of my agony, the girl's voice reaches my ears. "Prison and slaughter, not a protector's deeds. Be a true savior. Free the wives. Leave my people be."

Why can't this fool girl understand? Sacrifices must be made. Xié Shen seeks to destroy us all. I try to pull her fingers from my arms, but I can't get my hands to do what I want. The pain's too much. I have to hang on. She suffers too. I have to outlast her. She will not beat me. I must stop Xié Shen, no matter the cost.

Chapter 63
Qiu Lian – Helpless

"Tugs of the heart can be the most painful, most confusing, and most joyful—and sometimes all at once."
- Notions from a Royal Peasant

I want to scream at Meilin, "What were you thinking!" Instead, I clench at her staccato of sobs. Her screams make me quiver. Her spasms of agony tighten my chest and squeeze breath from my lungs. How is she even alive? Remarkably, the emperor appears to suffer even more pain and torment.

Watching Meilin's struggle paralyzes me with fear and helplessness. If I pull her free of the emperor's sword, she'll die. If I do nothing, she'll keep suffering. No one else knows what to do either. Father. Mother. Master Jin. The villagers. All stand in uncertain silence.

A chatter of whispers rises around me breaks the silence. Beyond the village square, across the field of grass, a beautiful young woman emerges from the bamboo grove dressed in a flowing plain white gown. I gasp. Two men walk beside her.

Dressed as a Gold Dragon Guard, Cai walks to her side and a step behind. Excitement, confusion, and joy surge and swirl inside me. He's alive! I fight the urge to sprint to him and wrap my arms around him.

On the other side of the woman walks Wei. He kept his promise. He came for me! A mix of more confusing emotions swell within and overwhelm me. Elation. Relief. Gratitude. Then I realize who the woman is. Ling Yuan, the Divine Lady Empress. Wei succeeded. He found the empress.

At a controlled, yet hurried pace, the three of them walk through the field of fallen Wives Divine and Shashyao. The shudder of the empress' shoulders tells me she's not pleased with what she sees. When she reaches the square, villagers cheer and shout. They rush closer to her but stop ten or so paces away before dropping to their knees and kowtowing face to ground in her direction.

The Divine Lady Empress beckons Master Jin to rise from his knees and join her. After a quick exchange of words, she rushes away toward Meilin and the emperor leaving behind Cai and Wei at the edge of the square. I want to go to them, to embrace them both. But that's not where I belong. I take a deep breath, exhale slowly, and hurry after the empress, following close behind. If there's anything I can do to help, I need to be there for Meilin.

Chapter 64
Qiu Meilin – Scent of Jasmine

"Sometimes the greater sacrifice is to save others by continuing to live."
- Pan Ru: Essays on Life

I quiver and clench when the healing ends once again. The sting of pain flares inside my belly like a white-hot fire. I'm drenched in sweat. I can no longer scream. I cringe and convulse at one assault of pain after another. My body twitches and trembles non-stop.

"No heart, no honor," I tell myself for the thousandth time. "Warriors never yield."

No matter his own suffering, the emperor refuses my pleas to free the Wives Divine and my people. My only hope is that my suffering will eventually strip him of his Chi and life. Of course, once he dies, I die too. That's the only thought that keeps me gritting through the pain. If I hang on long enough, my suffering and dying might actually be worth it, assuming the emperor can actually die. No matter, I won't give up. I'll keep battling.

Through my suffering, I hear soft footsteps approach on the cobbles. The scent of jasmine tickles my nose. Someone stands near.

A woman's voice mixed with sorrow and scolding speaks. "Sheepherder, look at what you have done!"

Sheepherder? Who does she mean?

She continues, "Shame. You have fulfilled your own prophecy. Do as the girl has bid you. Free the people you have made an oath to preserve."

Emperor Hu trembles. Agony creases his face. Gray colors his once dark hair. "Must. Protect." The words come out in a rasp, stuttered whisper. "The. Favored. Come."

"No," The lady says. "Don't you see? Xié Shen's favored one has already come. You have mistreated and dishonored your people. You have enslaved and imprisoned those who you should have loved and cherished. You have proclaimed yourself a god and have become a murderous tyrant. Can't you hear the laughter of Xié Shen rise from the depths of Kaioda as you have done his bidding in the name of your fight against him? You have become his favored one."

Hu does not respond.

Streaks of pain shoot in all directions from the blade's edge in my stomach. My grip on Hu's arms slips a pinky width. My fingers twitch and my entire body shudders. The healing from Hu is not enough. It takes every dab of will I have to stay conscious and hold onto the flesh of his arms.

The woman hovers over Hu. I see pity in her eyes, while a scowl deepens on her face. "Promise protection to these people you have threatened. Free the Wives Divine. Let them return to their homes. Let these villagers live in peace. Please, Xiang Hu, your zealousness has blinded you. Open your eyes to that horrible truth."

Hu's trembling intensifies, as does my own. Two's mercy, listen to her! My eyes close. I still hear my panting sobs and Hu's shuddered breathing. My fingers still clench, but I'm no longer certain they touch Hu's flesh. I'm dying. I feel it.

"Xiang Hu!" The woman's voice floats on the breeze like a faraway whisper. "You have spent so much of your life fearing the threats of Xié Shen that you have forgotten to trust in the Two and their Light. You can only hope to protect Dashi if the oaths you make and keep serve the Two and all their children instead of Xié Shen."

My heartbeat sounds loud in my ears. My body clenches in constant spasms. Spiking pain engulfs me. Hu's breath warms my face as words slip from his mouth in a garbled murmur I can't understand.

Even though it's like a distant echo, the whisper of the woman sounds clear in my mind. "That is enough."

What does she mean? The answer comes as firm, yet petite fingers grip my shoulders and pull me back. Pain screams at me as the edges of the sword rip away from my muscles and flesh. The pain erupts with thrashing frenzy and savagery as my fingers fly off of Hu's arms. Total darkness takes me as life flees me.

Darkness. Silence. Nothingness surrounds me. Until…

Warmth touches my cheek and speeds beneath my flesh and through my veins. Healing embraces me and restores me. When I open my eyes, a young lady hovers over me. The warmth of her bare fingers caresses my face. Her bright eyes and loving smile shine down at me, filling me with hope and peace.

"Wake up, young warrior," she whispers. "Your battle is won.".

Chapter 65
Qiu Meilin – Changed Heart

"Rise. Fall. Rise. Another day. Another chance."
- Private Journal of Qiu Meilin

Golden jays chirp and click at each other in the branches above in my favorite elm. In nearby holding pens, water buffalos whine and moan, begging to be milked. Up the village hillside, goats bleat non-stop, because that's all that goats know how to do. Anxious whispers surround me from the several groups of villagers scattered about the broken cobbles of the village square. The morning sun shines on my face, but I shiver at the chill that grips my flesh and insides.

A few paces away, the young woman—who I learned is Ling Yuan, the Divine Lady Empress Yuan—whispers with her husband, Emperor Hu. It is not a happy reunion for the royal husband and wife. Yuan no longer scowls. A faint smile even touches her kind lips, but there's no happiness in her eyes. She's so young and beautiful for a three-hundred-year-old woman. She looks no more than a few years older than Lian.

Sorrow and shame fill the downcast expression of the once proud emperor. Even with his newly gray hair, forehead wrinkles, and baggy eyes, the emperor still looks young for his age. But now a deep pain haunts the depths of his eyes. Is it the shame at having the one he loves discover his atrocities or leftover hurt from the intense suffering we shared?

Physically, I feel no more pain from Zhangchi's wounds, but mentally I'm exhausted. The constant ups and downs from severe pain to healing relief took an emotional toll on me. My hands still shake. I wonder if they'll ever stop.

"Meilin!" Mama's voice sounds sweeter than a songbird. Concern and relief fill her teary eyes. She grabs my hands and lifts me from my knees to my feet. She pulls me close in a snug embrace. "Thank the Two, you are safe. I worried so."

My arms and legs tremble at the warmth of her voice and the rush of joy that overcomes me. No more words pass between us. There is no need. Her eyes, voice, and hug shout all the expressions I hunger for from her.

When Mama relaxes her embrace and steps back, Lian squeezes in between us and wraps her arms tight around me until it hurts. I can barely make the words come out. "I. Can't. Breathe."

Lian loosens her grip, leans back, and laughs. "Sorry. Too much Chi. I'm not used to it yet."

"It's fine. I've had worse hugs. No matter how tempting, don't ever kiss a demon river rogue."

Lian cocks her head to the side and gives me a confused look. After a few heartbeats she smiles and shakes her head. "Oh, Meilin, you are always such a silly little duck. But you're my silly little duck. Thank you for saving me, even though I made it so hard. We have so much to talk about. I will always be in your debt."

"And guess what?" she says. Her eyes light up and her grin spreads wide. "Cai is alive!"

I grin back at her. "Yes, I know. We…" I stop. The way her eyes shine show she's not only happy that he's alive, but she still has feelings for him. My heart sinks. I should have known. Trying hard to smile, I continue. "You should go to him. He's missed you. I'm sure you'll have much to talk about."

Her grin widens as she nods in thanks right before she sprints toward the far edge of the village square where Cai stands alone. With her arms raised high as she runs, she shouts his name over and over again. When they crash together, their arms wrap around each other like they never plan on letting go. I close my eyes and turn away.

With a gentle touch, Mama's fingers light on my arm. "Meilin, do not envy Lian. You are still young. Soon enough, you will find a love of your own. I promise."

I smile to cover the pain inside me. Mama means well, but she has no eyes for what is in my heart. How could she? She has not seen all that Cai and I have been through together.

Oh, how I wanted to believe that things could work between Cai and me. All along I knew this could happen. I tell myself it should be enough that at least Lian is safe now, but it's not. I know that's all that should really matter. Now that our crazed emperor has stopped trying to kill everybody, maybe he could take a moment to use his healing touch on my aching heart.

Holding a small wooden chest before him, Father steps up to Emperor Hu. It takes me a moment to recognize the box. It's the bride price treasure box that Father accepted from Lord Zheng.

Father gives Emperor Hu a slight bow and places the wooden box at Hu's feet. "It was wrong of me to have accepted this. My greed made me foolish. This box has sat unopened on my porch since the day I received it. Every day I have prayed to the Two that someone might steal it. It almost cost me the lives of both my daughters. I will always carry the shame of what I have done, but perhaps returning this will allow me to gain back some of the honor I have lost."

With a frown on his face, Emperor Hu looks down at the treasure box and back up at Father. "The shame is mine." Hu's voice is meek and subdued. "I have wronged you and your family. I have wronged all of

Huyan. I'm glad your daughters are returned, but that will never be enough to repay you and them for what I have put you through. Please, keep the bride price. Knowing you have it, will at least ease some of the shame and guilt I feel."

Father's lips tighten. His body tenses. His fists clench at his side. Anger ignites in his eyes as he glowers at Hu. "I have no interest in easing your guilt. You tortured Lian. You tried to kill Meilin. You tried to kill us all. Keep your gold. I do not want it. By the Two, I hope your shame drags you down to the depths of Kaioda to burn with the demons you serve."

Father spits on the box at Hu's feet and storms away. Hu's eyes widen in rage. I fear Hu will pick his sword off the ground and strike Father down, but his rage only lasts a flash before the sullen look returns to his eyes.

With lowered head, Hu turns to the empress. "Oh, sweet Yuan, what have I done? I was a blind, witless fool. How can I ever pay for my crimes?"

A faint smile upturns the empress' lip. She takes Hu's hand in her own. "One step at a time."

Hu nods and squeezes her hand. "Yes. One step at a time."

In a loud, penetrating voice, Hu calls for the villagers to gather. They circle around him, but with a wide space between him and them. Now awake, the Wives Divine in their jade gowns and red veils gather also. The Mu Cu warrior approach close enough to hear, but do not join the circle. They stay apart with firm grips on their spears.

"Honorable citizens of Ning, I have wronged you this day. I have wronged you for many years. Centuries. For that I am sorry. I do not ask your forgiveness. I am not certain if my soul will ever be worthy of any forgiveness. Thanks to the courage of Qiu Meilin and the loving intervention and reprimand of the Divine Lady Empress, you are rescued this day from the blindness of my depraved heart.

"Your village bears no shame. Despite my accusations, your daughters, Qiu Lian and Qiu Meilin, have acted honorably. It was wrong to seek to take your lives or theirs. I rescind my judgments against you all. Any of you who have received physical harm or affliction from actions, I will heal. The physical damage I have done to your village, I will have repaired. I'm not yet sure how, but I will try to make right the emotional pain I have inflicted upon you too."

His gaze moves past the villagers toward the Wives Divine. "Honorable ones, you all know the truth of what I have done to you. No matter what you might believe, my intentions were good. I only sought to protect Dashi from Xié Shen. Using the Shen gifts from the oaths we shared seemed the best way. I felt it necessary to keep you asleep and hidden to keep secret the source of my power and to protect you from harm. I should have asked you if you were willing to make such a sacrifice. I was wrong not to."

The Wives Divine murmur as Hu speaks. Anger. Sorrow. Confusion. Those are just a few of the mixed emotions on their faces.

"Our marriages we're never finalized," Hu continues. "You have no commitment to me. You can choose to return to your homes or live at the palace. I cannot return the years of your lives that I stole from you, but I will make sure you live the rest of your days in luxury."

The emperor continues talking and apologizing for a while after that, but I stop paying attention. He sounds sincere, but I have doubts. It's hard to trust someone who tried to murder everyone you love. If he were really sorry, he'd give up his throne and lock himself up in a dungeon for the rest of his life. That said, I am happy that it appears he intends to do all that I asked of him. Not that I really had much to do with persuading him. The Divine Lady Empress is responsible for that.

After the emperor finishes talking, the villagers bring those who have been harmed to the emperor and empress to be healed. Others collect the cobbles used in the emperor's attack and attempt to repair the village square. My father works hard alongside them, his expression always grim. He has yet to look my way or speak to me since we stood together against the Shashyao. Why won't he talk to me?

"My young Pangze Wu, what an eventful day this has been." The strong arms of the short-haired warrior woman wrap tight around me as she lifts my feet off the ground. I cough, gasping for air. Liu Fen's embrace is almost as constricting as the Chi-powered hug Lian gave me. "Even among the greatest of our warriors, I have not seen such bravery as you displayed this day. I am proud to be counted as your friend."

"Thank you for your help," I say, once she sets me down and I can breathe again. "Your people saved many lives of our villagers. Now I believe I am in your debt."

Fen clicks her tongue and shakes her head. "No, Pangze Wu. You have my life bond for evermore. That will never change. You will always be welcome in the comfort of our boughs' embrace. I hope you will visit often."

A grimace tightens my smile. "What about your uncle? I don't believe Gu Zan shares your fondness for me. I'm sure he'll have me locked up if ever he sees me again,"

Fen laughs. "Don't concern yourself with Zan. When news of how you defied the emperor travels through the trees. The old goat will find it hard to not bow in honor of your valor."

I smile at Fen and bow my head in thanks. Silence hangs between us for several heartbeats. As it does, my gaze shifts to Cai and Lian. In the tall grass on the far side of the square, they sit close talking and laughing together. I want to be there, but I no longer know my place. Part of me hoped after I rescued Lian we could become closer again, like when we were younger.

It's ironic, as I drew closer to Cai these past few days, I feared our growing relationship would create a wedge between Lian and me. But now Lian is the wedge between my relationship with Cai. And Cai is the wedge between my relationship with Lian. I've lost them both. The hole that leaves in my heart is too hard to bear. In some ways, harder than what I endured in my fight with Emperor Hu.

I jerk my gaze away from them only to have my eyes fall upon Father working hard alongside the villagers to restore the cobbles in the village square. What is he thinking? Why won't he come talk to me? The pain and hole in my heart grows bigger.

The soft touch of Fen's fingers on my arm pulls me from my hollow yearning. "Pangze Wu, what is wrong? Are you ill? Do you need to rest?"

"No, I'm fine," I say, trying to smile. I open my eyes wide to keep any tears from escaping. My fingers tug hard at the folds of my robe behind my waist. I need to get away from here, somewhere faraway where punishing thoughts and longings can't follow. "You and your companions must be anxious to return home. I can take you if you like. I'm not needed here anymore."

Fen squeezes my arm. "That is kind of you, but we will travel home the traditional way—on our feet. It has been too long since we've journeyed far from our little village. We look forward to seeing and experiencing more of Gudai on our travels home. My sweet Pangze Wu, you will always have a place in my heart. May your paths always stay in the Mother Jade's watchful shade."

We embrace again and say our last goodbyes. Loneliness tightens my chest further as I watch her and her companions walk away, disappearing past the thick towering oaks at Gudai's edge.

I stand silent and alone for several heartbeats. Nearby, Emperor Hu and Empress Yuan continue to talk in low tones, but not too low that I can't understand their words.

Somehow Yuan makes her voice sound both firm and soft. "Give up and deny the oaths you have made with the Wives Divine. You do not need them. Be content with the gifts you and I share."

"The threat is still there." A tense anxiousness fills Hu's words. "How can I hope to stand against the demon lord and those who follow him without those gifts? It's impossible."

Yuan grips both his hands in hers. "You cannot beat Xié Shen on your own. You need the Two's help and the gifted warriors they will send. Just as they sent one to stand against you this day, they will send others to join the fight against Xié Shen."

"But…"

"It is not enough to free the Wives Divine," the empress interrupts. "As long as your strength relies on your oaths with the wives, they will be in danger. And you will be vulnerable. Let the oaths and gifts spread to any who seek to join the fight. Trust in the Two and the people of Huyan will become our strength. You have seen what one warrior sent from Heaven can do. Imagine what an army of Heaven's warriors can do."

A long silence rises between Hu and Yuan, but eventually the emperor breaks it. "You have given me much to think about, but as always there is wisdom in your words. I will give up the gifts I share with the wives."

Hu makes a hand in fist salute and looks upward. "By the Two and all the Shen with whom I have pledged a shared oath with the Wives Divine, I sever all bonds, withdraw all oaths, and give up all gifts shared with the Wives Divine, but keep all those that Yuan and I share."

No noticeable change occurs in Hu's outward appearance, but the energy in the air around him dims, less charged. He frowns and lowers his head. "It is done. By the Two, I hope this was the right thing to do."

Yuan smiles. "It can't help but be right. Come on, let us say our goodbyes and return home."

The Empress and Emperor walk away hand in hand toward the patch of grass under my favorite elm. Master Jin sits there, sipping tea and eating a sweet bun. I grin. It doesn't matter what catastrophe hits, Master Jin won't miss out on his morning tea and sweets.

"Meilin, may I speak with you?" Father's voice startles me. I didn't see or hear him approach. Dirt streaks the sides of his face and covers his ragged working grays. With head lowered and his gaze at the ground, he stands at my side with his hands behind his back. I lower my gaze too. I won't be able to stop the flood of tears if our eyes meet. I can't bear seeing in them the shame he always feels for me.

All across the square, the work and chatter of the villagers stops. I can feel their eyes on us. I had hoped for a private conversation with Father, but little of what happens in Ning is hidden among neighbors.

With hands behind my back, I grip the cloth of my robes to stop my arms from shaking. But I fail to hide the trembling in my voice. "Of course, Father. How may I honor you?"

Several heartbeats pass. Father doesn't answer. Why? He has never had trouble before telling me what is on his mind. I lift my gaze when he makes a muffled, snort-like wheezing sound. Back and forth, his bottom lip, moves slow beneath the tightness of his upper lip. His eyes still focus on the cobbles beneath my feet, but they have a faraway look to them.

My knees tremble. I want to run away. I want to disappear. "Father, please talk to me. I can bear your silence no longer."

His nose twitches as he clears his throat. His words come out in a low, quivering grumble. "Meilin, this day I feel more shame than I have ever felt in my life."

I tense at those words. Words that I have dreaded and feared my entire life. "But Father…"

"No, Meilin. Let me finish." His voice still quavers. "You have forced me to face my greatest fears. Fear that I am a failure as a Father. That shame weighs me down more than I can bear. Meilin, I have failed you. I tore you down. I should have lifted you up. I punished when I should have loved. I am a witless fool. Too many times my pride and greed would not let me listen to your wisdom."

With remorse, Father lifts his gaze to meet mine. Tears glisten the corners of his eyes. His voice softens. "Meilin, I was wrong. I am truly sorry I failed to show my love for you. By the Two, I will seek to love you better. Please forgive me.

His voice rises again with firmness. "For the first time in my life I have seen the face of true honor. That face is yours, my daughter. You have taught me much this day. Pain and death may follow one who stands and speaks against the silence. But nations die when their silence kneels to those who injure and corrupt."

Father holds his hands out to me, palms up. I stare at their calluses and the fingers that used to run through my hair when I would sit on his lap as a young girl. Those same fingers would clasp mine as we would walk the shores of the Pangbo at sunset to watch the patterns that starlings made as they dove and swooped above the river's glowing ripples. How many years has it been since I held those hands? Two? Three? More? Too many.

I release the folds of my robe behind my waist and place my hands in Father's. He grips them and falls to his knees, staring up into my eyes.

"Today, I kneel to the one who would not sit in silence. I kneel to the one with courage to stand. To speak. To act, when no others would. You live your life to do what is right, without fear and regret. You honor me. You honor our family. You honor Ning. You honor Huyan and all of Dashi. May the Two forever bless the name of Qiu Meilin, my cherished daughter."

Heartbeats of silence follow as Father holds my gaze. The pride in his eyes makes me shiver all over. Tingles warm the spine of my back.

Then Father, releases my hands and kowtows forehead to the ground three times. On the last kowtow, he keeps his forehead firm against the cobbles and does not move. Except for the whistle of birds and buzz of insects, silence grips the entire village square. Like a flowing wave, villager after villager falls to their knees and kowtow toward me. Mama. Lian. Cai. Master Jin. Even crotchety old Lo Jing and Magistrate Pang, every villager kneels and kowtows toward me. The Wives Divine kneel and kowtow as well.

Beneath my favorite elm tree, Emperor Hu and Empress Yuan remain standing. Emperor Hu does not smile, but with a slight nod of his head he gives me a fist in hand salute. Empress Yuan beams, her grin spreading upward from cheek to cheek. She also lowers her head, gives a fist in hand salute, and says loud enough for all to hear, "Thank the Two for Qiu Meilin, honored warrior sent from Heaven."

Chapter 66
Qiu Meilin – Shift in Power

"Change is hard. Not changing is tragic."
- Pan Ru: Essays on the Tenets of Light

Similar to the wedding banquet, rows of tables fill the outer courtyard decorated with red silk tablecloths, gold silk napkins, copper goblets and platters, and small Shen Breath lanterns. The savory smells of roast pheasant, plum sauce duck, ginger cabbage, and other delectable delights fill the air.

More than twenty thousand colorfully dressed lords, nobles, high ladies and important citizens sit at the tables, anxious for the feast to begin and anxious to hear the words of Lord Emperor Xiang Hu, Chosen of Heaven. While they wait, firecrackers explode, dancers dance, and suonas and drums play to entertain them.

The last time I was in the courtyard I wore a stolen set of blue servant robes. Today, I wear a flowing purple dress and a long floral green jacket with wide, purple-trimmed sleeves and a line of white petal flowers on each side twisting down from my breasts to my knees. My ponytails are pinned up with loose loops framing both sides of my face and then pinned on top into a twisting bun using ruby-studded combs of gold.

I would feel more comfortable in my scratchy peasant grays, but I can't complain too much. The silk is so light and smooth, I almost feel naked. I keep pulling at it to make sure it's really there. I could get used to the way it caresses my skin. And I love how it makes me feel so pretty.

But my dab of pretty is distant from the exquisite beauty of Divine Lady Empress Ling Yuan. Beaming with an ear-to-ear grin, she sits three seats away from me on her red Phoenix Throne atop the raised platform overlooking her adoring subjects. Diamonds and rubies sparkle in her hair and on the gold chains that dangle from the tiara pinned in front of her five peaked buns that resemble a peacock tail. Beneath a sheer gold lace coat embroidered with a scattering of fine swirling phoenixes, she wears a flowing ruby red dress with twisting vines of gold and jade trim running along her shoulders, bodice, cuffs waist, side seams, and hem.

Adorned in a magnificent yellow silk robe on his Dragon Throne, Emperor Hu sits next to the empress. He's smiling, but I can't tell if it's forced or sincere. Beside the emperor sits the ever-scowling, nasty looking Lord Zheng. Several others sit on the platform too, all-dressed in varying degrees of colorful silk finery. On the other side of the emperor next to Zheng sits some officials I don't recognize. Between me and the empress sits Suyin and her brother, Wei. On the other side of me sits three gray-haired Wives Divine who decided to live at the palace. And beside them sits Cai and Lian.

I smooth the folds of my dress on my lap, forcing myself not to look at either Cai or Lian. I haven't talked to or seen either of them since my standoff with the emperor eight days ago. Before leaving Ning, Empress Yuan asked me if I wanted to accompany her back to the palace.

"I could use a bodyguard I can trust," she said with a wide grin. "Plus, I need someone to tell me all that has happened over the past two hundred years or so."

My first reaction was to decline, but when I glanced at how friendly Cai and Lian continued to be towards each other I decided I could no longer stay in Ning. The past eight days in the palace have been interesting. I've enjoyed hearing about the first ninety years of the Empress Yuan's life—her rise from simple village girl to building the greatest kingdom in all of Dashi alongside the emperor until his paranoia and misguided vision created a divide between the two of them.

When I wasn't with Yuan—she forces me to call her Yuan instead of Divine Lady Empress, but I still struggle doing so—I spent most of my time in the serenity of the palace gardens. I've come to know Suyin and Wei a little better too. Apparently, they're related to the emperor and empress, but I'm not sure how.

Those two are so different. Suyin is serious most of the time, but once in a while she surprises with her dry humor. Wei is non-stop smiles and happiness no matter what goes wrong, except for when all of the sudden the smiles disappear, and doom and misery possess his soul for a bit of time.

When I ask Suyin about his depressing episodes, she laughs and says, "He suffers from a broken heart."

I'm not sure why that's funny to her, but I decided not to ask any more about his bouts of gloominess. But now not a dab a gloom shows on his face. He hasn't stopped smiling since he took his seat near the edge of the raised platform. And he hasn't stopped staring past me either. I can't tell if he's looking at Cai, Lian, Yuan, or the emperor. I'm not sure what that's about. Much about Wei remains a mystery to me.

A loud gong from the back of the platform pulls me from my thoughts and triggers a wave of silence to pass over the crowded courtyard. The emperor rises from his throne, and everyone drops to their knees, except for Yuan. The emperor grins, but motions with his hand for everyone to rise.

"Beloved citizens of Huyan." Emperor Hu grimaces when he realizes that few in the courtyard can hear him now that he no longer has the gift to amplify his voice.

Hu looks over his shoulder and motions for Lord Zheng to come forward. When Zheng does, he pulls from his pocket a short, but thick hollow bamboo rod. I can't read them from this distance, but a row of characters has been burned into the sides of the rod. Embedded along the top are a line of six round-side-up emerald teardrops and a line of six round-side-up ruby teardrops angled toward each other like those found on the hilt of Zhangchi blades.

Emperor Hu takes the rod, places one end near the front of his mouth, and speaks, "Beloved citizens of Huyan." His sound amplifies throughout the courtyard. "After a long absence, I am pleased to present to you Divine Lady Empress, Ling Yuan."

The crowd roars with approval. Yuan rises from her throne and steps forward to stand beside Hu. The emperor doesn't give any explanation for the empress' absence or sudden reappearance. Instead, he professes is dedication and love for her.

"Her joyous return has caused me to realize a few things," he continues. "For too long I have encouraged the practice of treating women as a lower class. Today, that stops. We are all children of the Two.

"Today, a new age begins and Innate Honor ends. We must respect all women as equals and honor them as divine daughters of the Two. We must cherish and exalt women for their many gifts. Seeing the good that one has to offer, does not lessen our own good. It strengthens it. It makes us better. The sum of our combined gifts—female and male—will make us a stronger, better nation. When we stand together, cherishing and building upon what the other has to offer, we cannot fail.

"From this moment on, women shall have full access to shrines of the Shen. Women shall be accorded the same respect and honor as men. Just as men, women must have unrestricted opportunity to lead in our villages, cities, and nation. Starting now, not only shall the Divine Lady Empress, Ling Yuan rule Huyan at my side, but she will take the lead in ruling. I will take a step back into the shadows, while she steps up as a glorious beacon for all of Huyan and all of Dashi to look up to and follow. Behold and honor, Divine Lady Empress Ling Yuan, Chosen of Heaven."

An audible gasp erupts from the crowd. Only one holds the title, Chosen of Heaven. With that pronouncement, the emperor has officially ceded his right to rule to the Empress. Her word, not his, will now be law. Even he will have to bow to her commands.

The shock on the faces of the crowd's twenty thousand is not limited to the men. The women look surprised and confused too. While some grin, none cheer their approval. This is a strange new thing. For many, accepting women as equals will be hard enough. Having a woman as their supreme ruler may be too much to accept.

Amid the murmurs and confusions passing through the crowd, Emperor Hu raises his hands for silence. Several heartbeats pass, but the crowd eventually quiets enough that only the coo of doves and the breeze rattling the branches of the courtyard trees can be heard. With all eyes on him, Emperor Hu drops to his knees and kowtows forehead to ground three times toward the empress. On the third kowtow, he keeps his head to the ground until all in the courtyard have dropped to their knees and given her the same respect.

All rise back up when Emperor Hu rises. He extends an open palm toward the empress and says, "Two's honor and hail your Divine Lady Empress Ling Yuan, Chosen of Heaven."

For a heartbeat there is silence, but a few cheers rise until little by little a roar of support spreads through the courtyard. When the crowds finally quiet, Emperor Hu hands Empress Yuan the bamboo speaking rod to address the crowd.

"What a glorious sight, you all are," Yuan says with a wide grin. "I cannot express how much joy fills me to be with you today." Yuan turns behind her and motions for me, Wei, and Cai to come forward and stand by her. "I would not be here today if not for the unselfish service these three have personally given to me. At great sacrifice and risk to their own lives, these three loyal citizens of Huyan have returned your Divine Lady Empress back into your presence. For this service to me and the kingdom of Huyan, I honor Qiu Meilin, Chao Cai, and Fan Wei each with the Great Phoenix Medallion."

From a pocket in her dress, she pulls out a jade medallion on a silver necklace. The jade of the medallion is carved in the shape of the great phoenix. It has a small, angled round-side-up emerald teardrop for the left eye and a small, angled round-side-up ruby teardrop for the right. Paired emerald and ruby teardrops also decorate the ends of the phoenix's three tail feathers.

Yuan places the chain over my head and onto my neck and whispers, "May the phoenix always protect you."

As she presents Cai and Wei their own phoenix medallion, she whispers something to each of them. As the crowd cheers, Yuan motions for Cai and Wei to return to their seats. I follow, but she stops me, pulling me close to her with her arm around my shoulders.

"I have one more thing I would like to say about this brave young woman before you return to your festivities."

The emperor steps close to me so now I'm standing between him and the empress with the eyes of more than twenty thousand people staring at me. I don't like so much attention on me. I like even less that I'm so close to the emperor. Despite his promises and supposed change in character, I don't trust him. My eyes fall upon the Zhangchi sheathed on his belt. Will he draw it to be rid of me.

That's one of a few reasons I wanted to wear my Zhangchi to the banquet. But I couldn't figure out how to make it look good with my dress. That didn't stop Suyin. With black leather, she strapped her Zhangchi to her back right over her flowing peach colored gown. I grin.

I've grown to really like that girl in spite of the fact that she tried to kill me once too.

Empress Yuan puts her arm around my shoulder and pulls me close to her. I really like Yuan too. I'm delighted that she will be ruling Huyan. I don't think the people realize how fortunate they are to have her. But they will find out soon enough.

"Wonderful people of Huyan," Yuan says into the bamboo speaking rod. "I present to you today, Qiu Meilin of Ning. Many of us would not be here today if it were not for her courage and determination. At the risk of her own life and through agonizing suffering, she stood against a great evil to save us all."

I smile to fight off the smirk that wants to rise to my lips. A big part of me wishes she would mention that Emperor Hu was, or is, that great evil. But now is not that time.

"For her valor and service to the people of Huyan," Yuan continues. "I hereby name her as Imperial Counselor of Huyan with all the authority, power, rights, and estates accorded to that title."

I have no idea what an Imperial Counselor is or does. It has to be sort of some honorary title that just sounds important, because I'm too young and too under-qualified to do anything too serious in the imperial government. Important or not, the crowd cheers and their approval makes me smile. I bow to them and return to my seat, grateful for the empress' kindness.

After the cheers subside, the empress continues, "There are many more things that I would love to tell you, but you have had to digest far too many words already today. I believe you would much rather digest the appetizing delicacies waiting to be served. May the Two bless you and enjoy the feast!"

Cheers thunder and an army of two thousand blue robed servants start bringing trays of food to the guests' tables. Servants carry a long table up the steps onto our platform, quickly followed by other servants bringing place settings. Amid the commotion of the servants' preparation, my gaze unintentionally turns toward Cai.

Our eyes lock for a single heartbeat. During that heartbeat, Cai smiles at me. It's an uncomfortable smile. A knot forms in my stomach, my flesh chills, and I start trembling. I turn away and rise from my seat as a servant places a covered plate of food on the table in front of me.

I step toward Yuan and whisper in her ear. "I don't feel well. Would you mind if I excuse myself?"

She looks up at me, concern in her yes. "Oh, I am sorry. Do you need healing?"

I shake my head, crossing my arms across my chest to try to warm myself and control the trembling. "No, thank you. I will be fine. I think I just need some time alone."

The empress smiles in understanding and nods, giving me approval to hurry away.

Chapter 67
Qiu Meilin – Honor and Hail

"Even when life seems most grim, the sun will rise again."
- History of the Descendants: Volume 1, Page 1

Trembling and still chilled, I sit in the shrine gardens beneath the shade of a blossoming peach tree on a patch of grass at the edge of a small pond. I slip my sandals off and dip my toes in the cool water. A colorful duck with a purple breast, yellow body, and a blue stripe running down the middle of its mostly white head quacks at me as it glides toward me. I'm not sure if the bird is welcoming me or yelling at me to go away.

Down the cobbled path not too far from me the blue tiled roof and rosewood walls of the Luxíng Shen shrine rises amid a bramble of berry bushes. I don't think I meant to come here, but I did. I can't help but think how Cai and I made oaths to Luxíng Shen a few days ago. Why is it so hard for me to stop thinking of him? Why did I let myself believe things would end up any different than they have? My world has changed in so many ways since that night.

I throw a small rock into the pond and watch it ripples spread. Although it's not Gudai, the pond, the garden's trees and brush, and all the sounds of birds and animal life remind me of the time Cai and I spent together on the river. How I loved snuggling in the shelter of the back of his boat with the warmth of his arms around me. How I longed to kiss him, but it was it all a wishful dream. A dream I never wanted to end. Oh, I am such a witless fool.

A squeal of laughter behind me jerks me from my thoughts. On the edge of the grass behind me stands a big orange ball of fur with big smiling teeth. "Snubby!"

I jump to my feet, race to the monkey, and scoop him up in my arms. I hug him close, the soft tufts of fur on his face tickling my cheek. "I'm so glad to see you little friend." He coos as I scratch the fur behind his ears. "Where have you been hiding? I've missed you."

Snubby's grin widens, baring all his teeth and sticking out his tongue with a chattering laugh. He pushes himself out of my arms, hops to the ground, scampers to the cobbled path, and howls up at the trees. He continues to howl and squeal, dancing from foot to foot and wagging his head side to side.

After several heartbeats, another chattering ball of fur drops from one of the trees in front of Snubby. The two snub-noses grab each other's hand and Snubby swaggers back toward me with the other monkey in tow.

A big smile fills my face. "I see. You have a new friend."

The monkeys stop in front of me, and Snubby lets go of her hand and starts jumping up and down, howling. His grin and eyes shout, "Do you like her? Do you like her?

I laugh. "Of course, I like her. She's my Snubby's friend, so she's my friend too." I hold my arms out to her. "Welcome to the family, little one."

The golden monkey grins and waddles toward me. I hug her close and she lets out a soft "oooh" as I scratch the fur behind her ear. Snubby howls, but I'm pretty certain it's a howl of joy not jealousy. The monkey rubs her nose against my cheek before slipping out of my arms and scurrying back to Snubby's side. They both jump up and down, grinning and chattering for several heartbeats before turning their back on me, jumping into the branches of the nearest tree, and disappearing from sight.

I stare into the trees as their howls and rustling of leaves travel further in the distance. I'm happy for Snubby, but the smile slips off my face as I wonder if I'll ever see him again. It's selfish of me, but I feel even lonelier than I did before as I sit once again at the edge of the pond, dipping my toes in its chill water.

I skip a rock across the pond and the colorful duck flutters its wings and quacks at me again. Part of me wants to quack back at it. Another part wants to bury my face in my hands and disappear.

"Hey, are you hungry?" I jump at Cai's voice. My feet kick the water, splashing myself.

He plops down on the grass beside me. I hug my arms tight across my chest and lean away from him. "Why aren't you at the banquet?"

Cai grins at me a beautiful grin that rips my heart apart. I want to punch him almost as much as I want to kiss him.

"You left in such a hurry I thought you might be hungry."

He sets a bundled silk napkin beside me and unfolds it to reveal a slice of roast pheasant and a leg of plum sauce duck. They smell wonderful, but I'm in no mood to eat. A quack from across the pond lessens my appetite even more.

I shake my head. "I left the banquet because I wasn't hungry, and I wanted to be alone. You're not helping with that right now."

"Gales and hails, Meilin. You can be as stubborn as an eel."

I smile, but there's no joy behind it. "I'm the stubborn one? You're the one who's still here after I told you I want to be alone."

Cai covers his face with his hands and shakes his head. When he removes his hands, a baffled expression scrunches up his face. "Meilin, what did I do?"

I want to shout. "Are you serious?" Instead, I lower my gaze and frown at the grass at my feet. "Cai, please leave. I really want to be alone."

Cai exhales long and deep. He shakes his head and slowly rises to his feet. He turns to face me. A thin frown lines his face. He's so close to me. Too close. I want to scream.

"No," he says, folding his arms across his chest. "I'm not leaving until we talk."

Delightful. The last thing I want to do is talk. I want to crawl into a hole and be left alone.

"Okay," I say, locking my gaze on him with no trace of a smile on my face. "What do you want to talk about? How you used to hold me, snuggle with me, and make me feel like you care about me until Lian showed up. Do you want to talk about that?"

Cai scrunches his eyebrows, sucks in his cheeks, and blows out a puff of air. "Lian thought I was dead. We were both happy to see the other alive."

My lips tighten. My fingers clench the silk of my dress behind my back. "And then you couldn't stop holding her. You couldn't stop being with her."

"No. Yes. That's not what I mean. Lian and I had a lot to talk about."

"What about us?" I shout whisper. "Don't we have a lot to talk about too?"

Cai takes a deep breath. Then another one, letting it out slowly. "Yes, we do. Remember, that's why I'm here. To talk to you."

Oh, yeah. I feel like a witless fool. An angry witless fool. "Fine. Talk. Then go away."

Cai stares at me. Frustration. Exasperation. Confusion. All show on his face. All the same emotions I feel. Several heartbeats pass in silence. The wind rustles the peach branches above. The duck quacks across the pond. Snubby squeals somewhere in the garden not too far away.

"Talk!" I want to yell. "Talk and then go away forever!" But I stay silent, clenching my lips together.

Eventually Cai's face relaxes. His eyes look at me with such caring that I want to melt, but it's pity not affection. A hint of a smile tips up the corner of one side of his mouth. "You were right," he says. "Lian did still love me."

My heart feels like it's being crushed. My stomach twists tight. I don't want to hear this. But I need to. That's the only way I can get over this.

"She only pretended not to love me to try to protect me. She had some crazy plan for us to escape to some faraway kingdom."

My heart tightens further. This is too much.

"That of course didn't work the way she planned. Still, we needed to talk through all our feelings, which can be quite confusing at times."

I don't need to hear anymore. I'm done listening. "So, you've talked it all out and things are back to normal, is that it?"

Cai grins and the grin breaks my heart. "Yes, Back to normal for you and me, not me and Lian."

My eyes narrow. I didn't hear him right. I'm certain of it. "What did you say?"

Cai grins wider. "I told Lian how I feel about you, and she told me how she feels about the gardener." He stops a moment and laughs. "In case you didn't know, Wei is no ordinary gardener."

"I don't care about Wei! What are you saying? How do you feel about me?"

His grin softens a bit, and he bites his bottom lip. "I care about you. I miss you when I'm not with you. I think about you all the time. I love how you never give up. I love how you always smile. Well, how you smile most of the time. If you're willing, I want to be with you and see where things go. What do you think?"

If I weren't in such a fancy dress, I'd roundhouse kick that grin off his face. "If you care about me, why did you hug Lian? Why didn't you come talk to me?"

His grin flattens. "You were busy with the empress and emperor. And Lian hugged me. I hugged her back because I was happy she was finally safe."

"I almost died with a Zhangchi in my gut, not to mention all the other ways the emperor tried to kill me. Don't you think I needed a hug too? Weren't you glad I was finally safe?"

Cai frowns. He lowers his gaze to the grass before my toes. "I was overwhelmed with joy that you were safe. I couldn't wait to tell you that. You're right. I should have gone to you first. I wish I had. But I didn't. I'm sorry. By the time Lian and I finished talking, you were gone."

My grip on the back of my dress lessens. My anger calms. "Why didn't you come tell me this all sooner? Why wait so long?"

"Since you left without a word, I knew you were angry with me. I didn't know what to do. I thought I had lost you. I didn't want to make things worse. I'm sorry. I'm here now. What do you say?"

I drop my grip on the back of my dress, step next to him, and grin. "I think you owe me a hug."

He wraps his arms around me. I wrap mine around him. I lay my head against his chest and let warmth, peace, and joy envelope me. Wondrous heartbeat after heartbeat passes. I never want to let go. I don't want this moment to end.

When it does, I step back and look up into his beautiful eyes. Then to his lips. I smile, step close, and stand on the tips of my toes and press my lips against his.

"I can't believe it!" The loud, impatient voice belongs to Suyin. "The empress wants you at the banquet and you're in the gardens brushing lips? They're going to float the lanterns to honor you and she wants you there to see it. So, show a little respect and get your slobber faces back to the courtyard before she sends the guard."

Cai and I pull back from each other and laugh. "Don't worry," I say. "We'll be right there."

The sun begins to set when Cai and I return to the platform. Throughout the courtyard people still feast on the array of delicacies and delights being served. Those at our table continue to enjoy their meals too. Lian and Wei both sit close to each other, holding hands and laughing as they share a peach. It's been years since I've seen Lian so happy.

In the sky above, the lavender moon Shi slowly overtakes her emerald lover, San, as they both rise to their apex overhead. When the radiance of Shi finally embraces San, completely encircling the gleam of the smaller moon, thousands of glowing lanterns of red and gold rise from the banquet grounds into the twilight sky. A chill comes over me at the breathtaking display.

At once, a roaring cheer rises among the crowd and they begin to chant. It's so loud and at first, it's not quite in unison, so I struggle to understand what they're saying. Then, Cai steps behind me, wraps his arms around my waist, and whispers it into my ear. I blush at the words, knowing they're undeserved. Still, I smile, grateful for their chanting praise. "Honor and hail, Heaven's Warrior. Honor and hail, Heaven's Light. Honor and Hail, Heaven's Might."

Epilogue
Ye San - Shi San Reborn

"The demon dragon's power comes from Shi Shen and San Shen. As such, it shares the lovers' curse."
- Forbidden Writings of Zha Zhi

As the sun begins to set and I step on the moist grassy shore of the Pangbo. The babble of its rippling current does nothing to soothe my misery. Neither does the slow thumping drum beating in the distance. Yemaren drums of mourning. In time with the beat of my broken heart, they sound every day before sunset—every day since Emperor Hu's slaughter of the Yemaren fifteen days ago. The more distance I've put between me and those slaughter fields, the fainter the thumping has become—as has the heart thump of my lovely Bing Shi has grown fainter too.

From heel to hair, black charring and bright red blisters and burns cover her once smooth skin. The lightning barely missed us both, but the scrub bush she stood near erupted in a blaze of fire, engulfing her body in flames. I treated her wounds best I could, but no one in the camp would help her, too busy caring for their own. No village from there to here had a living soul that could help. All slaughtered. All dead. I cannot let my lovely Shi fall to that fate.

Not knowing what else to do, I wade into the chill shallows of the Pangbo to above my ankles and lay my lovely Shi in the cool of the water, hoping for a miracle to save her.

"Oh, great and powerful god of shadows," I say aloud, not caring who hears my blasphemous cries. "The Two and their children have abandoned me, but you have always been true to me. Please hear my pleas."

"How may I help you?" The kind, smooth voice startles me. No one is in sight. A few heartbeats pass before I find the voice's source. A few paces away a small salamander, not quite as long as my arm, stands in the river's shallows. Its mottled, dark brown skin blends in with the riverbed's flat stones and pebbles, making it almost invisible.

"My son, tell me your plight and how I might serve you." The small lidless eyes of the salamander stare up at me without emotion, but the familiar voice is full of compassion.

My body clenches as I retell the story of Emperor Hu's lightning strikes and my lovely Shi suddenly being consumed in flames. As long as breath gives me life, I will never forgive Hu his crime.

The salamander flicks its long tongue in the air to snatch a passing fly. Its pale eyes stare at me as if it didn't hear a word. But I know the source of its voice heard. It has always heard me in the past.

"You would have me heal her? Make her whole again?" I squirm at the delight in his voice. "There will be a price and a boon to help you pay that price. Are you willing?"

My eyes fix on Shi as the clear water of the Pangbo courses over her ruined flesh and near lifeless body. Her chest barely rises with breath. Her eyelids twitch every few beats of her dying heart. Other than that, she doesn't move. My heart twists in agony. I cannot lose her.

"Whatever you desire, I will do. If you will but save her and reunite us."

"You will have your desire, but you must do as I say." Urgency fills the voice. "You must take another power brand. And with it, you will take the burden and power of all the emperor's broken oaths and serve me until your final breath. Will you do this?"

I nod my head. "I swear, I will do all that you ask."

A few paces away, small tendrils of fire erupt on the shore within a tiny spot of grass. My eyes linger on Shi only a heartbeat before the voice nearly shouts, "You must hurry. Before the sun sets."

I rush to the shore to the burning spot and slip off my right shoe. Below me, as the fire dies, where grass has burned away, lines of bright red burn atop the soil forming the characters for broken oaths paired with the characters for Xié Shen.

My body clenches and my foot screams with pain when I step on the burning lines and let the power brand sear my flesh. My heartbeat and breathing races as the searing sting continues even as the heat vanishes. I want to scream. I want to cry. The pain overwhelms me. Unable to walk, I crawl back to the Pangbo and push my foot into its soothing chill. Slowly, the pain subsides.

As I catch my breath and let my heartbeat slow, slivers of gold and scarlet blaze a thin line above the horizon and reflect upon the great river's end. Sunset's blaze mellows into misty blues and purples that streak across the sky and shimmer in the reflection atop the river ripples.

As the sun finally sets, directly above me, my namesake moon finally catches his lover in twilight's darkening sky. The spheres of glistening emerald and shining lavender become one. At that moment, unimaginable power and strength fills every vein and sinew of my being. But that is not all. My heart skips a beat. Water splashes paces away, as Shi rises to her feet. Her clothes still ragged and tattered, but from heel to hair her flesh his perfect and beautiful once again.

Confusion fills her eyes until she finds my gaze and grins. Splashing through the shallows, we rush into each other's arms. The warmth of her embrace fills and overwhelms me. Joy will forever be mine. We say no words. None need to be said. We have what matters most. Each other.

With the river's song, a chorus of cicadas and croaking frogs serenade our reunion. I never want to let go. Yet after several heartbeats pass, we step back from our embrace, but still joined by our gaze.

Soft and kind, her voice floats to me as the last light of twilight vanishes into darkness. "I knew you would save me. You always do."

I close my eyes and bow my head. Gratitude swells my heart. When I raise my head and return my gaze, pain fills my lovely Shi's eyes. Her limbs flail in every direction. Her skin darkens as ripples of black scales overtake her smooth flesh. Her body twists and contorts, growing longer and longer like an enormous snake. Magnificent wings sprout from her back. Tattered bits of Shi's clothes litter the river, floating away as a thunderous roar booms from the massive black long and sinewy dragon rising above me, beating its beautiful wings in the air.

Paces away, the salamander splashes its tail in the river. "ShiSan, the price has been paid. The desire filled. Now go. Serve me."

The great dragon rises higher and with a tilt of its wings, turns eastward and glides away with a joyful roar. With another splash, the salamander disappears beneath the surface into the dark of the flowing Pangbo.

The End.

Acknowledgements:

I'd like to thank first of all my wife, Denise, for always being there for me, including her willingness to read and give feedback on whatever I write, including this epic work of fantasy. I'd also like to thank my other alpha and beta readers, including Erin Cabatingan, Andi Bai (also my sensitivity reader), Spencer Baker, Leann Moody, Robert Liddle, Amy Nielsen, and Jason Warren.

About Ken Baker

Ken Baker has been writing professionally for more than 25 years as a published children's author and a freelance content strategist and writer. HEAVEN'S WARRIOR is his debut epic fantasy novel, although he has been writing fantasy for decades. He is best known for his published picture books; OLD MACDONALD HAD A DRAGON, COW CAN'T SLEEP, HOW TO CARE FOR YOUR T-REX, and BRAVE LITTLE MONSTER. He also writes science fiction, thrillers, YA middle-grade, and chapter books. He lives in the shadows of the Wasatch Mountain range. In addition to writing books, his loves include his wife, children, and grandchildren, as well as chocolate, ice cream, teaching, sports, and tropical adventures.

To learn more about Ken Baker or connect with him, visit www.kenbakerbooks.com.

Tell others about Heaven's Warrior

Loved Heaven's Warrior? Please leave a positive review about it on Amazon, Goodreads, or on your favorite social media platform. Thanks!

www.ingramcontent.com/pod-product-compliance
Lightning Source LLC
Chambersburg PA
CBHW060810120726
47909CB00006B/1853

* 9 7 9 8 9 9 3 0 5 8 7 0 2 *